W9-BBG-718

THE GOD
OF ENDINGS

THE GOD OF ENDINGS

Jacqueline Holland

FLATIRON
BOOKS
NEW YORK

This is a work of fiction. All of the characters, organizations, and events portrayed in this novel are either products of the author's imagination or are used fictitiously.

THE GOD OF ENDINGS. Copyright © 2023 by Jacqueline Holland. All rights reserved. Printed in the United States of America. For information, address Flatiron Books, 120 Broadway, New York, NY 10271.

www.flatironbooks.com

Library of Congress Cataloging-in-Publication Data

Names: Holland, Jacqueline, author.
Title: The god of endings / Jacqueline Holland.
Description: First edition. | New York : Flatiron Books, 2023.
Identifiers: LCCN 2022028769 | ISBN 9781250856760 (hardcover) | ISBN 9781250903853
   (Canadian, sold outside the U.S., subject to rights availability) | ISBN 9781250856777 (ebook)
Subjects: LCGFT: Novels.
Classification: LCC PS3608.O48437 G63 2023 | DDC 813/.6—dc23/eng/20220808
LC record available at https://lccn.loc.gov/2022028769

Our books may be purchased in bulk for promotional, educational, or business use. Please contact your local bookseller or the Macmillan Corporate and Premium Sales Department at 1-800-221-7945, extension 5442, or by email at MacmillanSpecialMarkets@macmillan.com.

First U.S. Edition: 2023

First Canadian Edition: 2023

10 9 8 7 6 5 4 3 2 1

For my children,
who taught me what love is and also fear

Suffer us not to mock ourselves with falsehood
Teach us to care and not to care
Teach us to sit still
Even among these rocks

—T. S. Eliot, *Ash Wednesday*

Then [*The Lord*] spoke to [Job] out of the storm:
"Who is this darkening my plans
With his ignorant words?
Stand up like a man, and brace yourself;
I will ask questions; and you, give the answers!

"Where were you when I founded the earth?
Tell me, if you know so much.
Do you know who determined its dimensions
Or who stretched the measuring line across it?
On what were its bases sunk,
Or who laid the cornerstone,
When the morning stars sang together,
And all the sons of God shouted for joy?"

Job 38:1–7, *Complete Jewish Bible*

THE GOD
OF ENDINGS

· 1 ·

WHEN I was a child, the dead were all around us. Cemeteries were not common in the early years of the 1830s. Instead, small, shambling family graveyards butted up against barns, or sprung up like pale mushrooms at the edges of pastures, in the yards of church, and school, and meetinghouse—until eventually you could look out across the village, see all those gravestones like crooked teeth in a mouth, and wonder who the place really belonged to, the huddled and transient living or the persistent dead?

Many folks found this proximity to death and its souvenirs discomfiting, but my father was the first gravestone carver in the village of Stratton, New York, which meant that the distillation of death and grief into beauty was our family business. Death, to me, was tied inextricably to cherished things: to craftsmanship and poetry, to my father and to the beautiful things he made, and I couldn't help but feel some tenderness for all of it. Even all these years later, I can still see those gravestones vividly. Drizzle-gray slabs of slate, smoothly planed and cool to the touch; grainy sandstone in its striated shades of red and brown and buttercream; soapstone soft enough to etch with a thumbnail, yet somehow able to resist the assaults of time and the elements; letters and symbols, crosses and cherub wings, and forlorn-looking skulls chiseled delicately into the surfaces; beveled edges smooth and sharp beneath the pads of my small, inquiring fingers.

Like the works of his hands, my father also remains vivid. When I remember him, he is working, always working, at his craft. His eyes and hands search a great heft of rock for its secret seams, and then, with wedge and mallet, he splits it open as one might split an orange. With great focus, he hammers at his chisels, patiently lifting away slow, stubborn ribbons of schist like potato peels to carve the rounded tympanums. With pick and file, he etches and sands and then blows the glittering mica dust into the air. Noticing me, his watchful daughter standing in the doorway, he looks up and smiles, but his hands are ever diligent; they glide along surfaces, feeling their progress.

When I was very young, I would go about with bits of stone in my mouth, enjoying the feel of the rough grain against my tongue. I have few memories of my mother, who died giving birth to a baby who died with her, but one of the memories I have is the sudden indignity of her finger in my mouth, swiveling roughly, fishing a piece of rock from it. Then she too became a gravestone: creamy yellow, reticulated by thread-thin veins of iron, embellished along the side panels with fine scrolls and rosettes, and with a centerpiece inscribed "Loving Mother," all of which I remember in greater detail than I remember her.

I am fond of those memories of my father, his shop, his gravestones, but they are tied to other, darker memories, and the mind, that imbecilic machine of associations, moves irresistibly from one to another, and before I can stop it, I am seeing myself and my brother, Eli, in a different shop, the smith's forge. I'm ten years old, my brother fourteen, the age of each of our deaths, and we're surrounded by our grim-faced neighbors who, out of the firm conviction that it will cure us of our afflictions, are forcing us to swallow the ashy remains of our father's burned corpse.

The fact is that I was a child at a hideous time, when the terror of death suffused all of life and against it people had little recourse besides their own dark imaginations. More than a hundred years had passed since the Salem Witch Trials, and still the habit persisted of encapsulating what was feared in stories. Stories, after all, have boundaries, and fear needs nothing more desperately than boundaries. Thus, a crop failure or injury might be construed as the work of demons, or the fruit of some unholy pact with the Devil, or punishment for one's own unconfessed sin. This was why when the wasting death—what is today called tuberculosis—came to our town, it arrived wrapped in a shroud of stories that were passed, like the disease itself, from hand to hand until they had both spread to nearly every town and village along the Eastern Seaboard.

The restless dead, it was whispered, were crawling up out of their graves at night and preying upon their own family members, dragging them down ounce by bloody ounce into the graves beside their own. This explained why entire families would crumble, one by one—strong, vigorous men and women watching their flesh fall suddenly away, their eyes receding into their skulls, the coughing and the blood. Who could blame people at a time when nothing at all was known about bacteria or the virulent microscopic droplets that sprayed forth from a sick person's cough, for seeing a perverse and ungodly malevolence at work—pattern, design, intentionality—in an entire family's slow, hideous demise?

This narrative of the malicious dead not only offered an explanation, it also suggested action that might be taken to stop what seemed unstoppable: if the dead were not quite dead enough, then the solution perhaps was to dig them up and put them more conclusively to rest. Exhumations began. When the second wife of the cooper fell ill, the deceased and famously jealous first wife was dug up for interrogation. On it went from there. Coffins were pried open, corpses examined, their appearances quarreled over. Why did the Wesley daughter, dead from scarlet fever in the early winter, look as though she'd been buried only the week before? Never mind that winter was only just relenting, and the girl was probably coming out of months of deep freeze, her flesh rosy with thaw. Why take chances?

People who knew, people with close ties to Europe and its intricate lore—young brides recently arrived from Häggenås and Blåberg, a grandfather from Lovön, a nephew from Bistritz—advised the rest on the best course of action.

"Break the arms and legs to keep them from crawling about in the dark."

When one measure failed to stop the descent of the living toward death, a new measure would be offered.

"Carve out the heart and examine it for the fresh blood of its victims, then you'll know for certain."

Then, "What use is certainty and how can it ever be had when you're dealing with the unnatural, the unholy? Cut off the head, and that will be that. To be safe, burn the heart as well. Then have all the remaining family members eat the ashes. Make the bodies of the living inhospitable, from the inside out, to the demonic."

My father, the gravestone carver, had spent his life helping folks make peace with death and he regarded this war with abhorrence, insisting at every opportunity in his gentle but stubborn way that our dearly departed bore no responsibility for the afflictions of the living and that fouling their bodies was a sin and an abomination. He may have persuaded some, but those who opposed him were louder, and when he too began to cough, I saw an ugly satisfaction in the eyes of those he'd reproved.

Deacon Whilt was one of these. The man, who had appointed himself commander in the war against the undead, and who took officious pleasure in bearing the arms of holy water and crucifix to the exhumations, came one day to my father's shop. He ambled about, picking up chisels to squint at their varied ends and knocking his head on the iron tools that hung by hooks from the ceiling.

"Word has it," he said, massaging the back of his skull where it had encountered the long metal handle of an adze, "they found a ghastly one over in Plattsburgh. Fat as a tick on a mule. Blood all over the creature's hellish mouth. They pierced the stomach and hot blood poured out for near an hour."

"And you believed this?" my father asked between hammer blows.

My brother, beside him, had paused at his work and was listening, open-mouthed and horrified, but a stern glance from my father flushed his cheeks and set him back to work.

The deacon frowned down at a smear of dust that had marred his black cassock and, taking out a handkerchief, began to sweep it off with controlled violence. "And what would you have me believe? That it is all mere coincidence? Six families in the next township, nine in our own, falling like a child's arrangement of dominoes—by *chance*?"

My father did not answer, and the deacon sidled up beside the stone my father labored over.

"Such lovely religious sentiments on your gravestones, Isaac, and yet their maker seems to deny the active influence of the supernatural in the affairs of this world. I might almost imagine you lacked a godly dread of the Devil and his works."

"Or imagine instead that I possess trust enough in God to drive out fear of a multitude of devils—real *or imagined*."

My father might have said more, but a cough welled up from deep inside his chest. He tried to hold it back, but finally could not and lifted his smock to hide the fit until it passed.

The deacon watched my father, his expression softening in a way that disturbed me more than his previous hostility.

"Your apron, Isaac," he said when my father had finished. "There's blood on it."

My father turned back to his work.

"Would that you might turn from your stubborn unbelief," Deacon Whilt went on, "which gives the demons free entry. We've lost half of our men already. Half again are as ill as yourself. At this rate, the village won't survive the winter. We need you well, and Eli too. We cannot afford to lose any more. Not one more."

He went to the window and gazed out at the two distant graves perched atop a hill and silhouetted against the pink blaze of the setting sun. My mother and baby sister.

"It *is* a vile business. On that we are agreed, but then the powers of hell are vile. We do what we must, not because it is pleasant, but because it must be done. You will have to dig them up."

"No," my father answered without pause or glance. "Never."

The deacon turned and let forth a sigh of great weariness, then made his way to the door. When he noticed me standing nearby, he put a damp hand of blessing on my forehead, which I struggled to endure without scowling or drawing away.

"I do hope you reconsider, Isaac," the man said without turning. "You'll all die otherwise."

. . .

"Papa?"

The deacon had gone and my brother was out filling the wood box, and my father and I were alone in his shop with the light falling and the hunks of stone set up on tables like islands in a stream. He was at a desk writing, something he did rarely on anything other than stone.

"Papa, what are you writing?" I asked, coming up beside him.

"A letter."

"A letter to whom?"

"To your grandparents."

"My *grandparents*?"

"Grandmother, anyway, and to her husband, Mr. Vadim Semenov."

"I did not know I had grandparents."

"You do. You met them once, but you were young, perhaps too young to remember."

"Why did I meet them only once?"

There was a moment of hesitation as my father tried to find the right words.

"Your mother loved her father very much. He was a good man, a minister, very pious and kind. After he died, your grandmother married again. Your mother was unhappy with the match."

"Why?"

"It came about rather . . . suddenly, and strangely. He is an unusual man."

"Unusual how?"

"Well, he's . . ." My father cast about uneasily and finally settled on, "He's no Protestant. I'll say only that. It's what upset your mother. She never imagined your grandmother would agree to marry a Catholic, or Eastern Orthodox, or whatever he is, though the man was—*is*, I imagine, still—quite wealthy and quite persuasive, but she did, without hesitation or discussion, almost as though she were . . . sleepwalking into the match. I'll grant you, it was strange. None of that seems quite so important now, though. I think even your mother would agree."

I looked down at my hands, where they nervously fingered a loose thread on the pocket of my apron, afraid to ask the next question.

"Why are you writing to them? Now? After all this time?"

My father turned to look at me and reached out for my hand, and the understanding that passed between us in that look and in that touch was so painful and clear that I could have believed that people did not need words to speak at all.

"Are you going to die, Papa?" I breathed. "As Deacon Whilt said?"

He looked down into his lap, took a rattling breath, collecting himself, then looked up at me again, a soft smile in his eyes.

"Be assured of it," he said. "As will you, as will everyone else you or I know."

He gestured with the feathered end of his quill pen at the gravestones leaned up against the walls of the shop in various stages of completion.

"*We all* pass from this world to the next, dearest: it is our lot as mortals and our privilege, and if the choice were mine to do it sooner or not at all, I'd not hesitate to choose sooner and be sooner in the presence of our Lord. You mustn't be afraid of death, Anna."

"I know all that, Papa. You know I do. And I'm not afraid of death, but I am . . . I am afraid of . . ."

I hesitated, struggling suddenly to speak. Overcome, I looked away, trying to tamp down the fount of breathless fear and tears pushing up forcefully in me.

"Afraid of what, dearest?"

My father opened his arms, still lightly white with rock dust, to me.

"Afraid of you going without me," I said, stumbling forward into them, "afraid of being left behind, without you."

Once in his arms, a kind of panic seized me, and I clung to him.

"I wish we could die at the same time," I whispered.

My father held me tightly for a long time in silence. Finally, he cleared his throat and wiped his face with the rag from his pocket.

"Our days are numbered by our maker," he said, his voice husky. "He's a number for me and a number for you, and each one holds a blessing if we've the courage to find it. You must not wish a day of it away. Though it's difficult, we must trust ourselves and each other to his gracious providence and his wisdom."

"I know," I whispered, my voice quaking, "but I'm still so afraid."

My father tilted my chin up. His face was pale and beaded with fine drops of sweat, and his eyes gleamed with a strange, unwell brightness. I could not hold my tears back any longer and I closed my eyes in despair as they fell.

"That's all right," my father said, wiping the tears gently from my cheeks with his handkerchief. "He can be trusted with our fear as well."

For a moment he just held me, then he stood up and walked over to his worktable. He picked up a chisel and held it out to me, knowing perfectly well that I could never resist helping him carve. I took the tool and let my father guide me to stand between him and the stone he'd been working on. He put his large, deft hands over mine to guide our strokes, and together we carved a fine, smooth bevel.

"What will we carve together in the world to come, you and I?" my father asked, wiping clean and looking down fondly at our work. "There'll be no more need for these."

"It's almost a shame," I said. "They're so lovely."

He smiled at me and then kissed my forehead, and his lips burned against my skin.

WE DID NOT DIG UP my mother or my baby sister, and my father did die. What's more, the sickness that had been quietly germinating in me and my brother bloomed into grave illness. Hollow-eyed skeletons, both of us, coughing up blood and thick white phlegm, and gasping for breath, we seemed sure to follow my father soon and bring all of Deacon Whilt's grim pronouncements to bear.

In those strange, bleary weeks, as my death circled in on me, I went into my father's shop to sit in silence among his tools, and the slabs of raw rock, and the gravestones he'd left unfinished.

As he'd neared death and lost his strength, his gravestones had grown smaller and plainer. The one he'd been working on when he died was little more than a flagstone squared off and engraved with a single line of poetry unfinished. It was from Donne's tenth Holy Sonnet, my father's favorite poem. My father's last stone had been his own.

I determined to finish the line. How many times had I carved with him, his hands guiding our strokes? Surely, after all that, I could do it on my own. With frail arms, I took up the lettering chisel and set about doing what I'd seen him do a thousand times. It was horribly difficult. Soon after beginning, I broke loose a button-sized chunk of stone that blemished the surface and I nearly gave up in tears. But then I tried again. I went on, though I did it poorly. Weak and easily exhausted, I took a fortnight to chisel the three missing words. Along the way, though, I determined to bury my father myself. I had already heard the deacon imply that my father's death was proof that he, the deacon, had been correct about everything, and I feared the vengeful pleasure the man might take in turning my father's remains into one of his undead enemies. I'd never let him do it. I would bury my father somewhere hidden, where no one could find or disturb him, and I would mark his grave with the stone he and I had made together.

On a wet day in early spring, I carried the grave marker—which, in my state, felt like a boulder, though it could not have weighed more than fifteen pounds—out of the shop, across the muddy fields, and into the leafless woods. I stumbled deeper and deeper into the trees, amid the plinking percussion of melting snow, the shifting bands of sunlight, and the lonely caws of watching crows. I stopped often to rest my burning forehead against a tree and try to regain my breath, though it went on as ragged and shallow as before.

Satisfied at last that I'd gone far enough, I set the marker down and myself beside it, and for a while I just cried helplessly while the mud seeped into my skirts.

"Papa," I whispered to the stone, "I'm scared. You left me behind, Papa. Trust God and his wisdom, I know, but I can't. I just want to come with you. They've dug up Mr. Harrison and Alice Brooke—dear little

Alice Brooke. And her poor mother was—Papa, I don't want to be here anymore. It's all so horrible. I can't *bear* to be here without you."

The water went on dripping and somewhere a cardinal trilled. Fever-drunk, I searched the treetops for the bird and spotted him, a bright red male high up in a tree, searching the valley arrogantly for what mattered to him. Suddenly I couldn't think what people were for, couldn't think what their lives amounted to besides misery. Like a bird, I looked down from high treetops at all the wretched villages of men and felt only blank confusion. Those pitiful beasts, I would think if I were a bird, those poor, sad creatures dragging themselves along the ground, passing their days laboring and fearing and suffering until death. Too clever to live in peace, too stupid to live well. They're better off in the dirt, finally quiet, finally peaceful.

"Why must we pass through this bleak world at all, Papa?" I asked aloud. "Please, Papa, if you have any power in it, let me die too and leave this place behind. There's nothing here that I care for."

The cardinal's call at last was answered by some distant listening bird, but mine was not, so I got up and started back home, thinking of how I would manage to move my father's body to the grave site. His shrouded, stiff corpse had been set in the barn for as long as the weather remained cold. The men of the town, who were spending so much sweat digging bodies up, saw no reason for haste to put one down, especially when the corpse might prove quarrelsome and need to be brought back up again.

If I could lift my father onto the horse cart, I thought, it would be easy from there, but I wasn't at all sure that I could lift him. I wondered if Eli could be trusted to help. Even if he could, I wondered, would his help be help enough, weak as he was? But the next day, when I went into the barn to see if I could lift the body on my own, it was gone.

"Eli!" I cried, running into the house. "Eli! Father's body! It's gone!"

My brother sat frail and chalk white before the fire. Around him and helping him gingerly to stand were gathered the deacon and men from several of the neighboring farms. They turned as one to look at me, and I knew immediately what they had come for.

"No," I said, shaking my head and beginning to cry. "No! We *won't*! *Never!*"

. . .

WHO KNOWS WHEN THEY DUG up the bodies, or how many of our friends and neighbors participated? Who was it that severed the heads from the bodies of our kin? Who placed their arms and legs against the cinder blocks to break them? Who cut out their hearts and sliced them open to search for the fresh blood of their victims? And what misgivings did they feel as they performed these acts on the husks of people whose lives had been so intimately entwined with their own? Whoever it was and whatever their sentiments, they had completed their grisly tasks by the time we were brought to the smith's forge for the burning.

My brother was too weak to stand, so Mr. Bird, the cooper, held him up as he inhaled the smoke from the burning hearts. I refused. They pulled me by the arms, but I bucked and clawed until they gave up. Then, when there was nothing left of the organs but oily ashes, Deacon Whilt scooped them up and placed them on my brother's coated tongue.

I thought my resistance had succeeded and that I would escape, only having had to witness this horror, but I was pinned suddenly. One man put an arm tightly around my chest and another around my head, holding me still. My lips were pried open, and my mouth was filled with soot. I sobbed, and the dust ran up into my nose and choked me. I gagged and screamed with weak rage and flailed my small fists at anyone within reach until I was dragged away.

"Guard carefully that girl," I heard the deacon say, "she behaves as one possessed of demons. They may not even wait until she is underground."

My brother, who had once been so strong, died soon after that, but I, a spindly little girl, just ten years old, and the one most would have picked to die first, held on. My illness and the quickly circulated rumor of demonism made me unwelcome in the homes of even our dearest family friends. I had nowhere to go but to the rectory, where the deacon oversaw my care with open loathing and instructed the house servants never to speak to me, look at me, or enter my chamber without a cross in hand. I lived in a feverish haze of illness, despair, and fear.

Then one afternoon, I was awakened from fever dreams by a commotion in the house. Voices high and agitated carried from the front of the rectory and up the stairs. Then loud, deliberate steps were coming down the hall. Into the room where I'd been spending my days tossing fitfully on a hard bed, and flanked by fluttering, alarmed servants, entered a white-haired gentleman in the finest riding clothes I'd ever seen. His eyes were the color of backlit amber, and his lined face was strong and arresting and somehow vaguely familiar to me. He strode across the room and lifted me from the bed. My body was frail and I, no doubt, weighed very little, but the old man lifted and carried me as though he were a youth carrying nothing heavier than a cloak.

Deacon Whilt stormed in behind the man.

"What is going on here?" he demanded of the servants. Then to the old gentleman, "What are you doing in this room?"

"I am this child's nearest relation," the man said in a voice large and roundly accented in a way that, like his face, was dimly familiar. "Her father wrote regarding his imminent death and requested that I assume guardianship of his children. I gather he has passed?"

"You are mistaken, sir," the deacon said acidly. "This girl is an orphan. She has no living relations."

The old gentleman pulled the folded pages of a letter from his coat pocket and pressed them to the deacon's chest as he carried my limp frame past the man toward the door.

"You, my good man, are the one who is mistaken."

The deacon stumbled along after us, looking the letter over and stammering protests, while I whimpered in drowsy confusion.

"Peace, child," the old man said, looking down at me, "I am your grandfather."

Then to the deacon, "Where is the boy?"

"The boy is dead," the deacon answered coldly.

The old man pressed my head to his chest as though shielding me from hearing what I already knew, and then started down the stairs.

Outside, the servants clustered, gaping on the porch, but the deacon hurried alongside Grandfather as he carried me to his coach.

"I *must* advise you against taking this girl into your home. She is oppressed by vile spirits. It could be she who has sent the others down to the grave."

Grandfather placed me in the carriage, tucking thick, soft blankets around me, then turned to face the deacon.

"What is it that you fear?" he asked in a tone low and serious.

In his gravity, the deacon's face was flushed and turgid, and he leaned forward to speak in a voice strained with intensity. "It is *widely attested to* that we, in these parts, are in the midst of an unholy epidemic, that Satan and his demons lie in wait to deny rest to those who depart from this world, to turn what should be God's glorious risen into tormentors of God's faithful."

"*Tormentors?* How torment?"

"There are some who, compelled by the prince of darkness, become restless after death. They crawl up from the grave to drain the blood of their living relations and bring them likewise into death and Satan's service. There have been nearly a hundred incidences in this county alone, all of them simon-pure and thoroughly documented."

"Drain the blood? *Ah, verdilak.* These are known in my country as well." Grandfather cast a wary sidelong look toward the coach. "This girl?"

The deacon nodded. "If she passes. *When* she passes. Who knows, perhaps before. She is one of unnatural tempestuousness already and resistant to all holy intercession."

Grandfather was very still for a moment, thoughtfully considering the man before him and his words, then, suddenly, he threw back his head and let out a great, full laugh, which set the deacon trembling with alarm.

"Koještarija!" Grandfather exclaimed, grinning. He turned, bemused, to the deacon. "*Rubbish.* This child is as helplessly ill with consumption as all the others. In the city, but *fifty* miles from here, the condition is treated with cod-liver oil, rest, and fresh air, but here, in this delightful little backwater, it is treated with exorcism and who knows what other nonsense. That a man of the church should revel in superstition like a pagan priest, well, I wish I could say I was surprised."

He took the fluttering pages of the letter from the deacon's hand, smoothed and folded them, and returned them to his pocket.

"Now, my little verdilak and I must away, but I thank you for your time and for the . . . *entertainment*." He gave another chuckle and clapped the deacon genially on the shoulder, then, turning, climbed up into the driver's seat of the carriage.

There was a whistle then, and a toss of the reins, and Stratton moved away behind me forever.

It took several hours to reach Grandfather's estate in Millstream Hollow, some twenty miles away—to me, an unimaginable distance. My father had told me that my grandfather was wealthy, but I had imagined it in the terms of our village: a large, thriving farm perhaps, with a pretty clapboard house and a carriage. But the three-story brick house with its porte cochere, towering glass conservatory, and half dozen chimneys would have astounded me with a grandeur unlike any structure I had ever seen if my sickness had permitted me to perceive it.

My grandmother's face, aged but very lovely, would appear now and then over my sickbed, accompanied by the sensation of a cool, damp cloth against my skin. More often, though, it was my grandfather who tended to me. He built up the fire, changed the linens, and sat for hours in an armchair in the corner of the room, reading poetry aloud in a strange rolling language and a low, resonant voice that wove in and out of my half consciousness. Sometimes, he sat close beside my bed, giving me odd commands.

"You are hungry, Anya. Your appetite is returning. You will eat."

And strangely, though I'd been turning my face from food for days, I would feel a sudden dim sensation of hunger and open my mouth to the spoonful of broth he held out to me.

The old man seemed possessed of limitless energy, and his presence, signaled by the smell of tobacco and leather and horse stable, became a near constant reassurance to me, such that I would whimper and toss whenever I awoke to find it absent.

Despite my improved circumstances, I grew sicker, thinner. My arms were bones draped in a muslin-like cloth of thin skin. My drenching sweat smelled of stale beer, and I could keep down only the thinnest broth. As a last resort, a doctor from Greenwich was brought in to attempt a surgery rumored to have helped some. He put an ether-soaked handkerchief to my nose and then cut a hole in my chest to let out the bad air while Grandfather held my hand, and I babbled dreamily. By the end of the surgery, my blood was stiffening rags littered across the floor, and I was only the worse for it. Like a boulder tipped over the crest of a hill, I careened toward death.

THERE IS A NUMINOUS SPACE that opens up just before death, a spectral herald with a trumpet blowing silence who announces the approach of a thing unlike anything that is. The air vibrates at a different frequency, the space grows colder, and there is nothing to do but wait. It was in this space, amid those vibrations and the grateful certainty of death, that I cracked my eyes open and saw a figure shrouded and hidden in the folds of a black cloak. *Death*, I thought with horrified certainty, so he is in fact real, and he does in fact wear a black cloak. But how could this be the way of it? Where was Jesus with all his ministering angels to carry my soul upward to paradise, as I'd been promised? Or had I committed some grave sin, and here was a demon to escort me from this fleeting world of suffering to an eternal one?

Terror completely unmoored from reality bobbed and ebbed in my last fevered scraps of consciousness. Time passed. Who knows, in that numinous space, how much of it? In terror, I closed my eyes. In terror, I slipped and stumbled along the border of waking and dreaming, unable to discriminate between them, but whether I was waking or dreaming, the figure was there, unmoving, its hidden yet heavy gaze fixed on my face. I wanted to scream, but all I could manage at last was a small, strangled cry of fear.

The figure rose. It moved toward me, not silently like a specter, but with footsteps softly audible against the floorboards. Tears slipped down the sides of my face, and my body shook with terror, bracing for the strike of a divine scythe, but for a long moment nothing happened.

Then there was a slight stir of breath and a motion, small like the muscle twitch of a snake coiling to strike. The black cloak fell upon me, and then my neck was in the grip of needles. Everything was confusion. I was confused by the needles in my neck, confused by this strange action of Death, and the fast, draining sensation of the blood and life running out of me, but most of all, I was confused by the familiar smell of my grandfather, the tobacco and leather and horse stable that told me he was near.

I AM TOLD THERE WAS a funeral: a pretty girl in a pretty dress with curled hair and a hole in her chest, candles in a dim parlor and unwilling guests passing through it quickly. My grandmother put a rosary in one of my hands, and my grandfather put a bell in the other. The rosary was of no help (my grandfather, when he tells it, likes to underscore), but some weeks later, when I was ready, I rang the bell.

I am told that on a clear night in spring, my grandfather, with shirt-sleeves rolled to the elbow and his collar dark with sweat from digging, lay down on the grass and stretched his arms out to a little girl in a dirty dress who sat crying in her grave. Finally, because she would not move, he had to climb down and lift her out.

Sitting on the moonlit banks of a stream, he fed her blood from a stoat and walked her patiently through the parameters of her new existence: henceforth, you shall live on the lifeblood of others, you shall bloom but never decay, you shall live free from the hidden enmity of the physical world, whose laws are conspiring always to bring an end to life. In Grandfather's telling of the night, it was all very touching and picturesque.

My own memories are patchy and far less idyllic. I remember dirt. I remember screaming. I remember *possum*—not stoat—and I remember the trembling, delirious haze of my mind clearing only enough to ask my grandfather, *Why?* Why have you done this? Why have you done this *to me*? And I remember his answer, the serene philosophical tone of his voice as he gave it.

"This world, my dear child, all of it, right to the very end if there is to be an end, is a gift. But it's a gift few are strong enough to receive. I made a judgment that you might be among those strong few, that you might be better served on this side of things than the other. I thought you might find some use for the world, and it for you."

He looked up at the moon, patted my shoulder almost absently, and said, "But if not, my sincerest apologies for the miscalculation."

· II ·

1984

IT'S early morning. The house is a quiet mountain, huge and still and lovely. A chilly October has etched the classroom windows with delicate arabesques of frost, and beyond them, the property is a panorama of autumn with sugar maples aflame, fallen oak leaves carpeting the grass in fire, and here and there, a witch hazel spreading gnarled black arms furred with innumerable yellow buds.

How curious it is that in nature, the most vibrant colors are those that precede death. The delicate pinks and blues of spring are wan in comparison to the dramatic crimson of the hawthorn berries or the bloody gashes of the buckthorn leaves in late November. Stars blaze pale in their infancy, but in old age they melt and simmer in reds and oranges just as the oaks and maples do. Youth, it seems, is a state of diffuse abundance, while death's approach concentrates.

Color is something I think a good deal about. I'm an artist after all, and this school that I run is an arts school for young children. Youth and death I think about even more than I think about color: the children I teach are *so* very young—three, four, five years of age—while I am, by most standards, very old (somewhere in the vicinity of a hundred and forty, I would guess). What's more, the children I teach will someday grow old, wither, die; I won't. I will remain just as I am. Forever—whatever that incomprehensible word means. All this, paired with the hushed stillness of dawn, has a tendency to make me contemplative in the morning.

THE LIGHT OF THE RISING sun slants through the long row of windows, glazing the tops of the four low, hexagonal tables, and my shadow, backlit and severe, slashes through the light like dark fingers, as I walk from one table to another, setting out paper for coloring and refilling the buckets of pastels in the center of each one. Outside, it's unseasonably cold, but inside, the classroom is overwarm as the antique yet everzealous radiators sputter and hiss along the walls and Marnie's morning glory muffins rise in the kitchen down the hall, filling the air with spice. In one corner of the room, an antique washbasin is filled with disparate scrap metal parts: the complex innards of broken clocks and radios, coils of wire, nubby screws, and Phillips-head screwdrivers enough to go around. Small and odd but uniformly delightful works of metal art sit on a shelf above the tub. In another corner, bolts of loose-weave fabric, large, blunt-tipped sewing needles, and spools of colorful thread are strewn across a table. Beside the table, costumes for dramatic play—tiny doctor's coats, carefully ripped pirate shirts, hats and shoes of every size and shape, as well as some of the children's own creations—spill from a wooden trunk where one of the house cats, Myrrh, lies on her side and bats at the knotted tassels of a scarf. A Mozart concerto—the music of optimal cognitive function—hangs in the gold-lit air. With the exception of myself, everything is queued up and ready for learning.

It's not been forty-eight hours since I last ate, and yet my stomach rumbles with my every movement like a push mower, and my thoughts all come around to blood. It's a nuisance I have no time for; the children will arrive any minute. I step across the rug, where the children will soon sit cross-legged for circle time, and reset the daily schedule that parses out the day's activities into bars of construction paper neatly labeled in French. Nap time for the children—*sieste*, as it is in French—is feed time for me. Six colorful bars separate this insistent hunger from its relief.

A minute or two later, the doorbell rings, and I make my way down the hall. It will be either Thomas and Ramona, a brother and sister who arrive early each morning to accommodate their parents' commute to Bridgeport, or Rina, the office assistant I brought on last year. Marnie, the sweet and blowsy older woman who prepares meals for the school, has her own key and lets herself in and out through the back kitchen door.

The house is huge, a three-story labyrinth of rough-hewn stone, and it takes me a minute to get from the back of it to the front. It's my grandfather's house, the same house I was brought to as a child. In that parlor right there beside the stairs, I lay dead in a coffin elegantly staged among white lilies and wavering candles. It must have been about a mile out back, past the creek, where I was buried. A few years ago, my grandfather asked if I'd consider returning to the States, as he was in need of a reliable caretaker. I had misgivings at first, old, all-but-forgotten memories I wasn't especially eager to bring to the fore, as well as a deep aversion to cooperating with any of my grandfather's schemes—they hadn't worked out well for me in the past—but then I had the peculiar idea of a school. (*Or was it Grandfather who had the idea, the sneaky bastard?*) I tried to shake the thought, find all the holes and impracticalities—there were plenty—and yet, finally, I agreed.

The bell chimes again as I approach the door, but before opening it, I take a second to tidy my appearance in the entryway mirror: russet hair pulled up in a loose chignon, bright blue eyes that draw more attention than I'd like, high cheekbones, and pale skin. Despite my considerable age, I have to dress thoughtfully in order to look old enough for this job. "You will bloom but never decay," Grandfather said to me long ago. It's proved true, and, at times, not particularly helpful. I think I should prefer to be eternally middle-aged and free to rent a car without questions. For added credibility, my office wall is decorated with framed degrees from European institutions—fakes, every one of them, but convincing ones—inscribed with my current name, Collette LeSange.

I check my teeth for lipstick in the mirror. My other teeth, curved, transparent, and magnificently sharp, are discreetly recoiled in the cheliceral furrow on the roof of my mouth. Ordinarily, I forget all about them, but when I'm exceptionally hungry, as I am now, I can feel them shifting ever so slightly, forward and back, tensed and ready for use.

From what I understand, the appetites of ordinary people—*vremenie*, or "the brief," as Grandfather calls them—can be capricious. Eating is as much a form of diversion as it is a satisfaction of biological need, and the desire to eat, even the impression of physical hunger, can be set off by mere suggestion. I've made the mistake too many times of mentioning food to the children and being immediately bombarded by claims of desperate, life-threatening hunger. This is not the way of it for myself. There's little entertainment to be had in a diet as monotonous as mine, and so I eat what I must, when I must, and without any special enthusiasm. For more than a century, I could have set a clock by my cravings, and a quart of blood every third day never failed to satisfy them. But suddenly and mysteriously, this is no longer the case. I press my tongue up against the roof of my mouth, but of course it does no good. Nothing will help but blood.

I tuck a loose strand of hair back up into my bun, turn, and open the door.

"Bonjour, mes petites canards!"

"Bonjour, Madame LeSange," the children mumble in a sleepy, syncopated chorus. They shuffle through the door and flop down on the rug to pull off their sneakers. Myrrh winds her way between them, rubbing against their backs in welcome.

With its gilt-framed paintings and tarnished silver, the old estate would seem an impenetrable bastion against time, but the children carry the year in with them. It's 1984, and Americans are in the grip of a feverish obsession with manufacturing. Everywhere you look the cornucopia of synthetics overflows its brim: plastic, rayon, hair gel, colors more like chemical reactions than anything found in nature—teal, magenta, neon—handfuls of glitter tossed at it all for good measure. Thomas and Ramona shrug off eye-injuring neon ski jackets.

Cubbies and coat hooks are in the cloakroom, just around the corner from the entryway, and Thomas and Ramona scamper off to put their backpacks in their cubbies, hang up their jackets, and swap their outdoor shoes for indoor slippers.

"Shall we go get the snack prepared for the class?" I ask the pair when they return from putting away their things. Ramona is smoothing the static from her wavy brown hair. She takes my hand and nods.

"Actually . . ." Thomas stands before me, tugging absently at the nagging collar of a cable-knit sweater. "Can I go read in the library instead?"

Thomas is a precocious reader, devouring books well beyond the typical skill level for his age. While I read to the younger children on the rug in front of the fireplace, he reads by himself, nestled against the pillows in the window seat. I recently introduced him to the Oz books by L. Frank Baum, and it's *The Emerald City of Oz* that he's anxious to return to now.

"*May* I *please* go to the library?" I correct him gently. "And, yes, you may."

He does an excited hop from one foot to the other and then dashes off. Ramona and I walk down the hall together and reach the kitchen just as the oven timer begins to chime.

"Ah, ce moment!" I exclaim. "What timing!"

Ramona knows the routine. While I go for the oven mitts, she hefts a folded step stool as tall as she is out from beside the stainless steel refrigerator and drags it over to the counter where the silver serving tray is kept. I pull the steaming muffins from the oven and set them on the counter. Ramona has placed napkins on the tray and is now making a careful stack of the small juice glasses beside them.

"Très bien, mon chou. Très soigneusement!"

Ramona watches as I remove the steaming muffins, one by one, from the muffin tray and set them to cool on the wire rack.

A striped tabby cat leaps up onto the counter and mews plaintively, lithe form snaking back and forth in agitation. With her sharp, gleaming teeth and thin whine of impatient desire, she seems, wordlessly, to speak for me in my frustrated, hungry state. Ramona gathers the cat in her arms, simultaneously stroking and scolding her.

"No, Heloise. Get down!"

The cat mock-bites her, sulkily and without force, and then begins licking the spot on the child's arm where she'd feigned aggression. Sniffling noisily, Ramona slides the importuning animal toward the edge of the counter and then off, carelessly trusting that the cat will land on her feet, which she does. Heloise casts a last brooding look our way, issues a final reproachful meow, and then slinks off to beg for succor elsewhere.

I hand Ramona a tissue for her runny nose, and she blows daintily, then rubs the snot-smeared tissue back and forth under it.

"Are those morning glory muffins?" she asks, pointing a chubby, no doubt snot-coated finger too close to a blueberry.

"They are," I say, and lift her tiny, light frame up to the sink to wash her hands.

"*Ooooh!*" she exclaims with the wonderfully immoderate enthusiasm of the very young. "I *yuv* morning glory muffins!"

"You yuv them?" I tease, laughing and tapping her button nose with a dot of warm, soapy water.

I set her back on the step stool and chuck her under the chin. She curls away, giggling. I arrange the muffins on a plate, along with the pitcher of milk, glasses, and napkins, and take the whole tray up in my hands.

"Do we have everything?" I ask her.

She nods brightly.

"Very well then, put the step stool away, please, and we can go."

She drags the stool across the floor again, struggles a bit to fold it and then to put it away.

"Do you have it, mon poussin? As-tu besoin d'aide?"

She gets the stool in place and, shaking her head, joins me at the door.

"Good job, ma belle. *Quelle force! Quelle détermination!*"

"Merci," she says primly, brushing her hair back from her face and following me out the door and back down the hall.

Even apart from my influence, the students at the school are precocious and generally well behaved—the children of upper-class defectors from Manhattan, who've abandoned the city for some ideal of the bucolic but have retained the need to achieve and display through their youngsters. As a result, they're potty-trained, most by professionals. Many have been tutored on letters, numeracy, preliteracy skills, as well as cooperative play. Harvard, it would seem, hangs in the balance of every tantrum or playground scuffle. Since the messy stuff has all been taken care of, the admissions process so severely winnowing, my program is then free to be exactly what I want it to be: European, neo-classical, but with a dash of Rousseau, full of song, dance, and art. In the afternoon, the sunlight pours through the cut-glass doors of the dance studio, glimmering on the delicate gilt hairs of the children's arms as they stretch and bend and flex them over their heads like little dandelions bending in a breeze. When the weather is fine, we troupe out to the garden in paint-spattered smocks to paint en plein air, and afterward the children eat lunch on picnic blankets beneath the flowering freesia that floats purple petals down onto the lawn around them, so that they look like a fleet of small gondoliers in a sea of restless lavender.

Very lovely. Very cheerful, as all preschool environments should be. I've made it so very deliberately, for my own sake as much as for the children's. After ample acquaintance with this world, I, personally, have found it to be quite a sinister place, a place where, more often than not, the strong crush the weak; sickness, hunger, and poverty prey upon the young and vulnerable; fools rule over the wise; and entropy moves all things ultimately toward disorder and decay. Nothing good I've known has been spared destruction. Everything I've loved I've lost, and not generally with sweet goodbyes and tearful embraces—violently, horrifically, such that it seems that to love *is to lose*.

But who can live looking such grim truths straight in the face every day for eternity? Not me. Not anymore. And so I've created, in this school, a kind of greenhouse: a lovely, if artificial, place of perennial bloom and beauty where I can live in peace, unheeding of the blowing winter storms outside. For a long time, I troubled myself with all the pain and suffering in the world. I struggled too long against the riptide of reality to the point of exhaustion, to drowning. What did it gain me or anyone? Nothing. Swim with the tide, not against, they say. Busy yourself in your greenhouse, remain untroubled, avoid becoming attached to any one blossom because the day comes when every flower fades, and then it must be cut off, tossed outside, and forgotten.

For this kind of lovely but detached existence, a preschool is really ideal. After all, can anything be more explicitly transient than early childhood? Preschool is the briefest imaginable thing. Two years overstuffed with energy, curiosity, momentum. The most buzzingly alive a person will ever be they are at three, four, five years old. Preschool is a line drive, a Slip 'N Slide, a mad dash to something else. Enjoy, but do not get attached. Eat, drink, and be merry, for tomorrow it all slips away to puberty and acne and angst. Once it's gone, forget it. New students are at the door, and we begin again.

BACK IN THE CLASSROOM, RAMONA makes for the dramatic play area, where she earnestly sets about layering herself in gauzy costumes. I wipe the glass of the terrarium where we keep a handful of furry caterpillars to observe their transformation into swallowtail butterflies. Hand, nose, and forehead prints are stamped across the glass: evidence of the great fascination and perhaps inarticulable sympathy that the children feel for these tiny creatures, who are performing their brief, miraculous transformations at only a slightly more dramatic rate than the children themselves.

A few minutes later the doorbell rings three times in quick succession. My guess is that there are several children huddled on my doorstep. Every child I've ever known has been afflicted with a desperate mania for ringing doorbells, pressing elevator buttons, and, if they can reach them, flipping light switches on and off.

I head down the hall again, open the door, and children pour into the house. In pigtails and parkas, with packs on their backs, bubble gum toothpaste on their breath, and fruity vitamins dissolving in their bloodstreams, they shake off mittens and make faces at one another. A few adults crowd the front stoop, but most of the drivers, nannies, and parents watch from behind the steering wheels of the cars lined up along the drive. I give the signal smile and wave, and they begin fighting one another for the exit like contenders in a chariot race.

"Madame! Madame!"

Annabelle, five years old and new this year, rushes to me and spreads her mouth wide in an extravagant grin. Her front right tooth is a gaping memory. I throw my eyes wide, take her pretty, brown face in one hand, and put the other to my forehead in theatrical dismay.

"Mon Dieu! Quelle catastrophe! Children, enfants, Annabelle's lost a tooth! Everyone, quick, look for Annabelle's tooth!"

The children giggle. A few of the younger ones watch in open-mouthed confusion from where they sit changing their shoes.

"Don't worry, Annabelle. It has to be here somewhere. We'll find it."

Annabelle laughs and squirms with delight. "No." She giggles. "I lost it last night."

She smiles her toothy smile again in evidence, this time sticking her tongue through the gap. I take her under my arm and hug her against my side.

"Ah, of course you did. And did you have a visit from la petite souris? From the tooth fairy?"

"Yeah! I got five dollars!"

I clutch a hand to my chest in shock, not entirely feigned.

"Oh la la!" I say, stooping down to help Sophie with a twisted sock. "You are une femme riche, très, très riche!"

As the children finish putting their things away, one by one they head down the hall to the classroom, where they can choose from the activities scattered around the room. A few stragglers remain in the cloakroom, working at stubborn knots in shoelaces, giving friends furtive peeks at their show-and-tell items, or simply sitting on the rug in a soporific daze.

Each year, about half of my students graduate—butterflies with new wings, fluttering off to the rest of their lives—and a handful of little caterpillars are newly enrolled. I have four new students this year. Chocolate-skinned and angelically beautiful, Annabelle is the daughter of the US ambassador to Algeria. She arrived on the first day of school in an actual tiara and threw a formidable tantrum during our first painting lesson, when a drip of Naples yellow landed on one of her saddle shoes, but after a few weeks of her theatrics being carefully ignored, she was able to, with what seemed like genuine relief, drop them and begin simply enjoying herself.

Then there is Octavio, who is adorable and funny and far too aware of both, and Sophie, who has already put her things away and run down the hall to play with the screwdrivers and scrap metal and sing show tunes to herself in her sweet little off-key voice. Her older sister is in musical theater, and so Sophie is always singing funny, unexpected songs like "Gee, Officer Krupke" and "Make 'Em Laugh."

Last is Leo Hardman—a pitiful little figure, it must be admitted, matchstick thin, sallow, and quiet. He hasn't arrived yet. It'd be surprising if he had. He's at least half an hour late to school almost every day. His nanny, a pretty young international student from Mexico City named Valeria, drops him off each morning, ducking her head and apologizing for their tardiness. The one time I asked about it, the girl told me in hesitant English that she gets to the house on time to pick Leo up, but that often Leo is not ready for school; sometimes he's not even awake yet.

"I wonder if his parents would consider having you arrive earlier?" I asked. "So you could help with getting him up and ready? I could suggest it maybe?"

"I ask them already," she said with a shake of the head and a shrug, "but they don't want."

I almost didn't accept the Hardmans into the school at all. Leo's very sweet, even if he's not the kind of hearty seedling I usually bring into my greenhouse of a school—too sickly, too vulnerable, and apt to cause me worry—but his parents were even further from ideal. The truth is, I'm careful primarily in my selection of parents, not children. I like pretty much every kid, even the rascally ones; they're too young to be blamed for their defects, and they're so incredibly responsive to consistency and kindness that reforming a genuine *enfant roi* can be just plain fun. Adults are more hit or miss, and when it's a miss, they're flat-out incorrigible. For my purposes, I want agreeable, pleasant, uncritical parents who will keep out of my way and turn in forms on time.

Leo's parents, Dave and Katherine Hardman, were all right on paper—a bond trader and an interior designer, respectively—no question of tuition payments being made in full. And in person, they were attractive and well put together. Dave was tall and barrel-chested, with angular features that gave him an imposing, hawkish look. Katherine was elegantly dressed and pretty, with dark hair that reached her shoulders and formed a soft heart shape around her face, and thickly lashed green eyes so large that they reminded me of a doll or cartoon princess.

She listened with rapt focus and answered questions thoughtfully, but her husband seemed almost as though he was trying, deliberately and even creatively, to make the worst possible impression.

While Katherine leaned forward attentively with one elbow on her crossed knee and her long, pretty fingers braced against her chin, Dave sat slouched back in his chair, thick fingers intertwined across his stomach, alternately yawning and looking around the room with an air of something between boredom and outright hostility. When he spoke, it was only to quietly contradict some minor point that his wife had made. Katherine spent most of the interview smoothing over these subtle aggressions and smiling excessively while the skin above the neckline of her shirt betrayed her embarrassment with its bright flush of color.

At one point, I asked Dave if he had any questions.

"Just how much?" he replied in a martyred tone. When I produced the tuition forms, he waved them away.

"Doesn't matter. Whatever it is, I'll pay it soon enough."

Through all this, Leo sat beside his mother, small and delicate as a baby bird, with large, droopy eyes, a chaotic mop of dark hair, and the sallow, unwell coloring of a Middle Easterner who's been kept from the sun. He was quiet, except for sporadic conniptions of coughing, which he smothered against the arm of his mother's jacket, leaving wet marks on the material. In the awkward lull after Mr. Hardman's last comment, he erupted into one of these coughs again.

"Are you not feeling well today, Leo?" I asked. "That's a nasty cough you've got."

The little boy just shrank slightly against his mother's sleeve.

"He has a weak respiratory system," Katherine said. "Always has, since birth. It's actually much better now. When he was a baby, I swear, he was constantly sick—bronchitis, RSV, ear infections, I mean, God's honest truth, you name it, he had it, sometimes more than one at a time. He spent a week in the hospital with pneumonia when he was two. It's *much* better now. This cough comes and goes, and he has some mild asthma, but it's nothing like it used to be. They used to call us by our first names at the emergency room."

She frowned down at the sleeve of her jacket, which she had just noticed was being used as a handkerchief.

"Did they?" Dave put in with a tone of disdainful skepticism. "Did they call you by name at the emergency room?"

"Leo," I said, ignoring the bizarrely antagonistic remark and the exchange of looks that passed between husband and wife after it, "can I get you a glass of water? Do you think that would help your cough?"

Leo again just looked at me with his big, dark eyes.

"He's also going through a bit of a quiet spell these days," Katherine said. "Leo, you heard Ms. Collette. Would you like water?"

"Honestly," Mr. Hardman said, leaning toward me and lowering his voice conspiratorially, "I think there's a bit of attention-seeking to it. Like mother, like son."

I wasn't sure whether he was referring to the cough or quiet spell, nor did I care. I felt suddenly seized with claustrophobia, as if the Hardmans' marital tension were a fifth and grotesquely oversized presence that left little room in the small office for the rest of us.

"May I take Leo for a walk? Just around the school?"

A walking tour with the child was a portion of the interview process usually reserved only for those under serious consideration, but I had a sudden burning desire to escape the oppressive tension of the Hardmans' company.

The adults rose to join us, but I motioned them back down.

"Please, stay. Rina will get you coffee and cream fresh from the farm down the road, where I take the children for regular field trips. Leo and I will be back shortly."

I wasn't sure if the timid child would come with me, but when I offered him my hand he took it, and we set off, touring the various rooms of the school, where he did listless wending turns, observing everything, half-heartedly touching a book here, a Hula-Hoop there, and responding to my questions with nods, headshakes, and stoic gazes. When we entered the art room, though, his whole countenance changed. His posture straightened. His lethargic gaze turned quick, bouncing around the room, taking in every detail with wonder.

"Try anything you like," I said, and he turned to me an expression of incredulity.

"Anything," I repeated with a nod. "Really, go ahead."

He bellied up to a table with a wooden model of the human form, an assortment of Conté crayons, pencils, and pastels, and looked to me again. I smiled and nodded. He took a seat in the little chair, picked up a stick of pastel, and dragged it across a sheet of paper, leaving a thick scuff of green behind it. He swapped it out for another and drew another line, then another. He studied the oily pigment. With his finger he smudged it, then he looked at the bright spot on his finger with alarm.

"That's all right," I said, handing him a cloth. "Our fingers are our most important instrument for art. If we're working hard, they're bound to get dirty."

He took a drawing pencil from a tin and began to draw. I stood silently behind him and watched. Most children begin drawing using tricks or strategies. A star is always two triangles inverted against each other. Birds in the sky are always wilting Vs. The sun is invariably a circle spoked with rays, like a bicycle wheel. Leo drew a house—an entirely common thing to do—but it was in no way generic; it had specificity and detail. I recognized it as a three-story brownstone, the type common in the city, where his family had just moved from. He drew people in front of the house—not stick figures, more like thin snowmen. Their faces and hair were intricate and fascinating. With the pencil he delicately drew some two dozen noodley strands of hair on each.

The family members were arranged from tallest to shortest, as is common: first a female with long hair and a pretty mouth, then a male with wild hair going up and out almost like the tip of a flame, followed by another almost identical but smaller, and finally a cat with varied blotches on its flank and face.

"Is that a picture of your family, Leo?"

He didn't answer, but just gazed down at the portrait and shaded a spot on the cat a bit more.

"It's a wonderful picture. Did you know we have cats here at school? Is that your cat in the picture?"

"Well, it was," he sighed heavily, "but Puzzle ran away, and then we moved, so she'll never be able to find me."

"Oh, I'm so sorry to hear that. That must have made you very sad. Puzzle was her name? That's a wonderful name for a cat."

He continued shading various parts of the picture without further comment.

"Is that your mother, there?"

A nod.

"And your father?"

He shook his head no and set about thickening the hair on the heads of the figures.

"What about that one, is that him?"

Another shake of the head.

"Where's your father, then?" I said with a laugh. Familial alliances and affections are often put on callous display in children's portraits. Leo just shrugged.

"One of these is you, I'm guessing," I said, pointing to the two medium-sized males in the lineup. "That one, am I right?"

A nod.

"So, then who is the other one?"

Leo turned his large eyes up at me, seeming for a moment to study me, then he shrugged again.

"You're a very good artist, Leo. *Very* good. Let's try something."

I reached over his shoulder and pulled the wooden form closer to him. I lifted the arms of the blank-faced person as though it were about to take a deep bow from a theater stage.

"Can you draw this for me?" I asked.

His eyes moved to the form, fixing it with his squinting gaze. His tongue pushed out from the side of his mouth and he hunched forward. His grip on the pencil tightened with intent. He drew the figure. In tight lines, from his painfully tight grip, it emerged, rigid and angular, but still remarkable for so young a child.

Next, I made the figure kneel on one knee, the bent leg foreshortened, a challenge even for advanced artists. Children will usually change the position in their drawing so that the problem leg appears at a different angle, a Picasso-esque solution to the conundrum of perspective. Leo didn't avoid, he didn't recast the leg as logic would suggest a leg should be, he drew the leg as he saw it: no longer a leg, but an assemblage of shapes that in combination equaled a leg. It was a child's drawing, to be sure, but it was astonishing nonetheless in its fearlessness, its freedom from the constraint of logic, its instinctive artistry. I held up the drawings for us to examine together.

"You have talent, Leo. Do you like to draw? Does this make you happy?"

He looked at me, his eyes seeming anything but happy, but then he nodded and a tiny flicker of a smile lifted the edges of his mouth.

"Well, let's go show these fantastic drawings to your parents, shall we? I think they'll be very impressed."

To my surprise, Leo shook his head. Cautiously he reached for the first drawing he had made of the house and his family, leaving the others in my hand. He took hold of an edge of the drawing and began folding it tightly. When it was coiled into a tight scroll, he stuffed it deep in his pocket.

"You'd prefer to keep that one just for yourself?"

He nodded.

"What about the others? May I show these to Mom and Dad?"

He nodded again, and I wondered if he perhaps thought his dad would be upset that he hadn't been included in the family picture. When we returned to the office, though, Katherine was alone. She offered a story about a forgotten but terribly important appointment Dave had had to dash off to, and we both pretended to be grieved by his absence. When I showed Katherine Leo's figure drawings, I wondered if he would pull the other drawing from where it was folded in his pocket to show her since Dave was gone, but he didn't.

Alone later, I contemplated Leo's figure drawings. They showed real talent of a kind I rarely encountered. I thought of Katherine and Dave Hardman, their marriage rotten and reeking like a bad piece of fruit. Plenty of my parents probably had less than blissful marriages, but they had the good taste and personal restraint to fake it in public. I thought of parent-teacher conferences with the Hardmans, of school field trips with them as chaperones. It was not appealing. However, I reasoned that men like Dave Hardman were not usually the involved-father, chaperoning types. I would probably only ever interact with Katherine, and I'd found her pleasant enough. The Hardmans were a gamble and more trouble than I generally liked, but the thought of working with a child with genuine artistic ability was enticing. I made up my mind and offered Leo a spot in the school.

It's turned out to be a spot that he fills only slightly more than half of the time.

Stepping out onto the front stoop and taking one final look down the drive, I wonder when Leo will show up today. He's always frustrated when he misses any of the painting lesson.

"D'accord, my sillies," I say, closing the front door and turning to the children still milling in the entryway or sprawled on the floor. "Are we ready to make our way to the classroom?"

"Mmmm, something smells sooooo good!" Octavio exclaims from where he sits on the floor, rubbing his tummy theatrically.

"C'est vrai. You're right," I say. "Is anyone else hungry?"

A gurgle from my own stomach joins the enthusiastic response of the children. The scent of blood is pervasive and tantalizing, and I, for one, am hungry.

· III ·

FOR a short time, I was kept in the small stone carriage house on my grandparents' estate. I passed the solitary hours of those days playing half-heartedly with a rag doll Grandfather had brought me or putting my eye to the crack in the wide blue shutters. From that crack, I could see the house rising up along the horizon, its great stone bulk dwarfing the surrounding pines, its five chimneys assaulting the sky. Most afternoons my grandmother, dressed in the black of mourning, went walking in the garden. From the window, I watched her pause to gently lift the trumpet of a lily or lean close, eyes closed, to breathe in the fragrance of a shrub rose.

"You understand that you must not speak to her," Grandfather said when he walked in one afternoon and found me standing at the window. "Yes, Anya?"

"Anna," I whispered with quiet belligerence. "My name is Anna."

My own impudence startled me so that my lip quaked and I struggled to blink back hot tears, but I felt a desperate need to hear my name, my born name, the name my father had called me by. Everything was so changed. Grandfather had changed it all, and now he would even call me by a new name? It was too much.

Grandfather laughed merrily, belly thrown out, as though I had said something delightfully funny. When his laughter settled, he held a hand up in front of him, spread his thick, blunt fingers wide.

"Rausium, Rhagusium, Rausia," he said, counting off on the fingers. "Raugia, Rachusa, Lavusa, Labusa. These are the names—just some of them, mind you—by which my country has been called."

He wagged a finger at me scoldingly.

"Names are like hats, Anya. You put them on, you take them off. If it's cold you wear a warm one. Old things will go by many names over time. Do not become attached."

He strode over to the shuttered window, glanced out through the crack he had come in to find me standing by.

"You must not speak to her. Ever. Let me assure you that to do so would not improve your circumstances, but may only jeopardize hers. I know this is hard for you, my child, and I am sorry, but it must be so. It *must* be so. Vremenie—those who die young—they are like babes. They are of limited understanding. Even good ones such as your grandmother. It is imprudent to confront them with matters they are incapable of understanding."

"What of me, Grandfather?"

"You?" he said. The look in his eye teetered precariously between amusement and irritation. "What of you?"

"I am beyond my understanding," I said. A tear broke loose from my eye, and I swiped at it furiously with my sleeve.

My grandfather gazed at me coolly, his eyes the color of dark honey. One corner of his mouth lifted in a faint smile.

"No," he said. "You're not. With much practice, I have learned to see what lies inside of men as others see what lies without, and, in you, I see a tremendous capacity for understanding. You understand *me*, for instance. You fought against your tears in my presence because you have sensed intuitively that I am a man who revels in strength, who has little patience with weakness and self-pity. I am also, if you had not sensed it, a man who is invigorated by battle."

Here he thumped a fist to his chest and took a great sniff of the air like an alpinist atop some great summit.

"The more I am resisted, the *stronger* I become! Those who oppose me would as well oppose the rising of the sun, or the crashing of the waves of the sea—*but* all who trust themselves to my stewardship may count on the most solicitous and unfailing care from me. *You* understand this, clever child that you are, and so I know that you will obey me. You will not speak to her or anyone save myself and Agoston."

His tone at certain points in this speech had struck me with a certain hardness, almost menace even, but now it softened and became kindly.

"You are lonely and unhappy. I know it and I am devising a remedy. Things will not remain as they are for long. Only trust me and keep my commands, yes?"

For some reason, perhaps because, as he had said, I understood him, I felt trembly and closer to tears than ever. I sat on the edge of my bed with my hands still in my lap.

"Yes, Anya?" he said, tilting his head to peer into my downturned face. "*Ah*, my apologies, *Anna*?"

There was a moment's silence.

"Yes, Grandfather," I said quietly.

GRANDFATHER HAD A BUTLER, AGOSTON, who was charged with seeing to my maintenance. Agoston was a tall, barrel-chested man with dark hair and a full, dark beard that held a single tuft of white hair on one side of it. Each day, he came in without knocking to replace the logs by the hearth, empty the chamber pot, and throw down a freshly slaughtered animal carcass on the wooden table, all with a grin on his face that seemed to me to hold a subtle menace. I was afraid of him and his grin, and so I scowled every time he came in, but this only made his grin wider and more frightening.

For a long time, I didn't eat. I couldn't. My stomach groaned, but it was unimaginable to me to cross the room to that animal, pick it up, and feel my new, hidden teeth unsheathe, shift forward, puncture skin. It was too frightening.

When Agoston would come in and find the rabbit or grouse he'd brought the day before untouched, he would grab it by its stiffened haunches and wave it luridly at me, jabbering in the indecipherable dialect that he and Grandfather shared. Then he would toss the thing back and catch the neck in his own grinning mouth, small streams of blood running casually down his chin. When I turned my head in disgust, he would laugh.

Rather than eat the food that Agoston brought, I snuck downstairs at night and gnawed at the dirty beets and carrots that were kept there for the carriage horses. The roots tasted strange and inedible in my mouth, but still I sat on the dirt floor, trying to force them down, then retching them back up and crying furiously into my pink, beet-stained hands. I could smell the blood of the horses, and it made me desperately hungry, which only added to my despair.

Despite Grandfather's warning, I was tempted still to go to my grandmother, to run crying out into the sunlight and the flowers, throw myself against her and bury my face in the soft wool of her black shawl. But after our conversation, Grandfather, taking no chances, made sure to accompany my grandmother in the garden. Though I was invisible behind the shutters, he managed to look directly at me, his eyes calm, but the interdiction in them clear and arresting nonetheless.

It was soon after that that I was roused from sleep in the night. Grandfather bid me to wake and get dressed. I looked at the traveling clothes he had brought for me, heard the warm snorting of the horses outside, their hooves tossing the gravel. Out the window I saw the dark coats of the animals gleaming in the soft light of the carriage lamps.

"Where are we going?" I asked—but when I turned back, Grandfather had gone.

In the lane, Agoston hefted a trunk up into the coach.

I asked again. "Where are we going, Grandfather?"

He held my hand and helped me climb up the carriage step. Inside, he arranged a blanket over the velvet skirt of my new Brunswick, the motions of his large hands deft and delicate.

"We are not going," he said, backing out of the coach and closing the door firmly behind him. "*You* are going. To my country. Agoston is going with you. You will be very happy there just as I was in my youth."

I clawed for his hand where it rested on the door sash.

"No, Grandfather, no." Afraid of the trouble I might be in if I made a stir, I kept my voice low, but the hysteria was clear in it, and the tears ran immediately down my cheeks.

"Please, Grandfather, *please*. I'll behave. I will never speak to Grandmother. Do not send me away. Do not send me alone."

"You will not be alone. As I have said, Agoston will be with you."

"Grandfather," I whispered, my hands shaking violently against his, "I do not wish to go with him. I am frightened of him."

"If you are frightened of him, you would as well be frightened of me, for I trust him as I trust myself. He is better than a brother to me."

"How long must I be away?" I asked, clutching at him and searching for his eyes in the dark. "Will you come for me after a time?"

"*Yes, yes*, after a time, I will come for you. Do not fret," he said soothingly, and tried to remove his hand from my grasp, but I clung to him, whimpering. Finally, he took both of my hands in his own, his grip both gentle and irresistible.

"Anya, I will speak now, and you will listen."

With those words and the force of his hands on my own, his eyes on mine, the will to do anything else escaped me. I felt my body and mind slow and go still. It was hard to tell whether his words had compelled me or something else, some invisible but overwhelming power emanating from his being. Satisfied, he went on.

"All of the beings of all of the realms of the world are divided thus—"

He held up two fingers. My hands, released, fell heavily in my lap and remained still.

"—Those who fear and those who do not. You have great power in you, lyubimaya, but you are afraid. The only unpardonable sin is sheltering another from the death of their fear. *I* will *never* commit such a sin. I will never hinder you from the death of your fear. Indeed, Anya, out of my great affection for you, I would hasten you to it. It is my gift to you."

Grandfather nodded up at Agoston, perched upon the driver's seat. There was the snap of a whip, and then the coach was in motion, and Grandfather disappeared into the distance and the darkness.

. . .

THERE WAS A SHIP THEN. A sailing packet in a harbor at dawn, bright sails, and the sunrise swelling on the horizon behind. It looked, to me, like a white-winged angel or some mythological ocean goddess, arms spread benevolently, pale robes filling with wind.

Agoston had a private cabin—a clean but narrow room with two narrow bunks stacked atop each other and a washstand—which was intended for us both. When we arrived, a porter led us belowdecks to it, but I wouldn't enter. Whatever my grandfather said, I still feared Agoston and despised him.

Agoston stood in the narrow room, his large frame filling the suffocating space like a hand in a glove, and tossed his head at the upper bunk, ordering me in. When I didn't move, he took a step forward so that he towered just inside the doorway, his head stooped under the low wood beams of the ceiling. Again, he tossed his head at my bunk. I remained where I was, gave a barely perceptible shake of the head. He looked me in the eye for a long moment, then his expression transformed horribly into that familiar grin. He laughed and, in a sudden, startling motion, slammed the cabin door shut.

If I had known what was to come, I might have more carefully considered sharing the cabin with Agoston. At Long Island Harbor, at least two hundred passengers boarded the packet and shoved their way into the tween deck with their bags and trunks, their young children and crying babies. A pair of enormous horses were backed fitfully into a narrow pen next to the bunks and fixed there with harnesses that creaked and jingled with their constant stirrings.

People eyed me curiously: a young girl in a blue velvet Brunswick that might have cost as much as all the contents of all their trunks combined, sitting alone on a hard bunk in steerage. Trying to attract little notice, I'd chosen an out-of-the-way bunk toward the back of the ship. I didn't know that the middle of the ship was where you wanted to be—where the rocking of the ship was least nauseating—or that we'd all soon be desperate for what small drafts of fresh air and sunshine came down from the stairway.

"Lord Jesus above, you're a curious picture, aren't you?" a woman exclaimed, lifting a little girl onto the bunk beside me and then setting a ruddy-faced toddler in a pudding cap onto the girl's lap. "You must be lost. These are hardly the accommodations for such a fine young lady."

I remained silent. The baby reached for the fringe at my elbow with a spit-slicked finger. The mother gasped and flicked the child's finger.

"Mercy! That velvet is worth our passage three times over. Don't let Jonas put a finger on her, or we'll be stuck in this ship for a month after we've made land."

The little girl, Mercy, perhaps two years younger than myself, shifted the child onto her other hip.

"Apologies, miss," she murmured.

"It's no bother," I said. "I don't mind."

The woman addressed her daughter, as though it were she who had contradicted her rather than I. "Her ma and pa are likely to mind, so you'll be careful nonetheless."

"My mother and father are dead," I said. "Brother too. All my family's dead. There's no one to mind but me, and I don't."

The mother, who had been busily organizing their belongings at their bunk, stopped midmotion and turned to me. She gave me a long, troubled look, pressed her lips together, and then looked away.

· IV ·

THE benefits of children interacting with animals are underresearched but widely accepted, and it's a rare preschool classroom that doesn't feature a cage of rabbits lazily chewing pellets, the intermittent squeak of a gerbil working diligently at its wheel, or, at minimum, a fish swimming small laps in a bowl. At our school, we have cats. The two that wander freely downstairs, Myrrh and Heloise, are hypoallergenic and very friendly. The rest are upstairs and are kept more for my purposes than for the children's, though a strong case could be made that their benefit to the children is significant, if indirect.

One by one, hour by hungry hour, the colored bars of our daily schedule come down, chipping slowly at the time before their afternoon nap, when my nagging appetite will finally be sated. We're fastidious in our routines, though, so I must go through the rituals of naptime—potty visits, a diaper or two for the deep sleepers, blankies, binkies, and stuffed animals administered with the exactingness of medications to patients in a psych ward—all while doing my best to ignore the impatience of my growing hunger.

The cats are ever at my side, soothing the children with purrs and affectionate rubs, picking dainty paths among the cots so that their tails bob up among them like submarine periscopes. The children reach for them drowsily from where they lie on the cots with their eyes dipping toward sleep. When the shades are drawn, the room deep in shadow, and the only sounds are the audible sucking of thumbs and the lazy rhythmic beat of slippered feet kicking against cot rails, I'm finally able to attend to my hunger. My blood teeth are poised and ready. Like the flood of saliva before a bite of food, there's no restraining them once they've sensed that a meal is imminent.

I rise quietly from the rocking chair, whose rhythmic creak eases the children each day to sleep. I pick my way slowly and carefully among the cots slung with blankets and slumbering children, surveying their progress toward sleep. One cot is empty; instead of being tardy today, Leo is absent. After bending here and there to straighten a blanket or retrieve a fallen pacifier from where it lies on the rug, I slip out the door and climb the flight of stairs to the second floor, and then another—a rickety pull-down ladder that descends in a creaking cascade—to the attic.

At the top of those last wooden steps, I put my hands, palm up, against the door and lift it upward slowly and carefully.

There is the immediate ammoniac odor of urine that no amount of scrubbing and airing has been able to eradicate. I open the door farther and the babylike mewing of cats is a thin, ragtag chorus.

Suddenly, Myrrh, who I didn't realize had accompanied me to the third floor, darts past me and up the stairs into the sun-flooded room, which her feline friends, some twenty or so of them, are filling with busy and delicate motion.

Cats stretch and yawn in the sunlight on the hardwood floor. They lick their paws and white-cotton underbellies on the windowsills. Atop the backs of couches covered in ancient drop cloths, cat tails twitch and hang curved in the air like question marks at the ends of wordless sentences. Twenty-odd pairs of diamond eyes turn and glitter my way. A few of the more sociable creatures leap from their perches and saunter over to greet me.

My hunger is impatient, but it wouldn't do to get right down to business. I've kept a variety of animals at different points in my life, and of all of them, cats are the fussiest. There are formalities, greeting rituals as strict and obligatory as those exchanged between foreign dignitaries. I sit down cross-legged on the floor and pass a few minutes petting the cats as they glide by, their movements akin in some way to sharks, sensuous and predatory at the same time.

At last, I take a treat from the bag I've brought with me, fold it in my palm, and give a low whistle. Whatever cats had remained where they were now leap from their spots and trot toward me. Myrrh, my pretty Russian blue, my beloved teacher's pet, is ahead of the rest as usual. She climbs elegantly onto my lap and settles in. I stroke her soft gray fur and she purrs. When I part the fur at her neck, she is obligingly still.

"What a good girl you are. So pretty and good."

When I'm done, she leaps down, extracts the treat from my open palm with her sharp porcelain teeth, curls up beside me, and begins to gnaw it.

Another cat climbs nimbly onto my lap.

· V ·

THE North Atlantic is a lunatic ocean, a raging, howling, hateful, cold beast. It isn't hard to imagine a predatory kraken rising up from its dark depths, enfolding the hull of a ship inside sensitive, ravenous arms—as if there could be any need for additional, imaginary horrors on the passage across the sea.

The tween deck was horribly crowded, damp, cold. Passengers received allotments of oatmeal, flour, rice, biscuits, and tea, but all had to cook for themselves in a single galley, and fights broke out almost immediately. Then a gale set in, and no one ate hot food at all because no one could cook with the ship climbing up the waves like mountains and then tumbling violently down again. Babies wailed, and children cried. When people were sick, there was nothing to do but put their heads out of their bunks, and so vomit covered the steerage floor and fed the rats that seized the opportunity to scrabble about boldly.

I lay on my back in one of the bottom bunks, where the vomit splashed up when the sick passengers let it fall, and the rats moved within reach. The little girl, Mercy, lay in the bunk above mine and peered down at me wide-eyed and trembling. Beside her in the same bunk, her mother held her baby brother and tried without success to soothe the screaming child.

Grandfather had said that I would never die. Was it true? And what would that mean if the ship was smashed to bits as it seemed constantly in danger of? I pictured Mercy, her mother and brother and myself sinking together in the frigid blue, the flotsam dancing slowly around us, the horses kicking as they drowned. They would all die—and I would watch them? Would it hurt, to be unable to breathe in the water and also unable to die? In my mind I saw the kraken rise up from the blackest depths, its suckered tentacles picking curiously amid the wreckage. I lay on my bunk, unmoving. I did not shake and cry quietly as Mercy did, but I thought that I was surely more afraid than she, that I would surely prefer to die than to be left in the sea with the kraken and a ship's worth of dead bodies.

After four days, the first storm finally passed, and we passengers all climbed gratefully onto the upper deck to feel the sun on our skin and also to slide two shrouded bodies over the side of the ship. One was a pregnant woman who had gone into labor during the storm and had been unable to deliver. Her husband stood to the side, stone-faced, but swaying too much for the gentle motion of the ship. He was drunk, and when he slipped and fell and then just lay there, the rest of the passengers looked to one another knowingly. The other body was that of a small child who'd choked on his own vomit as he slept. There was no minister on board, and so the captain took the hat from his head and offered a brief, pitiless eulogy.

"From the toils, Lord, of this world, to rest in the next."

"Isn't right," a woman beside me muttered as she made the sign of the cross. "Poor, sweet souls ought to have a decent Christian burial if naught else. There's no rest to be had in the sea."

DURING THE STORM, NONE OF the passengers had managed more than a few fitful snatches of sleep, and so on that first calm night afterward, we all slept to make up for it. It was the quietest it had been in steerage since we'd boarded—only a soft chorus of whistling noses, snores, and snorts—yet for some reason, I woke up.

Darkness at sea, when the moon is hidden by clouds, is a darkness more complete than any other, but my vision had changed with the rest of me, and so I could see something off at the far end of the quarters, a figure, it seemed, standing in the darkness. At first, the shape remained motionless so that I thought I'd only imagined that it was a figure at all, and I started to drift off to sleep again, but then it moved, quickly and silently, as if taking just a single large step to the left, then it was motionless again.

Awake now and rigid with fear, I lay still, peering into the far blackness, and trying to make out who or what it was moving about in the shadows there. With movements like those of a large predatory animal, the figure continued its start-and-stop progress, the motion and then stillness by which it was making its way slowly along the bunks. My first confused and childish thought was ghost or monster, but then, as my mind cleared, I thought thief: someone rummaging brazenly through folks' belongings as they slept. But as my eyes adjusted and I saw better, I could see the figure bending its head over the resting forms of the sleeping passengers as if giving each one a long good night kiss.

It was Agoston. I realized it suddenly, and the yawning darkness of his open cabin door when I looked that way confirmed it. He was feeding on the passengers, drinking from them, one by one, as a bee moves from flower to flower.

I had never fed from a human, or even witnessed it. During the storm, in desperation, I had reached a hand out and grabbed a rat that had scuttled close to my bunk. Then I'd yanked the filthy curtains closed around my bed and crawled back on elbows and knees to face the wall, where even Mercy, the little girl from the bunk above, wouldn't see if she climbed down unannounced for a visit, as she sometimes did. Fighting down my own sickness, I held the squirming, scratching, greasy thing tightly in my fist, then plunged my teeth into it and heard it scream. I had not yet learned delicacy.

My heart pounded as I watched Agoston's dark bulk continue down the row, drawing closer and closer. I scrambled out of my bunk and climbed up into Mercy's, where I positioned myself between her and her mother and brother, all of them sleeping soundly. I didn't know what I would do, only that I would not allow Agoston to touch them.

He came closer, his movements perfectly soundless, while it seemed that I could hear the blood and adrenaline sloshing riotously through my body. What would he do? Would he fight me? Would he bite me? And then laugh, grinning as my blood ran down his chin?

The black outline of his form was a single bunk away now, and, with dread, I was reminded of his great size, the thick muscle roping his arms so that he heaved a trunk as lightly as if it were a parasol.

A bead of sweat fell from my chin. I could barely breathe. And then the figure was before me, and for too long it paused there without moving. Then, finally, slowly, it leaned forward toward Mercy's mother, who lay on her back with Mercy's brother asleep and nestled in the crook of her arm.

I balled my hand into a fist, and when his head was in the bunk, hovering over the woman, I let it fly. My knuckles connected with bone, the sharp ridge of Agoston's brow. He jerked back suddenly, putting a hand up to his head, while Mercy's mother sniffed in her sleep and I waited in terror for the reprisal. A split second later, he thrust himself forward again. I gave a strangled yelp of fright and felt a strong hand clamp around my wrist. It yanked, and then I was flying forward out of the bunk, my limbs floundering in the air as I fell.

Before I hit the floor headfirst, I was caught at the waist and dropped roughly on my butt and heels.

Those hands that had yanked me into the air now grabbed me by the shoulders and lifted me to standing so that I was face-to-face with the towering figure. In the dark, I could just barely make out Agoston's face and see, to my surprise, not anger, or even Agoston's usual leer, but an actual smile.

He took one of my arms, bent it at the elbow, and pushed it backward. Confused and still afraid, I resisted, and he shook my arm, forcing it loose, then tried again. I didn't understand, but I stopped resisting, and he nodded approvingly, put his hand around mine, and formed my fingers into a fist, then pushed my arm back until it nested against the side of my ribs. Then he pulled it forward in a controlled motion until it landed squarely in the center of his own chest. He nodded, pushed my arm back again, and then again pulled it forward in a straight line to the center of his chest. I'd punched Agoston in the head, but apparently, I'd not made a good enough show of it; he was correcting my form.

He released my arm and touched his fingers to the same spot on his abdomen. Someone in a bunk snorted and turned over, and I looked in the direction of the sound. Agoston touched the spot again and muttered impatiently in his language. I hesitated, then brought my fist forward, slowly, as he had done. He shook his finger at me and slammed his hand forcefully against his chest, and then tipped his hand at me, not so much inviting as commanding me to punch him with all my strength.

In my mind a fog lifted, and in place of thought I saw the dark headstones of my family, four lined up in the snow. I felt the hands of my neighbors on my arms, around my waist, on my forehead and chin, holding me firmly while the minister placed ashes in my forced-open mouth. I saw Grandfather, a mild expression on his face as he sent me off into the darkness, and I felt *rage* flood, warm and lovely, through me. I narrowed my eyes at the spot in the center of Agoston's chest. I clenched my jaw, pulled back my fist, and then punched him with everything in me.

I felt the impact ring through my bones like a shock wave, ring through him, though he, not without effort, held firm as a wall. It was like the waves hurling themselves at some rocky coast, like the wind of a cyclone slamming into the houses, ripping trees up out of the ground. It left me dazed, this unaccountable strength that no thin-armed child had any business possessing.

With an expression of incredulous wonder, I looked up to Agoston's face and found him nodding with satisfaction, that pleased smile wide on his face, then he patted me on the head, turned, went back through his cabin door, and closed it behind him.

I crept back into my bunk but lay awake in the dark for some time, dazed and elated by the sensation of my own strength.

· VI ·

VANO is instructing me by candlelight. With his musical voice he speaks of Mokosh, the damp. As he speaks, his large brown eyes look from me to the body on the table and back, and his brown hands work at the cloth. The overlarge robes he wears make him look young and delicate, but he is older than I am and his solemnity makes him seem even more so.

Piroska is somewhere in the background, a shadowy bustle at work with her herbs and tinctures.

I'm dreaming, so many years later, but I feel everything I felt as a young girl in Vano's presence, all the awe and unnameable longing. I want to feel the liquid brown of his eyes in my mouth. I want to bury my face in the velvet of his voice and swim in the warm sienna of his skin, count his beauty like heavy coins, *clink, clink, clink.*

Please, Vano, keep speaking. Tell me everything. Tell me about myself and the world and all the obliging deities you see hiding in the groves, brooding on the high cliffs, lighting up the skies.

"Mokosh, the wet earth, mother of Mora," Vano says, and looks down at the effigy between us, the thickly bundled body of corn husks, arms of braided straw. He lifts a willow branch from a pile on the table beside it.

"Mora, who lives and dies, lives and dies, and lives and dies again.

Sacrificial child of death and rebirth, axle upon which the seasons and the lives of men spin. We bind her with willow branches, the beard of Mokosh's dark lover, Veles."

The candles flicker all around him, their light biting into the edges of his dark silhouette. The hearth is full of hungry fire. With a firm tug, he knots the willow reeds across the chest of the Mora doll. He places a reed in my palm for me to knot and for an instant I relish the warmth of his hand. Last, a necklace of eggshells around Mora's neck, and then Vano places her in my hands and leads me to the hearth.

"The seasons are doors. The seasons are windows, opening and shutting one after another," Vano says. "There is a truth unique to spring, unique to winter, to fall, to summer. No act of spring can occur in fall. Winter is for dying, descending, hiding, forgetting. For being emptied of all we have, in preparation for receiving something new. The ages are this way as well. Only the occurrences of this time are permitted to occur. The events of tomorrow are never early. Nothing comes to pass late."

Together, as he speaks, we feed the body of straw slowly into the hearth, the bristles of the arm lighting and curling in flame first.

"We welcome, for a time, destruction, chaos, death," Vano says as the thick stalk of body catches. "We do not fight it. We submit to it, for it is what the season demands."

I drop the flaming figure then, but Vano holds fast to it. He steps gingerly with it into the fire.

"No," I say, pulling at him in confusion. "No, Vano!"

He turns serene eyes to me, burning in the white heart of the fire.

"Vano! No! Stop it!"

"We each have our endings, Anya," he says calmly, his flesh burning and falling away, "which come in their appointed season. We can accept them or fight them, but nevertheless they come. He brings them. You flee from him, Anya, but Czernobog of the ashes, the one who brings endings, keeps all in his sights. There is no hiding from him."

The name Czernobog sends a wash of fear through me. I turn away from the leaping fire and the terrible, familiar sight and smell of burning, and the physical effort wakes me.

I lurch up gasping, grief and terror still surging through my body. A moment passes before I can accept that I am in my bedroom in quiet Millstream Hollow, New York, not in a hut of timbers and thatch in a forest somewhere on the other side of the world, not engulfed in flames and listening to the horrible sounds of the dying.

For many years, I was tormented by terrible dreams, my mind a dark cornucopia of nightmarish material, but some time ago my sleeping mind went mercifully blank. This dream, so vivid and emotional and out of the ordinary, leaves me shaken. I feel disoriented, split open, and vulnerable. I haven't thought of Vano or of the small, strange family we were a part of—me, Vano, Ehru, Piroska—in years, and yet there he was in all his grave beauty, as vivid and overwhelming as ever he had been.

Vano had been an apprentice of sorts to Piroska, yet he'd known more than anyone, things that couldn't be learned or taught, and everything he said was true if you could only make sense of it. Often even he could not make sense of what he knew—he spoke of fire for months before any of us understood why—but he trusted his knowledge: the signs in the moss, the patterned sand left behind the raking tides, the anything-but-haphazard crumbling of the peat clods in the hearth—and so did the rest of us. Even now, the instinct springs up in me to treat his words with seriousness, to search them for what they portend. We each have our ending. That's what Vano had said, but how could that be? There would never be an end for me, no matter how much I desired one. And what he had said about Czernobog keeping me in his sights, still pursuing me—a god from a bygone peasant religion thousands of miles and a hundred years removed. Absurd, yet still *terrifying*. Maybe I had believed it long ago. Maybe I had, for many years, seemed to feel his frightening presence, seen his brutal hand behind every tragedy, once even thought I saw his face in a river, but that was all behind me. Barely believable then, even less so now.

Those things and Vano too—his knowledge, his magic and prescience—they belonged to a different time, to a world that was more porous, more numinous. The world changed, expunged itself of mystery and divinity. Now people wear shoulder pads. They get perms. If they want to see wonders, they flip a switch, turn a dial. Their tea leaves rot in tea bags; they don't intimate the future by their arrangements at the bottom of a cup. Gods don't give chase, and seasons don't bring predestined endings. It was a dream, that's all, an echo—something perhaps meaningful at its origin, but dissolved into nonsense over time and distance.

I sit up, rub my forehead. In a tender daze, I look out the window. The sky beyond is still dark and clotted with a milky haze that hides the stars. I don't require much sleep. Four hours usually does the trick, and affords me a few hours to paint before the day really begins. Gazing out at the darkness, I feel Vano and the intense emotions of my dream clinging to me like a residue or an unseen ghost. But I've had enough.

"You're dead, Vano," I say to the room, the silent wood paneling of the walls, the four carved posters of the bed, the Oriental rug, and the wide, attentive windows. "You and Piroska, and my father, and Eli, Paul, and Halla. You're all dead, and I'm alive. I would trade places with you if I could, but I can't."

I let out a deep breath as if to blow it all away. Step down onto the cold hardwood floor.

"So, I guess there's nothing to do but get on with it."

MY STUDIO IS ON THE mezzanine of the conservatory. Looking down from the balcony, I can see the cobblestone paths winding among the landscaped tropical plants, the neat little pond orange-spotted with fat koi fish, and the children's small easels fanned out around the still life we've been working on. Heloise, the striped tabby, sits at the edge of the pond, watching the swimming fish longingly.

The paintings I'm working on now hang on the walls of the studio here before me: several small, rough studies and a couple of larger canvases in various stages of completion. It's a series of still lifes, portraits of gravestones: one moss-covered and nearly buried in thorny brambles with the light of the rising sun coming over its shoulder, one with the burned-down stump of a candle and a bouquet of petalless, decaying flowers in the grass before it, a hopeful bee investigating the dry anthers for pollen. Another is small and almost entirely obscured by bent blades of timothy grass. The birth and death years are faintly visible on the metal plaque, and the math, if you do it, comes out to four. There is a feeling—or at least I hope there is a feeling—of private, teeming *life* in the portraits. The weeds grow wild and greedy, the wind can be seen like sifting fingers in the bend and sway of the grass, and the bugs explore busily and without solemnity. I want the viewer to see (though no viewer will ever see) the cheerfulness of graves, the thoughtless serenity and peace of final resting places.

I'm setting up my materials, scraping the dried pigment from my palette, and wondering why already, first thing in the morning and having eaten only yesterday, I am feeling almost savagely hungry (*why* am I suddenly so *constantly* hungry?) when I hear a soft sound from somewhere in the house.

For a second, I don't think about it. I usually attribute odd noises to the roaming housecats, but Myrrh is at my feet and Heloise I saw down by the fish pond. It's too early for Marnie or Rina to be arriving. I pause my palette knife midscrape and listen. I try not to, but can't help think of Vano's words from my dream. No doubt it's the mention of the name Czernobog, whose soft stalking sounds so often in the past made my heart lurch in my chest, that has me listening so intently and foolishly now.

I'm about to scrape again when there's another sound, a squeal like a distant door hinge or squeaky drawer being shut. I set the palette knife down and get up. Trying to think of all the perfectly innocuous things that might make such a noise, I open the door from the conservatory to the second-story hallway. The east and west wings of the house are divided by a winding staircase, and looking down the hall to that staircase, I see nothing out of the ordinary.

I make my way down the hall, listening all the way. At the staircase, I peer down and up, but again silence. I follow the hall farther, and just as I'm deciding that it was nothing, just "house sounds" as they say, I reach my bedroom. My door is open. Odd only because I'm particular about keeping it closed. I'm a very private person who has to deal with the regular discomfort of having many people coming in and out of my house each day, so my bedroom I guard assiduously. It's possible I could have forgotten this morning, but it would be unusual. My gut tells me I didn't.

As I'm standing in the hall trying to recall my steps from the morning, a shrill scream leaps out from the silence.

Eeeeeeeeeeeep! Eeeeeeeeeeeep! Eeeeeeeeeeep!

The sudden clamorous siren shriek makes me throw my hands over my ears and a burst of cold sweat washes over me. An intruder leaping out from the shadows could not have sent a worse shock through me.

From the ceiling above my bed, and for absolutely no discernible reason, the smoke detector in my room has suddenly begun to sound its alarm.

Eeeeeeeeeeeeeeep! Eeeeeeeeeeeeeeeep! Eeeeeeeeeeeeeep! It screams, warning of smoke, warning of fire, though there is none of either that I can see.

· VII ·

SEVEN weeks to cross the Atlantic. How many storms blew over us? There would have been no use in even trying to count. And how many people died? I couldn't say that either. A dozen, maybe more, mostly children. A toddler wandered off while his mother was sleeping and then couldn't be found. Some guessed that the child had been lost out a scupper, but no one would ever know for sure.

Mostly, though, people got sick. The food rotted and festered with insects and maggots, rat droppings everywhere. The lice could be seen jumping from men's beards, and mothers combed them out of their children's hair, but it was only something to do. There was no escaping them. In the hull of a ship, there is no escaping anything.

Mercy had soon begun climbing down into my bunk, bringing with her a ratty, well-worn loop of string, pale and dirty like her own hair, for playing cat's cradle with. She would sit close beside me, teaching me how to make the many figures she knew and talking about her father, who she said was waiting for them in England.

"I can hardly wait to see my papa," she would say, lifting a string from one of my outspread fingers and then anchoring it on another. "I can barely remember him; it's been so long he's been away. I just pray the ship don't sink on the way and we don't fall sick and die."

But Mercy did fall sick, her mother and brother too: blistering fevers that radiated out from their bodies, delirium. I tended to them, but there was little I could do. I wrung rags of foul-smelling water into their mouths, unsure whether I was doing them more good or harm, and I fought my way into the galley to make porridge for them. I took to cooking during storms because at least then I only had to fight the storm and the motion of the ship instead of other passengers.

During one such storm, in the middle of the night, I was cooking for Mercy and her family. The pot was swinging and swaying over the fire and nearly spilling its contents, and the lantern on its hook was dancing and throwing wild, wicked shadows about.

"Mother of Christ, I could use a good meal."

I jerked my head up, startled by the voice that'd come from the doorway.

"It was my wife that did all the cooking. I haven't had a hot meal since they fed her body into the deep."

It was the drunk whose wife had died in childbirth. We'd all observed him in his bunk, drinking himself into a stupor with some hidden supply of alcohol, and we'd all known when the supply had run out because he'd begun moaning and tossing and starting quarrels.

"I'm very sorry for your loss, sir, but I've got uses for this porridge and there's none to spare."

The ship keeled nose-first into the deep trough of a wave. I tumbled to the floor and slid across the galley toward the man, who had grabbed the doorframe to keep from falling backward. He scooped me up and helped me back to my feet, but before letting me go, he ran his hand slowly down the length of my arm, shoulder to elbow. I pulled free, bristling, and strode back to the porridge.

"There are other needs that a man's got, that I ain't had met since my wife passed on. I seen you caring for those others. You seem a charitable type."

"Caring for your own family's not charity, it's duty."

"Those're not your family. Those pretty travel clothes. You're of a different class than them. You're alone here. *What* you doing alone here?"

I ignored him and scooped the porridge into a large bowl, trying not to let him see the shaking of my hands.

"They're not doing well," he went on. "Die likely as not. If you like, I could look after you. We could take care of each other."

I clenched my jaw, picked up the porridge and spoon.

"You're welcome to scrape out the leftovers," I said, pushing my way past him. "That's as much as I'll be doing for you."

I carried on nursing Mercy and her family, but I would look up to see the man from the galley lying on his bunk, watching me. He'd taken up directly across from my bunk, in a bed that death had made vacant, and I got little rest from his intrusive gaze. I went finally to Agoston's door and knocked on it. I wasn't sure how I would get Agoston to understand. I wasn't sure if, once he understood, he would care.

"Agoston," I whispered into the grainy wood. "I need help, Agoston. I'm scared."

There was no sound from within. I stamped my foot.

"Agoston, Grandfather said I could trust you," I hissed angrily. "Grandfather sent you to take care of me. He would not be pleased."

My eyes were hot with tears, but the door was unmoved—Agoston as well, it seemed. Wiping the furious tears from my eyes, I turned and walked back, passing the salon, where the captain was smoking cigars with the neatly dressed and groomed upper-class passengers from the cabins, all joking and laughing as if they had no idea what was happening in steerage—no idea that, on the same ship, mothers and fathers and children were rotting in their own filth and dying each day.

When I got back to my bunk, my throat went dry. The man from the galley was standing by Mercy's bunk, leaning against a beam, looking down and talking to her.

"Be off, if you please, sir," I said in a shaky voice. "She's just come about and she shouldn't be wasting her breath talking."

The man smiled at me and went on with Mercy, offering her his overly polite goodbyes.

"It's diphtheria she has, if you'd like it," I persisted.

The man just smiled at me again and started casually back toward his bunk.

"I think I feel it coming on, myself." I finished this remark with a sharp cough.

He tipped his head toward Mercy's mother and brother.

"They're not gonna make it. Two young girls alone on a ship, you'll need someone looking out for you."

"Like you did for your wife and child?"

The ugly shadow that came over his features was frightening, and I thought that perhaps I'd gone too far in provoking him.

"We'll be just fine," I said hastily, and climbed up into the bunk beside Mercy, where I ran a cloth over her sweat-drenched forehead and tried not to look over at the man.

"Mercy, dearest, I'm so glad to see you awake. You're so strong. You're going to be all right."

"Mama," she moaned.

"She's just resting," I lied. "Jonas too."

I leaned close and whispered in her ear. "You ought not to talk to that man. He's no good. You call for me if he bothers you again."

"I'm so glad you're not sick, Anna," Mercy said breathlessly. A tear slipped down the side of her face. "You've taken care of us."

"Shh. I'll go on taking care of you. I won't stop and I won't get sick. Get your rest now. No more talking."

In the days that followed, Mercy's brother began to recover. Her mother got worse. Then one morning I heard Mercy crying and when I climbed up into her bunk she was hugging and kissing and crying against the cold body of her mother.

On the deck, with a murky sun skimming behind smoky clouds, I stood beside Mercy, Jonas squirming in my arms because his sister wasn't strong enough yet to hold him. When they carried the body forward, the little girl turned and buried her head in my shoulder, weeping and shaking.

"You don't have to look, Mercy," I said. "The memory of that won't do you any good. Come."

I led her over to the other side of the deck, and we leaned against the rail with the whipping wind tossing our hair and her tears falling freely. The voice of the captain, monotonous from tired repetition, drifted to us, and Jonas squirmed and whined in my arms.

"Let's pretend," I said, struggling against my tightening throat, "that your mama is still back in America."

Mercy lifted her head, set her tear-stained eyes to looking out over the water.

"She had to send you on ahead, but she's coming on the next ship. She needs you to be strong and smart and look after your brother till she's with you again."

I sniffed and wiped with my sleeve at my eyes. "She's thinking of you. Both of you. Right now. Back in America, she's hoping you're well. She's praying for you."

From behind us there was a splash. Mercy gasped and turned, but I held her and shook my head.

"No, Mercy, no. She's not there."

I pointed out over the waves, where the gulls were wheeling just above the diminishing wake of the ship.

"She's there. She's packing your things and she's hoping for you. She's hoping so hard for you, that you'll be all right. Listen and you can hear her thoughts coming to you from over the water. Do you hear them?"

Mercy turned her large eyes up at me.

"'Mercy,' she's thinking, 'are you all right? You're not sick, are you? Do you have enough to eat?' Well? Tell her. Don't leave her wondering."

Mercy turned her eyes back to the horizon and wiped them.

"I'm all right, Mama," she called in a small, trembling voice. "I'm all right. I'm not sick anymore, Jonas neither."

"Tell her you're looking after Jonas and taking good care of him."

Mercy's eyes closed, her pale lashes heavy against her freckled cheek, and a tear dropped from them.

"I'm looking after him, Mama! I'm being real careful! And Anna's here with us. She's our friend and she's taking care of us, Mama, so you got nothing to be afraid about."

"No, Mercy," I said, taking her shoulder in my hand, looking into her wide eyes. "I'm not taking care of you. *You're* taking care of you, do you hear me? I'm only helping. I won't always be with you, so *you've* got to become strong enough to take care of yourself and Jonas."

Mercy's eyes filled with tears. She closed them and began to weep helplessly, and I pulled her to myself, hugging her angrily, hating the tears in her eyes and in my own, hating the world that I knew she didn't stand a chance in alone.

"You *are* becoming strong, Mercy. You are," I whispered into her hair, trying to make us both believe it. "You're going to be all right."

The little girl just went on crying.

THE MAN FROM THE GALLEY wasted no time. The night they put Mercy's mother over the side, I moved up into the bunk that she had slept in to be closer to Mercy and to Jonas, and that night I woke to hands moving over my body.

Startled awake, I slapped at them and sat up. The man stood at the end of the bunk. The moon above was in its last quarter and the skies were cloudless. Thick silver light poured brightly down the opening to the upper deck, so I could see him almost as clearly as by day. He was standing there, stinking of some liquor he'd gotten ahold of and weaving softly.

"Quiet now," he said. "This is quite simple. You and me is getting married tonight in a private ceremony. I'm being reasonable and fair, so you had better be good, or I'll throw the both of those little ones out the bloody porthole and not one person will be the wiser."

Mercy, who had fallen asleep crying quietly, let out a small, chugging sob in her sleep and squeezed her brother tighter in her arms. Jonas's eyes swiveled beneath their lids, and he sucked audibly for a second at his thumb. The man reached forward once more and grabbed me roughly under the arms, and in despair, I let him.

From the bunk, the man carried me across the room while I kicked and thrashed but only half-heartedly. I didn't want him to hurt Mercy or her brother and I didn't know what to do.

"I'm warning you, pretty, and I don't jest. No one will even notice those children are gone. Nor you, if you drive me to it."

He set me in his bunk, where I scrabbled to the back in a panic, though that was only trapping myself further. The steerage deck had thinned out by nearly a third with deaths, and there wasn't another sleeping passenger for at least three bunks on either side. But even if there had been, I doubted that anyone would intervene. The man had not been discreet in his overtures, and before, when I had scowled at him or told him off, the other male passengers had only laughed and the women averted their eyes. Most women ended up as the property of drunken, filthy fools, why should I be any different?

The man climbed up into the bunk and crawled toward me on knees and one hand, while his other worked at the buckle of his belt.

"Agoston!" I barked in a hoarse, whispered cry. "Agoston!"

"I said quiet," the man said, and cuffed me across the mouth, then he grabbed my ankles and dragged me by them until I lay flat on the bunk beneath him. I smelled the foulness of the man's breath and his whiskey and weeks of sweat. I tasted blood in my mouth and felt his frenzied hands moving on my clothes, pulling and tearing. He ripped the buttons off my blouse, pulling it apart, then with two hands he forcefully ripped the linen of my shift beneath.

"What in the name of all the bloody saints?" he spat, looking down at my exposed chest in the moonlight, the smooth expanse of pale, blank skin.

In the days after Grandfather had brought me back from the cemetery, I had discovered with confusion that my womanly parts had disappeared, the nursing parts and the place between my legs where a baby should one day come out. They were just gone, as completely as if they had never been.

An expression of disgusted outrage on his face, the man fumbled at my skirts. With his head tilted down and away from mine, the tendon at his neck stood out thick and tensed. I felt the rage rising in me again just as it had when I'd hit Agoston. A growl came from deep in my throat and then I lunged forward and bit, sinking my new teeth deep into his neck. He screamed and tried to wrench free, but I was locked onto him like a wild dog.

The blood poured from him. It spilled down over my face and ran into my eyes. Then I let go, and the man, holding his gushing neck and gasping, fell backward out of the bunk and landed on the wood floor, where he clawed at his neck with an expression of astonishment on his face.

There was the sound of people stirring in their bunks, and from across the room I heard Mercy call for me in a groggy voice.

"Anna?"

Then a man stepped out of the shadows, where he had been for who knew how long. He picked up the man from the galley as lightly as a sack and carried him quickly down the room to where the horses stood in their stalls. He lifted and tossed the man over the wood slats, where he landed inside with a straw-muted thump. Then, with the deft movements of a dance, Agoston—for I could see now that it was he—climbed up the slats, grabbed a whip from where it hung against a wall, and lashed the rump of the horse, making it dance and stomp while the man grunted and cried out beneath the hooves and then was silent.

Amid the sleepy exclamations of passengers waking up in confusion, Agoston strode calmly back down the room toward me and, passing the bunk where I sat stunned, he beckoned with a motion of his head for me to follow. I hopped down out of the bunk and followed him, holding back a gasping, spasming impulse to cry or throw up. Agoston held the door to his cabin open for me and then pulled it closed behind me.

Inside the cabin, he dipped a clean cloth in the lovely clear water of his washbasin and began to scrub the blood and filth from my face while I sat on the edge of the bed trembling and crying, no longer able to hold it back. When he had finished, he set the cloth down in the basin, where the water was now a murky crimson. He took my head in his bearlike paws, looked me in the eyes, and nodded, a gentle smile in his black eyes.

Then he left the cabin and returned a moment later with Mercy slumbering in his arms. He set her on the upper bunk that, from the beginning, had been meant for me, then he left again and returned with

Jonas, and the three of us children slept there on the bed—no thin sack stuffed with straw, but a blissfully soft feather mattress—for the rest of the night, curled into one another like kittens.

The captain and first mate knocked at the cabin door the next day. They stood there uncomfortably, cowed by Agoston's overshadowing presence, the tall mass of him, the still directness of his gaze, his expensive and immaculately tailored broadcoat. Agoston had had me and Mercy both put on the finest outfits from my trunk. Class would be our best defense against any wrongdoing.

"It's just that some says they might have seen you, sir," the captain said, squinting off to the side to avoid Agoston's gaze, "last night, in the tween decks where that man was trampled. Course, they were, by their own admission, sleeping and coulda been not knowing what they were seeing."

"He doesn't understand you." I spoke up from where I stood in the doorway beside Agoston. "He doesn't speak English."

"Well, you tell him—"

"I can't tell him anything. I don't speak what he speaks."

The captain squinted away, and the mate picked at a splinter in the doorframe.

"Well," the captain sighed finally. "The man was a troublesome drunk anyway. Stupid fool probably fell in himself. Good riddance."

He glanced in past me at Mercy, sitting cross-legged on the bunk with Jonas in her lap. "Too often it's the sweet mothers and children who don't make it, and the stinkin' mean drunks who pull through just fine. We'll call it justice and leave it at that."

But it wasn't justice that the captain spoke of, and I knew it. The captain was a coward, that was all. Most people, I was learning, were cowards, and most laws had nothing to do with justice. Justice was a private matter that you didn't expect anyone to execute for you. You did it yourself, or it didn't get done.

· VIII ·

"WOULD someone like to come up to the board this morning and help us with our calendar?"

The children, scattered cross-legged across the rug, shoot their arms up into the air. Fingers are spread wide and wiggling in every possible manner for emphasis; some of the children wear pained expressions in their desperation to be chosen. When I point to Sophie, there are the usual sighs of frustration, which always make me laugh.

"Quel enthousiasme! Je l'aime. You're all so awake and eager today!"

Sophie stands, her pink corduroy skirt crumpled up against her tights from sitting. Looking down and holding her chin-length blond hair back from her face, she picks her way through the obstacle course of other children. Finally, she stands before her classmates and, with their help, announces in both English and admirable French that it's Friday, the nineteenth of October, 1984, and the season is autumn.

"Children," I say as Sophie finds her way back to her seat, "is there a holiday coming up at the end of this month that you're all looking forward to celebrating?"

"Halloweeeeen!!" they scream with violence. Then there is a near-panicked clamor to share their costume plans, but I steer us away.

"In France, children, the holiday is called La Toussaint, or All Saints'

Day. All Saints' Day is a holiday for remembering loved ones who have died, and it's celebrated in different ways in many different countries, but if you were children living in France, you would get the day off from school and you would bring flowers and wreaths and candles to the cemetery to decorate graves and maybe have a picnic with your family."

"That sounds kind of like a holiday my family celebrates," Octavio chimes in, raising a finger in a professorial manner.

"That's right, Octavio. I was hoping you would tell your friends about it. What is that holiday called? The one your family celebrates?"

"It's called Día de los Muertos, and it's so awesome! You take flowers to the cemetery, just like you talked about, and you get to paint your face like *a skull*! Plus, there are these little skulls that are made out of sugar and chocolate and stuff, and we get to eat them!"

The other children are deeply impressed by this. They gape at one another wide-eyed and open-mouthed.

"Children," I say, "I have some pictures of Día de los Muertos, what Octavio was just telling you about, and of La Toussaint, the holiday they celebrate in France. Would you like to see them?"

In answer, the children put out their hands to be filled, and I pass around some *National Geographic* magazines with pictures of a Parisian cemetery festooned with colorful chrysanthemums, and another with a Mexican cemetery dappled in golden candlelight and long shadows. There is a picture of a lavish *ofrenda* that the children are fascinated by and another that shows festivalgoers in colorful dresses and with faces painted as skulls.

"So, Halloween," I say when we're done looking at the pictures, "is, *sort of*, about the dead, right? A little. There are ghosts and skeletons. And La Toussaint is about remembering the dead. So is Día de los Muertos. And all of these holidays happen around the same time, in autumn. Can any of you think of a reason why all these holidays that deal with death happen in autumn?"

"Because," offers Sophie, "there's already holidays in the other times. Like Christmas and Valentine's Day, and in the summer, you're too busy going to the pool and stuff."

"That's an interesting idea," I reply with a small laugh. "It's true that there *are* other holidays spread rather evenly throughout the year. Good observation, Sophie. Can anyone think of another reason? Something perhaps that is unique or special about the season of autumn that would cause people to think about death?"

"Halloween?" someone says in an excellent demonstration of circular reasoning.

"What happens in nature during autumn, or *fall*?" I ask. "What do you see when you go outside?"

"The leaves change colors?" Annabelle offers. "They fall off the trees?"

"They *die*!" Sophie gasps with the bright-eyed excitement of a sudden realization. "And the grass dies too!"

"All the flowers and plants die!"

"So, because so much things die in the fall," Thomas summarizes for us, "that's why there's all those holidays about death and dying and stuff like that!"

"Isn't that interesting?" I say. "And how clever you all are to figure that out! Well, this autumn season, we're going to observe what happens in nature in the autumn, and for open house, which is coming up very soon, we'll show your parents how they celebrate La Toussaint in France and Día de los Muertos in Mexico. We'll do art projects and baking projects, make our own ofrenda, like in the pictures. It's going to be très, très amusant."

"Can we paint our faces like skeletons?"

"Sounds like a great idea to me. What does everyone else think?"

Yes is the general consensus amid the joyful exclamations and fist pumps.

I glance up then and catch sight of Rina, my office assistant, standing in the classroom doorway. She is a short, plump, nervous woman, cute in the way of certain rodents, an adorable chipmunk or something of the like. Beside her in the doorway, tall and thin, especially by contrast, is Katherine Hardman. Beside Katherine is Leo. Leo's nanny has always dropped him off and picked him up. I wonder why Katherine is doing it today.

"Children, I'll be right back," I say, picking up the stuffed penguin we use during circle time. "Please pass around Monsieur Manchot, and on your turn, tell your friends what you will be for Halloween."

I leave the children to their task and go to the door, where Rina is already making a funny obsequious bowing departure.

"Leo," I say to the boy, "I'm so happy to see you. We missed you yesterday. Why don't you go join your friends so they can hear what costume you will wear for Halloween?"

"Okay," he says, and wanders quietly into the classroom to take a seat beside Annabelle. I turn back to Katherine to bid her adieu.

"Do you have a moment?" she asks. "I'm sorry, I don't mean to keep you . . ."

"Of course! It's no problem at all. Let's step out into the hall."

Katherine is dressed with the same casual elegance as the day I met her, in flowing slacks of some rich material and an equally fine blazer. Her well-cut black hair is neatly styled and her makeup is done, and yet there is something off in her appearance today. She looks almost overdone. Under her large eyes there are dark circles, like Leo's, but she's attempted to conceal them a bit too thickly with makeup, and her face seems pale and worn. She's holding a piece of paper, some kind of form, and behind it, two of the fingers on her left hand are bound in a splint, which she seems to be trying to conceal with the paper.

"Is everything okay, Katherine?"

"Everything's fine now, but I'll be honest, we've had a *rough* couple of days."

"I'm so sorry to hear that. What happened?"

"The evening before last, Leo fell and got a concussion."

"*Oh no!* That's horrible. How did it happen?"

"Oh, he just took a tumble down the stairs at home and, we think, probably hit his head on a step. It all happened so fast. It was really hard to tell, but well, then he had all the symptoms. He threw up, he was falling asleep, couldn't keep his eyes open. It was— " She closes her eyes and puts a hand up before her face as if to block out the memory. "It was horrible."

"You were hurt as well?"

"*Hm?*" She looks at me quizzically for a moment. "No. I wasn't—*why?*"

"Oh, it's just your hand. I thought perhaps you were . . ."

"Oh, this!" She holds up the injured hand, acknowledging it at last. "No, this was *me* being a klutz! I tripped last week and caught myself funny. I guess we're all a bit accident-prone lately. Anyway, I just wanted to give you this note from the doctor. It's a few things Leo needs to be careful about, symptoms to keep an eye out for. He hasn't had any symptoms since it happened, so I'm not expecting him to start now. The doctor said that children usually heal pretty quickly from these things."

I take the sheet of paper from her, begin looking it over. "Mr. Hardman was at home when this happened?"

"Yes, he was. And good thing. I was a total, shaking mess. There's no way I could have driven Leo to the hospital."

I glance at her. There's something brittle and false about her today, like someone who is sick or has had terrible news but must fake it through the day nonetheless.

"I'll look after him very carefully, Katherine, don't worry. I'm sure this has been hard on you too. You're probably exhausted. Maybe you should go home and get some rest."

"I think I will," she says, and for just an instant she gazes off into space contemplatively.

"Thank you," she says, gathering herself. Then she turns and walks down the hall to let herself out the front door.

I remain where I am for a moment, pondering the interaction, wondering what felt just the slightest bit odd about it. The word comes to me: *troubled*. Katherine seemed troubled. Not just distressed about what happened two nights ago, or nervous about Leo being all right today, but bothered by something, disturbed.

A yelp of conflict reaches me from the classroom, though, and I'm pulled from my contemplation of Mrs. Hardman. I turn and go back in to the children.

. . .

EACH DAY AFTER CIRCLE TIME, the children exchange their fashionable jackets and sweaters for white linen smocks, which they run around in more freely, looking like a miniature and unruly assembly of ancient Greek statesmen. I put on my painting smock as well and wheel out the gramophone to put on some Dvořák or Debussy, and we arrange our easels around a flowering jasmine or one of the potted citrus trees with their shiny clusters of lemons, limes, and mandarins.

Some days I set up a still life, draping a cloth across a table and then setting it with china vases, ornate tea sets, or bowls of fruit. Our pet finches, Turner, Sargent, and Mona, chirp and flutter in their hanging cage. The breath of the children and the exhalations of the hanging ferns mingle and fog the glass walls, making the room warm and humid and slightly tropical, so it doesn't seem like such a sacrifice to be indoors.

Today we're painting an ornamental bonsai. Its shape is something like a woman carrying two plates at her sides, one high at her shoulder, one low at her hip. Standing before my own canvas, I show the children how to first eliminate space, to slash freely with the straight edge of a flat brush all the canvas that is outside the form of the tree. It's counterintuitive. Students tend to resist this method, preferring to just jump in and draw the thing, rather than narrowing down to it, but then their proportions are invariably off and can't easily be corrected without starting all over.

After my demonstration, I make a wandering circuit among the easels. Thomas, who's been painting with me for a year already, has a very nicely proportionate tree developing on his canvas. Beside him, Sophie is assembling a vibrant colorful abstraction on hers. I do not think she is even aware of the bonsai tree before her.

I get to Leo's canvas and, for a moment, just stand quietly behind him, studying it. When a child's artwork is good, the impulse is to gush praise, but when a child's work is prodigious, it provokes silence, wonder, dismay. The difference between Leo's work and every other child's, even at this early sketch phase, is unmistakable. It's the ease of the line, the confidence of the strokes, the fidelity to the essence of the object portrayed.

Leo is absorbed in his work. Despite a recent head trauma, his concentration is as intense as ever. He has already eliminated the white space, sketched in the lines of the trunk and leaves, and is beginning to build up the pigment of the trunk. He alone has intuited the womanliness of the tree. There's a beautiful sideways thrust of a hip, the lazy arc of the arms bowed beneath the weight of the plates in her hands.

"Très bien, Leo. C'est formidable."

His focus is so singular that he seems not to have even heard me. I step closer.

"Move all around, Leo. Don't stay in one place too long. You'll lose perspective."

Perspective—language a bit advanced for a beginner. I rephrase.

"You'll lose the sense of the whole. Always move around."

I get a small nod from him, and then he heeds my advice, moving up to work on the branches above. I take a step back from Leo's easel.

"Don't forget, children," I say to the class, "to move around the canvas. Don't work on the same part of the picture for too long, or it will become uneven, unbalanced. You'll have too much pigment or detail in one place and not enough in another."

From Thomas and Annabelle, the oldest children, I get earnest nods of understanding. Ramona, between them, slathers phthalo-green stalks beneath bright yellow amoebic flowers. Her smock is a bright smear of painted handprints. The other two littles, Octavio and Sophie, paint unidentifiable, many-colored, many-legged creatures. Octavio, up front and unaware that I observe him, turns to Thomas beside him with his brush poised as if to paint on the older boy. His mouth is wide and his tongue hangs out mischievously.

"Ah, ah, ah," I cluck, and he turns the same silly expression—eyes wide, tongue still out—toward me.

"Hands and brushes to ourselves, s'il vous plaît. We paint only on our canvas."

Octavio mashes the bristles of his brush into his canvas deliberately and grins at me, and I work hard to keep a straight face.

From beside me, Leo lets forth a craggy, rattling cough.

"That cough, mon Dieu! Are you all right, Leo?" I ask him, patting his back gently as it pitches forward.

He doesn't answer, just goes on coughing. His eyes, when he finishes at last, are weak and droopy. He wipes his mouth with the back of his sleeve and then goes back to painting.

"Leo," I say, squatting beside him. "Your maman told me that you bumped your head pretty bad."

He turns to me and nods. His large, dark eyes are so serious and so tired looking.

"How are you feeling today? Is your head hurting at all?"

He doesn't answer for a moment, but looks up toward the ceiling as though checking the interior of his skull for pain.

"No," he says finally. "It's not hurting."

"Good. I'm so glad to hear that. Our heads are pretty important. We must be very careful with them. You will tell me, please, if it begins to bother you at all. Even just a little. Will you do that?"

"Okay. I will."

"How did it happen, mon petit?"

"Well," he says slowly, "first we were at the top of the stairs and then we fell down, all the way from the top. Really far. And—"

"*We?* Did someone else fall down the stairs too?"

"I fell and Katherine fell too."

It was a surprise to discover during the first week of school that Leo calls his parents primarily by their first names. It still sounds bizarre to me every time he does it, and I've not been able to bring myself to refer to them in the same way to him.

"Both of us," Leo continues, "but only I hurt my head. Katherine hurt her hand. These two fingers here," he says, pinching together the two fingers that she had bound in a splint. "And she also got a bruise on her leg. Right here."

"Your mom did that? She hurt those fingers, falling down the stairs with you?"

He nods quickly, then bends down, lifts the cuff of his pants, and points to his ankle. "That's where she got a bruise. And I got a bruise here." He puts a hand to his back. "And I hurt my head and had to go to the doctor."

After this demonstration, Leo takes up his paintbrush again, dips it into the small cup of water beside his palette, and swirls it about, clouding the water with brown.

"How did both you and your mom fall down the stairs at the same time? That seems sort of difficult."

"Katherine was holding me. She was—it was that she was carrying me. And they were kind of a little mad, so—"

"Who was mad?"

"Katherine and Dave. And then, she fell down the stairs, and me too."

"Dave, your dad?"

He wipes his brush on a cloth and shrugs, then dips the brush lightly into the puddle of dark green paint on his palette and lifts it toward the canvas.

"I guess," he says, and shrugs again. "Yeah, I guess so."

"You *guess*? Are we talking about Dave, your dad, or some other Dave?"

Brush still poised, he turns to me. "Oh yeah, him," he says, nodding seriously. "Yeah, Dave, my dad."

For a second, all I can do is blink in confusion.

"Okay, so your mom and dad were angry at each other before you and your mom fell down the stairs? How could you tell that they were angry?"

"They were, you know, kind of yelling, and their faces were mad."

"Were they hitting or pushing or anything like that?"

"Pushing a little, I think. And Dave was trying to take me away from Katherine, but she didn't want him to."

"Leo, I'm so sorry that happened and that you were hurt. That sounds like it could be a bit frightening. Was that frightening for you? Having grown-ups yelling and then falling down the stairs?"

He's quiet, and his eyes roll down to study the floor. "I don't really want to talk about it anymore."

"Okay," I say thoughtfully. "Bien, we don't have to talk about it anymore now. But if you want to talk later or another day, we can."

Leo lifts the brush again to his canvas and resumes painting, and I watch him but I'm thinking only of what he has told me and how it's at odds with what Katherine told me.

"Very good work, Leo," I say quietly. "Magnifique."

WHAT AM I SUPPOSED TO do now?

I'm asking myself this as I make my way up the stairs to the attic. It's nap time, which means that I'm finally able to satiate the hunger that has been inexplicably clawing at me since morning and also turn my attention back to what Leo has told me.

He's been seriously injured, and by his account of events, the injury resulted from some kind of physical altercation between his parents. He seems also to have made a liar of his mother. Tripped and landed funny, Katherine said of the splinted fingers. Nothing at all to do with Leo's tumble down the stairs. Why would she lie about something like that?

Could it be Leo, I wonder, who isn't telling the truth? When I think it through, though, it seems unlikely. The way the contradictory details came out was too natural to be a lie, and lying held no incentive for him. Could he have been mistaken? He might have been wrong, I suppose, about the fight that preceded the fall—a child might misconstrue intense conversation as a fight—but how could anyone who isn't given to hallucinations mistakenly think someone else fell down the stairs with them when they actually fell alone? And the details—"she hurt *these* two fingers," Leo had said, holding up the two fingers she'd had in a splint. No, he couldn't be mistaken.

But if I accept Leo's testimony as reliable, at least on the crucial points, then it's Katherine who's lied. But why? Why would she feel the need to deny that she also fell and was injured? I can think of only one answer: she wanted to make a problematic story, involving marital conflict and possibly even violence, into a simpler tale of childish clumsiness. She wanted to shield someone from responsibility and consequences.

I lift up the attic door absently and climb the last steps into the room, lower the door, and settle myself down on the floor. I run my palms distractedly along the backs of the cats that mill lazily around me. Full of the very suspicion Katherine wished to avoid, I'm now remembering every unpleasant detail of my meeting with Dave Hardman, the way he had contradicted her with plain hostility, those hard, arrogant features and insolent expressions of his, the way he sat in his chair looking uninterested, impatient, and sulky. In my experience the most dangerous men are almost always sulky. Why do women protect such men? Why do they go to such lengths to shield them from consequences?

I could imagine answers to these questions too, I'm sure, but I'm not interested. I'm too annoyed. I'm annoyed by this drama, and I'm annoyed at my involvement in it and the fact that I have no one to blame but myself. I knew the Hardmans were a rotten pair from the first. And now what? Domestic problems—abuse, neglect, child endangerment—dealing with such things involves going on record, filing reports, giving testimonies; it involves scrutiny, submitting to investigations by "the authorities." Authority to do what, though? Make Dave Hardman a good, kind man? No. Give his wife the inner resources to stand up to him? Not likely. Make a lot of trouble without solving any of it? Destroy everything I've worked to build while solving nothing? Most likely.

No, going to the authorities is not an option. The best I can do is keep an eye on the situation, hope that it's a one-off, try, perhaps, to get something out of Katherine. If there truly is a problem, she's the only one who can actually solve it.

· IX ·

THE ship anchored at last in Liverpool, and those passengers who were left alive and had managed already to pay for their crossing disembarked. All those who were still in debt for their passage, or for the passage of any family members who had died at sea, had to remain on the ship until they were paid up or purchased by the wealthy estate owners, who sent butlers to the docks to pick the strongest and most able for household servants.

In the damp, close fog of morning with the seagulls screaming low above our heads, Mercy and I leaned anxiously against the ship's side, looking at the old, smoke-smudged city of Liverpool and searching the faces of its bustling quay for her papa. I didn't know what the man looked like, though, and I wasn't sure Mercy did either. She told me that he'd be "tall" and "look almost just like me," and I wondered whether she knew these things for fact or only supposed them, but I held Jonas and squinted at the faces on the docks, looking for a tall man with fair features and hair like Mercy's.

Neither Mercy nor I, young and naive as we were, asked ourselves any of the practical questions I've asked myself since. Ships ran on loose schedules then, embarking whenever they managed to fill with cargo and passengers; how could Mercy's father know to be there at the quay just then? Letters made their way across oceans even less predictably than ships. How could we be sure the man was even aware that his family had embarked on the journey at all? But the worst question, which only time and experience eventually made me ask: Was Mercy's father truly waiting for them at all? What if the truth was that he was dead or a scoundrel who had abandoned them? I, myself, had been told a nice story—that Grandfather was looking out for me, that he cared for me and would come collect me soon—so that I would be compliant on a long journey. What if it was only a nice story Mercy's mother had told her to make a difficult journey easier?

Finally, it was time for those getting off the ship to do it, but when Mercy tried to follow me down the gangway, she was not permitted.

The captain slid a thick finger across his ledger book. "Passage for one adult only has been paid. That'll be your ma. There's two half fares left to be settled."

When he saw the look of fright on the little girl's face, he softened his tone.

"Not to worry, little one. You're a healthy, strong girl. Worst comes to worst, you'll be taken for a kitchen hand in one of these fine homes hereabouts."

"But my papa's coming for me. How will he find me?"

"I can leave word here at the docks if you like. If he asks after you, he'll find you. But he'll have to bring money. None's going to let go for free what they've bought and paid for."

"What about Jonas? What about my brother? Will they let me bring him along with me?"

"No, not likely. A baby's no use to anyone and lots of bother."

I could see the panic in the bloom of red spreading across Mercy's face and the tears pushing forward in her eyes.

"What'll happen to him? Where'll he go?"

The captain looked away. "He'll go to the orphanage, of course."

I took off running down the gangway to the wharf where Agoston was hiring a carriage and my trunk sat on the paving stones. I threw open the lid of the trunk and dug around until I found the rumpled velvet Brunswick and the mother-of-pearl rosary that my grandmother had placed in my hands at my funeral. I ran back to where the captain sat before his ledger book, chiding Mercy ill-temperedly to get out of the way so others might pass, and the girl stood shaking and close to collapse. I dumped the items on top of the ledger.

"Here!"

The captain's eyes flashed at the sight of the creamy pearls studded along the rosary.

"That's enough for their passage," I said. "Both of 'em, ten times over. Let 'em off."

The man pawed at the treasures appraisingly for a moment, then nodded Mercy along without even looking up. I grabbed Mercy and stopped her.

"It's *more* than the cost of their passage. You can give what's due to her."

The captain stared at me for a moment, measuring my insolence. I could feel the tension of violence in his body, his muscles taut and eager to strike, but he glanced over and saw Agoston's bulk at the bottom of the gangway where he was waiting for me.

"Anya," Agoston called in his deep voice. "*Ydziom!*"

The captain pushed back the lid of his money box and, without counting, dropped a handful of coppers into Mercy's small, cupped hands, more than they could hold, and some fell clinking to the deck. We stooped to gather them.

"Clear out," he barked.

It was on the docks there that I left Mercy, sitting on the damp wood, holding her baby brother on her lap, eight years old, paid for and alone, and waiting for a pa who may have come for her or may not have.

For many years after, I told myself that he did, that as soon as my carriage turned the first street corner and she was out of sight, her beloved pa came and took her and her brother home, where they made a life together, safe and happy. I tell myself no such stories now. Now I assume that the hungry universe, after much suffering and grief, ate both her and her brother alive and screaming. For that is the way of the world, and I, at least, will not be a teller of false and soothing stories.

· · ·

THERE WERE JOSTLING DAYS OF buggies, ferries on choppy water, and then the journey settled into long days and nights spent rumbling along an endless road. Dark green forests thinned out to broad moors and then angled up to rocky bluffs. Villages came and went. Carriages changed and the carriage drivers with them, taverns and languages also.

I had no idea at that time where I was or where I was going, and to this day it is still impossible to trace the route or name the destination with any precision. All I can say is that we journeyed east across Europe and ended up somewhere near the Carpathians, which heaped up at the shifting intersection of the Austrian Empire, Ottoman Empire, and Wallachian territories, what today might be eastern Serbia, western Romania, or northern Bulgaria.

The language barrier between us made it impossible for me to get answers from Agoston to the hundreds of questions I wished to ask, yet I had come to trust him just as I had trusted my grandfather, perhaps even more so, and I clung to that trust and to my grandfather's promise to come for me, when I had nothing else to cling to.

Agoston and I didn't need to eat more than three times a week. When we did, Agoston would signal the driver to stop. Climbing down from the carriage, he'd tear a handful of gorse grass up from the roots and feed it to the horses before walking off into the woods with a hunting rifle. By and by, there'd be the clap of buckshot, birds rising in the air, and then Agoston would call for me and I'd run off into the trees. There, he'd be waiting with a bleeding animal he'd run down himself, and another one that he'd shot and would carry back to the carriage as an alibi. I drank from voles, badgers, foxes, even deer, and I became accustomed, though never without some sadness, to the feeling of a warm, softly furred thing panting out its last breaths beneath me.

When Agoston and I would, at last, come stepping through the high grass toward the carriage, the driver would be searching the road anxiously before and behind. There were bandits, but more important, there were superstitions: spirits and demons and accursed-dead mischief-makers who were known to meet incautious travelers on these roads.

As we continued east, each new carriage appeared more elaborately adorned with charms and talismans than the last: crucifixes, bundles of dried herbs, bags rattling with teeth and fingernail parings supposedly shed by wandering saints. Sometimes we'd pass barren hillsides crowned in the distance with small rustic clapboard structures; whenever these eerie hovels appeared, the driver would cross himself and whip the horses to a gallop. I eventually learned that these were houses for the dead, built to shelter the souls of the deceased for a short time while they oriented themselves to the shadowy nature of the afterlife. Such souvenirs of the old pagan beliefs and practices were everywhere in these parts. Christianity had moved across the land, conquering all other religions, officially, but the beliefs and practices that had preceded it for hundreds of years were never eradicated completely; they merged with the conquering faith in strange ways or grew up, weedlike, about the edges and in the cracks.

At last, not just the spellings but the letters on the signs became strange, and Agoston began suddenly to be understood by the speakers. I discovered that Agoston was voluble, jesting and sparring with the innkeepers and merchants, who not only spoke like him but looked like him as well. They were big men with chests pushed out and they had dark, thick beards like Agoston, and dark, thick hair crawling across their forearms and up from the necks of their loose tunic shirts. Agoston began talking to me more too, but it was inscrutable gibberish all revolving around a single word repeated again and again: Piroska.

"Piroska?" I echoed uncertainly.

"Ya," he said, nodding. "Piroska."

"What is Piroska?"

He only nodded again. "Piroska."

The last hamlet we passed was a meager one, but it was wrapped around an enormous monastery, with towers and spires of brilliant green and gold. I'd never seen a more exotic-looking structure. The tops were round like fruit, but then sloped upward into sharp gold points that reached steeply up to the sky and glimmered in the sunlight.

In this hamlet, Agoston bought many odd things, candles and tools and bundles of rag paper tied with ribbon, a lantern and several dresses for me in the local style, and even a lamb and two chickens. He put these things and more into a coach that he drove himself, and for a full day, he pushed and coaxed it and the disinclined horses into nearly impassably dense woods, until we came to a tiny round clearing at the edge of which stood a house built from mossy timbers and roofed in thatch. A small unenclosed pasture filled what remained of the clearing, and in it, a shaggy pony with cream-colored hair falling down into its eyes chewed at grass, a cow and calf lapped at water from a pond, and numerous sheep lay folded in the grass.

Agoston pulled my trunk and as much else as he could hold down from the carriage and carried it inside the house, but I didn't follow. I stayed in the carriage, looking at the house, the pasture, the dark, dense woods all around, and the high craggy peaks that rose above them in the distance, trying to make sense of where I was and why.

There were bundles of dried herbs and flowers nestled amid the thatch of the roof. Hanging bells and stones wrapped in string dripped down from the eaves. On the dark wood of the walls and door were the darker shapes of symbols. They were hard to make out from the carriage, so I got out and walked slowly toward the house. I reached up and touched the rusty metal bells that hung easily low enough to reach. I studied the symbols on the wall—interwoven lines, diamonds, and triangles. Some were carved, others were painted or stained. None of them were familiar.

A shuffling sound from above made me jerk my head up, and I caught sight, just for an instant, of an eye peering down at me through a crack in the roof beams, then it was gone.

Agoston appeared in the doorway and beckoned for me to come. This time I followed him, full of dread and questions but with no way to ask them or understand the answers. The house was dark and small, just a single room divided into a few simple sections with wooden screens and a loft above the room.

There was a strange smell hanging in the air, sour and sweet, and when my eyes adjusted from the bright sunlight outside, I saw a kettle hanging over a low fire of simmering coals where the smell seemed to

be coming from. In front of it was the stooped form of an old woman. She stirred the contents of the kettle and then turned to us.

"Piroska," Agoston said, and held a hand out reverently to the woman.

The woman smiled so joyfully that the two of them might have been mother and son reunited, and with her gnarled hand she fondly patted Agoston's. Her face must have held a thousand lines in it and her hair was like white cotton, and yet, even in the dim light, there could be seen a remarkable glow to her face and eyes and even skin that made her look as though, under some veneer of age, she might actually be a young and radiantly beautiful woman, as though a spell of old age had been cast upon her, and she was at every moment teetering on the cusp of some miraculous transfiguration back to youth and brilliance. I remember vividly feeling in the light and warmth of her smile a calm and safety unlike anything I'd ever felt before.

There were five cups on the table and a small wooden barrel. Piroska uncorked the barrel and filled each of the cups with the dark, foamy beverage that poured out. The drink had the same briny smell that hung heavy in the room, and when I drank it, the taste startled me with its cold bite and sour-sweet taste. Like everything else, it was so utterly alien that I felt suddenly overwhelmed, stabbed with painful fear and sadness. I sat there choked, on the brink of tears.

The woman, Piroska, sat on the chair beside me. She had not been looking at me and I had made no sound, yet she turned to me as suddenly as if I had shouted and locked eyes with me. The look in her eyes was one of such tremendous compassion and tenderness that it seemed to pull, as if by force, the tears forward out of my eyes. Still holding my gaze, she reached toward me with her craggy hand. She put a finger gently to my cheek and with it scooped up one of the tears onto her fingertip.

She brought the tear-damp finger back to herself and bent her head toward it, studying it closely. She turned her head and bent her ear to it, as though listening. With her gnarled nose, she sniffed it several times. Then finally, she stuck her tongue out and delicately tasted it. When at

last she looked back at me, I was astonished to see tears bright in her own eyes.

"Oh, lyubimaya," she whispered. "Oh, lyubimaya. Lyubimaya."

It was a word Grandfather had said to me also. Piroska put her withered hook of a hand out again and stroked the back of my head gently, and that calm that I had first felt when looking at her returned and filled me.

"Vano," she said, nodding softly toward the door, then she tipped her head equally softly toward the loft above us. "Ehru," she said, a soft, contented smile coming across her face.

I was confused. I didn't know what these words meant, but a moment later a figure appeared in the doorway of the cottage.

"Vano," she said again, closing her eyes and smiling.

There was a shuffling sound from above us again, and a dark-haired head appeared at the top of the wooden ladder that led up to the loft.

"Ehru," Piroska said again.

And then, from two different directions, the loft and the door, there came toward the table the same boy. A tall, thin, dark-skinned boy. The most beautiful boy in the world.

· X ·

WE take a break from our still life of the bonsai to begin the construction of our class ofrenda. I always try to make our parent gatherings so dazzling and impressive that I hardly have to personally bear the discomfort of the parents' attentions at all. I'm not a particularly social creature to begin with, but I feel especially ill at ease when there are large numbers of adults in the school. I'm a very good teacher, and this is a very good school, but I'm also a total fraud, the school an elaborate stage set. I don't enjoy deceiving people, but I don't have a whole lot of choice in the matter. I either live honestly and alone, or I live in company as a liar. The choice is made, but I still get anxious whenever the artifice is examined too closely.

Today, I'm teaching the children how to make *papel picado*, or picked paper, a common adornment for traditional ofrendas. I call them from their various activities around the room to gather for instructions. Leo, first to the rug and sitting cross-legged and quiet at my knee, looks up at me and asks, "When are we going to work on our paintings again?"

He's not pleased to be taking a day away from his work in progress.

I reassure him that we'll be back to it tomorrow, and then, when all the children have gathered on the rug, begin to explain the day's activity.

"Yesterday, we learned that the purpose of the ofrenda is to remember and honor the people we love who have died, and that to do this you usually put a picture of the person on the ofrenda, but then we can also include anything that reminds us of the person, maybe a necklace that they wore, food they loved to eat, a soccer ball if they loved to play soccer."

The children are very taken with this idea, being that it strongly resembles show-and-tell but for the dead.

"My grandma died," Thomas interjects. "And she liked to watch the Giants on TV, so I would put a football, or maybe a remote control!"

"If *I* was dead," Octavio exclaims, bright-eyed and bouncing on his knees, as though sharing his dearest wish, "I would want a remote control and a whole TV for me! That way I could watch *Danger Mouse* from outer space!"

"Yours sounds like a fascinating conception of the afterlife, Octavio, and, more important, it seems like we're all getting the idea. Now, besides those reminders of our loved ones, ofrendas also include lots of beautiful decorations like flowers and candles and something called papel picado, which we're going to make today."

I show the children a few examples from pictures, give a quick demonstration of the process, and then send them off to their tables to get started. For a minute or two there is a noisy shuffle and scurry as the children take their places at the art tables, then organize and bicker over supplies, but eventually they settle down to work, raising their hands only sporadically with questions or to solicit help.

During a lull, when the children have fallen into a nice rhythm and are working with quiet concentration, I take up a stack of worksheets. They'll color them and fill them out at home with information about their deceased loved one—birth and death dates, relationship to the child, favorite things, and so on—and bring them back to school.

There's a great deal yet to do to prepare for the open house and All Saints' Day celebrations. I've scheduled a field trip for the morning of our open house, mostly to give the children less opportunity to make a mess of the school before their parents arrive. We're going to the Millstream Hollow historic cemetery, where, in authentic French fashion, we'll decorate the graves with flowers and candles.

The gentleman I spoke to on the phone seemed hopelessly baffled by my inquiry, and nothing I could say seemed to make the idea any more comprehensible to him.

"French holiday?" he gruffed into the phone. "The kids are going to do *what*? Decorate *graves*? What kind of school did you say this was? A *French preschool*?"

The man, at last, seemed to simply give up on understanding and declared, "Well, I never heard of anything like that, but I suppose it's fine. Just make sure you don't leave any of those candles burning after you all leave. There's two-hundred-year-old white oaks all around the place."

"Of course. Thank you very much."

"And bring those kids into the visitor center. There's lots they can learn about Millstream Hollow here. It's a historic site, you know. The oldest graves are from the mid–seventeen hundreds."

"We wouldn't miss the opportunity, sir. I look forward to it."

By Friday, nearly all of the children have returned their worksheets to me, identifying the friend or relative they wish to honor on the ofrenda. The makeshift tiers of the ofrenda, which we created from stacks of painted shoeboxes, are already filling up with photographs and small representative tokens. The photographs are mostly of great-grandparents, but there is one grandmother, an uncle, and a dog; the dog's collar and a well-chewed tennis ball rest near the photo. Only Leo has not brought in his worksheet or anything to place on the ofrenda.

On the morning of our field trip and open house, I ask him about it. He looks anxious and twists his hands before him in ways that seem to defy anatomy.

"My mom," he says, scrunching his nose and kicking one high-topped foot against the other. "She said she can't help me."

"Well . . ." I say, taken aback, "why not?"

He lifts his shoulders nearly to his ears and makes a face of total bafflement.

"I don't know. She just said no. She said it's moorrrdid, mor—mordid."

"Morbid?"

"Yeah. Morbid."

"Touché," I say under my breath with a small laugh. "Interesting. Okay."

"What does morbid mean?"

"It means having an unhealthy interest in unpleasant things. Like death." I sigh. "Very well, you can still help us with all the decorations. Unless—is there someone *you* would like to include on the ofrenda? *I* could help you, here at school, if there was."

Leo looks thoughtful for a moment. He goes on twisting his hands as though they were doorknobs, and he sucks at his cheeks, first one and then the other.

"Is there anyone? Maybe a grandmother or grandfather? Or even your cat?"

"My cat didn't die! She ran away."

"Ah, yes! You're right. I'm sorry, I—I misremembered. Well, can you think of anyone?"

Leo looks at me a bit sideways, still thoughtful and hesitant, as if evaluating my trustworthiness. I give him a small expectant look that says, *Well?* And he shakes his head suddenly, making up his mind.

"Okay. That's all right. Go get your shoes on with the other children, and then you can help me load the flowers into the van and we can be off."

THE DAY IS A GLORIOUSLY sunny one. The trees are at the height of their color, and the sky beyond them is recklessly blue. I park the van on the side of a grassy hill so that we can enjoy a short hike and a bit of exercise on the way to the cemetery. The children spill out of the van, bundled up in their hats and scarves, and I have them help me unload the pots of chrysanthemums and candles from the back of the van into a red wagon.

With the wagon loaded, we're off. Thomas wants to pull the wagon first. The other children run off across the grass, skipping, pushing, and pulling one another, and giggling. Octavio and Sophie are immediately immersed in some imaginary adventure game, pirates or superheroes or something of the sort. Annabelle is doing genuinely impressive cartwheels and, with each one, losing her headband in the grass. Other children are blowing the heads of dandelions or spinning in circles until they fall dizzily to the ground.

Why is it always at these moments, these pretty, careless moments, when the children, so well dressed and well fed and happy, are enjoying themselves most freely, that I find myself suddenly thinking of all the other less fortunate children I've known? Why is it always then that some intrusive memory elbows in, a memory of children in rags, children dull-eyed with fever, children orphaned and scared, children with bleeding mouths, bleeding sores, bleeding skulls? I had hoped that these happy children would help me forget all the unhappiness I've seen, that their laughter would drown out all the wails that still echo in my head, but sometimes it only seems to make it worse, to make me feel *more* keenly, like a sixth sense, all the suffering that I know continues every minute of every day, just *elsewhere*, elsewhere. It seems, unfortunately, that nothing can protect you from your own mind, your knowledge, your memories. The harder you fight to keep thoughts out, the harder they pound the battering ram to get in. If these happy children only knew the dark, troubled thoughts churning through their teacher's head on a pleasant sunny field trip, they'd stop their games and cartwheels, sink down in the grass, and cry.

"What a beautiful day!" I exclaim to anyone and no one, trying to force my spirits higher, trying to fake it.

Doing a quick head count, I notice that Ramona is not ahead with the rest of the children. Turning back, I see her some ten meters behind us, stooped over, picking a handful of clover flowers.

"Dépêche-toi, biquet!" I call to her, and she runs to catch up, her cheeks flushed and rosy.

Together the children and I crest a hill and pause at the top to take in the view. The treetops are a patchwork of crimson, umber, and sienna. To the west can be seen the well-kept pastures of my neighbors, the Emersons. Their grazing cows are brown specks against the green. Farther west of the Emersons, in a dense stand of pines, the finials on the roof of the school can just barely be seen and a small sliver of the conservatory is peeking out from amid the trees, the glass glinting in the bright sunlight. A cold metal wind sweeps us with its intimations of winter, as though the season ahead were a great glacier advancing slowly from just beyond the horizon.

"Regardez, mes enfants. Que voyez-vous?" I ask, pointing to the cows.

"Les vaches!" several little voices cry.

"Oui, les vaches. Et aussi les arbres," I say, pointing to the trees. "Et les collines." I make the undulating motion of hills with my hand.

"Et les nuages!" Audrey cries out, pointing upward at the clouds.

"Oui, Audrey. Les nuages, très bien."

We continue down the other side of the hill, where the cemetery lies at the bottom encircled by a low metal fence in the shade of what I have learned from one Mr. Riley are two-hundred-year-old white oaks. The children shout and exclaim and race down the hill. The sight of a cemetery is novel to them. It's likely that few of them have ever been to one.

At the sight of the blunt gray headstones standing in silent assembly like a regiment of forgotten soldiers, I, by contrast, am overcome by the strangest, most potent feeling of *home* that I have felt in years. I think of my father. I think of him with surprise that I had not thought of him sooner, surprise also that I had not recognized my desire to come to this cemetery as, at least in part, a desire to feel near to him. I look at the stones and I remember in a tactile way, a body memory way, more powerful than the memories of the mind, the first art I ever learned, that of stone carving—of gravestone carving. I feel suddenly overcome with a longing that is difficult to pinpoint or articulate, a longing for rest, for silence, for nothingness.

"But if I was wrong," my grandfather said to me on that night of my second birth, after he had "gifted" me with eternity, "my apologies for the miscalculation." Had any more egregious miscalculation ever been made? Was there ever a person more comfortable with final resting places than I, the gravestone carver's orphaned daughter?

Some of the children reach the fence that surrounds the cemetery and make as if to climb it. They could easily. It is really only a fence conceptually.

"Ah, ah, ah! Mes enfants! Let's use the front entrance like civilized young men and women, s'il vous plaît. Comme de bons garçons et filles Français."

The hopeful climbers back away from the fence ruefully and follow me around to the entrance and the visitor center. Inside the center, an elderly Black man looks up from where he is seated behind a desk and waves to us as we tramp noisily through the wrought-iron gated entrance, our feet scuffling through the fallen leaves.

When we have chosen the grave sites that we want to decorate and pulled the wagon up before them, the man comes out of the center and joins us in the grass.

"You must be Collette," he says pleasantly, and offers me his hand for a firm shake. "With the French preschool."

"I am. And you must be Mr. Riley."

"That's me. Good day to you, children!"

"Hi!" they shout back, and wave.

"Wait a second," he says, squinting suspiciously at the children. "Don't you mean . . . *bonjour*?"

The children grin, pleased as always with any adult who teases them.

"Bonjouuuuuuuurrr!!!" they cry in oversold penitence.

"That's better!" Mr. Riley exclaims. "If you go to a French preschool, you better know at least as much French as I do."

I nod in agreement.

"Thank you so much for allowing us to do this," I say.

"Happy to do it," he says. "Happy to do it. We don't get an awful lot of traffic here this time of year, so you all have livened up my day. And I can't wait to see how it looks when you all are finished."

The children are already earnestly hefting pots of chrysanthemums nearly as big as themselves out of the wagon.

"Hard workers," Mr. Riley says, giving me an approving pat on the arm, then he turns and heads back to the visitor center.

"Not all on one, mes petites, spread the flowers out among the three graves," I advise. "Who wants to begin placing the candles?"

"*Meeeeeeeee!*"

When we have emptied the contents of the wagon, and made the graves lush with a profusion of red, orange, and white chrysanthemums, I take a box of matches from my pocket and begin lighting the candles.

There is the audible click of a picture being taken, and I look up to see Mr. Riley, stooped behind the viewfinder of a camera.

"Isn't that lovely?" he exclaims. "You children have done an amazing job."

To me he says, "Is it all right if I take a few pictures to put up on the bulletin board inside so our future visitors can see the beautiful work you all have done?"

I don't like having my picture taken, don't like leaving a record of my unaging face lying about here and there, but what can I do?

"Sure," I say. "Of course, that's fine."

"Okay, everyone, get together now."

From behind the camera, Mr. Riley gestures for us to gather close for a group photo. The children huddle in and beam gap-toothed smiles at the camera. I stand to the side, smiling what I'm sure is an uneasy smile. When Mr. Riley counts to three, we all yell "fromage!" and he snaps a picture.

"Are you ready now to come inside and learn some very interesting things about the very interesting city of Millstream Hollow and about this very interesting and *very* old cemetery?"

"Yes!!!" the children cry.

"Blow out the candles, children," I say, "and then we can follow Mr. Riley."

Blowing out the candles proves to be the most desirable activity of the day, I think because it reminds the children of blowing out birthday candles, and there are a few small skirmishes over who will do it, but at last all the flames are extinguished, and the children are following Mr. Riley to the visitor center like a wobbly line of ducklings.

Inside, I take Audrey and Octavio to the restrooms while Mr. Riley shows the rest of the children some enlarged black-and-white photos of Millstream Hollow that are mounted on the wall. Audrey and Octavio emerge from the restrooms a few minutes later, and Audrey runs to join the others while I help Octavio with the top button on his pants. Then Octavio also runs to join the others.

Mr. Riley is a born storyteller and a natural with children. He is presently passing around a Civil War–style drum for the children to take turns drumming on, and while the class listens to him with rapt attention, I wander the room, looking at the other photos on the walls and at the various items that are displayed on shelves and inside glass hutches.

There are portraits of bearded mayors, captains from the Civil War; there is a photograph of the city's port, full of old barges and elegant sailing ships where today it holds powerboats and a fake showboat that takes people out for overpriced dinner cruises. There are pictures of some of the town's historic houses, including, to my surprise, one of the school, taken fifty years earlier. I probably shouldn't be surprised since the historic society is always pestering me to let muddy-footed strangers traipse in and out of the house for their annual historic home Christmas tour.

In one of the hutches, I see some items of particular interest to me: old iron stone-working tools, badly oxidized, chipped, and pitted with age. There are hand points, a half dozen chisels of varying sizes and weights, and a round hammer, the wooden handle dark with rot.

"These tools, Mr. Riley," I call. "Can you tell the children about these?"

"I most certainly can," Mr. Riley says, rising stiffly from the stool he'd been sitting on. He gestures for the children to follow him over to the hutch and, like puppies after a treat, they do.

"Take a look at these," he begins. "These tools are, we think, about two hundred years old. Gravestones today are made with big machines that cut and polish the rock like this, *jjjjjjjjjjjjjjjjjjl*," he says, running one hand smoothly and quickly over the top of the other. "So, graves today mostly all look the same, but a long time ago, they didn't have those fancy machines, so people called stone carvers or masons would cut out the gravestones from giant slabs of rock using these little tools. All of the gravestones in this cemetery were carved by hand with tools like these, not by machines. That's one of the things that makes this cemetery so special."

With that, Mr. Riley's presentation to the children is concluded. We thank him and look around, gathering a few dropped hats and mittens, then make our way to the door. I am herding the children out, and calling out our thanks again to Mr. Riley, when just before the door, I glance into another display hutch and catch sight of a small slab of rock, soapstone to be exact, approximately nine inches long by six inches wide. On it, neatly inscribed in the sure, lovely hand of a master stone carver, is a line of poetry from Donne's tenth Holy Sonnet. Below that is an amateurish attempt at the subsequent line of the poem. The letters are varyingly too faint or too deep and one of the letters is fouled by a deep pit. I can remember the disconsolate frustration of making that pit as vividly as if I had, only a second ago, made the errant stroke.

For a moment I can't speak. Leo is beside me, struggling with an inside-out mitten, but I lose all thought of the other children, who could be scattering to the seven winds outside the center for all I know. All I can do—all I *want* to do—is stare at the gravestone: my father's stone, and mine.

"Mr. Riley," I say, pointing to the stone lying behind the glass of the visitor center display case and struggling to find my voice. "What is this? What do you know about this?"

Mr. Riley smiles with real pleasure, nods, and lets out a whistle as he makes his way over to me and the case.

"Now that," he says, pointing at the stone, "might be my favorite thing in here, and all because it's so strange and I know so little about it. They found it about seven miles from here, southwest, at the construction site of a gas station. It was not over an actual grave site—no body underneath—but it is clearly at least a hundred and fifty years old. *At least.* Could be over two hundred. Soapstone, which is what this is, was never used all that widely. It was so easy to carve that folks didn't think it would hold up over time, but because of the unique mineral makeup of soapstone, turns out it is one of the most resistant stones against acid rain, so it in fact holds up very well over time, much better than marble.

"But what is so interesting about this is the carving. It's a line of poetry by John Donne, one of the most famous poets of the sixteenth century, but look at that top line. Perfect. The work of a master mason if ever I saw it. But then the line below it!"

He lets out a delighted laugh and slaps his leg in merriment. "Looks like a novice! It's a mess. Now what I think it is—which I have no way of proving, mind you—but I think that this stone is the work of a master and an apprentice. Practice, if you will. Like a little child." He gestures down at Leo, who is standing beside me and looking up at us. "Copying his letters in a little notebook."

He laughs again. "See, those are the little things that you find as a historian and they just, they *really* bring the past back to life. I love it. I love it so much. I'm glad you asked about that."

"Thank you," I say, fighting back the welling of tears in my eyes. "Thank you for that wonderful description. You're very good at what you do and you've made this trip wonderful for all of us. Truly."

"Thank you," he says. "And I hope to see you again this time next year."

"I would like that," I say.

· XI ·

SHORTLY after Agoston brought me to that small cottage in the dense center of a forest in a country I knew nothing about, he left me there. In a manner to which I was becoming accustomed, he offered no explanation of where he was going and no indication of whether he might return or when. This parting, following so quickly on the heels of the last, might have been devastating had it not been for the curious qualities of the family I found myself quite suddenly a part of.

The boy I had seen approach the table from two different directions on that first day was, in actuality, two boys: Vano and Ehru, Roma twins, with whom I would share Piroska's home and care. I had heard of twins, but I'd never seen any in life, so when they had appeared from opposite sides of us in perfect synchronicity and moved toward our table like a figure moving toward its reflection in a mirror, I was filled with confused astonishment and wonder. Looking back, it seems like that combination of feelings never really left me for as long as I lived in that house.

The twins had a dark and painful history. Like many Roma children, then and for hundreds of years before, they'd been kidnapped at a young age and sold for slaves. Certain unnerving qualities in the pair had caused them to be passed along quickly from owner to owner until they were sold to the very monastery that Agoston and I had passed in the last village.

In that monastery, the brothers had spent several years laboring, being forcefully converted to Orthodox faith, and being beaten. Ehru had it worse than Vano for various reasons; he would not speak and was of a stubborn, belligerent temperament, which provoked his keepers, but more provocative still was the matter of the food. Both boys were given a meager diet of gruel and occasional bread that in combination would only have sustained one of them. Vano ate what was provided and, over time, wasted away to skin and bones. Ehru refused the food and yet, somehow, put on pounds like a spring lamb. He was accused first of theft and punished. Then, when the possibility of theft was ruled out, witchcraft or dealings with the Devil were suspected, and the subprior in charge of discipline took zealous responsibility for beating loose whatever dark force gripped the boy.

After an especially violent spiritual intervention that left Ehru with several broken ribs and a leg bent horribly, the brothers, one battered and one near starvation, stole away from the monastery in the middle of the night during a lashing gale. The two children hobbled and struggled many miles in the freezing rain, until they finally collapsed exhausted less than a mile from Piroska's dwelling. Piroska, in the way that she had, sensed their distress, and going out into the blowing storm, found them near death from injuries, malnourishment, and exposure.

She brought them to her home and, there, splinted and wrapped Ehru's broken body and nursed them both. Vano responded quickly to her care, but Ehru did not. When she tried to feed him the same herbed broth that was restoring his brother, he gagged and spit and even vomited it up. He grew thinner and wilder, struggling violently in his sleep, rolling his eyes, gnashing his teeth, and groaning terribly.

Vano, once recovered, paced the floor, anxious and jumpy. He knew what his brother needed, but didn't dare hint of it to their kind new caretaker. This went on for several days until Piroska woke one night to find Vano dripping blood into his brother's mouth from a gash he'd carved into his own arm.

It was Vano mostly who told me the story, but Piroska commented once that it was a shameful lapse, her not recognizing what Ehru was and what he needed. After all, she'd had plenty of experience with his kind; she'd sheltered my own grandfather after his change, though he was an old man when it happened and not a boy, and it was his mind that needed mending more than his body (she shared little beyond this about my grandfather; his story, she said, was not hers to tell, and there were a great many versions besides, and only Grandfather knew which, if any, were true).

When Piroska discovered that bloody scene at Ehru's sickbed, she wrenched Vano away from his brother and bound the dangerously deep wound in his arm, then left the cottage. Vano feared that she'd abandoned them, or gone to get others to help her drive the boys out, but she returned, and when she did, she had something clenched tight in her hands: a small desman, tensed and panting and anxious to scrabble out of her grasp. She stood over Ehru, whispered a word seemingly to the animal, then took a knife and quickly cut into the creature, killing it. She poured the blood into Ehru's mouth then, and he, though half-asleep and half-feral, gulped at it with the greedy desperation of a starving baby.

After that, the boys remained with Piroska, and she cared for each of them in the ways each of them required. Calm, watchful Vano learned from her the special uses of herbs, how to listen for the sounds of things to come, how to prepare medicines and teas, poultices and tinctures, and the kvass they drank from the barrel. But silent, angry Ehru needed else from her. Him she taught to bellow out his rage as he felled timber or chopped firewood, to weep without restraint as he ran down the small game that was his sustenance, and to grunt out his grief as he ripped the feathers Piroska used for down from the birds Vano ate. As a mother might lead a child in practicing his letters, Piroska led Ehru in expelling forcefully, like a sort of spiritual bloodletting, the deadly, sickening rage that filled him. With time, Ehru's white-hot fury died down to crackling embers, so that he no longer flinched when a hand reached for him, and Piroska was able, at last, to coax speech from him again.

When I came to live with them, it was years later, and I learned the story from them slowly, in bits and pieces, just as I learned their language in order to speak to them. Grief for my father and brother and homesickness kept me quiet and withdrawn at first, but the steady goodness of my surroundings drew me out in short time, and the small, ordinary tasks that we performed together—tending animals, hanging wash, chinking the cabin walls, scraping pelts from the small, glistening muscles of rabbits and foxes—soothed me by their rhythm and familiarity.

Ehru and I shared much in common. We both lived off the lifeblood of others; we both possessed unaccountable strength and quickness. It was Ehru who taught me to use that strength and speed for hunting. He taught me to put off my mind and let my muscles take over, pushing me to run faster, jump higher, pounce with greater suddenness than I possibly could while thinking. Eventually, I too could run down the red deer and chamois as he could, and kill a wild tusked boar with only a knife and my bare hands.

I came to love Ehru like a brother, but he frightened me as well. He was wild like nothing I had ever known. Instead of fleeing danger, he raced toward it savage-eyed, shouting and goading fate. There was a destructive rage always brimming in him, barely contained and frequently spilling over, and when it did, he would chase bears away with his howl and fight wolves with reckless savagery. Afterward, dressed in blood, both the animal's and his own, he would laugh at the deep claw wounds across his body, the bone exposed through torn flesh.

Vano was not like me, not like his brother. Vano ate ordinary food twice a day. If Vano injured himself, it took time and care to heal, and whereas anger billowed off Ehru like thick smoke, Vano, with his powerful calm, cleared the air like a wind. Vano was vremenie, one of the short-lived, but there was little else that was ordinary about him. His gaze alone had extraordinary power, a way of settling on you and remaining, so that you felt he was seeing into you, opening doors and drawers in the most secret places and handling gently and tenderly the glass-fragile objects that lay hidden inside. When you spoke to him, he listened like a hunter listening for footfalls on distant grass, and nothing hidden by either false tone or false words could deceive him. To be near him was to feel that you stood naked and turned inside out, but he never betrayed the vulnerability that he, whether knowingly or unknowingly, extracted, like a poultice, from another. He was always careful with us, gentle, often far gentler to Ehru and me than we were to ourselves.

This piercing sight and sensitivity of his extended not only to us, his companions, but to the whole world around him: a seer, a prophet, a priest without ordination, everything that fell under his gaze was seen fully and understood just as well. I loved Vano too, but I did not love him only like a brother. I loved him in a quick, painful, breathless way that made me want to cry and shout and sing all at once and, most of all, do anything to be near him. Instead, I was quiet, uncertain, often awkward in his presence; I moved constantly toward him and away, as if tossed by tides of hope and embarrassment that shifted almost by the moment. This torturous love for Vano, which I carried so heavily with me always, seemed to be the only thing about me that he did not see like writing plain on a wall.

Vano would let me walk with him, through the forests and along the riverbanks and up to the rocky crags, and through every season, he would teach me things, or try to teach me things, things he learned from Piroska about the old Slavic gods that the monastery had driven into hiding and cast into disrepute, and the radiances that animated and connected everything, and the things that were coming, things the world and the creatures and our own bodies waited hungrily for. I collected every word he said, but I had no ear for the words in the wind, and the stars did not enact their sagas for me as they did for him. The only talent I evidenced, as Vano's student, was for mixing pigments from rocks and bark and berries, and painting the symbols of the abandoned Slavic gods that he taught to me: Belobog, the light god, whose symbol was like a nest of intertwining Ls; Czernobog, the accursed one of darkness, the bringer of endings, whose symbol resembled a goat's head with a diamond between its horns. And many others: Mokosh, the damp mother, and Veles, who walks through the forests and swims in every water.

Vano taught me also about Ehru. When they were very young, he told me, they had lived in a village in a land that was almost always hot. A wanderer appeared one day, and this wanderer had taken Ehru away into the forest and murdered him. Ehru's body was found, and he was buried and grieved by his family and village, but then, after a time, he had come back covered in soil and hungry only for blood. Because they were twins and thus presumed to be mystically linked, both of the boys were taken far from their home village and abandoned. It was not long after that that they were found by slave traders, carried a long way to this colder land, and sold. Ehru's life from early childhood, it seemed, had been full of brutality, and it had made him brutal, to himself most of all.

Once, when we were only teenagers, Vano and I watched Ehru throw himself down from a waterfall into a pool of white water churning around huge, sharp boulders. We fought the swift water, dragged Ehru's limp, bleeding body out, and set him on the grassy bank, where he lay unconscious for some time.

"*Why* does he do these things?" I cried in exhausted despair. "It's madness!"

Vano was silent for a moment, gazing down into his brother's still face. When he looked up at me, tears gleamed at the corners of his eyes.

"It has always been Ehru who has been chosen for violence. That man, that wanderer, he saw us both—I remember him—but it was Ehru he chose. And then in the monastery. They beat him so badly. They beat him to drive the demons out of him. They beat and tortured him in the name of Christ, *their own* beaten and tortured god of whom they knew nothing. They saw how quickly Ehru healed and they beat him all the more for it. There's none can beat as hard as those who beat to save. He would have died many times, I'm sure of it, if he'd been able."

Vano scooted toward his brother, then lay down beside the wet, inert body, his brown skin still glistening with river water.

"And now," he said, glancing up at me, "he goes on where they all left off, beating himself because he thinks that's what he was made for."

Vano's expression became pained and a tear ran off his nose. Face-to-face with Ehru, he called softly, "Bar"—the word in their language for brother—"small, sweet boy, where are you? Where have you gone? Come back. Do not harm yourself anymore. Do not do their evil work for them. In the name of the god they claimed but did not know, that

Christ, who suffered so much cruelty and turned it to mercy, *I* say to you, *live.* That's what you're *for.* Have mercy, brother; have mercy on yourself."

He began to whisper to Ehru in the language they shared, and I felt a burning wish that, for just a moment, it might be me lying there beside Vano on the grass, his mouth close and whispering benedictions in my ear. Cheeks burning, I got to my feet and left them.

· XII ·

OUTSIDE the Millstream Hollow Cemetery Visitor Center, the children are all alive and uninjured. Thomas has found a leaf bug and is holding it in his palm, showing it off to the other children while also keeping them at arm's length so that they won't steal it. I gather them, and we begin our tramp back up the hill to get the children's lunch sacks from the van for a picnic on the grass. As is becoming the baffling norm, I'm ravenous.

Annabelle is now pulling the wagon, but instead of chrysanthemums, Audrey and Sophie are inside it this time. Octavio and Thomas help push from the back, and Ramona is running alongside, showering the riders with picked clover.

I feel dazed, lost in the reverie provoked by stumbling upon my father's long-forgotten headstone. The vast span of time between now and then has fallen away as if it were nothing and I'm a child again, hefting the cold weight of that stone through the woods on a spring day long ago, searching for a place to bury my father where he would be safe from shovels and violation. I was so miserable, so sick and sad and lonely. I thought nothing could get worse for me, and yet now I look back and wish I could return to that time before everything changed. If I could go back, I would look my grandfather in the eye when he came to take me away and say, *go*. Leave me here. Whatever happens to me, even if they cut out my heart, burn me, feed my ashes to the ill, at least it will end. At least, eventually, I'll have that quiet, that peaceful nothingness that I long for.

Coming to myself, I look around at the children in their jean jackets and jelly shoes, bright pink scrunchies wrapped around off-center ponytails. How did I get here? What am I *doing* in *1984*? What will I possibly do with the 1990s? Dear God, *the 2000s*? It fills me with something close to panic, and I have to work to focus on other things to steady myself: the trees, the clouds, the children.

At the crest of the hill, Octavio stumbles in the grass. I'm taking his hand and pulling him back up to his feet when Ramona begins to shout.

"*Madame! Madame!*" she cries, running up the hill toward us.

"What is it, Ramona?"

Her cheeks are fiery, and her chapped nose is red and gleaming with snot.

"Leo!" she says, and points back to where Leo's small figure is halfway up the hill and hunched over, heaving.

I run back down the hill. The children follow, Annabelle dropping the handle of the wagon and the younger girls leaping out of it. When I reach Leo, he has sunk down into a low squat, arms wrapped around his knees. His pale forehead is beaded with sweat, and the blue of his little mouth matches the circles under his wide, frightened eyes. A high whine accompanies each gasping breath, and I can see the well at the base of his throat deepening effortfully.

"Leo, are you having trouble breathing?" I ask, kneeling beside him in the grass. "Nod your head for me if it's hard for you to breathe."

He turns his eyes up to me, and I see panic in them. He nods. The rest of the children have gathered around us in a silent, scared huddle. Ramona is right next to Leo, staring at him in unconcealed alarm.

He's having an asthma attack. Fortunately, I have an inhaler his parents provided in a bag along with some allergy medication for Thomas and an EpiPen for Annabelle. The bag is buried somewhere at the bottom of the backpack I'm carrying. I pull it from my shoulders and begin rummaging through the overstuffed pack.

"Leo, sweetie, we're going to take care of you and you're going to be just fine. I need you to do your best to calm your body and try to take the deepest, slowest breaths you can."

Leo is nodding his head over and over again helplessly. His eyes cast about in a drugged-looking panic, and the well at the base of his throat goes on sinking darkly as he struggles to pull air into his lungs. In the backpack, my fingers finally discover the bag, and I pull it out, sending other odds and ends tumbling onto the grass.

"Leo, do you know how to use this, or should I read the instructions?"

Leo doesn't answer. He's still gasping and turning his head from side to side as if in confusion. I take the tiny folded sheet of instructions and unfold it. There are paragraphs and paragraphs in a dense, fine type. I can't make sense of any of it. I finally just take the cap from the inhaler, put the thing to Leo's mouth.

"Breathe out, Leo."

He does.

"Now when I pump the inhaler, breathe in."

I pump the inhaler, and he breathes in deeply, but his eyes turn up to my face with a look of concern. I take the inhaler away from his mouth, but his breath continues ragged and gasping. Has it worked? I can't tell. The other children have tightened their ring around us. I can feel one at each elbow.

"Take a step back, everyone," I urge. "Give us some space. Leo, did it work? Did you feel the medication come out?"

He shakes his head, confirming what I had feared. Holding the inhaler up before me in the air, I give it a puff. Only the faintest wisp of mist comes out of the mouthpiece. I give it a good shake, glance back at the instructions; that's when I smell it: warm, liquid copper. A smell I know better than any other, and one that provokes as immediate a salivary reaction as meat roasting on a spit might for others. A thin stream of bright red blood falls suddenly from Leo's nose and spills down over the folds of the scarf around his neck.

The children gasp. Leo puts his hands to his face, and the blood slips slick through his fingers. He looks down at the red on his hands, and his shoulders begin heaving even more violently. He starts to cry. The children have hands to their mouths in fright. They look back and forth breathlessly from Leo to me. Ramona, beside him, begins to cry too.

"Everyone, take a breath and calm down. Leo, listen to me. You're fine. It's just a silly little nosebleed, nothing at all to be scared of"—my mouth is involuntarily watering, and I can almost taste the salt of the blood on my tongue—"but we do need to get you breathing calmly. I'm going to give you another puff from the inhaler. It won't be a lot, but it will be some. It will help."

I have no idea if this is true, but even a placebo effect would be welcome right now. I give him another puff from the inhaler, take his bloody hand and press it to the center of my chest, then take a slow, deep breath and blow it out as slowly.

"You feel that, Leo? That's my breath. We're going to breathe together, and I'm going to share some of my air with you, okay? I have lots of air and I'm going to give you some. Just keep your eyes on me and do what I do."

I take several deep, slow breaths. His red hand rises and falls against my chest. The blood is dripping from his chin, and I wonder briefly which he might pass out from first, lack of oxygen or loss of blood. He is looking right into my eyes, and I lead him through several more long, slow breaths.

"Do you feel it? Nice and slow."

His breath rattles out, jerky and gasping at first, but with each repetition slower and more even, and his eyes remain locked on mine. The children and trees around us fade. The blood grows brighter and brighter; it seems to expand, consuming my whole field of vision. I have to work to look past it, to focus on Leo's frightened eyes.

"There you go. Are you feeling it? All that good air in your lungs?"

His little hand rises and falls against me. His breathing is only faintly uneven now. The alarming purple of his lips has faded to a dusky blue, and then it's just a shadow around his mouth. The tears are still standing in his eyes and one slips down his cheek like a falling pearl, but he's no longer crying.

"There we go. That's better," I hear myself murmuring again and again in a kind of soothing loop.

I manage, at last, to pull my gaze away from Leo and the blood, and turn to the other children, who I'd almost forgotten were still gathered around us and transfixed. "We're all doing so much better just by calming ourselves and taking deep breaths."

Leo is sitting, dazed, in the grass, and Ramona and Audrey pour water from their water bottles on his hands to get the blood off, while I gather the spilled items back into my pack.

"Leo, would you like me to carry you the rest of the way up to the van?" I ask once I've gathered everything.

He squints up at me from where he sits in the grass, and with his large, dark eyes still sad and damp, he nods, and I take him up into my arms.

BACK AT THE HOUSE, I pass the children off to Rina, asking her to help them get ready for their naps. She catches sight of Leo, whose bloody scarf still hangs around his neck, and gives me an expression of alarm and an *okay* gesture before herding the children off toward the parlor.

I fetch a change of clothes for Leo from his cubby and then give him a moment alone in the bathroom to get changed. When he's dressed, I come into the bathroom, lift him up and set him on the bathroom countertop, then help him wash the crusted blood from his nose and mouth.

"How are you feeling now? Better?"

His chin quivers intermittently with feeling, but he nods.

"Does that happen to you often, Leo? Having trouble breathing like that?"

"Just sometimes," he says, "but I never had a bloody nose before. Why did my nose get blood? Does it mean I'm dying? I saw a mouse on the driveway one time, and his nose had blood on it, and Katherine said it was because he was dying."

"Oh no, Leo. No, it doesn't mean you're dying. Little boys sometimes get bloody noses, and it doesn't mean anything at all. You have nothing to worry about."

He says nothing, just stares ahead thoughtfully.

"Did it make you sad seeing that mouse that was dying? Or worried?"

His chin dimples a little and then he nods. "I hate when things die. It makes me so sad."

To my astonishment, his eyes fill with tears. "I wish nothing *ever died*," he says with passion, and then leans his head forward and starts to cry.

"Oh, Leo, sweetheart," I say, but I'm at a complete loss. "Leo, mon petit, can I give you a hug? You seem like you could use one right now."

He nods pathetically, and I take his small frame in my arms.

"You have nothing to worry about, dearest. I promise you, you are not going to die just because of a bloody nose."

"But everything dies," he says, sitting up again. "Did you know that? Katherine told me that everything that's alive dies."

"Just about," I admit, nodding softly. "But not before they've lived a nice long time. Not until they're old and they've done all the things they want to do."

"Sometimes things die when they're not old. Sometimes people do."

I'm feeling outgunned. I've run out of pleasant partial truths to offer this child as reassurance. Why is he so concerned with death? I wonder. Perhaps Katherine was righter than I realized in steering her son clear of "morbid" subjects.

"Well, my dear one," I say, taking his round face in my hands, "*today* we are both alive and we are here at school with our friends, and our parents will be coming soon for a party that is going to be great fun, but we must take a nap first, so that we're rested enough to enjoy ourselves. Okay?"

He closes his eyes and nods.

I lift him from the bathroom counter, set him on the floor, and offer my hand.

"Shall we?"

He takes it, and we head off to the parlor.

Once Leo is settled, I go to the phone to call Katherine Hardman. I want to tell her about Leo's asthma attack and ask her to bring a replacement inhaler when she comes to the open house this afternoon, but the line is busy.

Disappointed, I go upstairs to my room to wash up and change. I'm also smeared and spotted with Leo's blood. There are streaks on my arms and neck where he clung to me when I carried him, and a good-sized stain on the front of my blouse where Leo's nose continued to drip as we made our way back to the van.

I pull off the soiled shirt, and as I do, the smell of the blood overwhelms me. For a moment, all I can do is stand there with the shirt in my hands, my stomach rumbling, and the spots of blood staring up at me like so many red, suggestive eyes.

I do not drink the blood of children. I *do not* drink the blood of children.

Still, I stand there, listening as the spots beckon and my stomach growls in answer. Together they articulate suddenly and with almost brash clarity a fact that I've sensed for weeks now but have refused to acknowledge: my body is changing somehow; my hunger is growing. Whereas a few quarts a week was always more than sufficient, a pint a day is now inadequate. Thoughts of blood nag me incessantly, and the noises of my stomach vocalize the wishes of my body with all the perseverance of a whining toddler. My rations are fixed, though; an eight-pound cat has only so much to give. There, in the bathroom, considering a child's bloodstained shirt for longer than I should, I finally admit my situation to myself. I need more blood.

I lift the shirt to my nose, and the aroma invades my senses: fruity and metallic, sweet and savory. It fills my head. The blood of children is cleaner, less gamy than animals', and less tainted than that of adults, with their hair dyes, alcohol, and prescription drugs. Still, there's something slightly off about this blood: a vague, earthy taint, a cloying scent of sickness, like overripe fruit. Blood doesn't lie; and this blood tells me that Leo isn't an entirely well child.

With a sudden burst of determination, I open the laundry hamper and throw the shirt in.

. . .

THE CHILDREN WAKE FROM THEIR naps, and together we put the finishing touches on the class ofrenda. It has turned out magnificently. Between the candles and the souvenirs of deceased loved ones, red and orange marigolds richly carpet every surface. Constructed frames of tissue-paper marigolds line the edges of the photographs, which I've hung on the wall, and the brightly colored papel picados are draped between them. The gleaming, egg-washed loaves of *pan de muerto* that Marnie helped the children bake earlier in the week are piled on colorful plates. I think of my father's headstone back at the cemetery, in a case behind glass. What would I give to have it here? To be able to honor his memory in even just this small way?

The children will go with Marnie for the next hour to make *niflettes*, the traditional French cream-filled pastry of La Toussaint. They line up at the doorway to the kitchen and when it's time, Marnie—wide-hipped, gray-haired, and grandmotherly—ushers them in to gather around the island at the center of the kitchen. The ingredients, mixing bowls, measuring cups, and cooking spoons are all piled in the center, and under Marnie's gentle guidance the children will do everything. They will take turns sifting flour, cracking eggs, measuring spices, and cutting out the wreath-shaped circles of pastry dough.

Initially in these lessons, the little ones try to stick their fingers in the sugar or butter, but the older children, now experts with a year of such lessons under their belts, scold them in French, *Non! Non! Ne touche pas!*, just as they themselves were scolded by the older children in years past. It's very effective. The little ones, chastened, withdraw their fingers and thereafter keep their hands to themselves and watch the older children carefully for cues. Sometimes the herd mentality in people has its distinct advantages.

I was too busy with last-minute details to feed during the children's nap and now, as I'm tidying the conservatory, my stomach is doing uncomfortable and noisy acrobatics. This hunger paired with the impending descent of a horde of parents is making me jittery and anxious. I have a lot still to get done while the children are with Marnie, but the hunger is so distracting that it's a struggle to do anything. I feel unfocused, almost dizzy. I'm not used to battling my body in this way. After so many years of predictable health, any sudden change is unnerving, and I don't have the option of going in for a checkup. The thought of going over my X-rays with a doctor! What strange, extraneous organs might be revealed, or what dark expanses might mark out the spaces where other things ought to be?

The finches in their cage chirp and flutter white and yellow wings, and when I find myself staring at them transfixed, feeling myself much like a frustrated house cat, I decide that I will have to pay a visit to the attic during the children's baking lesson. I won't make it through the whole evening otherwise.

I take a stack of the children's most recent drawings to hang in the foyer on my way upstairs. As I walk past the closed door of the kitchen, I hear Leo cough. Marnie says, "Leo, dear, turn your head away and cough into your elbow, please. We don't want to get our friends sick."

Leo coughs again. This time the sound is muffled.

"That's the ticket!" Marnie exclaims. "This isn't a *germ* puff we're making here, is it?" she asks the children in a silly voice.

"No!" they answer gleefully.

"We're not making booger pastries for our parents, are we?"

"*Noo-ooo!*" they shout even louder, their childish giggles burbling out of the kitchen.

In the foyer, which doubles as the student gallery, I begin tacking up the drawings—pen-and-ink sketches of fall foliage: gum tree and black walnut seedpods, clusters of acorns, leaves, and such. The drawings of the first-years are wobbly and exuberant. Sophie's acorns are actually smiling. Ramona's drawing of a cluster of walnut leaves shows a promising level of detail. Annabelle's drawing is a neat and pretty still of three maple leaves—a bit *too* neat and pretty. She's drawing what she thinks she should, instead of what she actually sees. *Seeing*, it turns out, is always the hardest part.

I take Leo's drawing from the stack and pin his picture up on the board: a brittle milkweed pod with downy white tufts spilling from its opening and a stiff, dry stem. It's the most rustic and impressionistic drawing in the whole stack, and it's by far the best. There is no trace of the idea of the milkweed pod, only the pod itself. The husk is stippled with beautiful imperfections, and there's a dark, flat pool beneath it: the shadow of the pod. He's taking chances, getting better by the day. It's exciting to watch.

When I finally make my way upstairs and push up the door to the attic, the light shifts suddenly. A cloud obscures the sun, and the room goes strangely dark. The ammonia smell is there, as always, but another smell is subtly nested alongside it, a familiar smell that unnerves me even before I've consciously identified it. It's the smell of smoke, char, the aromatic signature of a thing burnt, finished. It's a smell I've smelled inexplicably many times before, though not in a long time.

A cat bolts past me and down the stairs, startling me, and then the smell fades and is gone, and I'm left wondering if it was ever really there at all. Disoriented, I climb up into the attic. It's still strangely dark. I think, for an instant, that I catch the smell again, but, again, it fades. The cats mew and pace anxiously. I take a step, and there's a sudden screech. A tabby darts out from underfoot.

"*Emile!* Oh, Emile! I'm sorry, kitty."

There's a palpable sense of unease. We all feel it, myself and the cats. I take a breath, trying to cast off the feeling, sit down, and as usual the cats come to me to be stroked, but there's a skittish tension in their arched backs. I take a treat from the bag, whistle, and welcome Myrrh when she steps gingerly into my lap. I drink from her and reward her, then Chaussie, then Miloz. The light continues to shift crazily as if the clouds are being carried along on a fast-moving stream across the sky. Brighter. Darker. Brighter.

Coco, a yellow-eyed Abyssinian, settles in my lap. The smell returns, and though I keep expecting it to dissipate, instead it grows stronger. Marnie and the children are baking, but they're all the way on the opposite side of the house. If something were burning in the kitchen, the smoke detector there would go off long before I would smell anything all the way over here. After the incident with the smoke detector in my bedroom, I went room to room, all throughout the house, replacing the batteries in every alarm, including the one in this attic. All is quiet, though.

Out the window, I notice a few white flurries fluttering against the glass. *Snow already?* In my lap, Coco is anxious, her body tense, and she's mewing plaintively. She jerks softly under my touch as I stroke her fur, trying to calm her, and also trying still to place the source of the smell. Vano's face from my dream, lit up in fire, flashes in my mind. Shaking my head softly, I think of the name and refuse to think of the name. It's not him. It can't be him. It is not what my memory, my long-buried and irrational fear suggest. *Czernobog.* The destroyer, the god of endings.

Brooding, I gaze absently out the window until I notice something odd about the flakes clustering on the sill. They don't seem quite like snow. The way they float upward again instead of sticking where they land.

At the same instant that I realize what those small, ragged white flakes look like—not snow, but *ash*—a scream of earsplitting noise explodes into the quiet. The smoke alarm overhead is sending out its shrill screech. In an explosive motion, as though she's been scalded with boiling water, Coco leaps up from my lap into the air, limbs flying frantically like a trapeze artist midflight, then she darts away and is gone, hidden in the shelter beneath an armoire. Likewise spooked, the rest of the cats have darted for shelter under furniture and drop cloths.

With the confusion of the cats and the siren still screaming, it takes a moment for the searing pain in my face to register. The cats are still hissing as I raise my hands to my face. With the tips of my fingers, I find the raised and hotly throbbing line of the scratch that runs all the way from my left eyebrow to my right cheek—a wicked diagonal slash across my face.

A shadow shifts. The room grows bright again.

As suddenly as it began, the smoke alarm quits its shrieking, and all is silence.

The cats settle. They quietly lick their paws.

My face drips blood onto the floor.

· XIII ·

MY grandfather never came for me as he had promised to, but soon enough I had no wish that he should. I was happy where I was, and would not have wanted to leave if I'd had the choice. Besides, if I mattered so little to my grandfather, if he could so casually usher me into this strange new existence and then set me adrift upon it, then why should he mean anything to me? Whatever faith or admiration I'd once had in him soured into bitterness and disdain.*

Piroska quickly became more to me than Grandfather had ever been. She was reliable in every way. In fact, in all the years I lived with her, she did not change *at all* from that first day that I met her. She

---

* I was not wrong. My grandfather has since confirmed (and unapologetically at that) that it was, indeed, on mere impulse that he'd made me what I would be forever. And of his promise to retrieve me, his response was almost charmingly blithe: "Though I have no specific recollection of the promise you speak of," he wrote in a letter not long ago, "I feel I can say with confidence that, no, I most likely had no intention of traversing half the earth to fetch a little girl. Many creatures on this earth bequeath precious life upon the young and then leave them to it, and those little hatchlings that manage to fight the surf and find their way out to sea on their own are only the stronger for it. But I will offer you now what no mother in the wild ever offered her babies: *Congratulations*, my dear. You've made it."

remained old, but never older, bent and hoarse, glowing and endlessly kind. What Piroska was, I never knew, whether she was like me and Ehru or like Vano or something else altogether. I never saw her eat, not the food that Vano ate, nor the blood that Ehru and I consumed. She drank the kvass and teas brewed from the leaves and seeds and flower petals she kept in wooden boxes, but if she ate anything else, I never saw what it was.

Unchanged too was her potent ability to soothe me with her presence. She knew, somehow better even than I, when I was feeling distress, and at those times, I would find a basket pressed into my hands and see another in her own—her wordless invitation to join her in foraging bugleweed and black elder, small balsam and hen-of-the-woods. Walking beside her through a glade with the grass wetting the hem of my dress, or kneeling at its edge, our knives working through the tough stems of mushrooms, I would find myself suddenly happy and realize that the sly woman had done it again.

Ehru, Vano, and I did not remain unchanged, though. Our bones stretched, we grew taller, and our faces thinned. We laughed a bit less, grew more thoughtful. I thought mostly of Vano. He grew larger to me, until he occupied nearly the entirety of my vision. I took all his words into myself like treasure, not wanting to miss or forget a single one. The only way I knew was Vano. All my senses filtered everything through Vano; but though he loved me warmly and with great care and tenderness, I grew smaller in his sight. His senses had become like great bowls into which the world poured itself, and he burned ever warmer with love for a spirit he had begun to sense all around him, a spirit that spoke to him often and caused him to miss my words. And I loved Vano so purely that there was no room for resentment. I loved him by helping him love the spirit and by listening to him attentively when he whispered the whispered messages he was receiving.

"There is a door, Anya," he began to say in the months before the end. "It is closed now, but soon it will open. We will step through it, and it will take us each where we must go."

"A door," I would whisper back, studying the cream of his skin in the firelight, the inkwells of his eyes. Vano was telling me what was to come, but I didn't hear it because I didn't care about what was to come. I cared only for what was right before me, for him.

Only take me where he goes, I silently begged Vano's beloved spirit.

"The dying leaves," he said another time, lifting a soft, rotting pile of them to his nose, "they smell of smoke, and the wind carries heat. Can you feel it?"

"I don't know," I said softly, ashamed that I could not.

In the evenings, he would watch the leap of the flames in the hearth and comment on the strange eagerness of the fire.

"The door is opening, Anya," he said on one of those evenings. "Something is coming, something important. The anticipation is everywhere. The rocks and the trees and the clouds, they're all chattering with it."

"They don't say what it is? The spirit doesn't tell you?"

He shook his head. "The spirit tells me only that it will be consequential and that it will be painful."

"Are you certain? Is there some way to know for sure?"

I regretted my question immediately. Vano did not answer, but his eyes darted to my face, and in them there was a troubled look as though he worried for me.

"Well, are you afraid?"

"No," he said, the worry fading from his expression. "The spirit says not to fear. The spirit has promised to be with us. It will not abandon us."

Ehru had grown also. He quickly rose above Vano's middling height and his tremendous strength became evidenced in large, sinewy muscles like the beasts in nature. He was a born predator, and it could be seen in his design. Unlike Vano, he had hair thick on his face and chest. The sweet boy lost inside him, the one whom Vano had beckoned that day by the water, had not returned. Ehru was calmer, quieter, but no more peaceful. I would come across him in the woods sometimes, sitting quietly on a rock, knife in hand, and slowly slicing strips of flesh from his own arms. He never looked up, though I knew he heard me coming. I could more easily have snuck up on a snow leopard.

Then he began to disappear. For days at a time, he would be gone and then he would return suddenly without a word of explanation. I didn't think much about it. Ehru was wild, the kind of person you expect to leave without a goodbye, the kind who surprises you every day they remain.

· · ·

"THERE WAS A MAN—"

It was I who said this, one evening in Piroska's hut, pausing at my work, scratching a pen nib against paper.

"—I saw a man today. I forgot to mention it."

I was the only one among us who knew how to read and write, and I busied myself often in the evenings with it. I transcribed Piroska's recipes with small drawings of the flowers, berries, mushrooms, and roots that went into her pot. I recorded all manner of diverse knowledge from Vano: the mythologies he dictated to me, the names that the monks had taught him for the Christian saints who now stood in for the exiled Slavic deities: Ognyena, who had become Saint Margaret the virgin; Yarilo, who had become Saint George. At present, Vano and I were working on a map of the summer constellations, placing the stars in their quadrants and tracing the shapes of the objects and beasts that they formed.

Ehru looked up from the wooden handle of the froe he was polishing with bundled horsetail. Piroska, at the fire, was skimming froth from the boiling decoction before her, but she too paused and turned her eyes to me.

"Where was this man?" Ehru asked in his gruff manner. "Where did you see him?"

"Standing on the point, near the sandbar where the brook runs into the gorge."

A look of concern passed among us like a solemn toast.

Vano, Ehru, and I each had our reasons for avoiding the village. The brothers had already risked life and limb once to escape it, and their stories, combined with my own grim experiences in my hometown, had made me mistrustful of towns in general. Nevertheless, Piroska had warned us many times to keep our distance and to avoid ever being seen by its people.

There was a time when the village women had trekked up the steep grade of the mountain and through the darkly gnarled woods to bring to Piroska sick children, barren wombs, or swollen bellies stuck fast with stymied births. She had done what she could to help them, until the belief took hold, helped no doubt by the teaching of the monastery, that the sacraments and prayer were the only holy help; all else came from the Devil and was administered by his consorts, who deserved no mercy save a quick passage to the eternal hellfire that awaited them.

"I am, to them, only a story now," Piroska had told us once with a smile. "My name frightens children to obey and keeps wanderers from these woods, so you see, the village and I, we help one another still."

"Did he see you?" Ehru asked me now, fixing me with his intent gaze.

"No."

"You are *sure* of this?"

I tilted my head irritably at him.

"I do not ask to patronize you, Anya," Ehru said, "only to be sure. You may not know that you are a beautiful woman now. If that man saw you, we could be certain that this glimpse of him will not be our last."

Embarrassed, I looked down into my lap, then furtively over at Vano, searching his expression for any reaction to this, but he only studied his brother thoughtfully.

"He did not see me. I am sure."

"What did he look like?" Ehru asked. "What was he doing?"

"A big man. No hair on top, but a large beard bound at the end. He was studying the ground, tracking something."

"Your infamy is fading, Piroska," Vano said to her with a smile. "You've been too well behaved. You should learn to send blight on their crops or cause their calves to be born still, so they'll leave us in peace again."

Piroska smiled at Vano, then to Ehru, who was still frowning, she handed a cup of her brew. "You are worried, Ehru?"

"Not worried," he said unsmilingly. "When you encounter a dangerous animal—and that is what those ignorant village fools are—worry is wasted; you must plan."

He took a sip from the cup Piroska had handed to him, winced at the bitterness of it, then nodded his approval to her. "Let us agree to take caution, yes?"

Piroska took the cup from him again and patted his arm fondly.

"Of course," I said. "We will."

"Yes, brother," said Vano beside me.

· XIV ·

TWO hours later, the classroom is busy with bodies and bright with chatter. As promised, many of the children have Día de los Muertos skulls painted on their faces and marigolds in their hair or pinned to their shirts.

The parents amble around, letting their eager, skull-faced children point out and explain various things to them. The ofrenda is a hit. The parents' mouths all drop when they see it, and some even become tearful, seeing their own family members so honored.

In the dramatic play area, Sophie drapes her mother and sister with capes and gives them pretend haircuts. Dr. and Dr. Snyder, Ramona and Thomas's parents, are in the foyer, milling around the student gallery and fussing over their children's artwork. Leo, I discovered with a pang, is waiting at the window by the front door, watching for his parents to arrive. As usual, they're late.

I'm walking an aimless circuit through the rooms, ostensibly touching bases with each parent, but in fact doing my best to avoid everyone. The cat scratch on my face began to heal immediately, but was horrific nonetheless. I had to choose between an enormous bandage across my face, or the spectacle of a garish wound steadily knitting itself together and healing over the course of an evening. I chose the bandage.

Harder still was coming up with an explanation for the injury. The parents would not be happy to hear that one of the cats residing in the school had scratched a six-inch bloody gash across my face. I would've had a petition barring cats on the premises signed by every parent in my hands by the end of the night. So, I concocted a feeble explanation involving a broken wire hanger in a closet.

I'm vaguely recounting this tale to Annabelle's parents, and they're looking at me with expressions of such concern that I feel nearly panicked to escape them.

"I could take a look at it," Annabelle's father says. "I was a medic in the navy for eleven years."

I'm opening my mouth to formulate some excuse when the doorbell rings and I seize the opportunity to escape down the hall. As I enter the foyer, heels clacking noisily against the wood floors, I catch a glimpse of quick motion, a dark blur streaking quickly around the corner from the closed front door to the adjacent cloakroom: something like a cat, but larger. I crane my neck to get a look in the cloakroom, but the doorbell rings again, so I abandon my investigation and open the door, where, to my great surprise, I find "the authorities" standing before me—a police officer, female, with dark hair scraped back into a ponytail and a gun on her hip.

"Can I help you?" I say, confusion plain in my voice.

"Hi. I'm not sure if I'm in the right place. Is this a school?"

Still confused, I blink and give her an uncertain nod.

"I'm sorry, I'm Samantha McCormick. Officer McCormick. I'm Audrey's aunt. Her parents are out of town for the week, and I'm watching her and her sister, so I'm on open house duty, it seems. Is that—am I in the right place?"

She seems nearly as thrown as I am. Her gaze lingers uncertainly on my face. The bandages, which I had momentarily forgotten, come back to mind along with a fresh wave of embarrassment.

"Oh. Uh yes, yes," I stammer, my hand going self-consciously to my face. "Please come in. I apologize. I confess, the uniform threw me for a minute. I was mentally reviewing my recent traffic-light conduct."

"Not a problem, ma'am. It happens all the time," the woman says, stepping inside.

She's a petite woman, perhaps a foot shorter than I am. Her voice, however, is not petite. Hers is a voice seemingly sculpted from crowd control and traffic direction, strong and flat and efficient.

"Am I crazy," she says, raising an eyebrow, "or was that a *skeleton* I saw through the window?"

Leo, with painted face, watching at the window—that *would* be a curious sight from outside. It must have been him too whom I saw flying around the corner so fast.

"Most likely, yes," I say with a laugh. "We're having something like a Halloween celebration today. Audrey can tell you more about it; that is, if you can pick her out from the pack of skeletons running around. You'll just want to head straight down that way."

I point in the direction of the classroom and dining room.

"*Right*. Thank you, ma'am."

The woman sets off down the hall, the thick bulk of gear arrayed across her body shifting heavily, like tectonic plates, with her movements. I'm hoping that I've come across as pleasant and totally at ease to this Officer McCormick; the truth is I'm *not* at all happy to have a police officer here in the school—in my home. There's nothing I can think of specifically that might come to her attention as amiss, but neither is there anything that is entirely on the up-and-up. My whole life is a lie, and that is probably also somehow illegal. All that can be done, though, is the proverbial "natural" act.

I close the door and head around the corner. The cloakroom appears deserted, just a disorderly rainbow of winter coats hanging from hooks, boots lined up—or more often flung—beneath, lunch boxes stowed in the cubbies above. Not a creature is stirring, neither cat nor child nor anything else. *And yet* . . . There is the soft yet distinct smell of blood that grows stronger the farther into the room I move. When I reach the opposite corner, I hear a soft sniff, and the sleeve of one of the coats before me quivers ever so slightly.

When I reach forward and try gently to part the coats, they resist me.

"I must say," I muse aloud, stooping down in front of the stubbornly immovable coats. "This is a very good hiding spot. It must be someone very clever who has found such a good hiding place?"

The coats part at last, but only slightly, and out from them peers a skeleton face, much smudged and smeared, but identifiable by its delicate heart shape and the wild, dark swirls of hair that rise above it. Leo isn't looking at me; his gaze is fixed on the door of the cloakroom with an expression of vigilant concern.

"Leo, is something the matter? What are you doing in here?"

There are footsteps in the hall outside the cloakroom, and Leo snaps the arms of the coats back in place in front of him. It's Thomas and Ramona's mother, Dr. Snyder, entering the room to fetch something from the pocket of her coat; when she sees me, she gives a smile that then transforms into a questioning look, wondering, surely, why I'm squatted down in front of a child's parka. I gesture toward the shoes and ankles that can be seen beneath the coats, and Dr. Snyder gives a quiet laugh of understanding before leaving the room with whatever she'd fished from her pocket.

"Leo, that was just Ramona and Thomas's mom, and she's gone now. It's just me here. What are you doing, silly? Why are you hiding?"

I try parting the coats again and this time they do not resist me.

Leo is facing me, but his eyes are still fixed on the door. The strain of his gaze and the white paint circling his eyes exaggerate the sallow, ever-present dark shadows beneath his eyes.

"Leo?" I say again, and his gaze returns to me. "Leo, what are you doing here?"

"Waiting for Katherine," he murmurs.

"You've picked a funny place to wait for someone. Are you trying to surprise her? Give her a good scare?"

His gaze had drifted back to the door, but when I say this, he looks to me again and nods vaguely.

"Well, you're missing all the fun. The niflettes are just about to come out of the oven. Won't you come with me?" I hold out my hand to him. "I don't want you to miss the treats."

Despite clear misgivings that are still visible on his face, it seems I have offered a compelling argument. Leo takes my hand and steps out from behind the coats. We leave the cloakroom, but his grip on my hand as we head down the hall is tight, and he's looking around warily as though expecting something to jump out at him any minute.

"How are you feeling?" I ask, hoping to distract him from whatever has him agitated. "After your asthma attack, I mean? All better?"

He puts a hand to his forehead and closes his eyes for a moment, miserably. It's an oddly adult gesture, but with the fingernails of a child, dark with dirt.

"A little not good," he says.

I pause outside the door of the classroom to give Leo's forehead a feel, checking for fever. Inside the classroom, Audrey is showing her aunt, the police officer, our class ofrenda.

"What do you think?" the little girl asks with a twirl.

The aunt tips back a framed photograph of Annabelle's dead dog. "It's . . ." she says, bobbing her head ambivalently. "It's . . . pretty weird."

Audrey laughs and twirls again.

Suddenly the warm little forehead under my palm is gone; when I look back to Leo, he's taken off in a flat run down the hall and then vanishes into the kitchen with the door flapping softly behind him. I look back at the classroom, at Audrey and her aunt. The little girl is now pointing out one of her drawings on the wall, and the aunt is standing with legs planted wide and hands on hips, looking at the drawing. Her handgun, matte black and dense, is holstered below the hand that rests on her right hip. Could it be this police officer who has Leo so spooked?

In the kitchen, Leo is at the island counter, hip height beside Marnie and looking impossibly tiny beside the woman's ample curves.

"Looky here, I've got an assistant!" Marnie exclaims with pleasure.

"I see that," I say, coming around the island and taking a moment to survey the splendor of platters layered with cookies and slices of various sweet breads. Leo is scooping cookies from a baking sheet with a spatula and great focus, possibly avoiding my gaze as well.

"Leo," I say in a low voice, "is it that police officer that has you so anxious? Or her gun, perhaps? I can see how that could be alarming. Guns make me a little nervous too. Is that why you were hiding?"

Marnie, behind Leo at the stove, overhears this and purses her lips sympathetically. Leo considers for a moment, his eyes turning toward the door and the classroom beyond it where Audrey had stood with her aunt, but then he shakes his head no.

"Okay," I sigh. I'm unconvinced, but what can I do?

"Well, I just want you to know, Leo, that that police officer is Audrey's aunt, and she's very nice, and her job is to protect people and keep them safe. That's what the gun is for too, just to make sure that if any bad guys ever try to hurt someone, she can stop them from doing that. You don't need to be afraid of her."

Leo looks up at me briefly and gives me a small, placating nod, then continues scooping the cookies from the tray.

"I'm sure she would love to meet you and tell you all about—"

I'm cut off midsentence by the vehement shaking of Leo's head.

"*No, please!*" he pleads. "*Please*, no."

FIFTEEN MINUTES LATER, I'M IN the dining room, doing my best to make conversation with several of the moms despite a long and growing list of distracting concerns: Leo, still hiding out in the kitchen with Marnie; my own anxiety about the police officer wandering my house; and my self-consciousness about the bandage on my face. Leo's parents are also now forty minutes late, and Rina, whom I'd tasked with calling them, finds me in the dining room.

"I called the Hardmans," she says, drawing up close so the other moms don't overhear, "but I only got a busy signal."

"That's strange," I say. "I called a few hours ago and got a busy signal too.

"Do we have a number for Valeria?" I ask. "Leo's nanny? If the Hardmans forgot about the open house, she should at least be coming to pick him up."

"We do, and I did call her, but she said she's no longer employed by the Hardmans."

"*What?*"

Rina can only offer a shrug and a look of bafflement before returning to her office.

I don't have time to contemplate this further. At my signal, half of the children begin to pass out plates and silverware to their parents with well-rehearsed decorum, while the others begin carrying the platters of sweets out of the kitchen and setting them on the table amid the marigold centerpieces. Kind Marnie has set Leo up in the kitchen, where they will have their treats together. I'm grateful. As much as I would like to attend to Leo, I have obligations as hostess. I sit with the Castros, Octavio's family, on one side and Sophie's parents on the other. Audrey and her aunt were seated at the opposite corner of the table, but when I look up again later, they're no longer there, and I feel a measurable degree of relief at their departure. One less thing for me—and Leo—to worry about.

Octavio's three-month-old baby sister sleeps nearby in a car seat draped with a blanket. When she wakes, I take her in my lap and give her a bottle so his mother can eat. The baby gazes up at me, her pink petal lips sucking at the bottle, her glossy eyes dark and thoughtful. Her fingers—so small and intricate with creases and dimples and fingernails—would require the finest round brush to paint in their delicate detail. She's beautiful, sweet, and warm, and, after the day I've had, it's remarkably soothing to hold her. And yet, at the same time, I feel a strange nettling uneasiness, almost tearfulness, that I can't quite place. I feel . . . *afraid*. That's what it is, fear. I'm afraid for this child, this *helpless*, *vulnerable* child, and, in a strange way, I'm afraid *of* her, afraid of the power she has, precisely by her defenselessness, to bring pain, such terrible pain, to those who love her. In my experience—*too much* experience—the helpless horror of watching someone or something you care for suffer far eclipses the pain of suffering yourself. What were her parents thinking, bringing something so vulnerable into this world of crimes and accidents, predators and catastrophes? Some part of me wants to keep her for my own, defend her violently against a whole sea of troubles; another part wants to put her back in her car seat and run as far from her as possible.

The hunger churns audibly in my stomach. Suddenly it seems to have permeated the marrow of my bones. The arms that hold the baby ache with it, and for some strange reason, the image of a hole—a small, dark, empty space that one might crawl into, a place of dreamless sleep—comes into my head, and with it a feeling of longing as excruciating as it is inexplicable. There is a sudden rush of heat, a flurry of tears blurring my eyes, threatening to overflow the brim, and suddenly I'm crying.

A tear falls from my eye and lands on the baby's cheek, startling us both. The room seems to grow suddenly quiet. The baby stretches and squirms, her mouth opens to let out a small, birdlike cry, and the tear sits there gleaming on her cheek like strange evidence.

"Oh, let me take her from you," Mireilla Castro says, wiping her mouth quickly and reaching for the baby. "You're so kind to give her a bottle while I sit here and stuff my face. And you haven't even had any. Look at how skinny you are. You need a plate of cookies more than I do."

Out of the corner of my eye, I see her quickly wipe the tear with her sleeve.

My chair scrapes noisily against the floor as I back it out too quickly and get up.

"I'm sorry," I say, "I've got some—something in my eye. Excuse me, please."

IN THE BATHROOM, I RUN the water and let the waves of disgraced horror wash over me. I look at myself in the mirror—my bandaged face, flushed with emotion. I pull the bandages gently from my skin. The wound has already healed to little more than a scrape. I study the face in the mirror, inquiring of it silently. *You're behaving like a crazy person. What's happening to you?*

It's no mystery what the parents must think: poor, lonely woman, no husband, no children. Of course she's on the verge of tears every waking moment. Of course she would hold an infant and weep. They couldn't possibly understand. I've been where they are before: happy, hopeful, totally naive of how insecurely I held the things I had, the things I loved. But unlike them, I'm not able to delude myself. Nothing we have is truly ours; it can all be taken at a moment's notice, and if you live long enough, you can be certain that it will be.

I envy these people terribly, it's true, but not for their children and families; I envy their brevity. I envy the low stakes of their choices. Whatever they lose, whatever they suffer, they don't suffer long. They get just a *little* life. Birth, some joys, some sorrows, then death to wash it all clean. Their race is a sprint, and so they are free to tear furiously out of the gate, to give it their all, hold nothing back for a few quick laps before collapsing in exhaustion and glory, but mine is an unending marathon. It's slow and steady for me. It's settle in. It's endure. "Eat, drink, and be merry, for tomorrow you die," the saying goes, but it's a saying for vremenie only; what I wouldn't give to live in such a way? What I wouldn't give to look in the mirror and find a wrinkle, a pair of crow's-feet creasing the corners of my eyes, any sign at all that there was an end coming for me too, a finish line toward which I might run recklessly. But there's always *this* face in the mirror—smooth, unblemished, a face free from the slightest evidence of the passage of time; a straight, flat line going on forever, never rising, never ascending, never culminating in anything, just moving ever forward. Slow and steady. Just endure.

For a moment, I think I will cry again, perhaps curl up in a ball on the floor and heave out the tears until I'm exhausted and finally empty, but that wouldn't do. There would be knocks at the door, a hushed silence when I emerged, questioning eyes, even, I'd be willing to bet, a sudden drop in enrollment. You can't send your child off into the care of an emotionally unstable teacher. So, I breathe it down, as I must, pat my cheeks and forehead with a wet towel, and practice a smile in the mirror. I toss the bandage in the trash—not necessary anymore—and walk out of the bathroom, off to convince a roomful of parents that everything is fine.

· XV ·

IT was Piroska who next glimpsed the man, closer this time than before.

"If I am the one to come across him next, the matter will be quickly resolved," Ehru said when we discussed it. "Anya, you too are quite capable of bringing remedy to this problem."

"By killing him?" I asked.

"Of course," he said without looking up. "As we would a wolf skulking about the pen."

"But . . . he has done us no harm."

"I assure you, he's done us no harm because he's not yet had the chance."

I did not argue with him, but the next day, as Vano and I gathered cowberries from a bush, I told Vano that I did not think I could do what Ehru wished me to do.

He looked me in the eye and smiled.

"Anya, the merciful," he said, his lithe hands moving deftly among the branches.

The look, his smile, and his kind words sent my chest buzzing as with the soft wings of a thousand bees, as if it were a hive. I longed to reach for the smooth hand before me, clasp it in mine. He would turn to me then; I would touch his face.

"Am I foolish?" I asked instead. "Is it foolish to take chances? If he's right . . ."

He held up a ripe cowberry, round and red and shiny.

"Mercy," he said, "is like a rare and valuable treasure; to find it and possess it, one *must* act foolishly and one must risk danger. That's what mercy is: loving your neighbor at risk to yourself, and that is what makes it so rare and so valuable." He put the berry in the basket and reached for another. "But I cannot tell you if you make the right decision. No one can decide for another what they are willing to risk."

I looked off into the distance, thinking about this, at the endless dark woods covering the mountains like thick hide on some humped beast's back. How endless and dark and lonely it all looked in comparison to Piroska's warm, bright hut. Should I kill a man to protect the home and people I loved more than anything? Or should I risk what I loved for mercy? I did not like to be foolish, even to obtain some rare and valuable treasure, especially when I already had treasure.

I looked back at Vano, but he was not thinking of me anymore. His keen eyes had caught sight of something. He narrowed them, tipped his head, and picked a beetle from its hiding place behind a leaf.

"But . . ." he said, lifting the insect so that its opalescent armor gleamed green and black in the sunlight and its crooked legs skated in the air. "I do not know that you will have opportunity to choose one way or another."

He studied the beetle as if it were an artifact of ancient importance. I looked too, trying to discern its significance.

"The pattern on its back," he said. "Look at it. Downward-pointing triangle, diamond above, those lines there: horns."

"Yes," I said, still baffled.

"And the legs, reaching forward and reaching back." He set the insect down on a branch, where it rested unmoving. "I've been seeing him everywhere."

"The man?" I asked. "You've seen him too?"

"No." He shook his head. "The god of endings. Czernobog. That is his symbol. Do you not recognize it? It presents itself to me five times a day. He is coming. I feel it. He does not always leave choices."

"What does it mean, Czernobog coming? What happens if he comes?"

"It's impossible to know exactly," he said, gazing thoughtfully at the beetle, which had resumed a slow, cautious crawl along the bough.

"It means," he said with a soft, resigned nod of his head, "something ends."

. . .

VANO DECIDED, FINALLY, TO CONSULT the saker. He had grown very troubled by the signs and messages he was receiving and he wanted greater clarity. I went with him. Vano lived at peace with everything. Deer in the glens didn't bother to raise their heads from the grass when he came near, and I'd once witnessed a wolf approach the hut with what I could have sworn was a penitent gait, to return a stolen lamb because Vano had asked it to, but still, the saker was a very dangerous animal with curved claws two inches long and a nature wilder even than Ehru's. I did not think the saker would harm Vano, but I would be there, nevertheless, to make sure of it.

With an offering of a live birch mouse, we set out and searched the cliffs along the river where the saker likes to nest, but we didn't find her or any evidence of her: no jumbled sticks jutting out from the rock fissures, no litter of feathers scattered from prey, so we made our way to the high western peak that looked down on everything.

There, climbing the rocky slopes, we heard the familiar scream of hot tempered joy that belonged only to the saker. We turned to see the sleek bird tumbling through the air like an acrobat, her wings like cupped hands cradling her falling body, and her claws struggling with some bit of dark fur.

The bird fell carelessly, as unconcerned as a fish falling in water, but then the bit of dark fur plummeted suddenly out from the bird's grasp. The saker abruptly ended her free fall, came up fast, and hurled herself back up into the air, pumping her wings hard in stoic defeat. With unimaginable speed, she flew past us and to a nest in the trees just a bit farther up the slope.

We climbed on, slowly and quietly and never taking our eyes from her, until we drew close enough and stopped.

The saker perched on a tree limb near her nest, which was really the nest of some other bird that she'd taken for her own in the same way that a queen takes whatever she likes as royal tribute. Her tough, dark claws were wrapped entirely around the limb of the tree, and she gazed at us with her black orb eyes—known to see more than those of any other creature—as though she'd been long expecting us.

Vano released the birch mouse from the small wooden cage he'd carried in his bag, and the thing skittered frantically forward over the rocks, causing the saker to bristle and stare, tracking its path. The bird tensed as one solid muscle and then dropped from the tree limb, grabbing the darting mouse with surgical savagery.

Keeping one eye on us, she jabbed her sharp beak at the small squirming rodent, severing some limb from body, then she lifted suddenly into the air. Setting the carcass in her nest, she turned her head this way and that, ruffled her feathers showily, and ate. Between each tearing bite, she fixed us with her hard stare until, at last, she took no more bites and only stared at us. Her mantle feathers bristled suddenly, and then she swooped forward out of her nest with a great flapping of wings and the same blistering cry she had made before. She skimmed smoothly down over the tops of the trees and away toward the monastery that loomed off in the distance.

Vano followed her with his eyes and I did too, until I saw, below her, a trail through the woods. It was a subtle thing, not the kind of blundering violent path a man would make, but more like an animal's trusted route to water. I stepped forward, searching it with my eyes, which were no match for the saker, but a near enough match for any animal short of it.

"Did she tell you anything?" I asked.

When Vano didn't answer, I turned and found him studying me.

"What did she say?"

"She said to follow you."

"*Me?*"

WE PICKED OUR WAY CAREFULLY along the path and in silence. I knew quickly, from the smell of it, that the path belonged to Ehru or had at least been recently used by him.

Vano followed me, but he was slow and hesitant, as though following the path was somehow painful to him, as though thorny brambles tore at him or the air grew thin and unbreathable, but there were no brambles, and the trail, though discreet, was level and easy.

Seeing him wince and draw in his breath shortly, I stopped.

"What is it?" I asked him. "Something's wrong. Should we turn back?"

"No," he said effortfully. "Please continue. Lead us."

I led on, Ehru's scent growing stronger in my nose, and another scent also, the scent of blood, but it was different somehow from the usual scent of blood, richer and more complex. I couldn't place it.

Vano and I both became aware also that we were drawing nearer to the hamlet that lay to the west of Piroska's hut and to the monastery, from which Vano and Ehru had fled years ago. The afternoon was waning and in the gathering shadows, the late autumn air carried a chill, but beside me Vano was sweating. He squinted and turned his head away from the assaults of something I could not see.

"What is it, Vano? What's hurting you?"

He wiped the dripping sweat from his brow.

"The heat," he said, and let out a long, slow breath. "It's getting so terribly hot."

He put his hands over his squinting eyes, letting them rest briefly. "And the smoke, the ash; it's difficult to breathe, difficult to see."

The air around me seemed clear and sweet with balsam, cool with the falling evening, but Vano's eyes between his thick, drawn lashes were bloodshot and painful looking. There was no way I could doubt him.

"We should go back," I said. "You're in more pain with every step we take."

"No, Anya. We *must* keep going. There is no alternative. It is toward a *time* that each step brings us closer, not a place."

We went on until, in the flush of sunset with the sky aflame and the monastery towers and domes rising sternly above the treetops, Vano stopped and fell back exhausted against a boulder.

"I'll wait for you here," he said. "It's not far."

I nodded and went on. I also knew that we weren't far. I'd begun to hear soft noises, the panting of mortal struggle, something dying; Ehru and his scent were close and also that rich and muddy blood smell. I feared what I would find. Ehru, I thought with dread, what have you done? What have you killed?

Then, with terrifying suddenness, Ehru, the swiftest and most cunning of all predators, was in front of me. But for once, *I* had caught *him* off guard. He didn't know it was me. When he saw that it was, the fierce snarl fell from his face, and he turned from me and stalked away.

"Ehru," I whispered, following him, "what's happening? Vano and I—"

Then I saw.

In a hollow formed from the roots of a tree, there lay a girl, and from the girl emanated the rich, meaty blood smell. She was young, likely not more than fifteen, with hair wet and matted against her head and a round belly to which her skirts clung, soaked with blood and birth water.

Ehru went to her and lay beside her. He took one of her hands in his, and with his other hand began to push her belly downward from the top. The girl had a stick in her mouth, and as Ehru pushed on her belly, she bit hard against it and stifled a scream.

I went quickly to the girl, pushed up her skirts, and saw, between her trembling legs, the breaching, bloody crown of a head.

I had witnessed births before, many years ago in the village. I'd never assisted with one. The girl was so small, her stomach so big. Any baby would be too big for such a narrow passage. Girls as young and small as this one had no business carrying babies.

"Get it out, Anya," Ehru hissed at me. "Get it out of her."

"It ought not to be in her!" I spat back at him in an angry whisper.

But I put my hands forward and worked my fingers in around the head. The girl gagged and groaned against the stick.

"Get it out, Anya!" Ehru snarled again. "*Get it out!*"

His blood teeth pushed forward, flashing at me threateningly.

I glared at him murderously but pushed in farther with my fingers, as the girl kicked weakly. The baby was stuck, too large across the shoulders for the birth canal. I felt for the baby's tiny collarbone, took it between my thumb and forefinger, and after a second's hesitation snapped it. Then, as quickly as I could, I folded the limp shoulder in toward the chest and pulled. For a moment, the head moved slowly, then suddenly it slid forward and out like a cork coming out of a bottle, and the rest of the body spilled out after it. I gathered the small, slippery form into my arms, not knowing whether it was alive or dead. It made no sound or movement.

The girl lay unconscious against Ehru, and he scooped her up into his arms in much the same way that I held the baby, then started back through the woods in the direction from which Vano and I had come. I stood there for a moment, stunned, then came to my senses and followed him. When we got to where Vano was sitting against the boulder, dripping sweat and waiting, Ehru went past him without a word. I tore my skirt and wrapped the baby tightly in the cloth, then Vano and I followed him back through the dark forest.

I thought that Vano's discomforts would recede as we moved away from the site of the birth, the threat of the village and the monastery, but they didn't. They grew worse. He said nothing, but his breathing grew louder, and he stumbled from time to time. When I reached out to steady him, his skin was slick with sweat and the muscles beneath jumped and twitched.

Piroska, knowing, somehow, as she always did that we were coming, had water boiling in the kettle and the bed ready for the girl when we reached the house. Ehru laid the girl in it, undressed her, and put a blanket over her chest and arms because even unconscious she was shaking. He took the kettle and, as if it were the cool water of a spring, dipped a cloth, wrung out the scalding water, and washed her with it. As the blood came off her skin, the green and purple of dark bruises became visible on the girl's legs. She had torn terribly where the baby had come out. Piroska held the point of a needle over the tip of a flame and then came over to the bed to sew her up, but Ehru took the needle from her and without a word turned back to the girl.

"Wait," Piroska croaked. She went to her shelves and came back with a small bottle. She put a drop of the tincture into the girl's mouth and then several drops on the girl's womanly parts. Then she nodded at Ehru, and he began sewing the girl's flesh with a delicate care I never would have imagined him to possess.

Piroska came to me where I sat by the fire, holding and rubbing the still-motionless bundle in the swaddle of my skirts. Vano squatted nearby, pushing the coals around in the hearth with the poker as if he'd lost something in the fire and was searching for it. His hair was as wet as if he'd just climbed out of the river. Sweat ran in rivulets down his forehead and his neck. Piroska touched his shoulder and he looked up at her, and there passed between them a look of wordless knowing. Piroska reached for the baby, and I handed the bundle to her, tears slipping finally from my eyes.

"I think it's—" I struggled against my closing throat to get the words out. "I think it's dead."

I went to Ehru where he was sewing the last stitches.

"Your child, Ehru," I said, averting my eyes from the girl's torn body. "I haven't felt it move. It hasn't cried. I'm afraid . . ."

"The baby is not mine, Anya. Do you still not know the way of things? The baby was put in her by the same one who put all these bruises on her body. The one you saw by the river, I don't doubt. I am certain, it was me he was hunting. He hunts nothing now."

I was too astonished by this to speak. He had known, or at least suspected, who the man was all along.

Ehru knotted the thread, then, with a sharp knife, cut it free from the needle.

"But the child will be mine," he said, pulling the blankets down to cover the girl's bare legs and smoothing them gently over her. "Just as she is mine, and I am hers."

Before the fire, Piroska had undone the swaddle and washed the baby—a girl—clean. She swaddled the child again in fresh cloth and put a drop of some other tincture in her mouth, and then she sat rubbing the baby's body vigorously and whispering into the child's ear. Ehru came over and stood beside her.

"She lives," Piroska said to him, "but only so much." She held her fingers close together. "Only so long. It was very hard for her. She feels she cannot go on."

She set the baby in Ehru's arms, and he looked down into the still-pinched, faintly breathing face.

"I go," Piroska said, "to get milk from the sheep."

"No," Ehru said. "There's no time for that. Or need."

"What do you mean?" I asked.

"We will bury this child tonight," he said, looking at me, and I realized that everyone was looking at me, Piroska, Vano, and Ehru.

"What do you mean?" I said again. "She might live. If Piroska feeds her, she might . . ."

I turned to Piroska, and the woman looked back at me with a gentle, compassionate smile as though I were a child in need of understanding. Vano too, gleaming with sweat in the firelight, just stared forward calmly. Neither of them seemed surprised. *Why?* How much, I wondered, had they known or suspected before tonight? Why was I the only one, as usual, who didn't understand what was happening?

"She might live," I said, choked with frustration.

"She *will* live," Ehru said. "She will live forever."

"*What?*"

"*We* will live forever, together." Ehru turned and looked at the girl in the bed. "They are my family now. Lada and I have spoken of it. Lada wills it also."

"You'll make them . . . like us?" I said, stumbling back into a chair, but I said it to myself. No one else was listening. Piroska and Vano were watching Ehru as he went to the bed and laid the baby in the crook of her sleeping mother's arm. If they had any opinion on the matter, they made no hint at it either through word or expression.

Ehru whispered to the baby in the language that he and Vano shared.

He kissed her on her forehead, then gently pulled one tiny arm free from the swaddle. He kissed her again on her face, on her hand, then he turned the arm over and put it to his mouth. The baby scrunched her face for just an instant as Ehru carefully punctured her skin with his teeth. Then he began to drink.

"No," I whispered. "No."

I stood up and paced, glancing over only now and then to see what was happening. At last, Ehru laid the baby's arm down, and the baby lay still, an ashy gray pallor to her tiny hand and face.

Ehru stood and walked out of the hut. I couldn't bear the stillness of the baby, the stillness of Piroska and Vano sitting silently in their chairs, listening intently to our futures, so I followed Ehru outside and found him splitting wood deftly into thin planks.

"You just . . . you just drank that baby's life away?"

"Yes," he said, then heaved the axe up over his shoulder and down through the wood again. "And I gave to her my own."

He looked at me then, and his face was the calmest and most at peace that I had ever seen it. He looked very like Vano, just as he had as a boy, but not for many years since. "It is an exchange, Anya. You take and you give. When you are ready, your body knows what to do and will do it. Your body always knows what to do, if you can only move your mind out of the way."

"But how can you choose this? How can you choose this for them? Life . . . *forever*."

He didn't answer, just thrust the axe gracefully forward, making the wood halves leap apart like a dance.

"Ehru, you and I are alike. I know you've suffered a great deal. I've suffered too. This world has not been kind to either of us, and yet we *must* go on in it. We cannot escape it. Is that what you want for them? Is that what they want? *Really?*"

Ehru rested the axe head against the dirt for a moment and shook his head.

"To starve a man would seem a cruel act, an unkindness, no?" he asked, looking at me.

"And yet, imagine that that starving man finally puts food in his mouth. How will that food taste?" He put his fingers to his mouth as though savoring some indescribable flavor. "I tell you, Anya, no matter if it is the blandest porridge, it will taste better than any dish that any well-fed king has ever eaten. And I ask you, in *that moment*, when the starving man holds that first bite on his tongue and discovers, as he otherwise could not, all the pleasure that food was ever capable of bringing to man, was the starvation that preceded it an unkindness or a kindness?"

He put a thick finger up before him.

"*He* will decide. And whatever he decides will be true for him."

He reached forward and turned the wood block, then threw the axe in another smooth arc. Like twin divers, back-to-back, leaping into twin pools, the halves peeled away.

"Your mind causes you suffering, Anya. Your fear of the pain you've experienced and of future pain. I have experienced much pain, it is true, but now . . ."

He straightened up tall. Waning crescent moons gleamed faintly in his eyes that might have been gathering tears. He pointed to the hut where candlelight glimmered through the windows.

"I am that man. I have tasted that first bite after so much hunger. I have no quarrel with the world. And I will give it, all of it, without hesitation, but you are right, Anya, they will have to decide for themselves just as I have. Everyone must decide for themselves whether this world and life in it is a kindness or an unkindness, a blessing or a curse."

Finished with the splitting, he fit the small wood planks against each other.

"Help me," he said. "Please."

Still unsettled and uncertain of what I made of his words, I came to him and knelt, let him guide my hands onto the wood planks so that I held them in place. Then he took a hammer and tacks and hammered the wood planks together, and together thus, Ehru and I built a coffin for his child.

He buried the baby that night. He placed a soft blanket inside the coffin. He pulled a string of bells down from the eaves, then he freed the baby's legs from the swaddle and wrapped the bells around the baby's ankles. Finally, he laid the baby on the blanket inside the coffin, nailed the final plank over the top, and, under the three-quarter moon, set the coffin into the hole he had dug among the trees just beyond the clearing of the pasture.

Back inside the hut, Ehru curled beside the girl, Lada, in the bed. Vano and Piroska sat in their chairs, Vano sweating through his clothes and flinching at odd intervals, and Piroska watching him intently and sipping at one of her teas. I lay down with a blanket on the rag rug that covered the dirt floor between them and fell asleep.

I WOKE SOMETIME LATER TO talking.

Vano was in his chair, still awake and gazing into the fire. He was speaking softly in his language. Ehru and the girl were asleep, and Piroska had also retired to her bed. Vano was speaking to the spirit, and he was weeping quietly. Every so often, he wiped the tears from his cheek with the heel of his hand.

"Vano, what's happening?" I whispered. "It's getting worse for you. It wasn't just the girl and Ehru and the baby, was it? There's something else. Something worse."

He turned to me an effortful half smile, but he was sweating and trembling so badly that the sight of it only made me more afraid.

"Getting worse is getting better," he said in a softly quaking voice.

"I don't understand." My voice was bitter. "I *never* understand. Are you in danger? Is something happening to you?"

"I'm sorry," he said, sensitive to my frustration. "These are things that are not easy to understand. What is coming is what has to come, and if it is what must be, then it is good, and we would be fools to want anything else. It's like"—he looked toward the bed where Lada and Ehru lay—"like childbirth. It leads you through pain and then greater pain, and you can't even be sure that it won't kill you, but still, there's nothing to do but trust it. Follow where it leads. To make any other choice would mean the stillbirth of our destinies, of the things we're meant to do."

"I don't *care* about destiny," I spat fiercely, "I *won't let* anything happen to you." Then suddenly I was crying, my face buried in my hands.

Vano's touch came gently on the back of my hand, and I looked up.

When I lowered my hands from my face, he did not let go of them, and, for a moment, his eyes held me with more tenderness than I'd ever known, and I knew suddenly that nothing had ever been hidden from him, least of all my love.

"I could . . . I could make you . . ." I struggled to speak, the words trembling and resisting utterance. ". . . like me. The way Ehru . . ."

He looked down at my hand in his.

"That would be a beautiful path," he said softly. "But my door does not open to it."

I closed my eyes, letting the tears stream down from them. The hollow of my chest ached painfully where it felt as though all my hopes had been cut out.

"*What can I do?*" I begged. "Is there *nothing* I can do?"

"Would you . . ." Vano hesitated. He looked suddenly weaker and more uncertain than I'd ever seen him. "Would you stay with me? Stay awake and keep me company? What lies ahead will take courage, but I don't feel courageous. You're so brave, Anya. Your company would be a comfort to me."

I could only wipe the tears from my face in answer.

"Would you just sit here, close, beside me, perhaps hold my hand?"

I moved next to him, my shoulder pressing against his. I took his hand tightly in mine. I had never been so close to Vano, so physically intimate, though I'd always desired it, and yet, somehow, sitting there clinging to each other, I felt more like a sister to him, he more like a brother to me than ever before.

He asked me to stay awake with him, and I did. For a while. Eventually, though, my head fell against soft wool, and in the dream that overtook me, I heard quiet words, a whispered benediction in my ear that, somehow, I never forgot.

"And you will go a new way," Vano's soft words said. "A way you have never gone before, a way you did not imagine you could go. You will see me then, when it's time. The spirit and I will come to you. Someday, when *you* need courage, I will be there with you. *I* will hold *your* hand."

· XVI ·

THE Hardmans never show.

The light dips deeper in its slant.

The cookies and treats disappear from the plates, leaving crumbs and smears of cream, and the first few parents make their excuses and depart with their children. When I'd reemerged from the bathroom, most of the parents had given me conspicuous space, pretending not to have witnessed—or been quickly informed of—my little breakdown, but a few of the less avoidant types offered me drippingly sincere good-byes coupled with looks of understanding and gentle pats on the elbow. Eventually, however, the busy confusion of adults and children moved to the entryway, then to the driveway, then they were gone. Except for Leo, who turns his little skeleton face up at me now and asks, for perhaps the tenth time in the last two hours, "Do you think Katherine is coming?"

With each repetition of the question, my answers had grown increasingly vague.

"No," I finally admit. "I don't think so. Something must have come up."

With a damp washcloth in one hand, I tilt Leo's chin up and begin wiping at the face paint, revealing swaths of damp reddened skin beneath.

"Maybe she's sleeping," Leo offers, bracing against the rough work of the cloth on his cheeks.

I cock my head to the side in surprise.

"What makes you say that? Why would she be sleeping?"

"She's really tired, so sometimes she has to sleep."

"Is she? She's really tired?"

"Yeah."

"Does your mom sleep a lot?"

"Yeah."

"And what do you do when she's sleeping?"

"I watch *Sesame Street*, or if I don't want to watch *Sesame Street*, I go in my room and color with my colored pencils."

"Do you do that by yourself?"

He nods. "Yeah, by myself or with Max."

"Who's Max?"

"I'll show you!" he exclaims, and goes running off toward the classroom. I follow him. He has run up to the ofrenda, and there, he takes a stuffed giraffe in a small brown T-shirt, which I hadn't noticed was there, from the display.

"Is that yours? Did you put that on the ofrenda?"

"Yeah! This is Max."

"Lovely to meet him. Why is Max on the ofrenda, though?"

"You said I could put something on there if I wanted to."

"Well, yes, that's right. I meant something for someone who had died, though. You know, that's what the ofrenda is for."

"Yeah, I know. He died!"

I have no idea how to respond to this, so after a confused pause, I just say, "Well, okay then," and change the subject. "Leo, what happened to Valeria? Does she not come to your house anymore?"

"No," he says, looking frustrated. "But I want her to."

"Do you have any idea why?"

He shakes his head. I take a deep breath and sigh.

"Well, let me get the rest of that paint off your face, and then I guess I will just have to take you home."

. . .

THE SUN HAS ALREADY DIPPED below the tree line when we gather Leo's things and walk out to my car. The days grow shorter now. In the blink of an eye, they'll grow longer. Shorter, longer, shorter, longer—the seasons rush past me like the smoothly shifting patterns on a spinning top.

I found the Hardmans' address in their file. According to the map in my glove compartment, they live south of the downtown, an unfamiliar area, but then I don't get out much, so there are many parts of town that are unfamiliar to me.

After fifteen minutes of driving the back roads, we pull into a winding and sparsely lit tract of huge but hastily constructed pseudomansions. I start searching for addresses on the houses. There are pools and tennis courts and horse crossings that traverse the road, but few streetlamps and fewer discernible addresses. After a couple of wrong turns, I pull up at last in front of a house that Leo confirms is his. It's dark and there is no car in the driveway.

I approach the door alone and ring the bell. The sound echoes into the expanse beyond the door, but no one answers. I knock on the door. There is the perfect stillness of absence, but I call out anyway.

"Mrs. Hardman? Mr. Hardman? Hello?"

A dog barks from a nearby backyard, and I wonder uneasily if it belongs to the Hardmans. Dogs are generally mixed in their opinions of me, but their opinions are always strong.

I walk back to the car, and it occurs to me that something might really be wrong. Perhaps Katherine was in a car accident on her way to school. What should I do? Find a pay phone and call the police station? Ask if there have been any accidents? Once again, I shrink from the thought of the police. It's a general policy of mine to steer clear of all bureaucracies and institutions that put you in a file that can be pulled up later. Calling the hospital is a more palatable alternative, but who knows where the nearest pay phone is?

"What are we doing?" Leo asks.

I sigh. "I'm just thinking for a minute."

"Are we going to go inside?"

"Well, no one is home at the moment, and the door is locked, so we can't go inside right now, but I hope we will be able to very soon."

He is quiet again, looking out the window at the dark houses.

Across the street, the blue lights of a television throw themselves manically against the drawn curtains in a living room window.

"You're being so patient, Leo. This day hasn't worked out the way we hoped, has it? But you've taken it all in stride. I'm very proud of you."

He smiles, basking in the praise with a transparency only children have and only for a little while.

"Are you going to come into my house? I want to show you some pictures I made with watercolor paints when Valeria was still here."

"That would be lovely, but we'll have to see what your maman says when she gets here. Out of curiosity, Leo, do you have a dog?"

He shakes his head. "No. I'm afraid of dogs."

"I must admit, I'm not overfond of them either."

"There's a mean dog next door, and when I go outside to play, he barks at me. I'm *really* scared of him, so I don't go outside very much."

"That's terrible. Is it that house over there?" I point at the house from which I thought I heard the barking.

"Yeah. His name's Vlad. He's really big and he even jumped over the fence before."

We sit in the car for another five minutes, discussing Vlad and then the general merits of various pets. I'm considering going up to the neighbor's house with the jumping lights and using their phone to call the hospital, or returning to my house with Leo, when a light flicks on in Leo's garage. The garage door gives a sudden loud lurch and then begins to open. The door is not much more than halfway up when a car comes squealing out from beneath it.

"Mom!" Leo shouts, and throws his door open, waving his small hand in the air.

The car has sped down the drive and into the street, but there it stops abruptly. Slower now, having noticed my car parked along the sidewalk with the headlights on and Leo waving from the passenger side, the driver pulls the car back into the driveway and parks, and there is a long moment of stillness.

I realize I've just witnessed a great parental gaffe, and my strategy will be the same as that of some of my parents this very evening: play dumb. I get out and come around to open Leo's door. I'm helping him get his backpack on when Katherine finally, some moments later, emerges from her car and begins making her way slowly toward us. She's wearing thin pants and a wrapped top that could very well be pajamas, and she's limping slightly.

"Were you here this whole time?" Leo calls out, and I wish I would have briefed him on the play-dumb strategy.

Katherine doesn't answer, just continues limping toward us. Her pants billow loosely in the cold wind, revealing how excruciatingly thin her frame is.

"We were sitting here for a long time," Leo continues, "and we rang the doorbell. Why didn't you answer?"

She still doesn't say anything but meets us halfway down the drive, where she stops and presses her hands together at her mouth in a gesture of mortification.

"I am *so* sorry," she says, her large eyes expressing her humiliation.

"Nothing to worry about, Katherine. Are you all right, though? You're limping. Did something happen?"

"God, I'm going to sound like such a mess. I'm not always this accident prone, I swear, but I got a piece of glass stuck in my foot yesterday, so I went to the doctor today to get it removed. *Dave* said he would help me out and pick Leo up from school"—she rolls her eyes up in frustration—"so I took a pain pill and lay down for a nap. Then I woke up five minutes ago to a dark house, no Dave, no Leo. I was in a total panic."

She takes a deep breath, tips her head to the side. "I can't thank you enough for bringing him all the way here. I'm *so sorry* you had to do that. *Ugh!* And you were probably worried. What a mess!"

"Really, it was no trouble, and . . . I hate to add to your concerns as it seems you've had a hard day, but we've had a bit of a day also. Leo had an asthma attack this morning and a bloody nose to go along with it—"

"Oh no," Katherine breathes, bringing her hands to her face again.

"He's got a bloody scarf in his bag, but otherwise, as you can see, he's fine. The inhaler, though. I had it on hand, but it didn't seem to work as it should. I'm thinking maybe it was empty."

"*Oh no*," she breathes again, and closes her eyes. "What a day from the absolute pit of—"

She mouths the word to me.

"Could anything else go wrong for us today?" she asks Leo.

Leo takes this opportunity to tug at her sleeve and ask, "Can Ms. Collette come inside our house? I want to show her my watercolor pictures that I painted."

There is an awkward moment of half-formed sentences and hesitation from both Katherine and myself, and Leo looking hopefully back and forth between us.

"Of course!" Katherine finally exclaims. "I think we owe her some hospitality for all she's done for us today."

"Will you come?" Leo asks, looking up at me.

I do not want to go in. I'm mentally and emotionally exhausted, but I can't possibly say no to the pleading heart-shaped face beaming up at me, especially after all *he's* been through today. Besides, I've been hoping for an opportunity to talk with Katherine and get a clearer picture of their homelife, and I'm not likely to get a chance like this again.

"I'll come in for just a bit, as long as you're sure I'm not intruding?"

"Oh my gosh, no! Please. We're so happy to have you. You have been, like, our own personal guardian angel today. You will have to excuse the mess, though. As you probably noticed, I haven't been the most on top of things today, and our house cleaner doesn't come until Monday."

WHEN KATHERINE APOLOGIZED FOR THE mess, she wasn't overselling it. The Hardmans' kitchen is all white and black and stainless steel, the kind of kitchen that is meant to be spotless, but this one is not spotless. There are dishes piled in the sink, a queue of stained coffee mugs around the coffee maker, crumbs scattered across the counter and kitchen table, and dark spots visible on the white tiles that alternate with black across the floor. I can tell that Katherine is self-conscious about it because she's padding gingerly about the kitchen on her hurt foot, tidying up as discreetly as possible while the coffee maker burbles and begins to spit decaf into the pot.

For my part, I'm wishing I hadn't accepted the offer to come inside; in the light of the kitchen, it's confirmed that Katherine's in pajamas, and I can see makeup smudges around her eyes and tiny flakes of mascara dusting her cheeks. I wouldn't want to be in her spot, entertaining in a dirty kitchen, nap-rumpled and injured on top of it all, and I'm sure she'd rather not be doing it either, but there's nothing to be done now, so I go on sitting at the table with Leo, who is nibbling a hunk of cheese and some baguette, and Max the giraffe, who is eating nothing. Leo is showing me his watercolors, which like the rest of his art are hard to accept as the work of a small child.

Katherine is making a valiant and skilled effort at small talk as she tidies, asking me about life in France and my transition to the United States. I get such questions all the time. Americans are fascinated by people who are not (or *pretend* not to be) American.

"Tell me," she asks in a confiding tone as she sweeps crumbs off the counter and into her palm, "is having kids as hard in France as it is here?"

I look up from the watercolor I'm holding in my hand and give her a reassuring smile.

"Actually, I think it's more difficult here."

"Stop," she says, tilting her head and squinting her expressive eyes into smiling crescents. Despite the mussed makeup, she's still very pretty. "You're just trying to make me feel better."

"*No*, I'm being honest. At least from what I've seen. In France, there's more tradition and consensus, for better or worse, about how to raise children. I get the impression that here, in the US, there's less agreement on how to parent, more passing fads, and so each family is sort of reinventing the wheel. That seems to me like it would be very difficult and stressful. I much prefer not having to figure out each and every thing for myself."

"Ah, so that's your secret."

I have so many secrets that, for a second, I'm not sure which one she is referring to.

"That's why you're so amazing with kids. Leo talks on and on all the time about how much he loves school and loves Ms. Collette."

I grin over at Leo, who ducks his head and smiles bashfully down at the table.

Things seem to be going well. Katherine is proving easy to talk to, so I decide to take a chance with a more pointed question.

"I was curious. Why didn't Valeria pick Leo up from school today?"

There's a pause while Katherine rinses the sponge that she's just used to clean the counter. After she turns off the faucet, she answers.

"Actually, we're between nannies right now. We had to let Valeria go, and we haven't found anyone to replace her yet."

"Where did Valeria go?" Leo asks, putting a crumble of cheese in his mouth.

"Oh, she probably just got another job, I would imagine."

Leo sighs. "Why couldn't she keep doing this job? I wanted her to."

"I know, Leo, and I'm sorry about that, but there are parts of the job of being a nanny that just involve the kid, and Valeria was good at those parts, but there are also parts of being a nanny that involve the people who hired you, and we had some problems with those parts."

Katherine puts a hand to her face to block Leo's view and mouths *stealing.*

My eyes go wide. I'm genuinely astonished. I never would have imagined Valeria as the kind of person to steal.

"I was *so* shocked," Katherine says, and then shakes her head in bewilderment. "*So* shocked."

"What were you shocked about?" Leo asks, looking up from the pictures spread before him.

"Oh, nothing, sweetie," Katherine replies, opening the refrigerator. Then to me she asks, "Anything in your coffee? Cream? Sugar?"

"No, thank you," I say. "Black is perfect."

I'm watching Leo. He has lowered his eyes glumly to his cheese.

"I wanted to show Valeria my new pictures from school," he mumbles.

I'm not sure if his mother hears him.

"I thought it was hard to find a nanny in the city," she says, "but out here, my God, it just feels impossible. It's such a vulnerable thing, you know, letting a stranger into your house, trusting them with your child. There's nothing worse than realizing you made the wrong choice, and now I just feel like, well, who can I possibly trust?"

"I can imagine," I say. "Perhaps some of the other parents might have recommendations?"

"I should ask around; that's a good idea. This has all happened so suddenly. I almost feel like I need a little time to recover. I just think I would feel so distrustful of anyone we hired right now. But then this isn't really the best time for me to be taking care of Leo by myself either. I have some health issues I'm dealing with."

"Oh? What kind?—*If* you don't mind sharing. Sorry, maybe that's too personal a question."

"No, no. Of course, it's totally fine. My back is messed up. I fell about a year ago and since then, it's just been this never-ending saga of doctors and X-rays and pain. I can't lift anything over fifteen pounds. Some days it's a struggle just to get out of bed."

Another fall. So many "accidents" in this household. I wonder if Dave ever has accidents, or if Katherine and Leo are the only clumsy ones.

"I'm sorry to hear that," I say, "and here you are alone tonight. Will Dave be home anytime soon?"

Katherine shrugs in answer to my question and makes a wry face. "He works late on Tuesdays and Fridays . . . and Thursdays and sometimes Mondays. Funny how that happens, isn't it? First it's one evening a week and then two and then all of them."

"I can't say I have any experience with that."

"Have you ever been married?" Katherine asks.

The coffee has finished brewing, and she's filling two mugs. Beside me, Leo has coughed and managed to simultaneously inhale cracker crumbs and spew them forth all over the tabletop in front of him.

"Not really," I say, distracted by Leo's watery-eyed sputtering.

"*Not really?*" Katherine says with a laugh, setting my cup of black coffee down in front of me.

"Uh, *no*," I say, coming to my senses. "No, I've never been married."

"Well, think hard before you do," she says, shooting me a meaningful look as she unscrews the cap on the cream to pour it into her own mug.

I'm curious about this. Does she wish she had thought harder before marrying Dave? Now doesn't seem like the time to get into it with Leo at the table, so I let the comment pass without response; instead I reach across the table and take Max the giraffe's two front hooves.

"Pat-a-cake, pat-a-cake, baker's man," I sing in a soft whisper, as I move Max's arms exaggeratedly through the motions of the song. "Bake me a cake as fast as you can."

Leo giggles, his head tipping back, the baguette lolling in his open mouth.

"Roll it," he continues as I do the motions with Max, "and pat it, and mark it with a—"

"M," I interject.

Leo grins and continues, "And put it in the oven for Maxy and me!"

"Leo!" Katherine barks at him suddenly, and both he and I look up in surprise. For a second, Katherine gives Leo a glare of incredulous anger, as though he has brazenly violated some well-established rule, but what it might be I couldn't begin to imagine.

He frowns guiltily and shrinks down in his seat.

"Sorry," he murmurs.

I have no idea what's going on, and to avoid gaping at them in conspicuous dismay, I turn and study a frame of pictures on the wall beside us. It's one of those wood frames with separate slots for several photographs. There's one of Leo with his mom at a wedding. He's younger, two or three, and wearing a tiny ring bearer's suit and tie. There's another of him buried beneath a pile of leaves, and a recent one of him riding a carousel horse, with Dave beside him and waving at the camera. Two of the slots are blank, with the black cardboard backing visible.

When I turn back, Katherine is again facing the counter, stirring her coffee and cream, and Leo has gone back to eating, though he's still sunk down in a hangdog slouch. An uncomfortable silence has pervaded the room.

"Sorry about that," Katherine says carefully, still not looking our way. "Someone is just not . . . minding their manners a little bit tonight."

I'm still baffled and unsure what to say to this, so I say, "Don't let me forget to get that inhaler from you tonight, if you happen to have an extra one on hand?"

It's a desperate attempt on my part to regain footing on stable conversational ground.

Katherine turns. "*Yes!*" she exclaims, obviously happy to take up a new topic. "Thanks for reminding me. There should be one in the cupboard. I'll get it in just a minute."

She reaches for her mug quickly, hits the handle but doesn't catch hold of it, and the mug falls from the counter to the floor with a dull crack of ceramic and the wet slap of coffee against the tile. The thin brown liquid spreads out from the shards of mug and across the floor.

"*Oh, good grief!*" Katherine huffs, and stamps her foot lightly in frustration.

"I'll help!" Leo exclaims, scrabbling down from his seat at the table. I get up to grab towels.

"No, Leo. The coffee's hot. I don't want you to get burned. Why don't you do me a favor and go watch some *Sesame Street* while I get this cleaned up?"

Leo, his helpfulness rebuffed, stands there looking sullenly at the mess.

"But I don't want to watch *Sesame Street*," he mumbles.

"Okay, well, it's really probably time for bed anyway, so go get your pajamas on and then you can watch one *Sesame Street* if you like, or just read books for a while in bed. Your choice."

Leo frowns and turns to leave the room.

"Good night, Leo," I call to him. "I'll see you on Monday. Thank you for showing me your paintings. They're wonderful."

He waves to me gloomily and then pads off across the carpeted living room.

I squat down and begin sopping up the spill with paper towels.

"*Oh, my goodness,*" Katherine sighs, picking up a glazed yellow chunk of mug. "I am just a danger to myself and others tonight, seems like. *Geez.*"

She looks up, and in spite of the bright illumination of the kitchen lights, her pupils are wide and round, and I recall the pain pills she mentioned taking earlier.

"Katherine, please, let me get it. You've got a bad back."

I wad up the sopping paper towels into a big ball and carry them over to the trash. Leo has apparently changed his mind about *Sesame Street*. Through the kitchen door, I can see it on the screen. The Count with his benign cloth fangs and his outlandish Transylvanian accent is counting "little batties," one, two, three—a charming portrayal of blood drinkers, that little cloth puppet, and quite preferable to some others I've seen.

I lift the lid of the trash can. Inside are the shattered remains of a large glass bowl, probably the source of the glass in Katherine's foot. Just more clumsiness, I suppose. Beneath one large shard of bowl, I can see, as if through a magnifying glass, Leo's Día de los Muertos worksheet— the homework that never made it back to school. It's crumpled, wet at one end, and blank except for the line where the students were to put the name of the deceased loved one. On that line, in Leo's handwriting, it says MAX. I drop the wet paper towels into the trash can on top of the worksheet and the bowl and close the lid.

Once the floor is tidied, Katherine pours herself a new cup of coffee, and we finally sit at the table.

"It just feels like it's been one thing after another since we moved here," she says, shaking her head and then taking a sip of her coffee. I notice that the splint that was on Katherine's fingers before is now gone.

"I've meant to ask you," I say, taking a sip from my own mug, "how has Leo been since his concussion? Have you noticed any symptoms? I haven't seen anything at school."

"No, nothing at all. Thank God."

"I'm so glad to hear that."

I hesitate, not sure how to say what I want to say next.

"You know, Leo mentioned . . . that when he fell . . ."

Katherine's eyes flick up to my face suddenly and then back to her coffee. She sets the mug down with an excess of delicacy and her neck does an odd pull-back motion as if she's tasted something bad. In an instant, in the space of a sentence, her body language has shifted from casual and at ease to guarded, and I feel I've made a mistake, but it's too late to take it back.

"What did Leo say?" Her voice is low and apprehensive, and her fingers are tracing the curve of the mug handle in front of her.

"Oh, it was nothing at all, just a very small comment he made about—about Dave seeming perhaps a bit upset at the time. He said . . . that Dave was trying to take him from you and then there was the fall."

"Ah," Katherine says thoughtfully, "I see. Did he say anything else?"

"Well . . . he also said that you both fell."

There is silence for a moment as Katherine continues to study her coffee, apparently deep in thought; I rush to fill it.

"Katherine, I could easily understand why you wouldn't want to share—"

"You asked him about what happened?" she interrupts, looking up at me with a pained sadness, almost a look of betrayal, and for a second I feel flustered, unsure if I've done something very wrong and hadn't realized it until now.

"*No, no.* It just . . . sort of . . . came up."

"It's okay," she says with a small but gracious smile. "I suppose you wouldn't be doing your job if you didn't."

"I mention it," I go on, "because I know that children can sometimes experience things in surprising ways, and I thought you might want to know how he interpreted what happened."

I'm hoping I've managed to walk the fine line I'm attempting: drawing attention to something without seeming to accuse or meddle.

"If I can help in any way," I continue, "or if there's anything *you'd* like to talk about . . ."

She lets out a long sigh. "It's all so much easier when they're babies, isn't it? Before they can understand the things that are being said around them. When they can be distracted with a TV show or fooled by ridiculous excuses no adult would fall for. 'The car's parked on the lawn because . . . Daddy was . . . cleaning the driveway.' You don't always realize exactly when they grow old enough and smart enough to put two and two together. To stop being fooled by your lies."

Katherine looks at me, then looks away. "If you do get married, make sure you don't love the man too much. Choose someone nice and pleasant, who you could take or leave."

She sighs. "He didn't *mean* to do it. I don't believe Dave would ever intentionally hurt either of us. It was an accident. There's just too much emotion between us, so we're constantly provoking each other, then things get crazy and . . ."

She looks at me again. "This is the worst thing that's ever happened, and I know it really shook him up. It shook us both up. We talked about it and we both agreed that things have to get better. He's really not a bad guy, we just . . . got off track somewhere. There was a line somewhere that we should have drawn, but we missed it. Well, we're drawing it now. I think we're going to start seeing a therapist, a marriage counselor, or whatever."

"Good," I say. "I'm glad to hear it. I really don't mean to intrude, but I appreciate your candor. It's not an easy thing to talk about, especially with someone you don't know that well."

"I feel like I can trust you," she says. "Anyone who is so good with kids has to be trustworthy."

She takes a deep breath. "I appreciate you telling me what Leo said. I do need to talk to him about it. I knew it at the time, but I chickened out. Told myself that I'd just be making it a bigger deal to him than it was, but I guess it was a big deal to him."

There is the sound of keys turning in the front door lock. Dave is home. Katherine and I both look in the direction of the living room like children about to be caught at mischief.

I rise from my seat at the table.

"I should really be going," I say, taking my coffee mug over to the sink. "It's late."

Dave walks into the room and looks first at me in surprise and then at Katherine. He sets his briefcase on the counter, still looking at us curiously.

"Hello," he says as he opens the refrigerator door and leans in to pull out a beer.

Dave is a mountain of a man—I had forgotten—and beside him, his wife seems like a spindly little aspen tree.

"Hello," I reply quickly. "I'm so sorry, I've stayed longer than I should have. I'll be going."

"Not at all," Katherine says cheerfully, a much better actress than I. "We should do this again sometime. It was lovely."

"Yes, that would be wonderful. Nice to see you, Dave," I say, and scoot past him.

Katherine walks me to the door and hands me a box that I realize holds an inhaler in it.

"Ah yes, thank you," I say.

"No, thank you," she says, opening the door for me, her eyes smiling genuinely. "*Really*. I mean it. I appreciate your . . . your . . . just your caring. About Leo, and about me."

"Of course," I say.

The door closes behind me, and the dog next door, the one Leo is so afraid of, begins to bark as I make my way across the lawn to the car. I drive home in the deep darkness—no moon at all tonight—thinking about Leo's home: Katherine and the things she told me, Dave, the glass bowl in the trash can, and Leo's worksheet. What does it all add up to? What have I learned? Then, near the end of my drive, just as I'm about to turn onto the lane that leads to the house, something occurs to me, just a small odd thing. If Dave works late every Friday, why had they planned for him to pick Leo up from school?

· XVII ·

"WAKE, Anya. Anya, wake!"

Ehru was shaking me by the shoulder, and I sat up before the hearth, frustrated with myself for falling asleep when I hadn't meant to. The girl, Lada, was awake and sitting with great effort on the edge of the bed. Piroska had dressed her in one of my dresses and was placing a cloak around her shoulders. Vano was standing at the window, grimacing and breathing slowly, and even from across the room I could see his thin frame jump and shudder.

"What is it?" I asked.

Ehru placed the girl's arm around his shoulders and helped her slowly over to the ladder.

"Help me get Lada up into the loft."

I stood up. "The loft? Why?"

"They're coming," he said sharply. "They're coming for her and for me. They're practically on the threshold. Hurry. There's no more time for conversation."

Piroska was moving about the hut quickly but calmly, putting things in a leather bag. Ehru placed the girl's hands on a rung of the ladder to support her and then climbed up quickly himself, then he lay over the edge with his arms outstretched to her.

"Help her, Anya," he called.

I came to my senses and leaped to her as her body sagged against the rungs, her strength more than spent from her laboring just hours before. I knelt down and seated her on my shoulder and then stood and began climbing the ladder with her there. She groaned in pain, and I felt the warm spread of liquid against my shoulder, which was the blood still coming out of her.

"We'll cut our way through the thatch and escape up the mountain to the north," Ehru said as I climbed. When he could reach the girl, Ehru took her under the arms like a child and lifted her the rest of the way. Piroska handed the leather bag up to him.

I went to Vano where he stood by the window. I could hear the shuffle of feet and the snapping of branches in the woods to the south, and here and there, the dancing glimmer of a torch or torches moving through the trees.

Vano's face was slick with sweat. His eyes gleamed so that he looked feverish, and the muscles in his face twitched fast and uncontrollably.

"He comes," Vano whispered, "Czernobog. The god of ends and of ashes. I hear him, just a soft sound like the flapping of flames. You would think it would be loud, the approach of one so powerful, but he comes softly."

"Make him go away!" I cried, beginning to panic.

"*Look!*" he said, grasping my arm suddenly. With terror, I followed his gaze and saw small white cinders flitting by beyond the window like moths.

"The men are almost here," I hissed, struggling to control my heaving breath. "We must go!"

"They are only doing what is appointed for them to do," he said. "As are we. They would not be coming if *he* were not."

"Bar!" Ehru's voice called out to Vano from across the room, and Vano turned to him.

"Bar," Ehru called again. It was the word for brother. His voice was gentle and his expression tender.

"Bar," Vano called back. Painfully, he smiled. "How I've missed you."

He took a panting breath, his eyes full of tears. "*Go*, brother! *Go! Live!* Be well with your family."

Ehru remained, struggling with some emotion, until Vano shouted again for him to go and waved him off.

Ehru nodded and disappeared back into the darkness of the loft.

"You have to go now, Anya," Vano said, guiding me firmly by the elbow toward the ladder.

"We have to go," I insisted. "*We* have to go."

When he didn't answer, I turned on him, but he took my face suddenly and roughly in his hands and looked me in the eyes with a frightening intensity. "There is no time for arguments. I will stay and you will go. Those men can't kill you, but they can make you wish you could die. They'll burn you and flay you and cut you to pieces, and then when you're well, they'll do it again. They'll call this work holy and entrust it to their sons. *Go now! Go with Ehru!*"

"You can't stay here," I sobbed in despair, but I knew he would. Vano never turned from a path he was set on.

"I can and must. Those men require Ehru's death. They won't stop until they have it. Ehru cannot give it to them, but I can. He is going through his door, and it is my part to shut the door behind him, so that they cannot follow. I will give them the death they seek from Ehru. I will do it joyfully, as I wish I could have when we were children. This is the gift the world has given to me: to die for my brother, so that he can finally live."

"You don't have to do it," I pleaded. "I'll kill them all."

"And all their brothers behind them in the village? All the men to hear about it for a hundred miles? There would only be more of them then, and more tragedy for Ehru and for you. You will do no such thing. You will go and not turn back."

For a moment, I just cried and clutched tightly at Vano's arms, trying to take him and hold on to him. Trying to keep him. A dark bead of sweat or tears, I couldn't tell which, ran down the side of his face, and without thinking, I reached for it. My finger came away with the deep red stain of blood. Then Piroska was at my side, taking strong hold of my arm. I turned to her, tears streaming down my face. She smiled gently at me, and though I did not want it, the peace of her smile edged forcefully, as it always had, into my despair. She lifted her hand toward the loft.

"Go, lyubimaya."

She walked me to the ladder. When I didn't climb, she said again. "Go, my love. Go. Live."

"Anya!" Ehru was calling me in a hard whisper from above. "Anya!"

I climbed.

The girl was on all fours, moaning softly with pain, beside a hole in the thatch that looked out on night sky and the dark, rugged profile of mountains. The stomp of feet was louder, and there was another sound like the soft flapping of a banner in wind, or like fire. Tiny white ashes drifted singly, here and there, and the smoke scent was steadily filling the air.

"Help her, Anya!"

Ehru had hopped down to the ground and was standing below, arms up to catch the girl.

"Lada, my love," he called to her softly, "jump. I will catch you."

I took the girl's arm and helped her to her feet and then to climb through the hole in the thatch. She was scared and frozen in her fear, and finally, I picked her up in my arms and tossed her down to Ehru, who caught her as if she were a bag of down, then he turned and carried her off into the night and the trees.

I stood there for a moment, watching them disappear and listening to the footfalls of the men approaching the hut from the other side. There was the soft tinkling of the bells that hung from the eaves and then the sound of the door opening, hard steps on the packed-earth floor of the hut. I looked at the red stain on my fingertip, Vano's blood. I turned from the sky and the wooded horizon, crawled back across the floor of the loft, and looked down through one of the cracks in the wood floor.

Four men, large, bearded, and thick-armed, had entered the hut carrying sickles and sod blades. The light glimmering in through the windows told me that there were more outside holding the torches. Vano and Piroska sat in their chairs by the fire, unnerving in their stillness.

"Where is the girl?" the leader of the men demanded.

"I'm sorry to tell you," Vano answered peaceably, "the girl has died. She is with Christ in heaven."

"You will not speak the name of our Lord, *demon*," the man spat back.

"Forgive me. She is with your Lord, then. She labored long in the woods near your village, and there, expired. The baby also."

"If truly she is dead, then half our work is done and she is in hell, where the lovers of demons go after death and where the two of you, a witch and a demon, are soon to return. We have tolerated your presence too long. Tell your master, when you see him, that the people of this land will tolerate no more."

One of the men handed skeins of rope to the others, and the men moved forward to bind Vano and Piroska to the chairs they sat in. The motions of the men were hasty and rough, as though they expected violent resistance, and even when the figures remained motionless and cooperative, the men still seemed skittish as though fearing some trick or trap.

"Bless you, my sons. Bless you," Piroska said softly over and over again to the men who worked at her ropes. "May this darkness not be held against you in the world to come."

Vano lifted his eyes and began speaking to the spirit in his language. I did not understand the words any more than I ever had, but I felt a power in them, and felt, along with it, the palpable presence of the spirit he spoke to; I realized that, all this time, I'd not truly believed that it was there. Now, though, like a camouflaged animal stirring from its hiding spot, like something always there but simply unnoticed, it revealed its presence, so that I could no more doubt its reality than I could my own.

The men seemed to feel it too and were unnerved.

"A demon's cries to the king of demons," the man said with agitation. "We'll not allow it."

He grabbed Vano by the jaw and forced open his mouth. With one hand, he pulled Vano's tongue forward; with the other, he lifted the sod blade high.

. . .

IT WAS BELIEVED IN THOSE days that if you didn't make sure a witch was good and dead before you burned her, she would take the shapes of worms and lizards and crawl out of the fire to work worse hexes upon you than before. If Vano wasn't a witch, the men were sure he was something equally wicked, so the men made sure, in many ways, that Vano and Piroska were dead before setting fire to their clothes and then the dry roof thatching.

I longed to push aside everything Vano had said and kill them all, but I didn't. I lay against the floor above my loved ones, weeping while the flames climbed the walls and swept in rolling waves across the thatch, until I was in a house of fire. I felt the burn of the smoke in my eyes, the choke of it in my lungs, the first bite of flame against my skin, and still, I didn't move. Vano and Piroska were burning, why shouldn't I burn with them? But eventually, just as Ehru had said, my body decided and moved me, against the will of my mind, through the fire and out the flaming hole in the thatch. It moved me sprinting across the pasture through the woods and into the cold waters of the river, where I gave myself up to the current, which knew that I needed both relief and pain and so simultaneously cooled my burns and beat me against its rocks, threw me into the sharp, lancing fingers of the tree branches hanging low over the water. At some point, I lost consciousness.

I finally awoke facedown in still water. I opened my eyes to open eyes looking up at me—a face the color of the muddy riverbed; beard and brows of drifting, black moss; eyes shot with squid ink. My scream erupted in a havoc of bubbles, and I lurched up out of the water, choking and sputtering, crying and wailing.

It was night still, or perhaps again. I had no idea how long I'd been lying there facedown in the water. The water was dark, and I could not know whether the face I had seen was real or imagined, though the vividness of it had in no way dissipated.

There was a pain in my leg, and I couldn't get my footing to stand. I flailed, trying to turn enough to see where the pain was coming from, but the angle and the darkness made it impossible.

For hours I struggled to keep my head above water, struggled awk-wardly to free my foot from whatever had it caught. I succeeded only at the first and it exhausted me. Reaching forward, I could just touch the sandy bank of the river sloping up beneath the water and some fist-sized stones there. I used this meager handhold to support myself for the hours until the birds began to chirp and the light of dawn began to seep slowly into my surroundings.

When it was light enough, I mustered my strength again to twist my body and try to see what had hold of my foot, and caught glimpses of a large boulder with which my foot seemed to be somehow painfully in-volved. I tried instead swimming down into the water and curling as if to do a flip and looking underwater. With this I had better luck, if it can be called luck, to see through the dim murk my foot held fast between an enormous boulder and another smaller one, and my blood a slow red haze drifting about it.

I tried to push the boulder, though to do so caused me tremendous pain in my leg. The boulder was too heavy, and in the water, I had no leverage with which to push it. I sputtered again to the surface.

I looked forward at the trees just beyond the riverbank, where I wished to be, more than one would think it was possible to wish for anything. I studied the sandy gravel of the bank, a dragonfly buzzing carelessly above the spume.

I screamed.

The dragonfly flew away.

· XVIII ·

"WILBUR never forgot Charlotte. Although—"

"What's those?"

The children and I are sitting in a circle on the wool rug before the fireplace in the library, all except for Octavio, who is standing, squinting at the small black-and-white illustration in the book I'm holding up for all the children to see, and pointing his small finger.

"Those are spiderwebs in the barn doorway. And those little *teeny* spots are Charlotte's children—all *five hundred and fourteen* of them!"

"How come she has so many?" Octavio asks.

"Well, life is very hard for spiders and many of them won't survive. Mommy spiders have to see to it that the world doesn't run out of spiders."

"I *wish* the world *would* run out of spiders," someone murmurs.

I smile sympathetically in the direction of the comment. "You know, the world used to be much harder for people and people, too, used to have more children for the same reason. Not nearly so many as spiders, though. Could you imagine? A mother stuffed full of five hundred and fourteen babies?"

There's a ripple of giggles and tiny tummies being pushed out in mock pregnancy.

It's the last day of school before Thanksgiving break. The first snow of the year lies across the grounds beyond the windows. I'm racked with hunger and also dreading the quiet stillness I know is about to descend on the house. Holiday breaks and the silent loneliness they bring are something I annually endure rather than enjoy. Leo seems to share my feelings. When I finish the book and set it down, he says, "I don't want Thanksgiving. I just still want to come to school."

"I will miss you too, mon petit. I will miss each and every one of you, but you'll have such a good time and I'll be eager to hear all about it."

Leo does not appear assuaged, but it's the best I can do. I'm struggling to soothe myself, trying hard to focus on the day, moment by moment, and enjoy these last hours with the children without casting forward to the dreary emptiness that lies beyond.

After story time, we put on boots and coats, hats and mittens, and go outside to enjoy the first snow. The children are determined to have a snowball fight, but this first accumulation is still loose and fluffy and won't pack, so instead they chase each other and throw powdery handfuls that glitter as they sift slowly to the ground or gather sparkling on hats and eyelashes.

Eventually, the time comes. It's three o'clock. The children's coats and backpacks are on. Cars are pulling up in the drive. A few children are going out of town—Audrey has been talking for weeks about the train ride she's taking to her grandmother's house in Burlington—and they are bouncing with excitement. They greet the adults who come to get them with shouts and hugs. Leo stands beside me, holding my hand. His head is hanging, crestfallen.

"It's only for a few days," I say, kneeling beside him. "You'll get to rest and eat good food and then in no time, you'll be back at school."

"But I just don't want Thanksgiving break." A wobble has come into his voice. The corners of his mouth are turned down, his little chin dimpled with sadness. "I want to go to school *every day*."

"I know, my sweet. I wish you could too."

"Au revoir, Madame LeSange!" Ramona calls as her father leads her and her brother out the door.

"Au revoir, biquet!" I call to her. "Have a happy Thanksgiving!"

The Hardmans' silver sedan pulls up in the drive. I turn back to Leo. His nose is running; it began when the temperature dropped below forty about a week ago and hasn't stopped since. I take a tissue from my pocket and wipe it.

"Leo, will you do something for me?"

He looks at me but doesn't answer.

"Will you draw a picture for me every day?"

He nods, dismally.

"It's five days until I see you again, so I'll be hoping to see five pictures. And I'd like you to draw just ordinary things like your bed or a shoe or a glass of milk, but pay close attention to it. Can you do that for me? I will *so* look forward to seeing them."

He nods again, still somber, and there is a knock at the door. I open it, and Dave Hardman is standing there. I do my best to smile and be pleasant.

"Hello, Mr. Hardman. I don't think I've seen you on pickup duty before. What's the occasion?"

"Katherine's not feeling great today," Dave says, and runs a hand through his hair. "I don't know if she told you, but our nanny is gone too."

"I did hear that, yes."

Dave rolls his eyes at this and presses his lips in annoyance. "So I may be on pickup duty more often until we find a new one. Come on, bud," he calls to Leo. "Let's get going."

I turn to Leo, struggling with my reluctance to send him off with this man—is Katherine really just not feeling well, or has she perhaps had another "accident"?—but aware also that I have no alternative.

Leo throws his arms around my waist, giving me one last hug.

"I'll see you soon, Leo," I whisper.

He lets go, walks out the door, and follows Dave down the steps and across the driveway to the car. As the car goes past, Leo waves to me, his face gray through the glass of the car window.

I go back inside, close the door, and lean against the wood, considering the house before me. Rina left early for a flight to Michigan, and Marnie too has been gone for hours. It's just me now, me and the unbroken silence, me and the dust motes swirling slowly over the stairs in a patch of window light, above me the maze of elegantly furnished and motionless rooms. For a moment, I'm swept by a nauseating wave of déjà vu, the too-familiar sensation of being buried alive.

THE NIGHT THE CHILDREN LEAVE, Vano comes to me again in a dream. We are sitting across from each other in the shifting, firelit darkness of Piroska's hut. He's sweating. The perspiration runs down the lovely thin ridge of his nose. It drips from the hair that hangs down over his eyes. I too am sweating. Scorching heat passes over me in waves, and the humid air is thick in my nose and mouth. We take turns flinching as what feels like tiny sparks kiss our exposed skin violently.

"He's coming," Vano says. "He's here already."

He doesn't have to say the name for me to understand that he's speaking of Czernobog. His words are spoken calmly, but they send violent tremors through my body.

"I don't believe in those things anymore," I try to assert with force, but my voice shakes. "I don't believe in *him*. I was young and impressionable; I thought I saw things that I didn't really see. Maybe I couldn't handle what I *did* see and so I imagined I saw other things."

"It makes no difference, Anya, whether you believe or not." Vano doesn't say this with reproach, only his old, gentle patience. Here I am again, failing to understand all sorts of things that I should understand already. "He is there whether you acknowledge him or not. He fulfills his purposes with your cooperation or without."

"But I—I have nothing left to end." My voice has gone shrill in my ears. Whatever remoteness I had managed to feign before now is gone. "He's already taken everything from me that ever mattered. I have hardly anything now. I have *been careful* to have nothing."

"To have nothing is impossible. A person may have little if they set their mind to it. More often, though, they are simply not aware of what they have. He knows, though. He keeps perfect inventory."

"Then all I have of value now are memories. Everything I love is in the past, in my mind. Will he put an end to that? Will he put an end to my mind? *My life?* If so, I'd welcome him. For once, I'd be grateful."

"We will see," he says, firelight flickering in the black of his eyes. "The seasons are doors. They open to what waits for you beyond. Your door is opening. I've come so that you can prepare yourself."

"Prepare how? For what?" I ask, my voice a scared whisper. "What is it, Vano? What's coming for me?"

"Prepare your courage, Anya. These things always need courage. An ending is coming to you. An emptying. A cup poured out. I wish I could tell you more, but it's all I know."

He pauses and his eyes smile. "Do you remember what I promised you?"

I don't. I shake my head no.

"That when the time came, I would hold your hand."

He puts his long, finely boned hand out to me. "Just as you held mine that night so long ago."

I take his hand, and some part of me must know that I'm dreaming because I'm amazed by the solidity, the softness and warmth of his hand in mine.

He smiles down at our hands interlocked.

"You see, I keep my promises to you. Will you make me a promise and keep it?"

"I'll try," I say, but I don't feel confident.

He smiles and nods. To try, it seems, is enough.

"Promise that when the time comes, you'll have courage."

He squeezes my hand before letting it go and rising from his chair.

"Courage, brave Anya," he says again, stepping past me toward the hearth. "But there are many kinds. You must find the right kind of courage."

I remain where I am, turning the word in my head—*courage*, when have I ever lacked it? Most of my life I've spent fighting, protecting, surviving.

I look up from my thoughts in time to see Vano standing before the hearth, hands braced against the stones on each side, and a jolt of despair runs through me. I leap up to catch him before he can do what he always does, but it's too late. He's stepping into the fire as through a low door, his garments crinkling in flame.

I reach into the fire to pull at him, but the flames that seem to cause him no distress sear me, and I pull my hands back. All I can do is watch him burn again and cry, my own wails high and thin and strange in my ears.

Then Vano's face is somehow no longer his. It has turned white like a spent coal, veined with fire. The heat coming off it burns my face. It leans toward me, soot eyes bulging and hungry. It grabs for me, sparks showering forward with every movement, and every spark sears my skin like a brand. I scream and try to get away, but the burning continues, and everywhere the fire touches, my flesh blackens and crisps.

I wake finally with a gasp, the dreaming and waking world smashing into each other in a confused collision. I'm lying on something hard. I don't know where I am, but the horrible pain of my dream has not stopped upon waking. My body is on fire.

With effort, I lift my head and realize that for some reason I'm lying on the rug that covers my bedroom floor, as though I'd been crawling to bed and had simply given up. I hear a soft, distant mechanical tone sounding with regularity somewhere in the house and soft moans coming from my own throat. The pain all over my body is so intense that I still cannot even comprehend it. Gasping, I sit up and look myself over, but for a moment I can't make sense of what I see. I'm bloody and my pajamas hang from me in shreds. The sleeves, the pants, everywhere the fabric is bunched and torn and crimson-soaked. The pain only seems to grow more intense with every waking moment.

Bloody hands shaking, I push up a sleeve and find my arm criss-crossed with bleeding red slashes, pocked with vicious gouges as if I had been snared by dozens of fishhooks that had then been ripped out again. My legs, when I examine them, are the same. For a moment, all I can do is sit there, staring in shock and trembling confusion until, at some point, it occurs to me. There is one animal I can think of that could cause such injuries.

THE HALL IS DARK, BUT the sound—I know what it is now, the stoic shriek of a smoke detector—is getting closer. When I turn a corner, it's louder still. Another step forward and then, suddenly, it stops. Silence, thick and nauseating. I don't know which is worse, the sound or the silence. I can see at the far end of the hall the pull-down staircase extending down from the attic to the hall floor. It shouldn't be. I make my way slowly, painfully, down the hall with my wounded arms tucked against my chest and trembling.

A creak from deep in one of the rooms along the hall makes me stop.

"Is anyone there?" I force myself to call. The silence that answers makes my head swim.

I nudge the door of a room open and see swift movement. A furred tail disappears under a sofa. Better than anything I'd been expecting, but my heart goes on pounding. I go into the room, lean over, peer under the sofa. Myrrh's pretty gray face peeks out from around a carved leg.

"Myrrh," I whisper, taking a step toward her. "Oh, Myrrh. I'm so glad to see you. I don't know what's happening. Do you know?"

I hold my arms out to her, desperate for the warm comfort of her fur, but Myrrh suddenly bares her gleaming teeth and lets out a strangled scream of fear. Her muzzle draws back in a rigid snarl, and her wide black eyes are fixed on me. She holds a tensed paw forward, and I see blood on it and on each sharp claw that she has extended threateningly.

"*Myrrh?*"

Her paw twitches warily. She hisses twice, then turns and darts farther into the darkness beneath the couch.

I back away out of the room and into the hall again. I run stumblingly to the attic stairs. From beneath a radiator, the dart of another cat startles me and there is another angry hiss. At the foot of the stairs, I look up and see the door at the top of the attic stairs thrown back wide—another oversight I would never commit.

I climb the stairs and when I get to the top, my hands crawl to my mouth in devastation. The room is wrecked—furniture overturned, upholstery torn with stuffing spilling out, a window has been shattered, and *the floor*; the floor is littered with tiny furred bodies, small torn furred limbs, and blood everywhere, puddled, smeared, and sprayed.

Cats. The bodiless heads of cats. The headless bodies of cats. I close my eyes and begin to cry, nausea sweeping over me.

When I open my eyes, I see one of the dead cats close at hand to my right. I sink to the floor and take the body in my hands. It's Coco, my beautiful Abyssinian. Her fangs are bared, and her eyes are fixed in a glassy expression of terror. Her body is a desiccated husk. It weighs nothing, easily less than a pound. It's been drained completely of blood.

I consider the room again and my body, the patchwork of wounds—*claw marks*. I lick my lip, and there is the taste of blood. For weeks, I've been waking up hungry, but I'm not hungry now. I drop my head down against Coco's body and weep into her blood-matted fur because I understand what's happened here. This attic is a henhouse after a fox raid, and *I* have played the fox.

· XIX ·

I spent days, maybe weeks, facedown in that river. I drowned many times. I woke many times to the face beneath the water. Was it a curious Veles, come to examine the disorderly creature disrupting the peace of his river, or Czernobog, the cursed, come to pay visit to his fellow accursed, or was it delusion? The figurative art of insanity? I dreamed. I raved. Occasionally, I gathered the strength and wits enough to scream.

The flesh of my fingers began to dissolve and fall away from my body. I searched, to no avail, for something sharp with which to amputate my foot. Defeated, I swam down and did what I could with my fingernails, but they were soft from the water and bent instead of cutting. If I could have reached my ankle with my mouth, I would have gnawed myself free, but I couldn't. My mind broke, and I became like the animals, and so when hands grabbed me suddenly and pulled my head up out of the water, I fought them with weak ferocity.

"*Frieden! Frieden!*" implored a voice, and there was another body in the water with me, pulling me. I felt part of my water-rotted foot tear and I screamed in pain. The pulling stopped, and there was a splash as the body dove under the water. I felt hands on my ankle, then there was a splash as the body emerged again from the water. I saw a man climb up the riverbank, dripping, and then I fell forward into the water and my delirium again.

There was fresh pain in my foot as the boulder rocked, and then another burst of pain as it rocked again and then tumbled away. I drifted for an instant, unmoored.

Again, I was pulled, but this time there was not the same horrific burst of pain, only the constant excruciating pain I had become used to. I was dragged up against the wet sandy slope and then the dry sandy slope of the beach. Then I was released and lay there feeling the small warmth of the sand and rocks, which I had forgotten existed in the constant cold of the water.

I vomited and then vomited again. Again and again, I vomited until the vomiting no longer poured forth water and instead poured forth screams, and then long, gagging wails, and then only soft, resigned moans.

I WOKE UP HOURS LATER warm, wrapped in a scratchy wool blanket that irritated my raw skin. There was a fire before me and when I saw it, I screamed and tried to crawl away from it.

A man, reclined on the opposite side of the fire, threw down a book and pen and came around the fire to me. The man spoke soothingly to me, but I didn't understand him, could not in all likelihood have understood him even if he had spoken to me in one of my languages. When I continued looking at the fire in terror, crying and crawling desperately away from it, the man finally took a pot and dumped the water in it onto the fire.

The fire hissed out, and only then did I become calm. The man rested on his haunches beside the steaming firepit, quietly studying me, and I slowly became aware enough to look at him. He was pale-skinned, but ruddy and freckled, and as thickly haired as Ehru, but his hair was gold flecked with red and brown. His eyes were blue and red-rimmed, tired-looking but kind—at once gentle and intense. His gaze searched me with bright curiosity, like hands.

He spoke to me again and when I said nothing, he seemed satisfied that I did not speak his language. He pointed to something beside me, and I turned my head to find a cup of water and a plate of food on the ground, some bread and a bit of roasted meat.

I turned away from it, and he said something that we both knew I didn't understand. Then he got up, but only partway, as if he didn't want to frighten me by rising to his full height. He made his way slowly and lopingly toward me. When he was close, he paused and put his empty hands out to show that he had nothing. I remained calm, and he reached slowly forward and pulled a corner of the blanket back, exposing my injured foot and ankle. It was horrific. He continued speaking and though I could not understand the words, I understood the tone and that they expressed concern for my injuries. He pointed to the lump of rotted flesh that had once been my foot and shook his head. He meant that it was very bad.

He reached to his belt slowly, one hand remaining up and open, and pulled out from a sheath a knife. He held it up, showing it to me and speaking softly, his empty hand patting the air between us soothingly. He was telling me that my foot ought to be cut off.

I shook my head vehemently.

"No!" I said. "No! No!"

He held his hands up in a disarmed gesture. He pointed again at my foot, then at his own, and ran his finger up his leg and all the way up to his chest where his heart lay beneath. With his finger he jabbed at the spot and slumped forward in a pantomime of death. It would kill me, he was saying. If the rotted appendage didn't come off, it would kill me.

I looked him in the eye, then shook my head.

"No," I said again. "No."

FOR DAYS WE STAYED BESIDE that firepit. I only lay there looking up at the sky through the fingers of the trees, trying to think of nothing, remember nothing. Sometimes, overcome, I began to cry and when I did, I would hear his voice, a sturdy baritone, come across the firepit, singing soft, strange lullabies.

Most of the time, he sat with the bound book in his hands, making quick lines against it with his pen. At other times, he wrote on small pieces of paper that he folded when done and added to a stack of others that he carried in his pack. At night, when it grew cold, he struck flint rocks above kindling to make a small fire, watching me the whole time and speaking in his strange language with his soothing voice. I let him do it and did not scream again. Each day, he came around the fire to examine my foot, and each day, he looked up at me amazed. It healed in three days as it should have healed in three months, if ever.

I was hungry. I couldn't remember the last time I'd eaten. Finally, when I felt that my foot could support my weight, I got up and started to hobble off into the woods. The man jumped up and tried to help me, but I motioned him away.

In the woods, alone and ungainly, it took me some time, but I was finally able, by lying silently in wait, to snatch a hare emerging from its hole. I drained it greedily of blood. Back at the fire, I tossed the furry carcass at the man, and he looked at me with wonder.

He roasted the rabbit for his dinner that night. When he offered half of it to me and I declined again, he looked troubled. He spoke and I understood his question without understanding the words. I pretended, though, that I did not.

After his dinner, he set again to making his marks in his book and this time I came around the fire to him. I held out my hand for the book, and after a moment's hesitation, he gave it to me. The page was littered with drawings: the nest of logs in the fire, the silhouette of the fire against the dark trunks of the trees, his own view of his leg and boot. I turned the page to see trees, his drinking cup, a grasshopper, a kestrel. And then there was a page of me. Me curled up in a blanket sleeping; me, in profile, eyes closed; a half dozen iterations of lips, eyes, nose that could only have been mine, though it had been years since I'd seen myself in anything other than a pool of water. I had grown. I was a woman. Ehru had told me so, but I did not believe it until that moment.

I looked at the man. He smiled and put his hands up in a *what can I say?* gesture.

"Good," I said, looking back at the drawings on the paper.

"Gut?" he exclaimed with an exultant smile and a laugh. "*Gut. Gut.*"

"Gut," I said, "good."

"Goooo-d," he said merrily. Then, after a moment, he gestured to himself and said, "Paul. Von Steinschneider."

"Paul Von—Von . . ."

He waved away my attempt at the second word and laughed. "Paul. Paul."

"Paul," I said.

He held a hand out to me, the warm smile still on his lips and in his eyes. I thought suddenly of Vano's eyes, of the blood I had taken from his face onto my fingertip, the precious blood that had washed away in the river. I thought of Piroska, with her smile of imposing peace. Tears gathered again in my eyes, and I wiped them roughly away.

"No one," I said.

"No one," he said, and smiled again. "No one. Gut."

THE NEXT DAY, AFTER PAUL had had his breakfast, he began packing up his camp things. He pulled from his pack a pair of pants and a man's shirt, one of very few changes of clothes that he had, and he set them beside me to wear in place of the torn, molded, algae-fouled dress that still clung to me. I went behind a tree to change, and when I came out again, he smiled and nodded his head and said something approving.

I watched him uncertainly as he packed up the rest of his things, the blanket, the plate and cup, the stack of folded letters he was ever writing, the pair of snowshoes that seemed out of place in the fall. I didn't know if he intended for me to go with him. If he did, I didn't know if *I* intended to go with him. But if he didn't, what would I do?

He picked up a stack of thin wood boards bound together with string, and I saw on the uppermost one that there were colors on it. I went over to look at it and found a thin strip of wood shaved from a tree trunk with a picture painted on it. It was a view of the trees and the river, the same river from which Paul had pulled me. Sunshine glinted off the surface like sparkling coins and the water seemed to move and twist among the rocks at the bottom. Clouds like castle ruins heaped up in the sky in the far distance.

I looked at Paul with his walking stick and rucksack, his chapped and callused skin and worn broad-brimmed hat on his head, bundle of paintings in one hand. Before he had been simply the man who had rescued me, but I saw then that he had been something before he rescued me and was something apart from me even now. He was an artist, making his way through the woods, alone and far from home.

I took some of his camp things and tied them up in my dress, so that I could share in carrying the load. He smiled at me, and together we started off.

· XX ·

A canvas is a separate place, a looking glass through which you may pass with only a little concentration. The dimensions don't matter. Even a small eleven-by-fourteen can trick the mind into forgetting that anything beyond it exists. I choose a thirty-by-forty, though—a rectangle the size of a window—just to be sure. I want to forget myself. Where I am. Who I am. What I am. I want time to pass with that strange, nonsensical speed of dreams and total artistic absorption.

My materials are laid out: jars of bright powdered pigments, linseed oil, turpentine, brushes. Many do not realize that painting is a deadly art. Pigments are almost always pure poison. Take lead white, for instance, perhaps the most commonly used pigment, which slowly gnaws at the kidneys, the nervous system, the brain. Then there are the greens— verdigreen, malachite, emerald, and Paris—with their steady, concentrated emissions of arsenic gas. Grinding azurite blue, which many a Renaissance apprentice did, produces mercury cyanide, and mercury cyanide in apprentices produces convulsions, paralysis, necrosis, death. And we've not even touched on the solvents yet.

Things have changed with time, of course. There have been advances, the viper largely defanged. During our lessons, the children use acrylics, a medium as harmless as Crayola markers. I'm old-fashioned, though.

For myself, nothing can compare to the brilliance of pure, deadly cobalt mixed by hand with linseed oil, and for some reason, it strikes me as fitting that art should cost the artist dearly, that the most beautiful things made by man should also be poisonous. It seems somehow consistent with what I've seen of this world and its men.

But then, of course, it's all no cost to me. I imagine I could slide into a bath of liquid mercury and climb out again unscathed. I'm a snake handler impervious to bite, and so it is with naked hands that I scoop out the powdered cadmium red, barium yellow, Prussian blue, sprinkle them onto my palette, and, with a palette knife, scrape and mix, mix and scrape the insidious, brilliant minerals with oil.

Once my palette is complete, I spread a thin wash of pigment across the entire canvas to even out the surface, then with a flat brush I begin to map out the dimensions: where the stone will sit in the space of the canvas, how large it will be. I slash the lines of the three-dimensional object. The shape doesn't feel quite right—too thick here, too narrow there—so I make new lines over the old. Closer.

Painting is a recursive process. You make an attempt, which is almost never it, so you make another attempt right on top of the first. It gets you closer, or it gets you farther. Either way, you attempt again. Somewhere between five and forty attempts, you find it. The shape you were searching for. To get it right the first time would be an incredible fluke, like a hole in one on a golf course; a pat on the back would be in order, but only a fool would approach the next tee expecting such lucky results again. The truth is something you work your way steadily toward through trial and error. Mostly error. To be too lucky too often would be to lose the joy of the work. Nothing but holes in one would make for a very boring golf game.

I'm beginning a new painting today, another in the series I had already begun. I'm painting my father's grave, the small simple flagstone-sized marker that he cut and polished smooth with the last shred of his earthly strength and that I also worked at with what I believed was the last of my own failing strength. I was so certain I was about to die. I was ready. I knew, even at that young age, what one could expect of the world (was *I* too lucky? Getting the lines right on the first try?), and I was content to depart from it.

I have photographs of the other graves in the series to aid me in painting them, but this one I have to paint from memory. It's a struggle. I'm not in the best mental state for such work. I'm a jangled mess, jumpy, covered in bandages and still hurting, trying not to think of what I've done or what I will do next. I don't know whether my lines are truly off, or whether the significance of the object and my longing for it only make me feel that they are. Portraits of our dearest loved ones are always the hardest to execute. They inevitably lack some je ne sais quoi that feels unbearably essential.

After many attempts, I step away from the painting in frustration. I'm hungry. I'm restless. I'm lonely. I'm scared. I am each of these things to what seems an unendurable degree; these feelings keep me chained to my body, to the reality of my life, the physical space around me; they deny me entry into the other reality of the work.

The windows of the conservatory are full of dusk. The sun is bleeding its final colors into the gauzy smears of cloud above the tree line. The Dvořák record I put on has long since lapsed into a grainy rhythmic shushing, as though I were a baby in need of settling. I feel like one: let down, deflated, anxious. I wish I could go on working, not stop until the children return to fill the house with life again, but I can't. I'm not making progress. Only getting frustrated, and, anyway, this layer of wet pigment must dry before anything more can be built up on it.

I gather my dirty, paint-smeared rags. I take a long time washing my brushes, massaging the cleaner slowly into the bristles of each one. Rinse. Massage again. Rinse again. I draw all these chores out because I don't know what I'll do when they're finished. Eventually, despite my best efforts, they're finished anyway, and there's nothing left to do.

I move into the library, build a fire, and sit in an old leather armchair, hoping to feel the reassuring presence of so many authors and characters from the books lined up floor to ceiling on the shelves. I take The Brothers Karamazov down from its place and try to force my mind to the words on the yellowed pages, but it's no use. This house is feeling more like a prison with every passing minute, and not an impersonal prison either, but a prison full of sinister personality. The house alone sees me, knows me, but it knows me as the wolf knew Red Riding Hood, as resistant, quarrelsome prey, a curious disturbance in its belly. Finally, I set the book down, giving up all pretense of reading. I'm too distracted by dread and hunger to be easily distracted by anything else, and I'm also listening, without meaning to, for a sound, a sudden calamitous *eeeeep, eeeeep, eeeeep*, or a flapping like a banner in the breeze, like the beating of flames in a white-hot furnace.

"He's coming," Vano said in my dream. "He's already here."

I feel the hairs on my neck rise just at the thought of those words, and I try to push them from my mind, but I can't. My dream of sitting with Vano had felt so vivid and real. Up until the end, it had felt too normal even, too quotidian, to be a dream. It was like Vano had just stopped in, from the past or beyond the grave, for a simple visit, a chat. And hadn't he said he would? I'd not thought about his promise in ages—to come meet me in some future season and hold my hand—if I'd ever really thought about it at all. He said so many things I didn't understand, but what he'd said in my dream about Czernobog, the god of endings, was clearer than I wanted it to be. An ending coming. An emptying. A cup poured out. Was it coincidence that I'd woken up then to find terrible destruction and loss? To realize that I did have something to lose after all, my beloved pets, and had lost it.

Yes, it was coincidence. That was all it could be. Just dreams and memories and nonsense. Czernobog was a myth, a story I believed when I was young and gullible. And Vano was . . . Vano must have been . . . just wrong. We were both wrong, to think that there could be some person or power interested enough to follow us across centuries and continents, to appoint for us our endings. For worse, and for *better*, I'm alone.

From the fireplace there comes a sudden, jarring pop, and deep in the fire, a log, breaking at the center, twists suddenly and falls, sending up a shower of sparks. The ashy white skin and fiery veins of the spent log remind me of Vano's face in my dream, when it was no longer Vano's face. I press my lips together, close my eyes, wait for my heart to settle down in my chest, but a single thought repeats in my head: I have to get out of here.

• • •

IT'S AN HOUR AND A half drive to New York City. The sun sets along the way, and the waters of the East River become a black mirror reflecting lit-up Manhattan. It's rush hour. The taillights of the cars creeping along the highway form a long red snake that shifts its endlessly jointed body as it moves. A light rain begins to fall, specking the windshield, and the red snake's jointed body blurs.

I know why I left the house, started the car, fled down the drive as though something were after me; I couldn't stay where I was, alone and waiting to drown in the tension between silence and sound. I do not know why I'm *here*. Perhaps just to see this red snake or the black mirror of the river or the glowing city that appears to be sunk in it, a gaudy neon Atlantis. The drivers honk their horns and the sound is like some avant-garde film score. I see their faces move behind glass. They're yelling. They're angry. It's all so curious.

I'm a tourist and so everything is image, sound, smell, without implication. What does traffic matter to me? I have no appointments, no meals growing cold, no babysitters at home racking up hourly fees. In this car on this highway, I've found everything I set out looking for, a crushing impersonal mass of people, cars humming and smoking, tires squealing—a multitude to dissolve myself into.

The highway is narrowing, traffic coming almost to a standstill. Up ahead the red and blue lights of police cars flash. An accident is narrowing traffic to a single lane. A van drives crazily along the shoulder, bypassing the congestion, and a small coupe follows its lead. More car horns sound. It calls to mind a flock of aggressive geese battling violently over bread crumbs.

A light on the dashboard flicks on. The engine is overheating. This is unfortunate, but not surprising. My car is a vintage Datsun, and it can be persnickety about spending too much time in low gears.

As soon as the next exit—Port Morris—appears, I coast down the off-ramp, take a right around the corner and onto a side street, pull over to the side of the road, and park the car. The rain is falling harder now, and after getting out to pop the hood and grab the jug of coolant from the trunk, I'm soaked. Unless I want the radiator to spew boiling water in my face, I need to wait to add the coolant, so I get back in the car. Through the back-and-forth slashing of the blades and the rain, I examine my surroundings.

I have no idea what part of New York City I'm in, not even which borough. The Bronx maybe? My headlights illuminate a street cratered with potholes and the side of a stone bridge netted with ivy and adorned with a loping white spray-paint scrawl. To the right of the car, the edge of the road slopes down into underbrush littered with bottles and cardboard, a rusted chain-link fence, and beyond it, train tracks cradling wide pools of standing water.

To the left of the road is a pair of stone tenement buildings, boarded up and elaborately graffitied. The one working streetlight on the block stands directly in front of the twin buildings; its cone of light perfectly illuminates a graffitied image of a grinning wolf, red tongue lolling out over its teeth and a lunatic sparkle in its eye. It's really pretty good.

What a strange place. Lovely—the old, dignified stone structures, the ivy—and ghastly at the same time. The street is empty, nevertheless I feel very exposed sitting in this car with the headlights on in the dark, in the rain.

The rain falls harder, so hard that I can no longer see anything through the windshield but a sloshing torrent of water. I'm watching it fall, listening to the pounding against the glass, when a shadow passes suddenly before the car. The passenger-side door handle rattles, and before I have time to react, it opens. The dome light flicks on, and there is the falling rain and a pair of very thin legs covered in a tight, shiny black material. A red pleather backpack is thrown in and lands in my lap and then someone is in my car.

A young Black woman has climbed into the passenger seat. She's shaking the rain from her thick braids, cursing creatively as she does. Her hands are up fussing with her hair, and the red leopard-print nails on her fingers are nearly as long as her fingers themselves. Beneath a bulky, bleach-spattered jean jacket, that tight, shiny material I saw on her legs covers her entire body, from neck to foot, like a thin layer of glossy paint, except in the front where it plunges down in a sharp V that reaches nearly to her belly button. She has white leg warmers on and white high-tops on her feet.

She goes on for some time tending to her wet hair and not paying me any attention, while I hold her bag. Finally, though, she turns to me, and her face is startling. It's shaped almost exactly like that of a Siamese cat, and her eyes are a lurid artificial green: color contacts. She is young, late teens or early twenties, and like one of the hologram cards my students collect, this young woman's face seems to shift back and forth between being beautiful and disturbing.

"What are you doing here, white woman?" she asks, tilting her head kindly as though speaking to a child. She closes her eyes for a long second as if listening to some music in her own head. "I mean, I knew you was white from the car, but I thought you was a dude."

Her eyes close again sleepily. "That's cool, though. I like white women. They're fun. They're fun to fuck with. They're so nervous. They like jump if you sneeze. Are you nervous?"

Her words are direct and somewhat unnerving, but there's something playful about her that makes it all seem somehow kindly meant.

"Nervous?" I ask, still thrown by her simple presence in my car. "No. Is there some reason you think I should be?"

"Probably." She nods her head in answer but then goes on nodding, lapsing into rhythm again with that inaudible music. Her eyes close. "Yeah, you probably should be."

"Why's that?"

She looks at me with an eyebrow raised. "'Cause you not in your neighborhood."

I look out at the rain, lean back against my seat. "I'm not the nervous type. Deep-seated anxiety, crippling existential despair, sure. Nervous? Not as much."

The girl grins and nods her head. "Yeah, I hear that. That's like how I used to be."

I almost laugh. How has this young girl had time to "used to be" anything?

"You ever read Sartre?" Her French accent on the name is impeccable.

"Jean-Paul Sartre? Yes."

"*No Exit*. You ever read that play?"

"Yes. I have. It's terrifying."

"Yeah, I was real down with that shit."

"You were *real down* with *No Exit*?"

She gives me a flat, almost impatient look and, chastened by it, I hurry to ask, "What did you like about it?"

"It's all about how people see you. All about being imprisoned by, you know, like people's perceptions of you. And that's all this. Everybody looking at each other and saying what they see, but can't nobody see theyself. It's the same at school, jobs, on the streets, on the train. Same everywhere."

"'The hell of other people,' as Sartre says."

She turns to me and nods. "And there's no way out. Even if the door opens, they're not gonna walk through it. It's like self-inflicted, you know."

"Hell self-inflicted; it does make a certain kind of sense, doesn't it?"

Her seat back reclines suddenly. She wriggles her shoulders, settling against it. Her eyes close again. "Heaven too."

"Heaven? How do you mean?"

The rain is gradually letting up, but this sleepy trespassing philosopher looks like she is about to take a nap in my car.

"You're in school?" I'm searching for something to say, some topic of conversation that might rouse her, lead perhaps to me dropping her off at some college dormitory.

"You ever met Adam?"

"Adam," I say, thrown again by the subject change. "Who is Adam?"

She turns her head my way and opens her eyes, and they are as startling as the first time I saw them. Her nose is splotched with freckles.

"Do you want to go to heaven?"

The question sounds vaguely threatening, but her expression doesn't look threatening. It looks serene. I give a small, baffled laugh at the absurdity of this entire conversation, but then fumble in my head for a response.

"If it's that or hell, I suppose I'd naturally prefer heaven."

"I didn't ask you what you prefer. I asked you, do you *want* to go to *heaven*?"

I hesitate, and the question hangs there in the air, so simple, so bald. I have no idea why she's asking me, but *heaven* . . . Do I want to go to heaven? Some perfect place on the other side of death. A place without brutality or sickness or loss. A place where children are safe, never orphaned or exploited or killed.

"Yes," I say, looking out at the gleaming street, the intermittent drops of rain pocking the puddles. "I want to go to heaven."

"Come with me then," she says, sitting up suddenly. She opens the car door and puts her backpack over her head to shield her from the rain that is now a soft, steady drizzle.

"Come on," she says again, with animation, waiting for me to open my door.

Getting this girl out of my car seems, in any case, like a step in the right direction. I take the keys from the ignition, open the door, grab the jug of coolant, and get out. She gets out too. I push up the hood of the car. It's very dark now, and I have to feel around in the nearly uniform black beneath the hood for the radiator cap. I unscrew it and almost blindly pour what seems like a safe amount of coolant in.

The girl has begun wandering slowly and unsteadily across the street.

"You coming?" she calls over her shoulder. I lower the hood of the car, let it slam down heavily.

I could get back in the car right now, drive away, leave this girl and all her nonsense behind. It's what I should do. Part of me is worried for her, though. Standing up, outside the confines of the car, her outfit looks frankly dangerous, and she's clearly ingested some kind of controlled substance, that much is clear. And what if the car she had hopped into *had* been occupied by "a dude" instead of me? How would that situation have played out? But what is any of that to me? Why should I presume that she needs anything done for her? She doesn't seem even remotely concerned.

"Where?" I ask, though I'm just buying myself time to reach a decision.

"I'm going to introduce you to Adam."

I open the car door, get in, and set the coolant down on the passenger seat. The keys rest in my palm. "*Adam?* Who is Adam?"

"Adam is *the exit.*" She spins around toward me, her arms angled out like the handles of a Grecian urn as she clutches her backpack still above her head. "Adam is the door."

"The door?" I tell myself her word choice, and the echo they carry of Vano's words from my dream, is only a coincidence. "The door to what?"

"To heaven."

This is craziness, I say to myself. I put the key in the ignition.

"Does blood bother you?" she asks.

· XXI ·

FOR a long time, I did little but watch Paul. He spoke to me regularly, and I began to understand much of what he said, though I made no effort to speak. I was still a bit animal. I had little interest in being human, if that's even what I was. I watched him cook in the mornings and evenings. I watched him take a hatchet and chop a shallow gash into the skin of a tree, then scrape, scrape, scrape the blade downward, until a small scroll or board fell away.

I watched him make pigments. I had gathered and made pigments before to paint the symbols of the Slavic deities, but those pigments I had made mostly from berries and some seeds. Paul would go walking, slowly, with his eyes on the ground and gather certain rocks and then crush and grind them with other larger rocks until they were only a fine yellow or red powder, then he would mix them with drops of an oil that he carried with him. Other pigments, ones that could not be found in the nature around us, he carried already pulverized in small jars—certain greens, blues, and a bright white.

I watched him paint, and at first this unnerved him, but I would sit there as still as a deer hiding, and eventually he would forget me. I wanted to observe every part of how he made those pictures. He was a marvelous painter, a wholly absorbed craftsman like my father, and there was something calming for me in watching him.

First, he would sketch what he saw on the wood with the burnt end of sticks, then he would unroll a leather cloth full of long, thin brushes tucked into thin pockets, and then take those brushes and dip them so delicately into the colored liquids he had painstakingly prepared, and finally he would begin putting color over the char sketches.

Weeks passed, and I went on watching, and I silently drew closer and closer in proximity to Paul while he worked. I wanted more. How did he keep the painting constant even as the sun made the shadows dance and shift across the landscape? How did he make the water move? Make the trees in the distance look distant?

Then one day, Paul cut a board from a tree, took a step to the right, and cut another one. At the fire, he blackened two sticks. Down on one knee, he held the tool out to me like a man presenting flowers to a maid. I took it from him, unable to conceal my pleasure. From then on, we painted side by side with the pigments and the leather pouch of brushes lying on a rock or tree stump between us.

When I painted, I was able to forget about everything else: the taste of ashes in my mouth; the blue of Mercy's mother lying motionless in her bunk; how small and helpless Mercy had looked sitting on the dock with her brother in her lap; Vano and Piroska and all that those men had done to them; the god of endings, roving the world, lifting homes and children and lovers and dropping them down his fiery throat. I forgot everything except what I saw in front of me—the trees and rocks and mountains, sunlight on one side, shadows on the other—and for a little while, I felt okay, at least until I finished painting.

ON A CHILL MORNING IN early autumn, Paul and I were sitting side by side, painting. There had been frost on the ground when we'd woken up, and the light felt pure and hard like glass. We had to cup our hands sporadically and warm them with our breath, and the wool blanket was draped across both our knees. There was a moment when the sun moved out from clouds; the light came skimming along the leaves and touched my skin with its warmth. I was feeling this when, beside me, Paul made a strange noise.

I looked over to see his hand jerk across his painting, the brush leaving a haphazard streak of brown across his beautiful forest landscape. I turned to him. He stared ahead over the top of his painting with an expression of blank astonishment. His mouth worked strangely, strange noises coming from it. I looked to the sky, where he seemed to be looking, but there was nothing there.

"*Paul?*" I said, making rare use of my voice.

The arm with the brush suddenly thrust outward again from his chest. His eyelids dipped, and he began jerking and trembling.

"*Paul!*" I cried.

He fell forward, knocking the pigments and brushes off the rock with him. On the ground, he lay rigid and quaking with his eyes still half-closed.

"*Paul!*" I cried again, "*Paul!*" and knelt beside him, pawing at his clenched and shaking body. There was nothing I could do, though.

Finally, his body went limp and still. His clenched jaw slackened, and from the corner of it, blood began to drip down his chin. I picked him up and carried him back to our campsite, where I covered him with the scratchy wool blanket and then built a fire.

He slept for hours. When he woke, he only cracked his eyes slightly and lay there wrapped in his blanket, gazing at me groggily until I noticed and smiled at him.

I came around the fire carrying the bound book into which I had been making quick lines with a pen. I took a seat beside him on the ground and held the book out so he could see my page of Paul. Paul asleep, wrapped in the blanket. Paul hunched over a wood panel, thin brush in hand. Paul's eyes squinting into the sun. Paul's rugged handle of a nose. Paul's full, bowed lips, his thick, bristly beard and mustache.

He turned his eyes to me heavily.

"Goooo-d," he whispered.

At the sound of his voice, something seized me, a painful surge rising up through my chest. Large, heavy tears began to drop from my eyes. I had been afraid. I only realized it then, that as he had slept and I'd built the fire and covered him carefully with blankets and drawn, I had been doing everything in my power not to feel the fear that he might leave me, that I might not hear his voice ever again. This eruption forcing its way violently through me was relief, horrible and painful. I wanted to run, run away from my fear of losing him and my joy at having him back. I wished I'd never met him at all, or else I wished to kill him, smother him with his own blanket, so I'd never have to be afraid of losing him again.

But Paul held his arm out to me, tut-tutting with gentle concern, and instead of running from him or killing him, I sank to my knees against him and cried into the coarse cloth of his coat while he stroked my hair and shushed me like a child.

"Did I scare you?" he whispered in his language. "I'm sorry."

LATER THAT EVENING, HE WAS able to sit up, attempt to eat the squirrel I had caught and cooked for him, but he'd chewed his tongue badly during his episode and it caused him pain.

"Was war das?" I said. What was that?

He looked at me, impressed.

"Was war das?" he repeated, seeming to both savor my words and ruminate on them. He set his plate on the ground beside him and stretched out on his blanket in great weariness. "Das . . . war . . ."

He looked into the fire for a moment, and then a tear fell from one of his eyes. Then the other.

"Mein problem."

I nodded.

"Problem," I repeated, to communicate that I understood the word.

He reached into an inner pocket in his jacket and pulled out a small square of paper. For a moment, he looked at it, then he held it out to me and I took it.

It was a daguerreotype. A picture in murky blacks and grays of a young woman as detailed and clear as if I were looking her right in the face. A boy in my hometown had told me once that such things existed:

pictures more perfect than anything a person could draw and made somehow with wood boxes and light. I'd called him a liar and a show-off, but here it was, exactly as he'd said. The young woman was pretty, with creamy skin and dark brows over intelligent, kind eyes.

"Johana," he said in a soft voice. "Johana. Ich wollte sie heiraten."

Knowing that I hadn't understood this, he clasped his ring finger and then put it to his heart.

"Aber . . ." he said, shaking his head sadly, "aber nein."

"Nein?" I said. No?

"Mein problem," he said, shaking his head and wiping the tears from his eyes roughly with the callused side of his hand. "Nein."

I sat there quietly, and as he often did, Paul seemed to forget my presence. Like one of the heavy packs he would drop from his shoulders after a long day's trek, he laid his head down and began to weep, and it occurred to me that he was out here in the wild mountains for reasons I didn't fully comprehend and he carried his own painful burdens that I didn't see. He'd taken care of me so well and in so many ways. He'd soothed me without me even realizing it. I wished I could care for him in some way, soothe him. I could not remember the words of any songs, and so I began to hum. It was a tune that Piroska used to hum, going about in her kitchen or beating the wash on the line. It had always calmed me, though until now I could not have brought myself to hum it for the pain of remembering.

Hesitantly, I reached my hand out. I was afraid. He cared deeply for this Johana; that was obvious. Perhaps he would not want comfort from me? But when I touched Paul's hand, he took it instantly into his own and clasped it.

Slowly and cautiously, like a forest animal sniffing the wind, I moved closer, lay myself down beside him. He lifted his blanket and drew me into his warmth. Nestled next to him, I put my cheek against his, feeling the rough bristles of his beard and his breath against the slope of my neck. In terror and despair, I lifted his face to mine, feeling his strong jaw beneath my fingers. I put my lips to his and felt the breaking, the capsizing of some part of myself; it slid away irretrievably, lost into him, never to be separate and safe again.

After that, we kept each other warm every night, and I drew often from his lips that precious and painful something that frightened me, but that I couldn't do without.

When he asked me next, "Warum isst du nicht mit mir?" Why don't you eat with me? I walked off into the woods and came back with a small furry creature in my hand.

I sat down before him.

"Mein problem," I said. "*Mein* problem."

Paul looked into my eyes and nodded softly.

I lifted the dead animal up toward my mouth and felt my hidden blood teeth move forward, knowing and ready. Holding Paul's gaze, I opened my mouth and let him see them. Then I gently punctured the skin of the animal and drank.

The shock in his eyes was faint, but I could see it nonetheless. I set the animal down and, frightened, so terribly scared of what he might say or do, felt the tears start down my face.

Paul reached out his hands, and with his strong, rough fingers, wiped the tears from my cheeks, then pulled me gently forward into his arms, where I lay weeping and listening to his song.

· XXII ·

HOW can I describe the room in which I now stand? Am I actually here, or has my unconscious, in its desperate craving, conjured this place as I sleep? No. It's real. I know because I can look down and see the bumps on my skin rising from the cold. I know because I can smell it.

It is, or was, an apartment in one of the abandoned tenement buildings I saw from the window of my car. The walls where they peek out from behind piles of rubbish—wood planks, a gutted dishwasher, salvaged and sagging shelving—are snaked with the jagged scars of ripped-out electrical wiring. A window is missing. The glass and frame are gone, and some of the wall surrounding it has been knocked out as if with a sledgehammer. A sheer red curtain is screwed into the wall and hangs over the hole; it moves in and out with the suction of the wind so that it looks like a glugging valve inside a beating heart. The floor is dark with grime, spent cigarettes, trash, and *hundreds* of paper towels crumpled up and splotched with blood.

Drops of blood can be seen spattered about on the floor. Also, there is a face on the ceiling. The face is nearly the size of the ceiling and belongs to the girl who brought me here, whose name, I learned as we were picking our way through the brambles and the dreary flooded courtyards to get to this place, is Dream. The face that belongs to Dream is painted on the ceiling in blood. There are long sheets of watercolor paper taped to the walls and to the wood planks, and on them are fig- ures and faces, most of them twisted and contorted as in pain, and all of them painted in blood. The room smells like a copper mine.

In one corner, a man—the artist, I presume—sits on a tattered gold armchair with a tourniquet cinched tightly around his intricately tattooed bicep. He is dressed all in white—white canvas pants like a sailor's, frayed white T-shirt, and there are smears and splotches of blood all over them. I wonder if he wears all white to make the appear- ance of the blood more shocking. If so, he has succeeded.

"Adam?" I ask once I have recovered from the disorientation of en- tering the room.

He laughs dryly.

"Sergio," he says, then selects a syringe from a collection of them that rest on a tray on a table beside him. Needle poised, he squints down at his forearm, searching for a vein or else for a patch of skin that has not been recently pierced and drawn from. It takes a second, but then he slides the needle in and the tube fills slowly.

I am left standing alone in the doorway, bewildered and hungry. Dream has thrown herself down on a flowered couch. Her arms cross over her head at the wrist and her nails fan out on the arm of the couch so that they look like a brightly colored tropical spider. On our way up to this place, she also informed me that she is the daughter of a dead supermodel—"You'd know the name if I told you," she'd said—a claim I received with some skepticism, but seeing her now, lounged on the couch with her long limbs draped disdainfully, it seems plausible.

I take a deep breath and move toward a painting hanging nearby: another portrait of Dream, but in this one she is laid out flat on a table, eyes closed and arms crossed over her chest as if being prepared for burial. A pink water lily is coming out of her mouth.

Music comes up through the floor, a sawing drone so loud I can feel its vibrations in the floorboards. On our way up to the third floor, we passed other rooms with people in them, more artists, perhaps, or va- grants or who knows what. We went by one room that was completely empty and completely dark save for a patch of moonlight coming through a window and a man sitting on a kitchen chair in the middle of the room, staring out the window and up at the moon. He didn't move. He didn't make a sound. He just sat there with his hands hanging down at his sides and his mouth slack. In another room, an artist was painting a female model wearing a wedding dress and a gas mask.

"You looking for Adam?" the man, Sergio, asks.

He has filled two vials with his own blood, capped them, and is now loosening the tourniquet. He looks up at me for the first time, and his eyes linger on my face, studying it.

"Yes," Dream interjects from where she lies on the couch. "She is, and I am too."

The man gets up from the chair. He staggers a bit and regains his footing, then walks over to a table strewn messily with art supplies: watercolor cups, tins full of brushes, gallon jugs of what looks like water, a dozen rolls of paper towels, and a roll of masking tape, which he picks up. He writes on the tape, tears a piece off, then another piece, and wraps one piece of tape around each vial of blood. He is dating the vials. He squats down, opens a cooler under the table, and puts the two vials inside. I see rows of caps inside the cooler. There must be twenty vials of blood in there.

He gets up, carrying a small toolbox, and crosses the room to Dream. With his fingers, he pushes up one of her eyelids and peers down at her eye. His wrist, I notice, is bound by a hospital bracelet. Dream bats his hand away.

"I'm ready," she says.

He kneels beside her, carefully opens the toolbox, removes and tears open an alcohol wipe, and like a Red Cross nurse begins prepping her arm to draw blood. I watch, hypnotized, barely able to believe what I'm seeing. I catch myself staring and turn back to the painting.

When he has finished labeling and storing Dream's blood, he walks over to where I'm studying a portrait of a bald man screaming as bloody tears run down from his clenched eyes. It is well done. This man is a shock artist, no doubt about it, but he's a talented one nonetheless. Still, right now I would prefer to tear the page from the board and eat it, paper and all, if I could. My mind has not left the cooler under the table. I can feel its presence like a fourth person in the room.

"When I painted him," the artist says, coming up close beside me, "he had just learned that his brother had put a gun in his mouth and pulled the trigger."

I glance at him.

"That scream"—he nods toward the painting—"it's completely real."

I study the painting again, the face clenched in agony. "Why do you do this? Why blood?"

"Because I'll never have children."

I turn to him and wait for him to go on. These delphic artists with their cryptic answers just begging to be begged to go on. It's kind of irritating, but I wait.

"These are my flesh and blood dispersed out into the world. They are me. My art *is me*. There is no barrier, no separation between the artist and the art. Or, in that case"—he nods again toward the painting in front of us—"the subject and the art; that one is painted in his blood. And that one"—he points across the room to a portrait of an eerily lifeless face with eyes closed—"in his brother's blood."

I study the portrait of the brother for a moment.

"But with no risk," I say after some contemplation.

"What do you mean?"

"You call these your children, propagations of you sent out into the world, but it's not quite the same, is it? These are safe children. No risk. You won't fear for them, hope for them, disappoint them, or be disappointed by them. No, artists are not parents. Close, perhaps, but not quite. Art isn't safe, but it's certainly safer than children."

"Are you a mother?"

"No," I say with a laugh. "I'm too cowardly."

"What is your name?"

"Collette."

"Well, Collette, allow me to introduce you to Adam."

He holds something out to me, a small pill resting in the palm of his hand.

"Ah," I say. "The door to heaven. I see."

He says nothing, just looks at me.

"Why do you call it Adam?"

"Its real name is methylenedioxymethamphetamine, or MDMA, but Adam has a more personable ring to it."

He moves his hand toward me, offering it again.

"Thank you, but no. Why were you in the hospital?" I ask, touching the hospital band on his wrist.

He laughs. "Hypovolemic shock."

"Hypovolemic. Low volume. *Blood loss?* Shock from blood loss?"

"It seems I've been a bit reckless in the gathering of my materials."

"How much were you taking?"

"Honestly, I don't know. As much as I needed."

"And an artist always needs as much as they can get. Mon Dieu, you're lucky you didn't shrivel up like a dried apricot."

He gives me a look—a gentle, lingering smile—that I haven't been given in a long time, but which I recognize instantly. I turn my gaze back to the painting.

"Are you an artist?" he asks.

"Yes."

"Medium?"

"Anything that makes a mark. Oils mostly. I confess, I've never considered blood. It would feel too wasteful to me, though."

"Ah, see, I look around at all the people just walking, riding the bus, standing in line at the post office, flipping each other off, and I think, what a waste of perfectly good blood?"

"Well, we're mostly agreed on that point."

He laughs. "May I paint you?"

He is giving me that look again. I glance over at Dream passed out on the couch. I glance toward the table where the cooler of blood rests in the shadows.

"Sure," I say with a shrug. "Why not?"

He has me sit on the floor, nested in a pile of blankets and crumpled newspapers like a chick in a nest. He is painting me in profile and with my own blood. He asked me and I said yes—*one vial*. It was a gamble, but two hours later, it pays off when he says he needs to pee. It'll be a few minutes, he says, because all the toilets on the lower floors are full.

He leaves, and I climb out of my nest. Watching Dream, who is tossing restlessly on the couch, I go to the cooler. I push back the lid and begin filling my hands with vials, then think better of it and just take the whole cooler. I should hurry, but the painting on the easel stops me. Watercolor paper taped sloppily to a wooden board, but it's a remarkable likeness, a beautiful portrait, truly. I put a finger to it delicately, draw it away, and then look down at the spot on my finger. The exquisite irony of the thing, my portrait painted in blood, as if all my life this painting was bound to be done.

It's a foolish thing to do, but I take it. I must have it. As he said, it is me. My image, my blood. I too will never have children. It's mine. I lean the board against the cooler and fumble quickly in my wallet for money. This artist, Sergio, is strong. He put himself in the hospital for his art. I don't pity him. He'll survive, but justice requires that I pay for his work. I throw a stack of bills down on his stool, take up the painting, and flee.

In the stairwell I hear him, a floor above me, talking with someone. I look up and see his hand on the railing, fingers ruddy with blood. I take the stairs steadily and quietly down, then outside, I run.

The night sky is rolling with clouds. The highway has cleared. I drive two miles before slowing and pulling onto the shoulder of the highway, and with the roving white beams of headlights passing rhythmically across the rearview mirror, I open the cooler, take out one of the vials, and throw it back. Then another and another. I tell myself to save the rest, then I drink them. When I'm done, I open the passenger window and, trying not to think of how my children would scold me for littering, I throw the whole cooler out. A bloody cooler is the last thing I need hanging about.

Forty minutes later, the road grows strange. Mice are darting across the country lanes. Not singly, thousands of them; they're dripping from the leaves of the trees like rain, their tails flailing as they fall. The moon is a white kite skimming low over the treetops, its string somehow fastened to the hood of my car, and there are children playing in the woods—I see their fingers at the edges of the tree trunks; their eyes peek around at me—though it is hours past their bedtime, somewhere between midnight and infinity.

My headlights wash suddenly over the strange, heart-shaped form of an animal in the road ahead of me. I slow as I approach and the moon, without wind resistance, plummets from the sky. I see ahead elaborately patterned feathers in a wing. A face turns over the shoulder toward me, wild black orb eyes and a dagger beak.

The saker sits in the road, ripping with enthusiastic violence at the innards of a mouse held in its claws.

"It's this way," she says, and lifts up into the air, red flesh still dangling from her talons. "Follow me."

Her wings flap slow. I follow her, to *it*, whatever it is. The moon soars fitfully back up into the sky.

· XXIII ·

A chill started to creep into the night air, and Paul and I knew that our clothing would soon be inadequate, so Paul began to consult a map, steering us slowly toward a town he saw on it. I had a phobia of towns and the people in them, and I made it known to Paul, but it was clear we would need supplies soon, so I followed where he led, full of dread and caution.

In the evenings, we huddled close together near the fire, and at night, we slept in his small canvas tent that shielded us from the wind and rain. We talked together more now in his language, which I could speak well enough, and he told me about all the unimaginable things that were now commonplace in the 1860s: cameras, and machines that did the sewing, and ships that used steam to move instead of wind, and even a wire that had been stretched across the ocean and somehow allowed the president of the United States to send a message instantly to the Queen of England.

Paul told me about his life before in his homeland, Austria, and how, growing up in his father's print shop, he'd exasperated his father by playing around with the inks and type forms to make pictures. He told me about the fits of shaking that had begun in adolescence, and how, when they seized him, he left his body behind and saw visions in the sky of bright angels and a divine emanation surrounding and passing through him and through everything. He told me about Johana, his love since childhood, and of how, when his fits of shaking became known to her family, their planned marriage was not permitted, and she'd been given to another man instead.

I listened and asked many questions, but I told Paul almost nothing of myself or my past. It was all accursed, and my name was still No one. When he asked questions, I changed the subject or simply went silent.

"I just want to *know* you," he'd pleaded once, close to frustration. "I *need* to know what's happened to you."

"But *I* need to forget," I'd answered, and then stalked off into the woods to be alone.

Paul had promised then not to ask me those questions anymore. He wanted to know, he said, and hoped I would tell him when I was ready, but he wouldn't ask.

But even though Paul stopped asking questions after that, I didn't forget. Memories and dreams of loss and violence chewed their way into my mind, like wintering mice, and I still sometimes thought I heard that sound like the flapping of a wild blaze.

"Do you hear that?" I asked once, sitting up in the dark, trembling.

"What is it? A bear?" Paul asked groggily, reaching for his knife.

"No. It sounds like fire."

"I banked the fire. It wasn't more than coals. We would see the light besides."

"I know. You're right. But do you hear a sound *like* that? Like . . . like . . . the whole forest is on fire?"

His answer had been no. Just as he and he alone experienced his fits of trembling and saw his heavenly visions, I was alone in hearing the sound of some great conflagration, rising up inexplicably out of the silence and then fading away back into it.

At night, by lamplight in the tent, Paul continued to write his letters that I understood now were to Johana, and I would fall asleep against his shoulder. Afterward, I would feel his hand against my cheek, stroking it gently as I dozed.

"You still love her," I said once when he was writing.

"Of course I still love her," he said. "If I did not still love her, it would mean that I had never loved her. Love—real love—cannot stop. It is one of the few things in this world that has no end."

He turned onto his side, toward me, and looked me in the eyes.

"If I did not still love her, it would mean that it was possible for me to someday no longer love you."

I felt a pain when he said this, like stabbing, inside my chest. My face flushed, and it felt hard to breathe.

"But that," he said, taking my hands in his, "is not possible."

He turned onto his back again and looked at the paper before him. "And because I am sure—*absolutely certain*—of her love for me, I can tell her about my happiness now, with you, and know that she will have only joy for me."

"You've written to her . . . about *me*?"

"Oh yes. Of course. When we were parted, she and I, her grief was as much for me as for herself. It was a good man that she married, and she knew she would have children and a warm home with him, but she feared that I would never have those things. For my part, I was certain of it, which just shows how wrong you can be."

He leaned his head toward me and kissed my forehead.

"I'm sure her life is full of happiness," he continued, "but I know that it would be fuller still if she knew of my joy, so I hasten to tell her. Look here."

He pointed to a line in the letter and read aloud:

"Such talent has my beautiful No one! She paints beside me, and her landscapes are so different from mine and yet still so true. It reminds me daily of all the many ways there are to see the world in front of you and to speak of it. It reminds me of my choices."

I smiled at his words, but I felt mostly shame. He did not know my real name; I'd still not told him, and now I'd made him sound foolish in a letter.

I turned over on my side and lay there in the dark, knowing that I should tell him. I should tell him everything—he deserved to love a real person with a name and a history like his own—and knowing also that I would not. I couldn't. Not with the god of endings out there, pacing in the dark, perhaps searching for me, perhaps dreaming hungrily of what he might take from me next. Anna and Anya, the two people I'd been, they'd lost everything in fire and horror and devastation. I couldn't risk it. I dare not breathe too heavily, step with too loud a footfall, attract attention by being anything more substantial than a ghost. If I were wise, I would care for nothing, possess nothing. My love for Paul, the way I treasured him in a hard, painful, frightening way, I knew was terrible folly. Already I was risking too much.

• • •

EVENTUALLY, WE CLIMBED OVER A ridge and found ourselves looking down at a small pocket amid the folds of the mountains. In the center of that pocket, a church steeple and the smoke of several chimneys rose from among dense pine and spruce trees. I was as close as I was willing to go, so Paul and I made camp a mile or two up from the nearest wisp of smoke, we put our paintings together in a single stack, and Paul took them up, along with his bundle of letters, and headed off to the town to sell the paintings and buy us warmer clothing and gear.

I sat there in our camp, alone for the first time since Paul had dragged me from the water. The wan white light of winter dropped down heavily from above the pines, and two woodpeckers, one near, one far, tapped their communications back and forth to each other across the distance.

I remembered the sound of the footsteps of the village men marching steadily through the trees toward Piroska's hut. A village like this one, with its sickles and sod blades and fire. What if they somehow discovered that I was here? What if they tortured Paul and got him to confess that he had taken up with a demon? *Tell us where she is! Lead us to her, so that we can slaughter you before her eyes and then light her like a candle that never burns down!* It was an irrational fear, but it still set me on edge, and made me anxious for Paul's return.

To pass the time, I set to work building a shelter for us to sleep in that night, something roomier and warmer than the simple canvas tent we usually slept in. I cut a few fallen logs to size with the axe, bundled and tied one end, and then, standing the bundle up, spread the logs at the other end to form the bones of a crude tepee as Paul had taught me. Then I set about gathering sticks and green boughs to cover the sides.

There were the usual sounds of movement in the woods as I worked. With my keen hearing, I could hear the claws of squirrels scrabbling up tree trunks eighty meters off, and so the forest was always full of sound, but then, at some point during my labors, it wasn't. One by one, the sounds dropped away. The squirrels that had been chasing each other across tree trunks and up into branches stopped their game, and the woodpeckers had ceased their communications. There was a series of squawks from a crow as it flew off, and then it wasn't heard from again.

In a kind of eerie silence, I finished the shelter, then I took out the book and pen and tried to draw in order not to think. It would work for a moment, and then I would look down and find the pen motionless in my hands, my mind having wandered again. There was the snap of a twig somewhere off to the left, and I wheeled my head around in that direction, breath held, waiting to see or hear something else, but there was nothing. I moved closer to the fire and put the wool blanket around my shoulders. I tried to breathe slowly, to restrain my fast-beating heart, my darting rabbit mind. I tried to calculate how long it would take Paul to complete his errand and return, where I could expect the light to be when he did.

I looked up from the fire and my heart jerked, startled by the formation of dry vines on a rock across the way, how face-like it looked. I tried not to see that dreaded face in my mind, the face that had been looking at me in the water—mud skin, black-shot eyes—I saw it all the same. Why had Vano ever told me of Czernobog? I wished that I'd never heard of him, never known of his existence or terrible power.

There was the sound of footsteps, so clear and undisguised that I looked up in hope that Paul had returned, though it was surely too soon.

"Paul?" I called, seeing no one. "Paul, is that you?"

I rose to my feet, the blanket falling back from my shoulders. My stomach was clenched with dread. I could not have been wrong in what I heard. The footsteps were clear and unmistakable. I stood motionless for a moment. Finally, I picked up Paul's hatchet, which lay on the other side of the fire, and with it I walked slowly, quietly into the woods.

The animals were hidden. Not a single bird on a branch. Nothing stirred.

"Is someone there?" I called unsteadily.

The answer came softly, and from somewhere directly in front of me, a small gentle sound: flapping, soft like a single flame wavering on a candlestick, but growing steadily louder until it approached the whipping noise of sheets hung on Piroska's line in a building storm—then surpassed it. It was the sound that sometimes woke me in the night and then kept me awake and listening, for hours. The skin of my face began to feel an inexplicable warmth that made me think of Vano and the way he had dripped sweat and flinched as if at the bite of invisible flames.

"*Czernobog?*" I hissed in a trembling whisper, daring to address him for the first time. "Is that you?"

The quiet but steady sound continued, and the heat on my face grew so that I took a step back. I turned my head this way and that, searching for some explanation, for the source of the heat and the sound, but there were only motionless trees and still gray rocks around me, yet somehow, despite what my eyes saw, my ears and skin told me that I was standing before some pillar or figure of invisible but billowing flame.

"What do you want from me?" I wailed in total despair. "*Why* do you *follow me?!*"

Then I saw before me, floating, turning in the air, a large flake of white ash drifting slowly, slowly down from the sky.

In terror, I lifted my hand to catch the drifting flake of ash, and it swirled with the perturbation of the air and then fell against my palm. Then, from among the trees somewhere behind it, something leaped forward at me suddenly, large and graceful as a dancer.

I cried out and swung the hatchet.

· XXIV ·

I'M running through snowy woods, or is it ash? I'm sweating and batting away the fine white flakes that swirl in front of my face and collect on my eyelashes. An indolent flapping like the beating of some enormous bird's wings moves along behind me, then beside me, then before me, patient, unhurried, hot. I run with terrible slowness. The moon looks down, a pale, pitiless face. Then suddenly there is the river. I fall into its wide black arms.

I wake facedown in water. My eyes open to open eyes. Mud face, gelatinous drifting moss, ink eyes. No expression. A face like eternity.

I scream and scream.

I wake up in my bed with a start and a sleep-strangled cry. Pain is radiating up into my wrists and forearms. In the half-light of morning, I lift my arms up, my hands hanging limp with pain. They look as though they, independent of the rest of my body, have been in a car wreck. They're brown with dirt and specked with grass. My nails, or what's left of them, are ragged and cracked and black with packed dirt and traces of blood. A small yellow leaf is glued with mud to the cleft between my thumb and pointer.

I sit up in panic, laying my dirty, aching hands in my lap like two shot doves and stare down at them in disbelieving horror. *Not again.*

What horrible thing have I done this time? I'm in yesterday's clothes, and there are streaks of dirt and grass at the foot of the bed. My shoes are still on and they're thickly caked with soil as well.

I undress and stumble into the shower, frightened and confused, and let the hot water massage my arms, watching the dirt slide away from my skin beneath the spray. The dirt makes the water swirl darkly around the drain, and blades of dried grass cling to the sides of the tub.

When the water stops running hot, I get out of the shower, bandage the worst of my injured fingers, and then dress gingerly. Buttons are difficult. What feels like an electrical storm is raging inside my skull, and the soft light of morning through the windows is painfully bright to my eyes; it makes me think of the questionable blood I consumed the night before. My memory of the night, beyond that point, is fragmented and bizarre: headlights on a dark country road, an erratic moon wheeling about the sky like a yo-yo, trees and grass and dirt. I do my best to scrub the muddy marks on the rug with a washcloth and pull the dirty sheets from my bed, though nothing is easy with my hands as they are.

When I go downstairs, the entire first floor is frigidly cold. Shivering, I go to the kitchen and find the back door that leads to the rear yard open and letting in an icy breeze. There are tracks, muddy shoe prints—my own, I can only presume—coming in from the door and running across the tile.

ALONE IN THE HOUSE, WITH days yet before the children return, the time passes like a slow fever dream or the agonizing detoxification of an addict. I try to work at the painting of the headstone, but my hunger is so acute and distracting and my mind so full of unease that I just end up pacing and puttering, and every mark I put on the canvas feels haphazard and off. I'm sure as I'm making it that I'll just need to undo it later. Every now and then, out the window, I catch sight of a cat. They appear singly, drifting aimlessly among the trees, scratching a raised back against the bark, meowing. I tried a few times to coax them into the house, but I may as well have been a wolverine. Immediately upon seeing me, the cat began hissing, turned, and fled. And who can blame them? Now I penitently put food on the back porch and leave them be.

In the absence of the cats, I'm forced to hunt. I spent probably twenty exhausting, ineffectual hours at it over the last three nights. I'm rusty. I've lost the knack for the job as well as the stomach. The first evening, I spent four, maybe five hours roaming miles of cold, hilly woods and caught nothing. Results the next night were better, but only barely: two squirrels and a rabbit, which were almost certainly a net caloric loss for all the scrambling and scrabbling I had to do to catch them. And, of course, wild animals I have to kill—I'm not about to try to feed from a rabbit while it's flopping about and kicking me in the head—but I couldn't help looking the softly furred, beautiful creature over and seeing it as my children would. As I drank, I could almost hear the children's high-pitched exclamations of dismay. *Why did you do that?* Audrey or Octavio would ask with wide-eyed horror. Because I *have to*, I insisted to the dead rabbit and to the accusing children in my mind. Because it's my nature. Because, like it or not, I'm a predator, a monster, and if it isn't this rabbit, my sweet, precious children, it's you as you lie sleeping soundly at your afternoon nap, lined up in your cots like so many dishes in a buffet line. What would you have me choose, children?

On top of that, the meal barely took even the edge off my hunger. By the next day, I was fully ravenous again. Then today, I was cleaning the bird cage in the conservatory, laying fresh newspaper and then filling Sargent, Turner, and Mona's little bird food cup with pellets, when Mona fluttered suddenly, shivering her tiny wings. In an instant of pure animal instinct, I grabbed her, and before I knew what I had done, she was in my mouth. I *chewed* her tiny body for God's sake, and her blood—what could she have yielded, an ounce or two?—ran down my throat before I spat the feathery pulp of her out in the garbage.

When the children return, spending hours hunting each night won't be an option, so tonight I'm trying something different. If I can't be trusted with my own domesticated animals and wild animals are too tricky, perhaps the solution lies in someone else's domesticated animals. I slip a small bottle of WD-40 into my pocket and bundle up. It's a two-mile walk to the Emersons' barn and it's cold out.

The shadows are deep in the woods between my property and the Emersons', and it's very quiet. Last week's snow has melted off and left only some dusty white rings around the bases of the trees, but they still call to mind my dream of fleeing something terrible and relentless through a forest of ash. I've had the dream twice now, and have twice woken up muddy and abused, with cracked, bleeding fingers and dirt tracked all through the house, the back door hanging open. There are a thousand questions—where am I going in the night? What am I doing? Why?—that I don't allow myself to ask. After what I did in the attic to my beloved pets, I'm not sure I could handle the answers. Fortunately, there's been no blood in evidence on me besides my own, a fact that I cling to for reassurance.

Here in these woods, making my way over rocks and tree roots and past the pliant arms of branches, I feel an uncharacteristic apprehension. My skin is tingling, I'm sweating at the neck and armpits, and I keep realizing that I'm holding my breath. I'm afraid, but it's ridiculous that I should feel so. I've spent a good portion of my life in the woods, much of that alone, so the idea of being scared should be laughable; the problem is, I don't feel like I'm alone. My dreams of being pursued through woods just like these ones, and Vano's pronouncements that Czernobog is near, it's all messing with my mind. There's too much overlap between dreaming and waking life; it's hard to know what's real, and that uncertainty gives the waking world a sinister, dissimulating feel. The moon above me, it's so pretty and bright—so like that pitiless moon face in my dreams that I can't be certain, even now, that it's real. What if I *am* dreaming, and the chase is just about to begin? An owl hoots somewhere nearby, but even that sound seems to stir some memory from a dream.

What if I'm going crazy? I wonder, momentarily aghast. What if there's a limit to how much a mind can hold without breaking under the load? If I were truly to go crazy, what would I do? Where would I go? In what padded cell or what institution would I live out my days, calling through the food slot in the door to the blank-eyed orderlies? *Please! You don't understand! I cannot eat this food! I need blood! Please, just a little. I'll wither to a husk unless I have blood! Someone, please, have mercy!*

With relief, I emerge from the wood into a cleared expanse of rolling hilly pasture. Trying to shake off the clinging sensation of having unseen company, I climb the low fence that keeps the Emersons' cows in. The barn will be a half mile south. I know my way around. I've been on the Emersons' property countless times, even in their barn.

They are an old and very kind couple, who have extended an open invitation to the school to visit any time. Each year, I bring the children to see the cows and help May Emerson milk them. Henry Emerson gives tractor rides out to the copse of fruit trees where we pick cherries in the spring.

They are such a generous couple. The kind who would give anything they could spare to anyone who had need. If the request were not so bizarre and alarming, they would probably even give me the blood of their cows. But, of course, it is bizarre and alarming, and it's their very generosity that fills me with misgiving. To be caught abusing the trust of generous people who have shown you great kindness is the most inexcusable betrayal of all. I'm so tired of finding myself in this position: wanting to do good—*be* good—but simply unable, forced instead to lie and deceive, sneak and steal.

The large building rises up in the dark ahead of me. The ground surrounding it is muddy, pocked with puddles that have collected the melted snow. The dark house is about a hundred yards away, silent and still.

I pull the bottle of WD-40 from my pocket and oil the hinges of the barn door before sliding them carefully open just wide enough to permit me through. It's warm inside. The smell of hay and manure and fur is sweet and reassuring. I remember watching Vano milk Piroska's cow. He would seem to have an entire whispered conversation with her before laying a hand on an udder. The goats that I kept in France come to mind as well, but less fondly; they were stupid, difficult creatures, always squirming and trying to get a taste of my hair as I fed from them.

I haven't made a sound, and the cows asleep in their stalls go on dreaming silently as well. I remove my coat, hat, and gloves so I can move more easily and quietly, and then go to the first stall. I oil the hinge, slide the latch, and go in. A large cow, caramel brown with cream-colored ears and legs, is curled on her side in the straw. Her pretty head rests on her delicately crossed front legs, and her large ears, thin and ovate like the leaves of a birch tree, are turned up. They twitch slightly as I creep across the straw to her. I get down on my hands and knees and nestle behind her. I don't dare kneel in front of her where her hoof-shod legs lie folded in against her belly. I'm not interested in a kick in the ribs should she wake. With a finger, I gently search out the strongest point of pulse on her neck and then I put my teeth where my finger was. There is an extra layer of hide and fat that take more work to pierce, but my teeth are adequate to the task. Her ear flicks, but she doesn't wake.

With my head nestled comfortably against the soft pillow of her shoulder, I drink, feeling at once tremendous relief at having found an abundant supply of blood that won't be missed, and also total ragged exhaustion at the sad state of my existence, the lengths I have to go to simply to survive.

AT HOME THE NEXT MORNING, I sleep well past the time I ordinarily would. My experiment the night before had gone off without a hitch, to my immense gratification, and I'd fallen asleep hopeful that drinking my fill from the cows before bedtime might help me sleep soundly and keep to my bed through the night. When I wake, though, I find that it hasn't. My hands are filthy and smeared with blackened blood. It hurts just to look at the ragged torn state of my fingernails, and there's a bloody, dirt-crusted gash on the sole of one mud-spattered foot. For a while, I just lie in my bed and cry.

Finally, though, with the sky out the windows a predawn purple, I get up and move numbly through what is becoming a grim routine of washing, bandaging, dressing, and then going downstairs to put things back in order down there. In the kitchen, I close the door that's wide open in spite of my having both locked and barricaded it the night before. I clean the muddy tracks from the floor and then sit, exhausted in every sense, at the kitchen table. In silent stupor, I watch a woodpecker, black-and-white spotted and with a red tuft at the back of his head, *tap-tap-tap* at a tree, then pause and listen before *tap-tap-tap*ping again. He flutters off finally, and the grounds beyond the window are still and solemn feeling. I'm paralyzed in the silence, trying to rouse myself to action, to do something, *anything*, other than sit here waiting for the next horror, or for the children to return and almost succeed at turning my thoughts away from myself and my increasingly unbearable life.

The tick of the kitchen clock asserts itself from the thick, suffocating quiet. The second hand stabs loudly, almost manically, as it approaches the twelve. Having noticed the sound of this clock, I become aware of the syncopated clicks and ticks of a half dozen clocks on the first floor. The sound is so like a heartbeat, the beat of the wolf's heart, Red Riding Hood's only distraction. Why do I have all these hellish clocks anyway?

Rummaging in a kitchen drawer, I find a screwdriver. I won't survive the next three days with all these clocks. I pull the kitchen stool over to the doorway and climb up. I'm just pulling the clock from the nail it hangs on when a riotously loud ring shatters the silence and nearly sends me off the stool. I recover my balance, but the clock slips from my hand and crashes to the floor. I jump down from the stool, grab the phone from its cradle, and answer as I stoop to pick up the clock.

"Hello?"

"Hello, is this Madame LeSange? Or should I say Ms. Collette? Gosh, I always get all confused about what to call teachers."

"It is," I say, beginning to recognize the warm, effusive voice on the other end of the line.

"This is Katherine Hardman," she says, confirming my guess. "Leo's mother."

"Katherine, how are you? How's Leo?"

"Good, good, we're all very good. How has your holiday been? Have you been enjoying the time to yourself without all our little monsters chattering and clinging to you?"

"The holiday has been . . ." I search for a positive adjective. "Quiet. You may not believe this, but I actually miss those little monsters terribly when they're not here, and I very much look forward to their chattering and clinging."

"My God, you are a saint. Well, once you hear why I'm calling, you might regret saying that," she says with a laugh.

"Oh?"

"Well, absolutely no pressure whatsoever, but Dave and I managed to get an appointment with a really highly recommended marriage therapist in the city today—they had a cancellation and we were on a wait list—but since we let Valeria go . . . we don't have anyone to watch Leo. It might be totally inappropriate for me to even ask you, and if so please tell me, but I just thought I would give it a shot and see . . . if you weren't busy . . ."

I glance at the clock and screwdriver laid out before me on the kitchen counter. A long crack now runs across the face of the clock that wouldn't be there if I were very busy.

"You'd like me to watch Leo while you go to your appointment?"

"I know it's a long shot, but I just thought I would see . . . I know Leo would love to see you too."

It *is* a strange request, and some part of me recognizes a subtle breach of propriety. Perhaps I should say no, and yet all of me leaps up desperately to say yes. A person long stranded on an island would not welcome the sight of a ship on the horizon as much as I welcome the thought of a day spent with Leo instead of alone in my quiet, empty, unnerving house.

"Yes, I should be able do that."

She lets out a great breath in relief. "Oh, I would be so grateful. And Leo will be so excited! You are his absolute favorite person in the world. And we would pay you, of course."

"Please do not think of it. It would be my pleasure. When should I arrive?"

· XXV ·

PAUL'S footsteps did not frighten me when he returned, trudging heavily through the darkened woods. I knew them from a great distance. He stepped into the perimeter of firelight, his arms heavy with bundles and a new pair of snowshoes on his back.

"Ahh, it smells good," he said. I had built a fire and had meat roasting over it for him. "I am very hungry."

"You were long," I said.

"Were you worried? I'm sorry." He began setting things down and sorting through them. "It took many hours to sell enough paintings. But they did sell. Very well. Your picture of the birch alone took enough for these snowshoes, which you'll be glad to have soon enough."

He carried my new things around the fire to me.

"A sweater of thick wool. *Very nice*. Here, put it on now."

He knelt beside me with the wool garment in his hands, then he saw me up close in the firelight, a bloody gash in my arm, my shirt torn.

He threw the things in his hands down in alarm and knelt before me, taking my face in his hands.

"What happened to you?" he cried. "What happened?"

I turned and looked over into the shadows behind me. He followed my gaze, and when he saw the wolf carcass gutted and skinned and stretched out in the grass, he started in fright and then looked back at me, horrified.

"This animal attacked you?"

I nodded.

He took my head in his hands and turned my face this way and that, examining my wounds in the firelight.

"Is that all? Are you hurt anywhere else?"

I showed him the bloody tear in the side of my shirt, and the deep gouge beneath it.

"I'm so sorry!" he exclaimed over and over again.

"I'm fine," I said, "really, I'm fine. Nothing is that bad, and it will all be better soon."

"No, no. I feel terrible. I should not have left you alone."

I gave him a look, just a small smile, and he turned again to the wolf. Its eyes were glassy, its mouth frozen in a murderous snarl. A bloody hatchet wound had cracked its skull and a cut of its meat was sizzling on the fire and making the air fragrant. He put his hands on his thighs and laughed.

"What am I saying? I only pray that you are there if ever I am attacked by such a creature."

WE LAYERED ON THE WARMER things that Paul had bought over those things we already had. Then Paul ate his dinner of wolf, while I scraped the animal's hide, which would be very useful as a warm blanket.

Paul sat quietly, and his face, when he didn't know I was looking, appeared dark and bothered. I wondered whether he was still troubled by the attack, or if we'd not made enough money from our paintings after all.

"What is it?" I asked.

He looked up at me but didn't answer.

"You seem troubled," I said.

"It's nothing," he said, and tossed a tiny pine cone into the fire. "Just. Unkindness."

"Unkindness? What do you mean?"

He let out a deep sigh.

"I am a Jude. Do you know what I mean by this?"

"Jude?"

"A son of Abraham. An Israelite."

"Ahh, yes. Yes."

"This, it would seem, is a terrible thing to be."

"Why?" I asked, though hearing him say this had conjured vague memories from my childhood days in my hometown of some sense of ill repute associated with Jews, though I could not remember what it was if I had ever known.

He shook his head and frowned. "I do not know."

"Did something happen? Did someone . . ."

He nodded. "Some men came to where I was selling our paintings. They looked at me. They asked me my name. I told them. They asked if I was Jewish. I said yes, and they told me to pack up. They said that their town was not a town that had any interest in Jewish paintings."

"What did you do?"

He shrugged.

"I packed up. It didn't matter. I had sold almost all of our paintings by that time anyhow. I guess *someone* was interested in Jewish paintings, eh?"

"That's horrible. Why would they do that?"

"I don't know. But it was the same back home in Salzburg. We used to say that you cannot be received by both God and men. To know God and be known by him is to be reviled by men. It was just something to make us feel better, I always thought. But I sometimes wonder now if it is true.

"When the quaking seizes me . . . I tell you, *I see* God. God shows me things and he calls to me. The world is full of beauty, but in all the world there is no beauty like the beauty he shows me. It is like I become *one* with everything, and everything becomes one with him. And yet, it is because of this that I have been despised, cast out. I have had my life in community taken from me. It *has* begun to seem that the holiest places are at the end of the most difficult paths, and that union with God is very costly."

"It seems to me that you're lucky," I said quietly. "Your exile has been compensated for with ecstatic visions—union with God. What consolation is there for one who is despised by men and God alike?"

He scooted closer to me, took me in his arms.

"They aren't just for me, you know—the visions. I see, *on occasion*, what is always there is always true. It's all there right now: this world the lower branches of a beautiful, fruiting tree, and the perfect glory of God filtering down through the branches, radiant creatures filling the air, everything singing with joy, and all of it pulling us up, me and you, into love."

He laughed softly, threw a twig into the fire. "I used to never speak of it. I knew it made me sound like a madman. But then, it stopped mattering. People thought I was mad no matter what, so I stopped hiding it. I began just to offer it, to say 'the glory and the love that surrounds you, that you breathe in with every breath, it's there, if you want it.' What I see is yours as much as it is mine—if you want it."

He looked at me and smiled. "But *you*—now you've upended my entire theology. I have my God, I have my painting, I have my love, I have the world. It's too much goodness!"

He threw his hands up merrily. "I'm not paying nearly enough for God. I must be doing something wrong."

I leaned back against him, his chin resting on my head, his arms and scent of wool and pine around me. In the tent that night, under our new, warm blankets, we clung to each other, and I kissed him as he ran his hands joyfully over the strange body he seemed to love in spite of its strangeness. Later, when he was asleep, I turned to him.

"Anna," I whispered so faintly that he might not have heard me even if he'd been awake, "it is Anna you love; Anna who loves you."

If Paul heard me, it was as in a dream, but I spent a fitful night afraid of what other ears might have caught my words, wolfish ears pricked up suddenly. How far might the hearing of a god stretch? Was Czernobog— the only god who cared for me—galloping toward us already, circling in on our camp? I woke many times in the night, certain that I heard his approach, padded feet scampering in the dark, preparing to pounce and take what I had dared to assert as mine. I lost sleep in vain, though;

he did not strike that night, and I should have known that he would not. The god of endings does not come when he's expected; he prefers to take by surprise.

For instance: a bright day in winter, unexpectedly warm, just after a tremendous snowfall. Paul and I, with snowshoes fastened to our feet, pushing our way up, laughing and panting, to the highest point we could reach. On a high rocky ledge, looking out over the great white snowy bowl of the world rimmed with ragged clouds and the sky rose pink beyond, Paul took my mittened hand in his.

"All of this, *ours*," he said, sweeping an arm out across the view. "Can you imagine? We must be kings and queens."

He breathed deeply, triumphantly; smiling, he surveyed his kingdom, the most benevolent king who ever lived.

I tried to be like him—I was *always* trying to be like him. I took a deep breath slowly. I looked down at the world and smiled.

I sniffed. "Think there might be someone out here," I said. "I smell smoke."

He made no answer, and I turned.

Paul was staring ahead blindly into the sky, his mouth agape, awe-struck and overcome by the sight of all the bright angels of God ascending and descending on their gleaming stairs. He fell to the ground, quaking with the uncontainable glory of it all, and I fell beside him.

Eventually, many hours later, I got up again. Paul never did.

Midsentence, midembrace, at the height of your hopes: that, you see, is when the god of endings likes to do it.

· XXVI ·

I pull up to the Hardmans' house at eleven and park on the street. When I went to get into my car this morning, I had discovered a cracked head-light and beside it a fresh and sizable dent in the front fender. I have no idea what from. The tale of Dr. Jekyll and Mr. Hyde comes to mind: a single man split in two, upstanding citizen by day, fiendish hell-sprung monster by night. Is that me? Running wild, getting in accidents, who knows what else?

I step out of my car at the Hardmans', and as I do, I see movement from the corner of my eye, a black figure rushing toward me. I turn. In the side yard of the house neighboring the Hardmans', a large German shepherd—what did Leo say his name was?—has leaped up, two paws against the fence, to bark savagely at me.

I turn and look the dog directly in the eyes. I'm the alpha, and if there is any instinct in the creature to submit, he will turn heel and slink away. For a moment, we study each other. I look into him and he looks into me. Neither of us like what we see. There is no instinct for submission in this dog. He wants to kill me. On principle. He goes on barking defiantly. I move on, thinking again how fortunate it is that this dog doesn't belong to the Hardmans.

In the daylight, the house looks larger. It's very modern, all smooth-planed angles dashed with skylights. The roof slants sharply downward like a ski jump, and from the long window that runs down beside the length of the front door, I can see all the way through a sunken living room and out a wall of sliding glass doors to the backyard.

When I ring the doorbell, I see Leo scamper over to open the door. The knob turns, the lock clicks, the knob turns again as he struggles with it, then it finally opens and his small, darkly mopped head peeks out.

"Te voilà!" I say, smiling at him.

He grins and runs into my arms.

"Mon beau. I'm so glad to see you. I don't think I could have made it all the way to Monday."

He smiles up from where he's nestled against my side.

The inside of the house is cavernous and sunny with tree-filtered sunlight pouring in through the two skylights and the sliding glass doors. The living room is well furnished but sparse, decorated in beiges and flinty metal grays, and it sinks down two carpeted steps even as the steeply vaulted ceiling soars high above it. A spindly floating staircase descends into the middle of the room. It's all so vast and airy that it almost feels as if you could float away in it.

"How are your drawings coming along? Have you been doing them as I asked?"

Leo nods vigorously. "Yeah. I did seven already."

With effort, he works to hold up seven fingers.

"Seven? That's more than I even asked you to do! You must show me."

"Hello!" Katherine calls down from the second-floor landing.

The last time I saw Katherine, she could have only been described as a mess, but today she looks like she's just stepped out of a print ad. She wears an elegant champagne-colored silk blouse and dark slacks, and as she comes down the stairs, she's fastening a string of small pearls around her neck. Her big green-and-brown-mottled eyes, which were expressive even on pain meds and just up from a nap, are perfectly made up and sparkling.

"I really can't thank you enough for this," she says, tilting her head as she draws up beside me in the entryway.

Up close, I'm always struck by some quality of bone-china fragility that Katherine has to her, like a small, fine, delicately painted teacup. The center of her chest just above the neckline of her shirt is concave, the bones of her clavicles knobby and pronounced, and thin strands of threadlike blue vein run close under the surface of the skin beneath her eyes. She is an elegant assemblage of bones.

"Honestly, I was getting a little stir-crazy at home, so I'm very happy to help. Though, I must say"—I turn to Leo and shake my head sadly—"it would be much easier if this petit garçon were better behaved."

Leo looks up at me and grins.

"Are you joking?" he asks, a dimple appearing in one cheek.

"Of course I'm not joking. Tu es un fripon! Un coquin! Nothing but trouble for me all day long." I turn my nose up in mock disdain.

"You're joking!" he shouts, laughing and tugging at my arm.

"Yes, of course, I'm only joking. If you were a doughnut, I'd gladly take a dozen."

I glance over and find Katherine gazing at Leo with an odd focus, almost as if she were a stranger observing some unknown child at a park. She snaps from her thoughts and turns to me.

"I'm not entirely sure how long we'll be. We have the drive to the city, the drive back, the appointment itself is an hour. Is there a certain time you need us back by?"

"I have nothing else planned for the day, so take as long as you'd like. In fact, I was wondering if I might have your permission to take Leo to the Neuberger Museum. It's not far, just up by the college. A twenty-minute drive or so. It's a small collection, but quite good, and I thought this budding artist would enjoy it."

"That sounds fabulous. I'm jealous. I wish I could go. Let me just get you the spare key and some cash for lunch."

She goes into the kitchen, her heels noisy against the tile, and returns with a key and two folded twenties.

"In case it costs anything to get into the museum," she says.

"Leo, get your coat," Katherine and I say at once.

• • •

AN SHORT WHILE LATER, LEO and I arrive at the museum. The Neuberger is generally a tranquil place, but today, perhaps because of the holiday, it is especially subdued.

The building is a low gray concrete slab surrounded by thin, leafless poplars. Why Americans insist on housing beautiful works of art in such belligerently drab buildings, I'll never understand, but I'm glad that modernism hit France only after its architectural style was already firmly established and enshrined in law.

On our way in, a nylon banner advertising a temporary exhibit— artists and their unsung siblings—is rippling in the wind on the sidewalk. We enter the building and stop just inside to take off hats and coats.

"Now Leo," I say to him, "it isn't altogether fair, but because you're a kid, the people working here might worry that you are going to touch or break something, so when we walk through the galleries, we should fold our arms behind our backs, like this."

I turn to show him my arms crisscrossed behind my waist. He crosses his in imitation.

"Then the gallery attendants will look at you and think, *my goodness*, what a very grown-up and well-behaved little boy, which, of course, you are."

And so we go, walking like strange birds through the galleries with our arms folded behind our backs.

"Going to a museum is just like a treasure hunt," I tell him as we enter the first gallery: American 1750–1900. "We go room to room and spy out the most beautiful treasures. Do you see any pictures you like in here?"

"That one!"

The gallery attendant, a Black woman in the signature maroon blazer, smiles at Leo's enthusiasm from her post beside a Winslow Homer.

It is a William Merritt Chase that's captured his attention, a plate draped with two beautiful, shining fish. The fish in front has the sallow luminescent cream color of candle wax. The one behind is silvery gray with scales that shimmer like sunlight across the ocean.

"William Merritt Chase," I say approvingly, "you've picked an excellent one, Leo. I've always been of the opinion that he never quite got his due. What do you like about it?"

"It looks like real fish!"

"How very astute."

We study the painting in silence for a moment.

"What's ass-toot?"

From behind us, I hear the gallery attendant snort.

"A*stute*. It means perceptive—good at noticing the really important things. It's one of the best qualities a person can have, if you ask me."

We go on hunting from room to room, searching for treasures. In the Dutch Still Life gallery, he picks out a painting of hunting dogs, and another of fruit: peaches dripping juice, oranges with bright stippled rinds, fat dark grapes and luminescent green ones spilling out of a glinting glass bowl.

"Now, I'm your painting teacher," I say, pausing at the still life of fruit, "and so I think we must have at least one small painting lesson for my young artist. Look at this picture. Extraordinary, isn't it?"

Leo nods with enthusiasm.

"The drawing is perfect, perspective, proportions—all flawless, but do you know what makes it truly incredible?"

"*What?*"

"It's the range of light and dark. And by range, I mean that the darkest points are *very dark*, and the lightest points are *very light*. Look at those grapes—so black you can barely see them, and the shadows under and around the bowl—extremely dark, the depths of the abyss. And then look at that glint of light on the rim of the glass, one single speck of the purest, brightest white you've ever seen. And it's the *contrast* between them, the difference, you see, that makes this painting so *dramatic* and so beautiful.

"What's more, you'll notice that there is much more darkness in the picture than light, but the darkness has the effect of pointing to, in a sense *exalting*, the light. It almost seems to make our eyes hunger for it."

I pause for a moment, studying the painting, awestruck by its dark, hideous depths and bright pinnacles.

"This is an important lesson for an artist like yourself. Does it make sense, Leo? What I'm saying?"

"*Sort of*," Leo says, squinting up at the picture as if distrustful, "but not really."

I laugh.

"Perhaps I've not explained it well. Make your darks as dark as you can, and your lights as light as you can. If a picture is all dark or all light or all just sort of in between, it will be . . . *blah*. Does that make sense?"

"Oh yeah, that makes sense," he says, and then does a slow-motion pantomiming walk to another painting.

"Liiiike thiiiiis oooone?" he asks, his speech now in slow motion as well. "This one is kind of like you said, kind of in between and blah."

At the "blah," he folds forward, arms hanging limply.

He is hopelessly silly, but he is right. The painting before him is too uniformly light, pale grapes and peaches against a yellow wall—a rare blunder for the Dutch. The absence of any significant darkness makes the light indistinguishable. The painting is bland and forgettable.

"You clever boy. I do believe you've got it."

WE COME NEXT TO THE room where the visiting exhibit is on display. Leo is so dazzled by *Wheat Field with Cyrpesses* that he runs up to the painting, and the gallery attendant, this time a white-haired gentleman, clears his throat and shoots me a stern look.

"Walk, Leo. We must walk, my sweet."

I come up beside him and regard the van Gogh.

"This is my *most* favorite picture."

"Mon petit artiste, you have excellent taste. This is a painting by Vincent van Gogh, one of the greatest artists who ever lived. Tell me what you like about it?"

"I don't know." He shrugs. "I just like it."

"As good a reason as any, I'd say."

"The clouds are all swirly-whirly."

He swirls his hands in front of him to illustrate his point.

"Yes, I like that too."

Next to the painting is a display of items under glass, and among sketches, letters, and journal pages covered in van Gogh's tight scrawl are two photographs set side by side. They are old black-and-white portraits of two teenage boys with thick, wavy hair, prominent brows, and sulky-looking mouths. Vincent and his older brother, Theo.

"Look, Leo, here is a photograph of Vincent van Gogh, the artist who painted that picture."

Leo joins me at the display, and I point down at the photograph on the left.

"Who's that?" he asks, pointing to the other picture on the right.

"That's Vincent van Gogh's older brother, Theo."

"His brother?"

"Yes, his brother."

"Bincim Vango had a brother?"

"Vincent van Gogh. Yes, he had a brother. That's him right there."

"Did Vincim van Gogh's brother die?"

I glance over at him.

"Well, yes. Eventually, he did. They both did. They both lived and died before you were born."

"In the water?"

"What?"

"Did his brother die in the water?"

"What do you mean? Like, *drowned*? No, I don't believe he died in water. Why do you ask that?"

He shrugs. I get down on one knee so that I'm at his height. I go on looking at the picture beneath the glass, trying to act nonchalant. Children, I find, are often more comfortable talking when they're not being looked at directly.

"Do you know someone who died in the water?" I try to ask this as casually as possible.

Beside me, I see him nod his head softly.

"Who?"

He is quiet for a moment, and I turn to him. He is sucking his bottom lip and contemplating. He leans toward me suddenly, cups his hand to my ear, and whispers, "Max."

· · ·

AFTER AN HOUR OR SO of walking the quiet galleries of the museum, Leo begins to get squirrelly, so I buy him a smoked salmon sandwich with cream cheese from the museum café, and we put on our hats and coats and take the food outside to eat on the benches. It's crisp and lightly windy, but there won't be many more days this mild before the consistent bitter cold of winter sets in.

My head is as swirly-whirly as those van Gogh clouds. I'm not sure what to make of what Leo said back in the gallery, but I don't want to press him. He is suddenly happy and silly, climbing all over the benches, balancing on the short curb that lines the sidewalk, and telling me knock-knock jokes that make no sense.

"Knock-knock," he says as I unwrap the cellophane around his sandwich.

"Who's there?"

He looks around, casting about for an answer.

"Museum."

This is not our first time through this stand-up routine, and I know approximately how this joke will end, but I oblige: "Museum who?"

"Museum-booseum!" he exclaims, and dissolves into giggles.

"*Ah! C'est drole!* Je ris si fort qu'il fait mal!"

I pretend to laugh and hold my sides as if in pain. He hops down from the curb and starts to cough. It's a shallow, easy cough, though, not his usual phlegm-filled, racking cough, and I realize that he has been a little healthier lately.

When he finishes coughing, I pat the bench beside me and he plops down. I hand him his unwrapped sandwich, and he takes a bite. As he eats, he bounces his bottom on the bench seat over and over. I do not think I have ever seen him this cheerful and energetic.

"Tu aimes le sandwich?"

"Oui," he says, bouncing and chewing. He picks out a bit of the pale pink fish and holds it up to me.

"What's that?"

"C'est saumon fumé. Smoked salmon. Do you like it?"

"Yeah," he says, and pops it into his mouth.

"Did you enjoy the museum?"

He nods vigorously, his eyes going wide.

"Good. I'm *so* glad. You were a wonderful little museum companion."

"Yes. I was," he says, and I laugh.

"Maybe someday *you* will have one of your paintings in a museum, and people will come from all over the world to see it."

"Yes!" he exclaims, bouncing. "And my brother too. People will come see my brother."

"Your *brother*?" My tone is light and silly. "Who's your brother?"

"Max!"

"But I thought Max was your giraffe?"

"Well, he's my giraffe now, but before he was my brother."

I pick a tiny piece of salmon out of his sandwich. "May I?"

"Sure," he says.

I hold the salmon to my nose and breathe in the smoky salt smell.

"So, was it your brother, Max, who died in the water, then?"

He takes a bite, nods, and then turns to me with a finger to his lips.

"Shhhh!" he hisses. "We don't say that."

An ache of sadness trills through my body. It rings down my arms and through my fingers. Tears prick at my eyes, and it takes work to blink them away. Leo is not wallowing in grief, however; he is eating his sandwich again and bouncing, but I feel shattered on his behalf, bereft and heartbroken. I feel like I should say something. There is something that he needs to hear from a responsible, caring adult like myself, but what is it? *Yes, Leo, the world is a miserable, hard place, be thankful you only have to spend eighty or so years in it?* Or, *don't expect much from life besides sorrow and pain and you won't be disappointed?*

These cynical perspectives are not what he needs. What he needs is the same thing I need, which of course I wouldn't need if I knew what it was, so instead of anything helpful, I say, "Oh, I'm sorry. I didn't realize."

I look at the trees, the sunlight sparkling through them as it shifts with the motion of the bare tossing branches. The few remaining leaves that cling to the branches are recklessly flame-colored. The fallen leaves have collected on the ground and in twin ponds cut out of the pavement, where they form colorful tessellations across the surface of the water.

How tactless of the day to be so beautiful. How dare nature go on innocently insisting on the world's loveliness, even as Leo and I speak of what may be a dead brother? It's not lovely. It's certainly not innocent. It's just a spinning orb of pain, where the most vulnerable suffer most of all. It's too despicable. I'm swept by a familiar feeling of disgust. I'm so tired of this place; I don't want to live here anymore.

"Can I give you a hug, Leo?" I ask.

He nods, and I put an arm around him and lean my chin against the side of his head. He burrows against me, a bite of sandwich still working in his mouth, and sighs a deep, contented sigh.

"I love you," he says, his head tilted against my shoulder. His words take me by complete surprise, and for a moment I cannot find my footing amid the mixed emotions—happiness, sadness, alarm—that they inspire.

"You're so sweet, Leo," I say, smoothing a wild lock of his hair with my fingers. "I—I love you too."

And then there is that dread again, the same strange despair that overwhelmed me as I held Octavio's baby sister—some deep, unnameable fear.

THE FIRST BLUE BLUSH OF dusk is settling when we return to Leo's house. The dog next door rushes the fence again to begin his incensed barking. It frightens Leo, and he presses himself against my side as we walk past. Katherine's beige Saab is in the drive, but Dave's silver car is not. No lights are on. I knock, and when there is no answer, I unlock the door with the spare key, and we go in. Beyond the sliding glass doors, the tall, thin birches in the backyard are ghostly in the fading light.

Katherine's purse and keys are sitting on the kitchen table, but where is she? I'm not sure what to do. I go with Leo up to his room so that he can show me his drawings. His room is sparse as well. There is a bed with dinosaur blankets, though I have never heard Leo express the slightest interest in dinosaurs, a small bookcase with four or five books on the shelves, and a low table beside a window with Leo's art supplies strewn across it. Cardboard boxes are stacked in one corner of the room.

"Leo, how long have you lived in this house?"

"I don't know," he says, pushing aside crayons and coloring book pages from where they lie on the table. "I think maybe ninety-nine days or something."

I laugh. "Hmm, let's try again. When you moved into this house, was it in the fall when the leaves were changing colors, or the summer when it's hot, or spring?"

"I think it was in the summer."

He pulls loose pages out of a large sketchbook and spreads them across his table.

"One, two, three, four, five," he counts them, jabbing a finger in the air toward each, "six, seven. See?" he says.

I come over and take a seat in the low chair beside the table. I lift each drawing one by one and study them carefully. One is of the trees seen through the sliding doors in the living room. The trunks are patched with peeling scaly bark. Another is a pencil drawing of his bed. He has drawn the rumpled folds of the bedding and the shadows nesting among them in abundant detail. There is a shoe, laces looping down on the sides; a potted dumb cane with its bladelike leaves pale in the middle and dark along the edges. He has drawn ordinary things, just as I instructed him, but they are extraordinary.

"My goodness, Leo," I whisper, "*my goodness.*"

He is standing beside me, looking breathlessly back and forth from the pictures to my face.

"Look!" he says, pulling the pages from my hands and flipping until he finds the one he wants, a drawing of a cluster of grapes with tiny paisley-shaped drops of condensation running down their sides.

"Just like we saw at the museum-booseum!"

He laughs at his own joke, hands the drawings back to me, and does a silly twirl with his arms warbling up and down so that he looks something like a nauseating carnival ride.

"Well, I think you take the prize for the silliest artistic genius the world's ever seen."

"What's genius?"

"It means someone who is extraordinarily gifted at something."

"Gift? Like for my birthday?"

"No, gifted as in extremely good at something."

"*I?*" he asks, putting a hand to his chest in a gesture of disbelief that I find comical. "*I am?*"

"You are certainly gifted at drawing and painting. *Genius?* Well, it will take time to tell, but maybe. You very well may be."

His mouth is open wide in a ridiculous expression somewhere between surprise and alarm.

"Oui, mon pitre, but don't let it go to your head," I admonish.

In response, he does a cartwheel off the side of his bed.

I leave Leo in his room for a minute and tiptoe down the hall to Katherine's room. The door is open and inside the room deep blue evening light is coming through a sliding glass door. A large bed is strewn with craggy heaps of white bedding, and peeking out from amid the bedding, ribbons of Katherine's black hair are spread across a pillow.

I back out of the doorway and return to Leo's room, where I sit beside him at his little table, watching him draw and pondering the situation. I have nowhere to be and the thought of returning to my house and its silence is not at all appealing, but it feels awkward to be here while Katherine is sleeping in the other room.

An hour, maybe more, goes by, and I'm just glancing at my watch, thinking that I will either need to make Leo dinner or go wake Katherine up, when there is a light rap at Leo's door.

We both look up and Katherine is there in the same outfit as earlier but with a few more wrinkles than before and a large wool sweater draped over her shoulders. Her hair is slightly crumpled on one side.

"My goodness, I slept longer than I meant to. Have you two been here long?"

"No, not too long," I say, and depending on what scale of time you're using, this is true.

"I'm getting hungry, Mama," Leo says.

From the doorway, Katherine raises an eyebrow at him.

He smiles and groans, and says, "*Katherine.*"

"Let's go get you something to eat then," Katherine says.

Leo jumps up and runs out of the room, headed for the stairs and the kitchen.

"He calls you Katherine," I say, walking with her out to the landing and then following her down the stairs.

"Yeah. It's a funny thing, I know. I always hated 'Mama,' even before I had children. I would hear some kid in a grocery store say 'Mama' and a shiver would go up my spine. I don't know, just too babyish or saccharine or something. And then, sure enough, I have a kid and what does he end up calling me? Mama. Well, one day, I was just like, *no, enough*. You can call me Mom; Mommy's kind of on the line, but fine, whatever. But he said, kind of as a joke, Katherine, and I was like, well, that's my name, why not?"

In the kitchen, Katherine opens a cupboard and takes out a box of Ritz crackers for Leo, who is filling a cup with water from the sink. I take up my purse from where it rests on a chair. Katherine turns and sees me holding my purse.

"You sure you don't want to stay?" she asks. "Have something to eat? I can't thank you enough for hanging out with this one today. I forgot to ask, how was the museum?"

"It was great!" Leo chimes from behind a very full cup of water that he is walking slowly to the table.

"And how was he?" Katherine asks, nodding toward Leo.

"He was wonderful, as always. And I appreciate the offer, but I should be going."

"I'll walk you out," Katherine says, setting the crackers on the table before Leo and then pulling a pack of cigarettes and a lighter from her purse before following me toward the front door.

"I'm really sorry about the nap," she says. "I wasn't planning it, but I got home and the house was so quiet and I felt *totally* wiped out after our appointment. I hope I didn't keep you here too long."

"No, it was no problem at all," I say, taking my coat from the coat closet and putting it on. "Did it go all right?" I ask cautiously. "The appointment?"

I don't want to intrude, as much for my sake as hers, but I do want a sense of whether Leo's home life might improve, however slowly.

Katherine glances in the direction of the kitchen, where we've left Leo with his snack. She opens the front door and we step outside.

"It was . . . *okay*," she says, pulling a cigarette from the pack. "I'm sorry, do you mind?" She gestures to the cigarette.

"No, go ahead."

"I'm down to one a day," she says from around the cigarette as she holds it in her mouth and lights it. She blows the smoke carefully in the opposite direction from where I stand. "But that *one* will be damned if it's going to let me go without a fight."

She takes another drag. "The therapist was good, *I think*?" she says through the exhaled smoke. "It's hard, though . . . finding the right level of . . ."

She searches for the word. "*Transparency*. You know, I want the therapist to know enough to be helpful, but I don't necessarily want to say too much, and then Dave feels like I'm putting all his dirty laundry out there or something, and then he doesn't want to go anymore, and we're right back where we started."

"Ah, yes. That makes sense."

"He's a very private person, and he likes me to keep things private too, especially if it concerns him. Now me, on the other hand, I'm more of an open book. It's kind of my nature to be more forthcoming, which is why it's so nice to have someone like you to talk to. So, you know, all that to say, it's a bit of a balancing act. We'll see how it goes. But I'm really so grateful to you for giving up your day and helping to make it happen. Hopefully we can find a good, reliable babysitter soon, so we can go consistently for a while. Get things a little less chaotic around here."

She bends over and stubs the cigarette on the stone step of the porch.

"Well," I say, pulling my keys from my purse, "if you have any trouble finding one and you need my help again, just let me know."

There is a loud dog bark, this time from the opposite direction of the neighbor's house. Katherine and I both turn toward the sound and there is that damn German shepherd again, this time being walked on a leash by a rotund white-haired older man. The dog barks again and strains a bit at his leash. Katherine gives the man a neighborly wave.

"Evening!" she calls out to him.

The man nods and pulls back at the leash that appears to be all that is keeping the dog from charging forward and gleefully mauling us.

"That horrible dog," Katherine says under her breath, still managing to smile at the man as he and the still-barking dog go past. "He wasn't out the day we did the walk-through of the house, otherwise we might have made a different decision."

"He does seem a bit high-strung," I say. I'm glad when he and the man disappear into the garage next door.

"Anyway, that's kind of you to offer," Katherine says, turning her smile back to me.

For a moment I forget what I've offered, but she reminds me.

"I'll keep that in mind if we have trouble finding a babysitter."

· XXVII ·

I carried on after Paul much as I had with Paul. In some ways I became Paul, a stalwart lonely artist, wearing the same dirty pants every
day, taking my hatchet to the trunks of trees, searching the ground for
particular rocks. But there was a difference between us: I had not Paul's
peace, nor his unflagging trust in the goodness of his god, the beauty of
his god's creation with all those bright spirits filling the sky. I could not
accept that he was gone. I kept looking for him across the fire, stretched
out long and propped up on an elbow, tossing twigs into the flames. I
kept expecting to feel his hand on the back of my head, and in my sleep,
my hands searched restlessly for him.

Missing him was not sweet. I was bitter and angry. I made careless
mistakes that caused me injury. Cutting wood one day, my axe skipped
and I split my thumb nearly in half lengthwise. I sat there laughing and
screaming at intervals, emptying my lungs at the sky and pouring out
my blood onto the ground, and it wasn't until I had, in a rage, kicked
down my shelter and the wooden stand that held my waterpot to boil
over the fire, spilling the water and extinguishing the fire, that I calmed
down enough to stop howling and bind the wound.

I thought of Ehru, at times like those, and all the harm I had watched
him do to himself, and I felt with fear that I understood now why he'd

done it. To harm yourself, to lose all aversion or resistance to pain, to in fact welcome it, was to take all the power away from those who would hurt you. Those monks—*this world*—they could do nothing to you that you weren't already glad to do to yourself. I knew it was a kind of sickness, this way of thinking, but I could feel myself slipping down into it, so instead, I tried to feel nothing. I concentrated on emptying myself of all thought, all care, all memory. I pushed out Paul and Vano and Piroska and my father. I refused to think of them. I became only a pair of eyes. I fixed my gaze on something before me and then reproduced it in pigments with as much fidelity as I could, and while I did this, I was able to feel nothing and have no thoughts, and it was a relief.

At night, I waited insolently in the silence for Czernobog, that divine highway robber. I watched for ash to drift down around me and sniffed now and then for that scent of smoke where nothing burned, but I smelled only forest smells: pine and wood rot and the sweet perfume of monkshood and primrose. The god of endings knew his business too well to be fooled; he wouldn't waste his time on me now. I had nothing of value left for him to take, no joy worth the trouble of ending.

When and for how long was I alone in this place, wandering? I have asked myself this question. I have tried to reconstruct a time line, sync the events of my life up with those of the distant, forward-moving world, and it is very hard to do. Piroska had kept no track of the days. She'd measured time out in the increments of what mattered to her: the budding of the boughs and vines, the births, the blooming and harvesting, then the withering, the gathering to wait out the freezing and the dying, and, eventually, the budding again. I, likewise, measured the passage of time by what mattered to me: the storms and disasters I weathered; the shelters I built and dwelled in sometimes for months, sometimes for years; the towns I accidented upon and skirted carefully around; the times I failed to skirt far enough and was chased by dogs who came snarling at me into the woods or packs of ruffian boys who tried to pirate my shelters for their own amusements.

In those many years after Paul, I lost track of time, or, you might say, *belief* in it. What need had years for numbers? Why bother to cut and count the interminable like a loaf of bread? Perhaps I lived in the truth then and have only since returned to the shared delusion of hours, minutes, seconds, past, present, and future.

There was, however, one incident, small and strange, that tied, as a tent is tied to tentpoles, the formless substance of my life to the larger structure of history. I was sitting high on the forested shoulder of a mountain one day, quietly painting the peak above, when I heard an unnatural buzzing sound. I looked up, shielding my eyes against the sun, and saw in the sky above me a flying thing. It looked like a black metal dragonfly, all silly teetering disproportionate wings with a long, slender rump trailing after. It was a plane, though at that time I would have had absolutely no framework for conceiving of such a thing or language for expressing it.

I left my things where they were and ran through the trees after it. I climbed upward toward the peak, trying to keep the bizarre object in my sights. I had made out the round shape of heads—*people* were riding in the thing, a thing that seemed to be not much more than a big metal bathtub, somehow held aloft.

Emerging from the trees onto the high, arid slope of the peak just below the summit, I watched mesmerized as the plane churned its way forward through the sky. It wasn't until it was far off, just a small black X of wings in the distance, that my gaze fell down to the broad valley that lay below it. Stretched out before me for perhaps a hundred miles lay a battered and smoldering land violently cut and stitched as if by careless surgery, and from the long, ugly cicatrix that ran in a straight line all the way to the horizon, there streamed countless noxious yellow plumes of smoke.

It was the front of a war larger, more carefully designed, and more machinelike than anything I could have fathomed. "The Great War," I would later learn to call it, as if it were something magnificent and noble rather than ghastly and sad. I had reentered humanity's delusion of time and territories. With a few steps, I'd traveled forward without knowing it into an unfathomable and horrifying future of flying contraptions and war trenches and poison gas.

It was too much for me. I turned away. I went back into the quiet woods where the trees and the rocky escarpments and snowy ledges and I could remain a while longer apart from time and so-called civilization. I sat back down at my painting, picked up my brush, and resumed my forgetful art.

. . .

UNLIKE PAUL, I DID NOT keep my paintings. I kept *his*, the small stack that remained of them, and also a bundle of his letters, but my own works I left where I painted them, a trail stretching away behind me—works of art destined to decompose back into the forest floor, to become one again with what they had been separated from in order to represent. Art is a strange thing in that way. The artist must step away from the thing, create a thing that is not the thing, in order to express a longing for the thing. And somehow, in that, there is an experience—even if only the briefest taste—of union.

I came eventually to a place where the woods became entirely pine and mountain caps soared overhead white with snow even in the warmth of late spring, and the grade of the mountains I trudged up became steeper than it had been anywhere else. It was a difficult, punishing path, and so I followed it and was surprised when, at the edge of a wood higher up than I would have expected to find such a thing, I came upon careful rows of woody vines festooned with broad, glistening leaves and heaped with fruit. It was a vineyard.

I shrank back, alarmed by the orderly humanness of what I'd stumbled upon, and turned away to leave. But there came a sound of childish laughter from somewhere in the middle of the vineyard, and a strange rattling, jangling noise that provoked in me not even a guess as to what it might be. Curious and hidden as I was by trees, I hesitated and peered down at the vineyard. After a moment, a bewildering amalgam of machine and child jounced into view. A skeletal frame of metal perched atop large, thin wheels was conveying a young girl and boy about. It was a bicycle, and the children on it were careening over the uneven dirt between the rows of vines in shrieking, giggling merriment.

I watched them for some time, found myself smiling faintly at their pleasure, laughing softly when the boy nearly went forward off the handlebars, then regained his balance with triumph. Eventually, the boy *did* go tumbling off the bike and sat sprawled in the dust crying over a scraped knee. The girl helped him up, turned the bike around, and with an arm around his shoulders led him and the bike away through the vineyard.

I had been avoiding people and villages for so many years. I had not walked freely in one since I was a girl and the idea of doing so was terrifying. But the bike and the children, the laughter—they had stirred something, shaken loose something long-buried that glimmered now in the murk of my memory: child happiness. The feeling I'd had at seven years old, swimming through the air on the tree swing with my brother's hands on my back pushing me upward, my feet reaching for the green leaves, or twelve years old, running alongside Ehru, certain that I was faster than anything under the sun. That glimmer of feeling—*what was it? Was it joy?*—flickered so bright and startling that all I could do for some time was sit there and try to hold it, keep it from fading.

I made camp nearer to the village than I ever did normally. At night, staring into the flicker of my fire, I thought of it, the children, the bike, the loveliness of that vineyard that I wanted to despise but could not. I heard the children's laughter in my ears and dreamed of laughter in my sleep. The next day, I told myself I would only watch. I would spy out the village, get a bit of a show, and then head back off into solitude and safety. For a day, and then another, I lurked along the periphery of the town, watching the people go about their errands and make their social calls. I saw more bikes and more children. I saw shops from which people emerged with long loaves of bread. From another shop there emanated the reek of fish, while the front window of another was draped with ropes of sausage. The men wore clothes very different from those Paul had worn. They had small, flat black hats on their heads and jackets that folded across their chests snugly, like envelopes. The women wore dresses in an extraordinary array of colors, their ankles were visible below the hems of flowing skirts, and their lips were as red as cardinal wings.

In the mornings, fruit merchants carefully stacked pyramids of oranges, apples, and lemons beside crates of raspberries and strawber-ries and bilberries. The flower merchants spread out buckets of flowers on the cobblestones like bright quilts. Spice merchants opened sacks of finely powdered spices in a hundred colors and stabbed metal scoops into the center of each one. It was all irresistibly beautiful. There was a tall building with a sign in the ground-floor window that read CAFÉ, which seemed to be the morning gathering place of the town, while a tavern near the center seemed to be the gathering place of the evening.

Just the thought set me trembling, but I decided that I would try to enter the town, try to walk its streets like any other person, perhaps even try to find a courier where I would finally send Paul's letters and some of his paintings to Johana or Johana's children or her children's children. I owed that to him. I should have done it long ago.

I did my best to tidy myself. I found a stream and bathed and washed my clothes. I braided my long hair, and then, rigid with fear, I ventured into the town.

In the street, people bumped and bustled and bikes sped past at alarming speed with their little bells ringing. I saw a large mechanical carriage that moved in the slow, blundering way of an ox but honked like a goose and held people inside. If people had figured out how to ride a bathtub through the sky, I supposed I shouldn't wonder that they had found a way to ride one over the ground. Voices called out in a language that had a slippery sound to it, and some eyes followed me, a woman in men's clothes and loaded down with a rucksack and snowshoes in summer, but no one spoke to me. I decided to try the morning gathering place, the building with the sign in the window that said CAFÉ, in the hopes that they might take letters there. I entered the building. There was a long wooden counter along one side of the room. Spread across the rest of the room, tables and chairs were scattered, and men were sitting at them, drinking and smoking cigarettes.

A young golden-haired woman wearing an apron stood at a table, briskly stacking dirty dishes on it. I approached her, then paused, dis-tracted by the dress she was wearing. It had tiny, perfectly identical roses all over it—several hundreds of them. For some reason this baffled me more than almost anything else I'd seen. How was it possible to get so many identical pictures on a dress? To paint them by hand would take a year if it could even be done, and then it would be much too expensive to be worn by a barmaid.

She looked up and said something to me that I, of course, did not understand, but her tone was pleasant, so I took out the stack of Paul's letters and held them tremblingly out for her to see. She spoke again and threw her thumb back over her shoulder, gesturing at the door. I looked at her apologetically and said, in Paul's language, that I did not understand.

She looked up.

"Es-tu Allemand?" she asked, her eyebrow arching. She snapped her fingers, searching for the words in German. "Deutsch? Kommst du . . . au Deutschland?"

I shook my head. I didn't know where Deutschland was, but I knew I wasn't from there.

"Bon!" she said, with what looked like relief.

"You understand my language?" I asked.

She grimaced and pinched her fingers close together in the air.

"What about English?" I tried.

"Anglais? Ahhh! Votre accent. Vous êtes Américaine!" she exclaimed with sudden eagerness. She clutched her heart rapturously. "J'adore James Cagney et . . . et Barbara Stanwyck et tous les acteurs Américains!"

This too was nothing but a stream of indecipherable sounds followed by a couple of unfamiliar names. Even if I had spoken French at that time, I still would have been at a loss. I had not yet seen an electric lightbulb, much less a motion picture; it would be a revelation when I got to watch a film for the first time and discover what a movie actor was. I shook my head vaguely.

The young woman seemed to finally accept that I would not understand her, but she untied the apron at her waist, tapped at the stack of letters in my hand, and gestured for me to follow her. On her way to the door, she called out to an old man who sat smoking and conversing expressively with another man at one of the tables in the corner. He waved to her without looking up.

Outside, the woman led me back through the square, with its bustling crowd of morning shoppers, down a narrow cobblestone street, and into a shop where the walls were covered with hundreds of small, metal mailboxes, and a man with oiled hair leaned across a counter, speaking with another man with hair of a similar luster.

The first man stopped his conversation midsentence and looked me over from top to bottom with a raised eyebrow as though personally affronted by my appearance, but the woman who'd brought me said something in a sharp tone that got him cooperating. She took the letters from me, and I hurried to pull the paintings from my rucksack that I had intended to send along with them. When the woman turned and saw the painting at the top of the stack, she gasped and her eyes went wide. She reached for the painting and, with my assent, took it up lovingly in her hands.

"Oh la la!" she breathed, holding the small square of wood and looking back and forth from it to me. Hungrily, she snatched the other paintings from the stack one by one and spread them out on the counter. She said things first to me, then to the two men, who were peering down at the paintings with nearly equal fascination. The woman even called to the young man working in back sorting mail, and he came and joined the huddle of admirers.

They murmured to one another, pointing out small details in the works as though they were professional appraisers of fine art. When they looked up at me, smiling and nodding their approval, there was nothing I could do but flush with a discomfort that they surely took as modesty. I would not have enjoyed the attention even if the paintings had actually been mine, but they were not mine, and there was no easy way of explaining this; besides, I realized that the paintings were turning the situation quite unexpectedly and dramatically in my favor. Instead of navigating suspicion or disdain, as I had feared I would have to, I felt suddenly warmly—almost *too* warmly—welcomed.

The postmaster finally put the paintings back in a stack and carefully wrapped the items in brown paper, tied the paper bundle with twine, and said something to the woman. She turned to me and held out her hand for money. I flushed again. I didn't even know what the currency was here, much less have any of it. But the lady, seeing my embarrassment, pulled a few coins from her apron and put them on the counter. The postmaster tipped his head to each of us, this time with far more cordiality, and turned away with the package.

The woman motioned for me to follow her back to the boarding-house, and because I didn't know what else to do, I followed her. There, she pulled out a tall chair for me and set a "café" on the counter in front of it. Gently and with a smile, she tucked a loose strand of my hair behind my ears and turned her head, examining my face, and I likewise examined hers. She was not a woman to stand out in a crowd, but her features, when you studied them, were pleasing. She had a kind of golden skin with soft freckles that matched her strawberry-blond hair. Her soft blue eyes were fringed with strawberry lashes, and below a slightly snub nose, her teeth were even and pretty.

"Vous êtes très, très jolie," she murmured to herself. "Et, bien sûr, nous aimons les rousses ici. Toi en robe, et les hommes bouront toute la journée.

"J'ai besoin d'aide," she said more loudly, no longer speaking to herself, but trying to communicate some idea to me. She sucked at her lips and squinted into the air, trying to think of the words in a language I spoke. "*Hilfe*," she finally said—Help.

"Ich will hilfe." I want help.

"Hilfe," I echoed, conveying to her that I understood the word, despite my having no idea what she was trying to communicate.

"Ici." She gestured around us. "Dans le café." Then she looked at me expectantly. "Du . . ." She held a hand out toward me. "Hilfts . . . moi?" She rolled her eyes at her own mishmash of French and German.

She was offering me a job. It was unexpected and very intimidating, but, I thought, if I wanted to stay in this town for any amount of time—and I did, though it seemed to defy all rationality—I would need money.

"Ja," I finally said, and nodded timidly.

She squeezed my hand with enthusiasm and immediately got up and crossed the room to speak with the old man at the table. There was low talk and glances my way, and I heard the word *artiste* and saw the young woman gesture toward the bare walls of the café, as if with a wave covering them in works of art.

When she came back, she gave my hand another excited squeeze and then motioned for me to follow her. She led me up a flight of stairs, down a hall, and into a small room with a chest of drawers and a tall bed. The woman asked me a question, which must have been whether or not I wanted the room or liked the room, and I nodded, scarcely daring to believe my good fortune in having been provided with lodgings in addition to a job. At the same time, I was mildly terrified by it and the sudden intimate proximity to other people that it implied. I told myself, though, that there was nothing to prevent me from leaving at any time if I disliked it.

The woman gave me a dress to put on—another of those miraculous things with a thousand identical yellow and red flowers—and with a brush she dusted a colorful powder on my cheeks to make them look flushed. She offered to put lipstick on my lips, but the idea seemed repulsive to me. I demurred, and she laughed and then led me back downstairs, where she put me to work with her in the café, cleaning and clearing dirty plates and occasionally breaking them, to the disapproval of the old gentleman in the corner, who was her father and the owner of the café and attached hotel.

The woman's name was Anais Chambrun, and I was now her assistant in the various duties of the café and hotel, in exchange for which I received room and board and a small amount of money each week.

From Anais, I learned that the town, which lay precisely on the eastern border of France, was called Chamonix-Mont-Blanc, after the snowy peak that rose up vertically above it; that it had a movie house— where I learned more in just a few hours than my poor brain could handle about the distance the world had come since I'd last truly lived in it—and gas station for the handful of automobiles in the town and for the tourists who came by car to ski the famously pristine mountain slopes; and also that the city was excessively proud of the fact that, fourteen years earlier, it had hosted something called the Olympics, where people from many countries had traveled to Chamonix to compete at things like ice-skating, skiing, and bobsledding.

I was extremely grateful to Anais, but equally overwhelmed. I was a stranger from the past thrust suddenly into a loud, bright future of perpetual motion and information. News arrived every day to Chamonix from all corners of the world about earthquakes in Africa, civil wars in Asia and Spain, and annexations in other parts of Europe, and the people—*common people*, who had nothing to do with any of it—took it all into their heads and formed opinions about it and argued about it in the café. They threw out strange words and names like Manchukuo, Molotov-Ribbentrop, Anschluss, and Sudetenland.

When I was growing up, my town received plenty of gossip from the surrounding towns and the occasional news from the city; I'd also grown up hearing tales of America's war for independence from the British, but that was as international as it ever got. Anais would scan the newspapers that were left crumpled on tables and throw comments in among the arguing men that set them roaring, but I let it all slide past me like another foreign dialect and one I had no intention of learning.

Anais, herself, was bright and cheerful and looked out for me as though I were a beloved stray puppy, but she was also, at times, too much for me. She moved and spoke quickly, and laughed in sudden loud bursts that made me feel perpetually spooked, and there were days, too, when she struck me as shamefully lazy. I would be at work on the wash, the ironing, the cleaning of vacated bedrooms, and not see Anais for hours. Then I'd walk into one of the bedrooms and find her sound asleep on the bed. At other times, if her father, Monsieur Chambrun, was away from his usual spot at the corner table of the café, Anais would sit down heavily in a chair with a pot de crème to rest and eat until the very moment her father returned through the door. Each time she would apologize profusely and tell me that she'd not slept well the night before or believed she was coming down with something. I didn't mind doing the work while Anais slept or rested, but it gave me an impression of her as indolent, and indolence, I'd been well trained in childhood, was among the most inexcusable of vices.

Living in such close quarters with so many people after so many years of solitude left me more exhausted still. I had difficulty sleeping, waking with a wild start every time the café door slapped closed beneath my window or some inebriated patron went off singing down the road. Before long, I felt frayed and worn thin. I saw summer ripening on the mountainside and knew that life in the woods would be easy and quiet, and I was tempted to abscond into them again. I was teetering on the brink of leaving when two things happened that held me back. The first was that Anais surprised me with a small portable painting easel and then gave me a day all to myself to go paint.

"You deserve it," she said warmly when I tried, out of courtesy, to refuse the gift. "I take such horrible advantage of you. You do *all* the work around here. Don't think I don't know it. It's selfish really; I'm only trying to appease you because I need you so desperately."

I hugged her and thanked her and then gathered my things as fast as I could and left to paint far off in the quiet of the woods, and I discovered something strange that day. I was happier than I'd ever been in all those many years when painting alone in the woods had been my daily life. After Paul's death, I'd remained alone out of fear and because there seemed to be no other choice, but I'd carried a terrible feeling with me all that time, like a bitter gall in my mouth that had tainted the taste of everything. Painting then had been not a joy but only a relief, an escape from the noxiousness of every other moment. And somehow, I'd been oddly blind to it, but now I saw it. That terrible feeling had been loneliness, a potent, paralyzing loneliness, and it had been poisoning me slowly and insidiously. Now, going out into the woods with my gift from Anais, painting all day, then returning to her welcome and praise of the work I'd done, I felt the peace and quiet I'd longed for, but also something deeper: joy.

Anais was very proud to have a painter living and working in her establishment. It had been Paul's painting that had so impressed her, but she was no less pleased by my own. When I returned to the café carrying oddly shaped boards of rough wood with my landscapes painted on them and she realized that I was carving boards of wood from tree trunks to paint on, she showed me where I could purchase canvases—the first I'd ever seen—at two francs a piece. My finished paintings she hung on the walls of the café, and to my surprise and gratification, the tourists who came to Chamonix with money to spare began to buy them. Soon I became known as Chamonix's resident artist, which seemed to be a thing of no small significance here where everyone shared a curious enthusiasm for art.

THE SECOND THING THAT HAPPENED and kept me in Chamonix was that I discovered why Anais seemed so lazy. Anais was sweeping the floor of the café one day. She bent over to scoop the mound of dirt and crooked spent cigarettes into a dustpan, and two buttons popped off at once from the front of her dress. She flushed so red that her freckles disappeared, and her eyes darted over to her father where he sat at his corner table, but the man was shaking his head and waving away the forceful argument of the man across the table from him and had taken no notice. Embarrassed and trying to conceal the gaping opening in the front of her dress, Anais begged me to watch the café and then hurried upstairs to change her dress. Some time passed and she didn't come down, so I went up to check on her. She was in her room, rummaging frantically through the dresses—every dress she owned from the looks of it—which were strewn across the bed.

"None of them fit," she said tearfully, collapsing down onto the bed.

I stood quietly in the doorway, unsure what to say.

"None of them fit here." She cupped her belly in her hands. "What am I going to do?"

"Do you want to try one of mine?" I asked.

Her eyes, red and bleary, turned toward me, and she laughed bitterly.

"Yours aren't going to fit, and even if they did, I'd just be in the same spot two weeks later."

"Anais," I said uncertainly, not knowing how to broach the subject, how to ask a question that seemed unaskable. "Are you . . . what I mean is, are   "

"Yes," she said bitterly, looking up at the ceiling from where she lay. "Yes, I am."

I crossed the room and sat down on the edge of the bed. It'd been such a long time since I'd had a female friend. I wasn't sure what I should say, what I should do. She put an arm over her eyes, but I could see tears rolling down the side of her face beneath.

"Can you tell me—"

She shook her head back and forth, the arm over her face moving too. "Don't ask me who, Anna. I cannot possibly tell. It was a *stupid*, *horrible* mistake, and he is a married man with a family. It would do no one any good if it were known."

There was silence, and I chewed my cheek thoughtfully.

"Whatever happens, Anais," I said in a low voice, nearly a whisper, "I'm here for you. If there is anything you need, I will do it. Anything. You've been such a friend to me. I never imagined I would have such a friend."

Anais rolled over, set her head on my lap, and squeezed my legs in a strangely positioned hug, and for a few minutes, I stroked her pretty red-gold hair, until she finally sat up, wiping at her eyes, and rose from the bed.

"I've been avoiding wearing this," she said, lifting a half apron from where it was draped over a chair, "because it draws attention to my middle, but I guess at this point, it's a choice between that and popping all my buttons and putting my girdle on display for all to see."

I tied the apron loosely around her waist for her, and we looked at our reflections in the mirror, two redheads, one fair, one dark.

"I can't tell a thing looking at you," I said, tilting my head to the side.

"Oh, just give it time," she replied, and then grabbed up the pot of rouge from the dresser and swept some fresh color onto her pale cheeks.

The weeks passed in Chamonix with a steady quiet rhythm of laundry loads and dish tubs, beds made and bottles of wine poured out into glasses. I scrutinized the faces of all the male patrons, trying to figure out who might have gotten Anais pregnant, but there were simply too many candidates. Anais was clever and vivacious and pleasant to look at; all the men loved to flirt with her and seemed even to enjoy her wry wit when she mocked and scolded them with a wicked gleam in her eye and her bright laugh ringing out like bells. I kept an eye also on her belly, but it was still early. The popped buttons on her dress were probably due to

· XXVIII ·

THE children return. Ramona has gotten a haircut, an adorable little bob with bangs. Thomas finished *The Emerald City of Oz*, and when I place the next volume, *The Patchwork Girl of Oz*, in his hands, his expression could be that of a young King Arthur laying hold of Excalibur. Octavio reportedly fell out of a Power Wheels and landed on his face, and he has returned to school with scabs across the end of his nose and a gray tooth that I am told could fall out at any moment. The rest of the children are all perfectly, wonderfully the same but for the collective inch they've grown in just a week. In their presence, my spirits are immediately lifted. The past week was hellish. I felt tight and twisted, wrung out and desolate, but the children's return, their happy prattle and restless motion filling the rooms and halls again, acts as a potent balm.

In their absence, I dutifully transformed the house and grounds into a Currier and Ives scene: wreaths hung on every door, candles in every window. A ten-foot tree stands lit up and decorated with bells and red ribbons in the crook of the spiral staircase. When the children arrive to school and see the tree, their eyes and mouths go wide and round.

I was glad for the distraction of decorating, but it was also an unhappy reminder of the next school holiday—this one even longer than her sudden craving for pot de crèmes more than anything else, and she also took to wearing a full apron loosely tied, beneath which little could be detected. After some weeks, she was feeling better. She regained her energy and worked nearly as hard as I did without complaint, so that no one could have guessed from her vigor that she was with child. There came a day, however, when she decided it was time to tell her father.

"He'll discover it sooner or later," she said resolutely. "And I prefer for it to be *him* who is caught off guard when it happens, rather than me."

"How do you think he'll take it?" I asked.

Anais sighed, and then one of her eyebrows lifted in an expression of almost haughty defiance.

"The poor, sweet, old fool. Of all the men who love me—and there are *many* men who love me; this is all too clear, no?" she said with a wry smile. "My father loves me best. He'll take it. He'll holler and curse, certainly, but then he'll take it."

She was right. Both the café patrons and I heard indistinct shouts echoing off the walls upstairs, the *clomp-clomp* of agitated footsteps, and a slam of a door. I brought people their delicate cups of espresso, sugar cubes perched on tiny spoons, smiling and acting as though I heard nothing, knew nothing. Then eventually there were footsteps on the stairs, and Anais appeared at the bottom of them wearing that same defiant arched eyebrow that dared anyone to make inquiries. She set to clearing dishes, smiling and jesting just as she ever did, and a few moments later Monsieur Chambrun himself came plodding down the stairs looking gruff but effortfully composed. He squared his shoulders and made his way across the café. When he passed me at the bar top, he gave me a stern look.

"You knew about this?" he grumbled at me under his breath.

I only pressed my lips and looked down, but he was already moving on toward his spot in the corner, uninterested in my answer. But when he passed his daughter, who was gathering a stack of saucers and cups from a dirty table, he reached out. Without turning his head toward her or saying a word, he gave her elbow a small squeeze and then a pat, before continuing on his way, some argument for his companions already forming in his throat.

the last—that looms ahead. School will soon be suspended *again* for an unfathomable two and a half weeks. Just the thought of it leaves me short of breath. Best not to think of it at all. In the meantime, we have gingerbread houses to bake and decorate, ornaments to make, and a holiday dance recital—a medley of dances from *The Nutcracker*—to prepare for.

BY THE END OF OUR painting lesson later that day, I'm frustrated by the cinching band of hunger that is tightening around my waist. The children are gathering up their soiled brushes and palettes smeared with acrylics. Their studies of a potted hellebore are resting on their easels to dry, and all the while my gut is wringing itself. My skull feels as though it might crack, my forehead splintering in shards of bone right down the center like a dry branch. Invisible thumbs are attempting to bore through my skull to press prints into the putty of my temporal lobes.

I went to the Emersons' barn last night, specifically to avoid this very thing today. The cows and I have fallen into a comfortable rhythm. There's something very soothing about resting against the warm hides of the animals, feeling their rib cages rise and fall with their steady breath, drinking deeply and at a leisurely pace—or perhaps that's just an indication of how low I've sunk, that I take such comfort in the closeness of cows. But what's the point, if it doesn't keep me from feeling brittle and ravenous all day with the children? I'm being smashed in the vise grip of a hunger I've never experienced before and don't understand—*Why do I feel this way?* What must I do to *finally* feel sated?—and every solution I come up with grants me only a fleeting reprieve at best.

In their baggy smocks the children are shuffling over to the big tub sink to wash their brushes when Audrey suddenly points a horrified finger at the birdcage.

"Look!" she exclaims.

The rest of the children turn to look in the direction of her finger, and Thomas cries, "Mona is gone!"

Mona, being the only female, was the drabbest bird of the three, and the only one that could be easily identified.

"Mona is *gone*."

The cry rises as both question and statement in anxious and beseeching tones from all the children.

"Where's Mona?" Audrey asks me point-blank.

My hands are doing strange things, clasping and unclasping and gesturing in unconvincing bewilderment.

"Well," I say. Then I let my hand fall from the puzzled position it has assumed at my chin, dropping the pretense of ignorance. "Mona, I'm terribly sorry to say—well, unfortunately . . . Mona got out of the cage as I was cleaning it. She—she flew away."

"Did she fly away in here?" Thomas asks reasonably, and a few of the children look up, searching hopefully for her amid the rafters.

"Um. No. I took the cage outside to clean it, and she flew off into the trees. It was a bad idea, and I certainly won't do it again. But maybe she'll come back, or maybe you'll see her in the trees. She's likely very happy out there."

All eyes turn glumly to the barren trees beyond the conservatory windows, except mine, of course.

"I'm sorry." I say, "I'm so very sorry." And I mean it more than they can know.

We practice our dances, we paint, the children bake holiday treats with Marnie. I am visiting the Emersons' barn at least four nights a week, feeding quite immoderately each time, and still I feel like I'm wasting away. My mind slips constantly back to blood. I can hardly hear a word Marnie or Rina say to me over the thundering drumbeat of their pulses, the roar of the rushing rivers of their veins, the chambers of their tender hearts *glug-glug*ging as the valves open and shut.

One day Rina holds a folded newspaper out to me, but for a moment I'm too distracted by the sight of the lovely blue tributaries of blood running down her arm, twisting at her wrist, and fanning out over her upturned palm to understand that she means for me to take the paper from her and read something in it.

"Isn't that the cemetery you went to with the children?" she says, helpfully guiding my attention away from her veins and to the matter at hand. "For the field trip a few weeks ago?"

So it is. An article in the local paper reports a nighttime break-in and theft at the very historic cemetery we visited for La Toussaint. Kindly, gray-haired Mr. Riley is even featured in the story's photo, arms crossed with a look of stern disappointment. Small in the background, I can actually see the photograph he took of myself and the children posed before the candlelit graves on a bulletin board behind him.

"It *is*," I reply. "Poor Mr. Riley. Why on earth would anyone want to break into . . ."

Before I can finish the sentence, my father's headstone pushes forward in my mind. No. There can't be any connection. A strange coincidence, that's all.

". . . break into such a place?" I say, finally completing my thought.

NAP TIME THAT DAY, AND every day now, is like an hour-long tug-of-war with the darkest, hungriest parts of myself. At the hour that my body has come to expect relief from its hungers, it instead must busy itself with other things: tidying, pacing, determinedly *not* thinking of the seven horrifically vulnerable children lying quiet, prone, and inert in a room just down the hall. At times, the image of the attic, blood-spattered and littered with small animal parts, flashes in my head, and then the thought of the savage damage I could inflict on the children fills me with a breathless horror and a panicked urge for flight, the urge to run from them without word or warning as far as I can, as far as the desire to protect them from my terrifying self might send me.

It doesn't help that I'm also tired. I wake up several times a week muddy and bloody and so filled with frightened despair that I'm now beyond tears. I've barricaded my bedroom door, barricaded the hall, the back door. It seems that whatever I'm strong enough to move when awake, I'm also strong and sensible enough to move in my sleep. What am I doing on those nights when something calls me to go wandering outside? *Breaking into cemeteries?* Breaking into God knows what else? And why do I keep returning so physically misused?

It feels like every bolt in the construction of my life is suddenly coming loose, every rope fraying. I find myself at times waiting in tension, almost listening for that final snap, when the last rope rips and I'm in free fall.

These things go on, and the days pass, and the holiday break looms large and dismal, and yet it also carries with it the hope that then I will have time to figure everything out, solve all my problems, and regain my footing. I can't continue like this with my hunger growing and my white-knuckled control over it every day closer to failing. I've been here before. I've seen how this ends—too many times. Self-control is such a weak, paltry thing, while the monster inside is so powerful and tireless. Is there any hope in trying to subdue it, or do monsters simply have to be hidden away from the innocents deep inside labyrinths where they can rage and feast with abandon?

TWO DAYS IN ONE WEEK, three days in the next, Katherine calls and asks if I can watch Leo in the evening. Sometimes it's for marriage counseling, sometimes for doctor's appointments or physical therapy for Katherine's back. I should perhaps be put out by this, but I'm not. I'm grateful. Even if Katherine were not as effusively appreciative as she is, or if Leo's face did not light up as brightly as it does each time he greets me at the door, I would still infinitely prefer the evenings I spend with Leo to the ones I have to pass alone. I'm afraid of my house, afraid of the darkness and the silence, afraid even more of those shattering eruptions of sound that send me fumbling up and down stairs and along dark corridors, searching for some demonic alarm that has sounded by inexplicable command and then stops just as inexplicably—and then those moments afterward, when the avalanche of silence falls on me again, and I'm buried. It gets so that I'm not sure what I would do without the evenings I spend at the Hardmans'.

On one of these occasions, Katherine calls me crying, and when I arrive, I find her in the kitchen. Her face is tear-streaked, and she clings to a glass of wine on the table in front of her as if seeking from the brittle object support for her whole weight. She looks up at me and smiles unconvincingly, but this attempt at cheerfulness seems to inspire fresh tears, and she presses a wad of tissues to her eyes while they flow.

"What is it, Katherine?" I ask, taking a seat across from her, but she doesn't answer and instead rises and goes to a cupboard to get a second wineglass, for me, I suppose, which she places on the table.

Katherine has let me into her confidence quite deeply, but I've never seen her like this. I've not, in fact, seen anyone like this, so emotional and raw, in a very long time. I'm not sure I remember how to be someone's confidante, or *friend*, if that's what Katherine and I are becoming.

Katherine's head sloshes around in what may be a slightly inebriated gesture of uncertainty. "Oh, I don't know how to explain it exactly. It just feels like the wheels are coming off. I was so optimistic, certain that things would work out in the end, but now, it's like it's hitting me for the first time that they really might not, and there might not be anything I can do about it."

She sniffs and dabs at her eyes again.

"With Dave?" I ask, and from behind her tissue, she nods.

"He won't go to counseling anymore. He just told me. Said it's not working, and he's not going to waste any more of his time on it. He seemed so cold and uncaring. Like it didn't matter at all."

She looks over at me and seems to grow embarrassed. "I'm sorry, Collette. It's so unfair of me to dump all of this on you. You've already helped me so much. But I—I don't really have anyone else I can talk to about this."

"Don't be silly," I say, though another voice in my head agrees with her; it is a lot, and I feel very much out of my depth. "You don't need to apologize, Katherine. You're going through so much. If I can help by listening, I'm glad to do it. Did Dave give you any reasons? Did he say why?"

"He didn't say why, but I know. I messed up and told the therapist something I shouldn't have. Dave freaked out, called me a liar, swore up and down to the therapist that what I'd said wasn't true. The poor therapist didn't know what to do! Gave us this speech about how therapy only works if both parties are being honest and how it wasn't her job to figure out who was lying and who was telling the truth. It felt like she was about to dump us. It was so stupid of me. I should have known that he was going to react that way. Now I've ruined whatever chance we had of making progress."

"What was it that you told the therapist that got him so upset?"

"That I was starting to feel afraid of him. Because of the stairs incident, among others, and because the other night he tried to suffocate me."

"*What?! He tried to . . .*" My voice has risen sharply with alarm. I catch myself, look toward the living room where Leo is sitting obliviously in front of the TV, then continue in something closer to a whisper. "He tried to *suffocate you*?"

"Well, okay," she says, putting up her hands to backtrack, "I shouldn't say that—and this is exactly why he got so mad when I said it to the therapist—to be totally accurate, I should say, he put a pillow over my face *like* he was suffocating me for five seconds or so and then took it away, so he wasn't *actually* trying to suffocate me, but, I mean, *I* didn't know that at the time. For those five seconds, I thought I was about to die."

"As *anyone would*," I reply with force.

I sit thinking for a moment, a look of unconcealed distrust on my face.

"How do you know, Katherine, that he wasn't actually trying to suffocate you and then just came to his senses? I mean, let's be honest, this is *not* the first time he's done something to harm you."

"He said it was just a joke. We were having an argument in bed, and he was frustrated with me, and it was a 'joke,' like, '*I could just kill you!*'"

She lifts her glass to her mouth. "Ha ha," she says flatly, and then takes a drink. "I told him he needs to work on his material."

"Do you believe that, Katherine? You were there, did it feel like a joke to you?"

She gazes off into space for a moment, her mouth twisting slightly with thought.

"I don't know," she finally says. "There are times when *I* could imagine putting a pillow over *his* face. Even now," she says with a soft laugh, "I wouldn't mind seeing the look on his face after *I* played such a joke."

"But you haven't done it," I rebut. "There's a vast distance between thinking something, even wanting something, and actually doing it."

She accepts this argument with a small wave of her shoulders and then studies the wine in her glass.

"Katherine," I say hesitantly, "have you ever thought about just leaving? Joke or no joke, what you're talking about is *very* alarming. I can't help but think that the better wager is to take it too seriously and be wrong, than to take it too lightly and be wrong."

She's silent for a moment, thinking, and my mind turns to Leo, sitting there in the living room. What would become of him if Dave put a pillow over Katherine's face and didn't stop after five seconds? Suddenly I think of what Leo told me at the museum. I had cast the whole thing aside in my mind, preferring to chalk it up to childish nonsense, to imaginary friends, or imaginary brothers. I had enough to deal with on my own, and besides, I could never get to the bottom of it even if I tried. Leo treated it as a strictly held secret, and neither Katherine nor Dave had ever mentioned anything about another child. I'd never seen a scrap of evidence anywhere of Leo having a brother. But what if what Leo said was true? What if he'd had a brother? A brother who nobody talked about, who had died "in the water"? Could it be possible that Dave, who's knocked Katherine and Leo down the stairs and done who knows what all else, had something to do with that death?

I realize with a start that I'm rushing ahead of myself, but a powerful dread for Leo rises up in me nonetheless. What if he's in danger? What if Katherine isn't the only one whose safety I should be concerned about?

"You have to think about Leo too," I say quietly. "What would happen to him if something ever happened to you?"

Katherine purses her lips anxiously.

"I don't know," she says fretfully. "Everything we have is his. He makes all the money. I used to have a great career doing design, but I haven't worked in several years. I feel totally out of touch with the industry now. And the thought of being a single mother, *ugh*, it's *so* scary . . . plus . . . I know it's unfortunate and probably hard to believe, but I love him. Maybe I shouldn't, and I'm just being dumb, but I don't believe he's a bad man. *Flawed?* Sure. Kind of an asshole? Fine, but I can't stop believing that we could get through this if we really tried, that we could be happy. Maybe if we went to a different therapist, and I promised not to bring up that stuff . . ."

I close my eyes in frustration. It all seems so obvious to me, but she's the one who must make all the choices.

"I just wish I knew the *real* reason that he won't go," she says, pouring the remainder of the bottle, about half a glass, into my cup, which I've not yet touched.

"But you told me the reason was—"

"I don't mean that, I mean . . . something's changed. He doesn't *care* anymore. What happened in therapy was just his excuse to stop going. There's something bigger going on. That's what's killing me: his coldness. I think he's having an affair. He doesn't want things to get better because he's already got something better. That's how it always works with men. They never stop caring, they just stop caring about *you.*"

I am beyond frustration now. If Dave, on top of everything else, is also having an affair and that still doesn't tip the scales of Katherine's heart away from him, it seems certain nothing will.

"I mean, *who needs to work that much*?" Katherine continues. "He 'spends the night at the office,' just about once a week. *And* I just learned that there's a female research analyst, who apparently has been there for six months and works very closely with him, and somehow he's never spoken her name to me once. He's got plenty to say about *Jim* and *Tom* and the rest of the boys, but not one word about this female colleague."

"Katherine," I say, determined to give it one last try. "I know this will be much harder to hear than it is to say, but maybe it's for the best. He's hurting you and scaring you, and he's done the same to Leo. If he wants to go hurt and scare someone else, well, maybe in the long run it would be better for you and for Leo if you just let him go."

She smiles softly, but it's a bitter smile.

"You're probably right," she says, and takes a last drink of wine, draining the glass. "But before I make any decisions, I have to *know.*"

She rises unsteadily from the table.

"Know what?" I ask apprehensively.

"I have to know what's really going on. I have to know if he's cheating on me. I *have* to. I'll go crazy if I don't."

She walks out of the kitchen, and I follow her to the entryway, where she goes for her coat.

"Where are you going?" I ask. There is the slightest wobble to her walk, a fluidity to her movements that makes me worry about her driving in this condition.

"To find out," she says again, putting her purse strap on her shoulder. "He said he'd be sleeping at the office tonight. Well, we'll just see if that's true."

"Katherine, can you find out what you need to know tomorrow? Ask Dave directly?"

Whatever she is planning, I don't think it's a good idea.

She opens the door.

"If I'm right and he's cheating, I can find out tonight. He'll be with her, probably complaining about his crazy wreck of a wife."

"Katherine, I really don't—"

"I just have to know," she says again. "Maybe then I can take your advice and leave him."

And then the door is closing behind her.

THE REST OF THE EVENING I'm distracted, wondering what Katherine is doing and fearing the results. Leo asks me questions that I miss the first time, too deep in my own thoughts, too busy waiting for the sound of a key in the door and reassurance that all is well.

At bedtime, Leo becomes quiet, his expression forlorn. Pulling his pajama shirt down over his upstretched arms and head, I poke the side of his belly and wait for the laughter when his head pushes its way out the collar, but instead his chin is dimpled with sadness and tears are beginning to run down his cheeks.

"*Oh no*," I say. "Leo, what is the matter, mon petit? Did I hurt you?"

Leo shakes his head no, but goes on crying.

"Please tell me what is wrong?"

Leo pulls Max the giraffe from where he lies on the bed and presses the stuffed animal's nubby fur to his eyes.

"What is it, dearest? Please tell me."

"I waited all day, but I never got even one thing, or even candles."

"Candles? *What?*" I ask, brushing the hair gently back from the side of his face where the salty wet of his tears has plastered the dark strands to his skin. "What is it that you were waiting all day for?"

Finally, he lowers the giraffe from his face. His eyes are red and glossy with tears and sadness.

"For a present or some candles or cake or something."

I take a breath, let it out. I don't want to ask the question. I don't want to hear the answer.

"Leo . . . is today your birthday?"

He nods, his chin dimpling again and new tears filling the corners of his eyes.

I could weep. This beautiful, sweet little boy waiting so patiently for a birthday celebration that never comes because his parents are too consumed with their own personal drama to think of it.

Instead, I smile as widely and happily as I can.

"Leo, how old are you today? Are you *six years old*?"

Leo nods.

"*Sacré bleu!* This is the most wonderful news I've ever heard in my life. I cannot believe that *I* get to celebrate your sixth birthday with you."

Leo is looking at me uncertainly. He's hugging Max tightly to himself, but he isn't crying anymore.

"Get up! You can't possibly go to sleep! Here." I turn my back to him. "Your royal chariot awaits to chauffeur you to your magical, middle-of-the-night birthday celebration."

It's such a sad charade, and I feel close to tears even as I grin and exclaim over him, but I can only hope it fools him—fools him into happiness. I think of Katherine's words: at some hard-to-discern point they become too old to fool. After that they just begin to play along. Is he at that point tonight? Whether he is or not, I have to try.

For a moment he stands on his bed considering, then he climbs on, Max dangling over my shoulder, and we make our way back downstairs, singing "Happy Birthday" loudly in English and then French, on our way to the magical, middle-of-the-night birthday celebration that I will have to conjure up somehow.

HOURS LATER, LEO IS ASLEEP on the couch beside me where he drifted off as we were watching *The Hunchback of Notre Dame* with Lon Chaney on the classic movie channel. The portrait I drew of him and Max—the only present I could think to give him—is still in his hands, and a half-eaten tiramisu that I found in the refrigerator is on the counter in the kitchen with a tall white candle stuck in the center of it. Hopefully the sight of it will jog his parents' memory and Leo will at least get a belated and apologetic celebration tomorrow.

I'm just coming down the stairs from carrying Leo to bed when Katherine pushes open the front door. Looking tired and defeated, she puts her coat away and kicks her shoes off. I'm tired too. This is all too much for me. I'm unused to involving myself so deeply in the lives of others. It's so terribly draining. At the moment, I don't care anymore where Katherine's been or what she's found out. I'm angry that she and Dave forgot Leo's birthday, and I'm relieved that she's home and no catastrophe has occurred tonight.

I gather my things to go. Katherine is at the kitchen sink, filling a water glass at the faucet, putting a pill in her mouth, chasing it with large, desperate gulps from the glass. She's upset, shaky, and I can tell she's been crying, but she's home and safe, and I have nothing to offer her. How did I even get here in the first place?

"I'm going to go," I say, standing in the doorway of the kitchen. Though I shouldn't, I can't help but ask, "Are you okay?"

"He wasn't there," she says in a knowing voice, gazing at the gleaming metal faucet in front of her as if she were speaking to it. "Wasn't at his office, but *his car was.*"

There is something strange, kind of languorous about the way she is talking, the way she is hanging to the edge of the sink with one hand. My guess is that she had a drink somewhere along the way tonight.

"Where was he?" she goes on. "That's the question. Where was he? And with whom? Maybe he was with *Janelle. Janelle.* That's her name. That's the name of the coworker, who is so very insignificant that she can't even be mentioned despite their working very closely together for the last *half year.*"

The bitterness in her voice and eyes is enough to choke me by proximity. I should feel sorry for her. I know it's easy for me to discard Dave. I feel nothing but loathing for him, but Katherine is his wife and she still loves him. It isn't as easy for her to be rational as I wish it was. I know this, but right now, I'm too tired and too fed up with all of it to care.

"It's late, Katherine. You need sleep. Nothing is going to change tonight. Everything will be better dealt with in the morning."

She looks to me, but her gaze is vacant, her thoughts elsewhere. When her eyes fall on the tiramisu on the counter with the candle in it, I hope she will remember Leo's birthday, say something about it, but it seems not to register. She turns back to the sink, then the dark window above it that sees nothing in the dark, only reflects herself back to her.

"I hope you weren't saving that dessert for something. It's just that Leo told me that he had recently turned six, so we had a little celebration."

Katherine is silent, still staring ahead, but her eyes are focused, thinking.

"How nice," she finally says, and turns a feeble smile toward me. "That was so sweet of you."

There is no devastating moment of realization, no agonized contrition, oaths to make it up to Leo. For a moment I wonder if she's heard me correctly—should I repeat myself? But no, I've put it out there as plainly as I dare. I know that I should pardon her; here I am, witnessing what is quite possibly the very moment of hitting rock bottom for her entire life. Do I really want to add into the moment motherly guilt and shame? And yet, I'm just confused by it, or by its absence. In that moment of quiet, something seems to move into the space between the two of us, some haze or distance or unfamiliarity. She has disappointed me, and I too have somehow disappointed her, but how is for each of us unspeakable. We're both too old to fool and too tired tonight to play along.

I leave her in the dark kitchen. I leave Leo in his dark bedroom a floor above. I leave the Hardmans' house deep in shadow, and part of me wonders if I'll ever return; part of me senses that maybe I shouldn't.

· XXIX ·

IT was a great relief to me when Anais's father finally knew and when I could rest assured that he was not going to throw her out into the street as many fathers might have. He grumbled and glowered at the two of us plenty—I seemed to be somehow implicated in Anais's crime in the old man's mind, or perhaps he was vexed at me for claiming, in all honesty, that I did not know who the father was when he asked me—but he was also touchingly considerate of his daughter. He often asked Anais when she'd eaten last. If it'd been too long, he forced her to take a break and have some food. He began to help more around the café, occasionally even serving and busing tables in order to give Anais a rest.

Though I would not have liked to admit it, it was a relief also to no longer be the only shoulder for Anais to lean on. I was happy to do it. I'd meant what I'd said to Anais, more even than I'd been able to convey. She was very dear to me, and yet the intrigue, the drama, the emotion, it drained me, especially on top of the constant strain I already felt from the noisy, hectic, crowded environment I worked and lived in. I looked desperately forward to my weekly escapes, when I left the cacophony behind and walked out into the quiet woods to paint.

On one of my outings, I came across a small, dilapidated cottage set beside a stand of almond trees. The roof sagged in spots, and pigeons were nesting in the chimney. It reminded me somehow, with its soft, old slouchiness, of Piroska's thatch-roofed hut, and as soon as I saw it, I longed deeply for it to be my own. In the evening, when Anais asked where I had painted during the day, I described the spot and the house.

"Ah, yes," she said with a scheming look in her eye. "The Pierret place. You know, that would be a nice place for *you*, Anna."

"What do you mean?" I asked, acting as though the thought had never crossed my mind.

"Nah, nah, listen to me," she insisted. "It's a good size for you. It's out where you like to paint. You wouldn't have to walk two miles every time you wanted to go out. You're basically independently wealthy now as Chamonix's most illustrious painter in residence—thanks, I feel I must add, largely to me—and besides, I'm fairly certain you could get it for a song; it's been sitting out there empty for so long."

She set down the rag she'd been wiping the bar top with and leaned against the back counter. One hand rested on her belly, which was still discreet but often seemed to draw her hand thoughtlessly to it none-theless.

"Why is it empty?" I asked.

"The son grew up and moved away to Lyon. When the parents died, it was just left to sit. Kind of out of the way, after all."

"But why would I move at all?" I asked, shrugging and gesturing around at the walls of the café and then significantly at Anais's belly.

"Anna," she said, giving me a wry smile. "It's no secret that you don't love living here. Mon Dieu, you jump out of your skin every time the door slams shut. You are an *artiste*, my dear. You need space and time and quiet, not clattering dishes and drunk men slobbering on you. I know it. Surely you must know it."

"But you're . . ." I looked around, but the crowd in the café was thin and no one was near enough to hear. "You're pregnant, Anais. You need my help around here. I don't know how you did it all on your own be-fore, and I can't imagine how you would possibly do it with me gone and your belly out to here!"

"Ah, you're a good friend," she sighed, and patted my hand across the bar top, "but I'll be just fine. I'll hire a new girl, someone better at flirting than you are. I swear, you are the most uptight beautiful girl I ever met. The men have all given up on you."

I laughed. She was right and there was no denying it. The attentions of the men in the café always made me sweat and search in a panic for something to busy myself with on the opposite side of the room.

"As a barmaid, let's be honest, you are just comme ci, comme ça," Anais continued, shrugging her shoulders this way and that, "*but* you are a *magnificent* painter."

I could do nothing but smile down at my hands where they rested on the table, grateful again for Anais and her friendship.

"Now if you take it into your head to move off to *Paris* or go wandering off in the woods again, *then* you can expect some stern words from me, but just down the road, *pah* . . ." With one hand she brushed the concern away. "And when you get lonesome, you can come back and wash linens with me. You are quite good at that."

THE NEXT WEEK, ANAIS AND I went for a walk to have a look at the house.

"I'll put a little swing in that tree," I said, pointing to the closest of the gnarly armed almond trees, "and you'll come here with your little son or daughter—"

"Oh, it's a girl," Anais said confidently. "I'm quite sure of it. They say girls steal their mother's beauty, and look at me!" She pulled down at her cheeks so that the rims of her eyes sagged comically. "I haven't had a decent-looking day since this little boarder moved in."

"Nonsense," I scoffed. "You're prettier than ever, Anais."

"Well," she said with a lift of her brow, "whether yes or no, I will have a little girl. I know it, and I'm never wrong."

I laughed. "Okay, well then we'll push your *daughter* on the swing, and we'll have picnics in the grass, and when she gets older, maybe I can teach her to paint."

"You almost make it sound wonderful," she said, putting one hand to her belly and the other over her eyes to squint up at the peak of Mont Blanc, which seemed to rise straight up nearly from where we stood.

"It *will* be wonderful," I said quietly. "You're going to be a wonderful mother."

"I think you're right," she said, tilting her chin defiantly, but in the next moment she seemed to shrink again. "I just need to get through everyone else finding out. There will be a moment, suddenly, when *one* person puts it together, and then it will go out, *pshew.*" She swept her hands forward in front of her as if describing the path of some powerful blowing wind or the fallout of a bomb. "And everyone will suddenly know all at once."

She took a deep, uncertain breath and looked sidelong at me, seeming to seek confidence from me instead of the other way around, the way it usually was.

"Maybe," I answered, "but your father already knows and I know, and we'll both be with you through whatever comes."

She nodded, looked away, and gave a small sniff.

"Maybe *war* will break out like everyone's saying and then no one will have a thought to spare for a barmaid's big tummy."

I gave her a puzzled look, and she laughed.

"*Hitler?*" she said, looking incredulous. "*Mussolini?* The fascists right there and there." She jerked a thumb first toward the bottom of the mountain where the border of Italy lay, then north toward Austria and Germany beyond it. "You really don't have any idea, do you, you sweet, innocent dear? Oh, you artists," she said, laughing again, "heads so far in the clouds, you've got rainbows coming out your asses!"

I laughed too, relieved somewhat to have my ignorance exposed and attributed to sweetness and innocence.

"Anyway," Anais said, her wonderful haughtiness returning, "those people need me and my wine more than I need them and their opinions. Two days sober, and they'll be back and greeting me with curtsies."

"That's right," I said. "There can be no doubt that you have the upper hand."

She tossed her head, shaking all other thoughts from it, and looked up smilingly at the mountain peak before us.

"Such a view!" she exclaimed. "You'll practically be printing your own francs with all the lovely landscapes you'll be making."

"Right," I said, and laughed.

"You will still hang them in the café, won't you?" she asked, turning her shaded gaze my way.

"Of course, and you'll still *sell* them for me, won't you?"

"Of course." She smiled deviously up at the mountain. "For a small commission."

I looked up at the mountain, unable to keep from smiling. Paul came to mind, and, for once, I didn't push the thought of him away. I wished for his company here. Thoughts of how well we would share the cozy little house and how well he would paint Mont Blanc with its twisting white peaks, and how he would say that all of these things—this house, this friend, this pretty village with its kind people who bought my paintings— were all too much. Too much goodness.

Beside me, Anais took a cigarette from the pack in her coat pocket and lit it. Shielding her eyes against the sun and trailing a plume of white smoke behind her, she stomped away through the tall grass, shouting at me to come look at some outbuilding she'd discovered behind the house. I didn't move, though; I was distracted by the acrid burn of the cigarette smoke that had wafted into my face and the sudden pounding it had prompted from my heart. I was busy waving it away and telling myself that smoke didn't mean anything to me anymore.

• • •

ANAIS SENT SOME MEN OUT to work on the house for me. Old men and loafers from the café who didn't have regular jobs. One of them was Monsieur Seydoux, a man with a subtle limp, who worked odd jobs and who might have been handsome—dark, curly hair and bright blue eyes—had he had a more pleasant disposition, but he was snide and touchy when sober, and sensual and hot-tempered when drunk. He was a regular in the café, and often let his gaze linger on Anais and on me in a hungry, appraising way that made me uncomfortable. When he came to work on the house, he was no less attentive. He took frequent water and cigarette breaks in the house and made strange conversation, ask- ing me about my friendship with Anais—"You two are very close, no? The prettiest girls in Chamonix and thick as thieves as well?"—while I cleaned and swept the floors and turned my back on his intrusive gaze, trying to walk the line between polite and cold.

When he and the others had finished, I thanked them warmly, but made sure later to tell Anais that I disliked Monsieur Seydoux's attentions and preferred to avoid his company whenever possible. I knew him to be married and the father of a number of children, and his brazen eyes filled me with indignation.

Anais usually had a tart, ready reply to anything, but when I told her this, she was uncharacteristically quiet for a moment. She set her jaw and wiped forcefully with a bar rag at the ceramic demitasse she was drying.

"Yes, you should be careful of that scoundrel," she said after a moment, her lips pinched with suppressed anger. "I should have known better than to send him out to your house. He's a cad and shiftless on top of that. Has a thing for redheads too. I should have wondered why that that club-footed gimp was so eager for hard labor on a Saturday, when every other day he's inclined to do nothing but sit about in the café. Monsieur Seydoux won't be bothering you anymore. I'll see to *that.*"

I was caught off guard by the vehemence of Anais's response, and for a second just looked at her in silence, wondering. She felt my gaze on her, and after a moment gave a noticeable swallow before jerking her head off to the right.

"Clear that table for me, would you? I'm almost caught up on dishes."

"Oh, yes, sorry," I said, and scrambled off to do as she'd asked.

BY LATE SUMMER, I WAS able to move into my little cottage. For the first time, I kept domesticated animals—two goats and three sheep—to feed from, and with much practice, I became adept at feeding gently and sparingly and rewarding the animals so that it became as simple and routine as milking cows. I went among my neighbors politely but maintained a careful distance. It helped to be Anais's friend and it also helped to be known as the town artist; it allowed for some small degree of eccentricity and a bit of freedom from the usual expectations put on women. My neighbors knew my work—many of them owned some of my pieces—and that allowed them to feel that they knew me even if they did not.

For a little while, it seemed that life in my new home would be simple and perfect. I spent my days sitting in a field before my easel and my nights in my parlor with books borrowed from the village library, doing what I could to catch up on the decades of history and literature I'd missed. Anais visited me on rare occasions when she could get away, but more often I went to see her, and we caught up as she went about her duties in the café. She had hired a new girl, Elodie, but perhaps regretted her choice. The girl was pretty and lively and chatted well with the patrons, but she seemed incapable of talking and working at the same time, and Anais was constantly having to direct her back to her work or shoo her off upstairs or to the kitchen, where there were fewer distractions. Anais's midsection was growing thicker all the time, and I could tell she was worrying more about the day when her secret would no longer be secret. But then, all at once, she wasn't.

It was a strange, surreal day. Something big had happened, and in the streets people were huddled around newspapers, shaking their heads and pulling the smoke anxiously from their cigarettes, then throwing the butts down with bitter force. The headlines spoke of Germany's invasion of Poland, of an ultimatum issued by England and France that Germany had now defied.

I found Anais in the café. She was sitting slouched at the bar, in front of a glass of wine, though it was only a little past noon. Her elbows were propped on the bar surface, and she held her forehead up with one hand as she drank. It was her usual habit to greet every guest who came through the doors, but when I entered, she did not even look up. All this was very unlike her and it filled me with dread as to the significance of those headlines in the paper.

"Anais," I said, pushing through a tight band of men clustered near the door and drawing up next to her at the bar. "Anais, what is it? What's happening?"

She barely turned to me, and her expression was clouded and bitter.

"Oh, it's just war," she said darkly, as though such things were all that was to be expected of life, and then she lifted the wineglass for another drink.

I studied my friend's profile in confusion. She looked exceptionally pale, her soft brown freckles suddenly standing out darkly on her nose, and her eyelids seemed heavy.

"Anais, are you okay?"

She took another drink, drained the glass, and then reached for the neck of the wine bottle that peeked up from the other side of the bar top. Behind the bar, where Anais ought to have been, her father stood instead. He took the bottle in his own hand and, with a look as dark and dismal as Anais's, poured wine into his daughter's glass, then squeezed her hand before moving off down the bar to fill another glass.

"What is it, Anais? Is it the war? Are things very bad?"

She gave me a small sidelong glance, and her eyes were red and swollen.

"The fascists are welcome to everything, for all I care," Anais slurred belligerently.

Monsieur Chambrun overheard this provocative statement from a few feet down the bar, and he and I exchanged concerned looks over Anais's head.

"Anais, what's going on?" I whispered, leaning close to her.

"I've lost the baby," she said quietly, and then she crumpled, head in hand, against the side of my arm, tears running down her face.

"Oh, Anais."

I put my arm around my friend and my cheek against the top of her head. "Oh God, Anais, I'm so sorry. When? When did this happen?"

"Yesterday. I had cramps all evening, and then"—she lifted her wineglass, but then set it down again without taking a drink—"out she came. I saw her. Can you imagine? Only the size of a bean, but I could see the little spots for eyes, the beginnings of arms and legs. She was right there."

I couldn't think of any words that could possibly be equal to the moment, so I just held her closer against my side. Behind us, the group of men grew loud, and one of them bumped Anais with his elbow. I turned around, and it was Monsieur Seydoux. He didn't apologize. He barely even glanced at Anais before returning to his conversation with the other men.

Anais set her jaw and glared darkly forward.

"Curious, isn't it?" she said, one eye trembling softly with rage. "That I hate the bastard even more now than I did when he got me pregnant in the first place?"

I glanced back toward Monsieur Seydoux and then again to Anais, and the hard, unblinking look in her eye seemed intentionally not to deny what she could see I suspected. She pulled herself back up to sitting and wiped at the tears on her face.

"I suppose I should be glad. Solution to all my problems, right?"

I gazed down at the smooth, oiled bar top for a moment.

"Was it a problem?" I asked, looking over at her. "That didn't seem to be the way you felt about it."

She stared ahead, no longer looking bitter, only sad and far away.

"No," she said. "I knew I should be afraid, but I wasn't. I loved her. I wanted to push her on that swing."

With one hand I pulled the long curtain of Anais's beautiful strawberry hair around, set it neatly on her shoulder, and smoothed it.

"I know," I said, tipping my head again to rest it against hers. "I wanted that too."

I WENT MORE OFTEN TO visit Anais after that. She bled for several weeks, and for many weeks after that she continued to look thin and unwell. Some days her cheeks were fiery red, but it wasn't rouge, and when she did not bat my hand away, I found her forehead warm to the touch. The café around her had slipped into disorder, with dishes piled up and floors unswept. Anais did not have the strength or the will to carry it all as she always had, and her father and Elodie could not make up the difference. I helped out whenever I came, but only on the condition that Anais go upstairs and rest. I was very worried about her. Lost babies could cause infections or other problems and take the mothers with them, but Anais had made it this far without the village discovering her pregnancy and she didn't want to risk word getting out now by seeing the town physician. From the woods, I brought my friend what medicinal plants I could find—rowanberries and herbes de la Saint-Jean—but otherwise, all I could do was lighten her load in the café and watch over her through the dismal months that followed as her health, at times, made small gains and at other times deteriorated.

In worry and unease, autumn slipped into winter, and winter went on and on. Passing time in the café once more, I heard plenty of talk about the war, but I still found it all difficult to make sense of. The Soviets, whoever they were, had invaded Finland, wherever that was; German boats that went entirely underwater were sinking Allied merchant vessels, and next door to us, Italy, which had allied with Germany, was making show by mustering companies of soldiers along the border just below Chamonix. And yet the papers and many of the villagers called it all a "phony war." France, I was many times assured, had two impenetrable barriers protecting our borders from Germany: the dense forests of the Ardennes to the north and the fortifications of the Maginot Line along the one-hundred-mile border with Germany to the southeast. And Italy, the enemy we could have hit with a well-aimed stone, seemed to be the least concerning of all: "the barking runt bitch of Europe" was how I most commonly heard it referred to, and Monsieur Chambrun would often declare with relish that "those Italians couldn't make it up Mont Blanc if we dangled down ropes to help them."

"Hitler's a *damn fool!*" others shouted. "And he'll realize it soon enough, if he so much as winks at France."

An armistice would be agreed to any day, the men said with confidence, and it was unthinkable, above all, for any threat to actually come to France.

"We are *French!*" they would drunkenly declare, which seemed to be synonymous with untouchable. I was too ignorant and too preoccupied with Anais's fluctuating health to bother with forming an opinion of my own, but I had to admit that when you looked out over the still valleys falling away below Chamonix or up to the high, arid, white slopes of Mont Blanc, what they said seemed true enough. It felt impossible to imagine anything in Chamonix but peace and tranquility forever.

Finally, spring came, and both the mountainside and Anais seemed to flush with new life, but the joy of warmth and budding leaves on trees and pleasant strolls with my friend in the sunshine was tempered by the news of more countries falling to the Germans. In April, it was Denmark and then Norway. In May, it was Luxembourg, then the Netherlands, then Belgium.

On a fine day in September, what seemed likely to be one of the last warm days before the chill of autumn moved in, I was gathering my supplies to go painting. I hadn't been out in quite a while, and Anais, the last few times I'd visited her, had had better color and higher spirits than I'd seen in a long time. She'd made the acquaintance of some nuns who ran the village orphanage and had gone on several occasions to read and play with the children. This seemed to do something powerful for her. She was not the bright, laughing, gregarious girl she had been, but she'd regained a soft, subdued version of her old smile, and her eyes now looked out thoughtfully and were no longer empty and bitter. For the first time since she'd lost the baby, I felt that she would be all right in both body and spirit. With the weight of that worry lifted from me, my thoughts had gone, with longing, back to painting. I was just pouring linseed oil from the large jar of it I kept on a shelf into a smaller, more portable one when a loud knock at the door startled me.

I opened the door to find Anais, her face tear-stained and her expression stricken.

"Anais, what is it? What's the matter? Are you all right?"

"I can't stay long. I've got to get back to the café, but I just thought you should know, and I knew you wouldn't unless I told you." She paused and took several heavy breaths. "The Germans are in France. They've invaded."

My mouth fell, and my eyes searched Anais's face as I struggled to think through all that this meant.

"It's actually happened," I murmured. "They all said it couldn't."

"They're *all* a bunch of fools; that should be no surprise," Anais replied. "But that isn't all I've come to talk to you about."

"There's *more*?"

Anais pressed her lips and cast a look to the side before going on.

"The teacher's left the school. She's left Chamonix and likely France altogether."

Confused, I waited for Anais to go on. The school and the orphanage shared the same building, the village children and the orphans learning together; Anais must have learned of the teacher's departure from the nuns, but I couldn't see what the significance was, or what it might have to do with me.

"She's a Jew. They say that the Germans are rounding up all the Jews. They disappear and nobody sees or hears from them again. Some say Hitler's trying to get rid of them. *All* of them. The nuns need someone to come to the school to help with the children. But with so many of the men gone and the women all doing the men's work in addition to their own, well, I thought of you."

"*Me?* A teacher? But—but I don't know anything. Why *me?*"

"They're not too concerned with education right now. No one in all of Europe is learning any damned arithmetic at the moment. It's mostly just to watch them, keep them distracted. I would do it, but obviously I'm too busy with the café."

She pulled a cigarette from her pocket and fidgeted with it, but couldn't seem to focus enough to even attempt to light it. I took the matches from her, lit one, and held it out. Fine lines like thin, bare branches formed on her mouth around the cigarette. They used to disappear when she took the cigarette from her mouth, but now they remained, ever so faintly. In just the year or so that I'd known her, my friend had aged, subtly, but I had not. Never would. How long, I wondered, before Anais noticed? Before everyone noticed?

"Some of the children are Jewish," Anais went on, giving me a mean-ingful look. "At the orphanage. Their parents have been arrested or gone missing *or worse*, and they've been brought here for hiding. No one's sup-posed to know, but I'm telling you because you're going to teach them and the other children and look after them with the nuns. You're the only one in this town who hasn't anything to do all day. Will you do it? Please?"

As soon as she'd mentioned Jews, I'd thought of Paul looking soberly into the fire after he and his "Jewish paintings" had been thrown out of town.

"I'm a Jew," he had said, "and apparently that's a terrible thing to be."

I hadn't really known what to make of all he'd told me—I still didn't—but I understood now that it was a larger thing than I had previously imagined. It wasn't just an "unkindness," as he'd called it, in a town here and there. It was something huge and murderous, a stomping, snorting beast pounding its hooves across whole countries and continents.

I thought of the orphans Anais spoke of, Jewish children, despised and punished for being Jewish, just as Paul had been.

"They're so beautiful, Anna, the children," Anais said, wringing her hands, her face suddenly anguished. "And they're so scared. The Germans are after them, and they have no one to protect them but a couple of elderly nuns. Will you come?"

I took a deep breath. Let it out.

"Yes," I said to Anais. "Yes, I'll do it."

A FEW DAYS LATER, THE very day that Paris fell to the Germans, I became a teacher to some twenty pupils of various ages. Most of the Chamonix children had said goodbye to fathers and older brothers who'd gone off to fight for France, but the Jewish children had said goodbye to everyone and everything. They were beautiful children with beautiful names that I would remember all my life: Jacov, Hadassa, Michiline, and Mendel. They were close-lipped and watchful. Two of them did not speak French, and I had to translate everything I said into German for them, which inspired the fury of some of the other, older students, who had quickly learned from their parents to despise all things German.

"What are *Germans* doing here?" Alain Seydoux, one of Monsieur Seydoux's children, demanded. "The Germans are murdering babies and people in wheelchairs, and we're supposed to sit next to them in class?"

The smaller children, and some of the orphans too, shrank down in fear at Alain's blunt announcement of a rumor, which I had heard too, and it was no small task trying to convince the children that they would hear many rumors but should not assume any were true and also to explain to them the difference between these German orphans and the German army that was rolling across France in tanks.

It was an exhausting first day, and aside from mediating conflict, I had no idea what to do with the children, so at first, I shared with them the things I'd learned from the books I'd been reading, or gave rambling summaries of plays and novels, but *Hamlet* was not nearly as compelling in summary as it was in full. The children were restless and agitated and quarrels broke out frequently between them. I cast about for a different approach. When I went to Anais for advice, she said, "You must know *something*, Anna. Whatever it is, teach them that."

So, the next day I began with a drawing lesson that, to my surprise, was enthusiastically received. After that, I took the children out for a walk in the forest, where I taught them to spot hen-of-the-woods mushrooms and pheasant's back, lemon balm and wild celery, and I taught them how to test unfamiliar plants to discern whether they were edible or poisonous. I knew how to survive in the woods, and it occurred to me that survival might now be a valuable skill to possess.

Then I thought of another thing I knew, the only bit of history I was familiar enough with to teach, the American Revolution. I taught them in stories, just as I had been taught, about the outrage of the Quartering Act and the rebellion of the Boston Tea Party, about oxcarts loaded with canons crossing hundreds of miles of wintry terrain to force the British from Dorchester, about the militias that were formed at a moment's notice by limping farmers and Quaker ministers and slaves fighting for their own freedom no less than the country's, how they rushed off and beat one of the great military powers of the world with little more than farm tools and rifles, belligerence and conviction.

As more news arrived about German advances farther into France, and with it more rumors of barbarism and brutality, and as the children waited for word from their fathers and brothers, I found myself saying things, always under the guise of history, to encourage them.

"The biggest army," I told them, "does not always win. When people are fighting for their freedom, for their families and their homes, for things they love and believe in, they fight harder than it makes sense to. They fight harder than anyone could predict or prepare for or defend against. The British wanted to win the war, and by all accounts they should have, but the revolutionaries *had* to win. Everything depended upon it. They simply *had to*, and so they did."

I was afraid to give the children hope, even as I did it. I knew the truth just as Anais did: that what is hoped for is not always what comes to pass, that darkness too often prevails, and that horrible evil and tragedy habitually befall the least deserving. Their fathers and brothers could very well all die. Yet I also believed what I said, that none fight harder than those who fight for what they love. I hoped they could take comfort at least in knowing that their fathers and brothers were fighting hard for them and that their fight was no small thing.

It seemed to help the children. It seemed to unleash some belligerence in them, some belief in their own power to fight for what they loved, even if it was only their own fear that they were fighting.

By winter the Germans were in Lyon and Grenoble, and scattered battalions were marching closer to Chamonix all the time. The resources of the nearest towns were being requisitioned for the Germans. Trade was cut off. We had only what we raised or hunted. The café was digging deep into its stores of wine and mixing them with water. Elodie left with her parents and a younger sister for Marseille, where it was said one could still get out of France, but Anais and her father no longer needed extra help; the rooms in the hotel were mostly vacant.

To help feed the orphans, I slaughtered my goats and sheep, one by one, and gave the meat to the nuns. When they were all gone, I began a new evening routine: I went to see Anais at the café, get whatever news was to be had, and then I went out to hunt. I fed myself, and then I did my best to bring back whatever I could for the children and for Anais and the café.

The first time I hauled a dead deer to the back door of the café, Anais looked at me with a mix of wonder and horror.

"Anna, my very dearest of friends, who *are* you?"

Anais knew nothing about dressing or butchering animals. The process was difficult for her and such a mess (not to mention a waste of perfectly good blood) that I knew as I helped her that I could never expect the nuns to manage it, so I added it to my duties and used the outbuilding on my property for the tedious and unpleasant work.

On one of these nights, I wandered in my hunting farther than usual from the village. On the outskirts of a little town called Coupeau, I came upon a small military camp: some two dozen tents pitched in a moonlit stand of pines.

There was the orange flicker of a cooking fire, the smell of frying pork and onions (stolen, no doubt, from a nearby farmhouse), and the choppy cadence of German conversation. I was hidden in the trees, surveying the camp, when about ten meters to the right of me a branch snapped.

I turned, and across the distance and through branches my eyes met those of a soldier just turning from the tree where he'd been urinating. His hand was frozen at his zipper, and for a moment we both stood like statues, staring at each other and calculating. My situation was not good. This man alone would have been little cause for concern—I had a hunting knife attached to my belt, which I carefully slid back behind me and out of view—but the whole camp of other men who were within a shout's reach, and who I wagered were more likely to assist their comrade in his endeavors than to assist me in mine, were cause for concern.

Then the soldier began to come toward me.

"*Halloo*," he called softly in German, studying me and approaching slowly, as if I were some bird he intended to coax and catch before it flew off.

"Sprechen sie Deutsch?" the man asked.

I made no answer, only continued to watch him as he drew nearer.

"Are you lost? Pretty lady?" he said in German, pushing past the needled branch of a fir. "Do you need help finding your way? Do you need help finding your way to my tent?"

I gave no sign that I understood him and let him continue to draw near. Best to play vulnerable and afraid.

When he was finally close, almost within arm's reach, he smiled the contented smile of a man sitting down to a feast and began slipping off the rifle slung across his chest.

"If I'm not the luckiest bastard in all of France."

"*Juden!*" I hissed suddenly.

At the unexpected word and the sound of my German, the man's expression became startled again.

"Es verstecken sich Juden," I said. There are Jews hiding.

For a moment, he only stared at me in confusion, recalibrating to a situation that was no longer what he had thought it was.

"You are looking for them? I know of some," I said. "I know where, but you must come with me now. It cannot wait. Soon they will be gone."

"*Jews?*" the soldier said, eyeing me with a mixture of suspicion, hunger, and amusement.

"They are this way," I said, pointing out farther into the woods.

He thought for a moment, glanced in the direction of his own camp, and I could read the calculations of his mind on his face. Either way, Jews or no Jews, he liked the idea of our moving out farther from camp, where we wouldn't be heard or disturbed, as did I.

"Yes," he said finally. "Very well. Show me."

"This way," I said, and I took off running through the trees.

"Hey!" he cried in a muted shout. "Not so fast!"

He began running after me, his uniform and gear shuffling and rattling noisily. I swung behind a tree, and as he came running past, I grabbed him from behind and slit his throat so fast that he did not let out even the smallest cry, just collapsed forward into the snow like one of those army tents, the poles removed suddenly.

Chest heaving, limbs shaking, I looked down at the man where he lay prone and bleeding onto the snow. I searched for the fear or remorse that I expected to feel, but I did not find it. This man hated Paul, hated my children, wanted to find them, take everything from them, kill them. This man might have bound Vano and Piroska to a chair if his comrades led him there to do it. At a command, he might have lit the match and watched them burn.

I bent over him in the snow, like a wolf at a carcass, and drained him right there. If I'd been a wolf, I would have howled, long and slow at the moon and all the despicable things beneath it that ought to have feared me. When I was done, I stripped the body of any useful supplies and left it where it had fallen.

Did I ever actually form a plan? Was there ever a moment when I made a deliberate decision to protect the children in my care by spending my nights hunting down those who hunted them? I don't think so. I just followed a feeling: the hard, cool calm I felt when I looked down and saw one less German soldier in the world. And whenever the children seemed afraid, whenever the papers delivered news of some further encroachment, some enemy victory or Allied defeat, some new regulation or mandate for handing over Jews, I would go, driven out into the night, looking to soothe the fear of the children and my own, which was new and quick and hot now that I had something at stake in the fight, something I cared about.

And it *was* soothing—running them down, stabbing them, strangling them, watching them drop to their knees as if in confused prayer, watching the blood spill out across the snow. Ehru rose up like a ghost, hunting alongside me, and I felt again our kinship, or my desire to be akin to him: brutal, thoughtless, possibly mad. Perhaps it is only a certain kind of soldier who experiences a hard, druglike calm in the act of killing, but I discovered that I was now that kind of soldier. It gave me a sensation of infinite power, as though I could murder and feed my way through the entire German army, with all I cared for sheltered safely behind my skirts.

With pride and pleasure, I listened from the shadows as the *soldaten* smoked together beneath the stars and whispered their speculations about desertion, or a French resistance cell, saboteurs within their own ranks, or what some of them were starting to call the Nacht Bestie: an inhuman monster, beast, or phantom that was patiently hunting them, nesting amid their bones back in some fetid den.

Nacht Bestie. I confess, I have always loved that name.

· XXX ·

NEARLY a week goes by without a call from Katherine. Somehow, I'm not surprised.

Sometimes Dave, terse and unexpressive, drops Leo off (notably on time) for school or picks him up, but mostly Katherine does. When it's Katherine, they're invariably late, sometimes by a lot. At pickup, she's warm and casual but makes no mention of anything personal. It's as if we've never known each other or had a conversation beyond the superficial. I wonder if she and Dave have patched things up. Perhaps my suggestion that she leave was some unpardonable breach or maybe she was more embarrassed than she let on at having forgotten Leo's birthday. Either way, it's probably all for the best. I miss those evenings spent with Leo—my evenings at home have not grown any more bearable—but I don't miss the headache of being his mother's confidante. I'm content with superficiality.

Instead of going to the Hardmans', one afternoon I take a trip to see Mr. Riley at the cemetery. I'm seeking reassurance that I had nothing whatever to do with the break-in. When I arrive, Mr. Riley, in a knit hat and thick gloves, is spreading mulch at the base of rosebushes wrapped in burlap for the winter. The leaves have all fallen from the oak trees, and the graveyard is no longer shadowed and cove-like. Now it's a tapestry woven in the textured browns of plant husks and barren branches all washed in wan winter light.

Mr. Riley sees me and smiles, but I know immediately that I will not get my wish. I will not be cleared of involvement in what took place here. He has something he wants to tell me—*me* specifically.

"Hello there," he calls as I approach. "I'm so glad to see you, my dear, but I must tell you that it is with a heavy heart that I greet you today."

He puts his gloved hand out for me to shake when I'm near enough, and I take it.

"I have terrible news. *Terrible* news."

"I think I may have heard it," I say. "I saw the paper last week."

"But my dear, only *you* will grasp the *true* tragedy of it all. Do you remember that stone that I showed you? The little, strange, no-account grave marker that I said I thought was the work of a master and an apprentice?"

"I do," I say, bracing myself for what I know is to come.

"We stood right in there," he continues, pointing abstractly in the direction of the visitor center, "and talked about it. My *favorite* artifact, and wouldn't you know it."

"They took that one?"

"They took that one, and *only* that one."

My expression is one of deep regret because I am full of deep regret. Mr. Riley, who thinks I'm merely being sympathetic, pats my shoulder.

"I'm so glad you're here," he says. "You're the only one who would understand."

"You said that was all they took. Was there any other damage to the property? Did they break anything getting in?"

"They didn't break anything getting in. You know, I've never been too fussy about locking up. Mostly I do, but sometimes I forget and, you know, I don't sweat it. We're so far out here, and I've never had any problems before, but I guess the door wasn't locked because it was just swinging in the breeze when I got here. I knew something was up right when I arrived, though, because there's a little statue out front, a little cherub right next to the parking lot, and it was knocked over and split in two, like someone ran into it with their car. Wasn't like that the day before."

I think of the dent in the front bumper of my car and the cracked headlight beside it, the height, width—yes, that's about the damage you'd expect from running into a two-foot-tall statue.

"I guess I should be grateful we didn't lose more than that. But you know my heart hurts. It *hurts my heart* that someone would do that, and *why*? Just can't make sense of it."

"Yes, it is very strange and saddening. Again, I'm so sorry."

We both consider the grounds for a moment in silence, a brief act of shared mourning.

"Well," I say at last, "I—I came by because I wanted to help if you would allow me. I'd like to pay for any damages you may need to have repaired. I'd love to replace that cherub statue for you to begin with, or if it'd be easier, I can just make a donation and then you can use it however you see fit. Whatever would be most helpful. We enjoyed our visit here as a class so much, and when I heard about what happened, I felt more terrible than I can say."

"*Oh, my goodness*, that's so kind of you," Mr. Riley exclaims, taking my gloved hand in his and patting it like the hand of a well-behaved child. "That's so kind. Look at that, my faith in humanity takes a blow, and here you are, come to restore it just like that. Bless you, my dear. Bless you."

Mr. Riley's faith in humanity, I think as I walk back to my car, has been restored, but what about my faith in my own? And the stone, my father's headstone—if I was the one who took it after all, then where is it? What have I done with it?

MR. RILEY AND MY CEMETERY break-in are of course on my mind again when two nights later I'm back in the Emersons' barn. Breaking in. Doing precisely the thing for which I'd just expressed and *truly felt* such deep contrition. Trespassing on friends, stealing from the sweet and unsuspecting—it seems at times that virtue is a kind of luxury and that, desire it as I may, I simply lack the wherewithal to possess it for my own. Instead, it's my lot to wrestle with just how despicable I'll allow myself to be.

With my hunger satiated, I put on my things and leave, sliding the door silently back into place, then I make my way past the Emersons' house, dark and still, headed toward their pasture and, beyond it, my own property. In a few minutes, I'm walking toward my house through the long, unbroken stretch of trees, when a sudden smell stops me short. It must be after midnight, much too late for anyone to be burning leaves or enjoying bonfires, yet there it is, pungent on the wind: smoke.

Though I don't want it to, it all comes back to me (smells are so powerful that way): Vano trembling and dripping sweat, the face in the river, the sounds in the woods just beyond the circle of firelight, the drifting ash, and through all of it, like a backdrop, the empty final scent of char and the sound like invisible wings of flame beating the air. Why is it all coming back to me now? There were so many years of silence, so many years devoid of the inexplicable, that I'd become sure, *gratefully sure*, that it had all only been nonsense in the first place. Sure, I remembered it all as clearly as I remembered anything. And had believed it then—no, not believed, unless one would say that they are, every minute, "believing" their senses. I *experienced* it, just as I am experiencing these things now, but I don't want to. I want to believe that the girl I once was was simply impressionable and overly imaginative, but then what is there to say of the woman I am now? The woman who is living every moment in fear, scrambling from room to room in her house disconnecting smoke detectors to no avail, catching glimpses of floating ash in the air, smelling smoke? How can I discredit her?

I walk on, trying to ignore the smell that only grows stronger, hoping it will dissipate, though it does not. There is a rustling in the trees to my left. I click on my flashlight and point the beam at the sound. It's nothing, I tell myself. It's nothing. It's the wind. It's a squirrel. A branch snaps, and I whip the bar of light toward it, and there is no movement, no hunched figure carved from coal peering blindly around a tree trunk, but in the jaundiced circle of light, at the base of an ash, there is a single glove the color of wine—one of my gloves, which I put on in the hope of preventing injury to myself during my night escapades. What is it doing out here? And the better question, what was *I* doing out here when I dropped it?

I hunt around for a few minutes, turning the nosing beam of the flashlight here and there over leaf piles and into the scrub and the crook of a jack pine bent over like an arthritic old man, searching for the other glove or for any other evidence that might elucidate my nighttime activities, but I find nothing else.

FOR SEVERAL DAYS IN A row, it is only Katherine who is dropping Leo off and picking him up. On one of these days, she takes me aside.

"I did it," she says meaningfully. "I asked him to leave."

I feel as dizzy as a yo-yo with Katherine's unexpected intimacies and inexplicable exiles.

"Katherine, I don't know what to say. If you feel it was the best choice for you and for Leo, then I'm very glad," I offer diplomatically. "Has he agreed to go?"

"Yes. He's gone. I told him to go Wednesday, and he's been staying at a hotel since then."

"And . . . how are you feeling?"

"I'm petrified. I hope I can stick to it. He knows all my weaknesses and he just tosses me around so much emotionally. One minute he seems like he can't wait to get out, the next he's holding my hand and saying we can get through this. He knows just what to say to get me doubting myself, letting him back in."

"You're stronger than you think, Katherine. You'll stick to it if that's what you need to do."

"Keep telling me that, please. I'm going to need it. The truth is, I don't have all that much practice being on my own. You know, I met Dave *two days* after splitting with my ex, who I'd been with for years. I used to tell myself it was just coincidence, but now, well."

"What's the next step for you, then?"

"Oh, filing, lawyers, divvying up assets, all that wretched, awful stuff. Actually, I was wondering if you might be available to watch Leo sometime this weekend so that we can meet with our lawyers?"

I hesitate, trying to think of some excuse or way to demur.

"It really shouldn't be long, and if this interview I have next week with a potential nanny goes well, it might be the last time I have to impose on you. Leo's missed having you over too. He keeps asking when you'll be over, but I'm like, honey, I just don't have any reason to ask Ms. Collette and I can't just ask her to babysit for no reason."

I look over at Leo, sitting in the cloakroom beside Thomas, both of them putting their outdoor shoes on. One last time really *would* be nice.

"All right," I say. "Yes, I can do that. Have you told him? Have you told Leo?"

"Not the truth. Not yet. I told him Dave's been on a business trip. I want things finalized before we officially tell him. Just in case. In case of what, I don't know," she says, and laughs. "In case Dave miraculously transforms overnight into an amazing husband who desperately wants to stay with his wife and treat her like a queen. Or even just like a regular goddamn human being."

She catches herself at the profanity and puts a hand to her mouth apologetically, but none of the children are near enough to hear her.

"Well, I guess there's no special rush," I say. "It seems wise to try to think each thing through before you do it. Just let me know when I should be there. Sunday, I presume?"

THAT SUNDAY, TO MY SURPRISE, Dave is there when I pull up to the house. His silver sedan is parked in the driveway, and he's loading boxes into the trunk. He sees me pull up. Had he not, I might have circled the block slowly and waited for him to leave. With misgivings, I get out of my vehicle. I wonder if Dave wonders how much I know. He must. I wonder how dangerous he ought to be considered. Men in his position, and with his tendency toward physicality, have been known to do crazy things. Katherine may persist in believing that he's "really not a bad guy," but I'm not remotely convinced.

"Afternoon," he calls, but there is no pleasantry in his voice or his face as he scoots and shoves the boxes in the trunk.

"Good afternoon," I reply, doing my best to sound pleasant and ignorant. The dog next door has taken up its usual determined barking. Dave looks toward him.

"What the hell is Vlad's problem?" he mutters.

Vlad, I think, ah yes. The Impaler. What an adorable name for a dog.

I start up the drive, but as I'm passing him, Dave puts out an arm and stops me.

"You know, this might not be my place to say, but at this point, screw it."

I take a step back from him, as though he has pulled a gun on me, and glance around uncomfortably. I really do not want to have any kind of serious conversation with him, but he continues.

"I see her pulling you in. You're here all the time taking care of Leo, and that's kind of you. I'm glad Leo has you around. It's sure as hell better than him being alone with her, but I gotta warn you, it's not a good idea to get too close to that woman."

I'm totally taken aback by this. "I have no idea what you're talking about," I say with unconcealed scorn and move toward the front door.

"All right, fine," he says, turning his attention back to straightening the boxes in his trunk. "But don't say later that I didn't warn you. I've seen it *many* times, and I'm starting to feel like an asshole for not telling people what they're walking into."

I should ignore him, refuse to hear another word, and proceed straight up to the house. It's what Katherine would want me to do, and what I, in her place, would want a friend to do. Still, I can't resist.

"Seen *what* many times?" I ask, clearly conveying by my tone that I'm not likely to believe anything he will say.

He lets out a breath, sets his jaw. "Seen her suck people in, use 'em up, then turn on them. Get rid of them. It's your turn now because she just finished doing it to our nanny."

"Valeria was fired for stealing."

Dave gives a contemptuous snort. "Valeria wasn't stealing. Valeria was a saint, but she witnessed one of Katherine's tantrums, saw her throw a fucking bowl at my head, so she had to go. That's why you're here now, and I bet you're a better deal too. Does she even pay you? *At all?*"

Indignant and vaguely embarrassed by Dave's correct guess that I'm not being paid, I cast about in my mind for a response, something to prove him the liar I know he is, but all I can think of is the broken bowl in the trash can around the same time Valeria stopped showing up to get Leo from school.

"Every word out of her mouth is a lie," he goes on before I can formulate an argument. "Big things, little things, doesn't matter. She doesn't know how to talk without lying. It's how she gets what she wants from people. You're telling me you really haven't noticed?"

"What about *Leo*?" I ask, regaining my footing and suddenly ferocious. "Is *Leo* a liar too, then? Because it was *Leo*, not Katherine, who told me that you pushed them down the stairs and that's how he got a concussion."

"*Leo* said *I* pushed them?" He gives me a look of hard skepticism. "No. I don't believe it."

"He said Katherine was holding him, and you were angry and fighting and tried to take him from her, and down the stairs they went."

"Well, *that's* true enough. You know why we were fighting? Because Katherine was stoned out of her mind on pain meds, just like she is"—he points a finger accusingly at the house—"right this very minute, I might add. *And* she was drunk and carrying him around on the landing, which I didn't think was a good idea. When I tried to get her to put him down, she got all belligerent, and what ended up happening is precisely why I was trying to get her to put him down in the first place."

"You tried to suffocate her!" I throw at him with some desperation. I'm violating all kinds of confidences, but I can't let him win, can't let him manipulate and lie his way out of everything I know he's done. "And then when she told the therapist, you called her a liar. Why should I believe anything you say?"

Mouth open, eyebrows raised in incredulity, Dave looks, for a moment, genuinely spooked.

"She said that? She *actually* told you that?"

I don't answer, just hold my ground, my expression flinty.

He closes his eyes and shakes his head. "Oh God, it would almost be funny, if it wasn't so completely *fucked* up."

"Of course you'll deny doing it," I say, "and since I have no way of knowing one way or another—"

"Of course, of course," he says, waving the hypothetical denials away.

"But how about this? We've never even been to a therapist. Ever. Not once."

I feel as though I've been slapped. I'd expected him to deny trying to suffocate her or calling her a liar; I had not expected him to deny that they'd ever been to a therapist at all.

"But I . . . I've been coming over . . . for weeks, so you two could . . ."

Dave lets out a soft, sad laugh. He tilts his head and gives me a look of simple compassion.

"I'm sure you have. I'm *sure* you have. This is what I'm talking about. This is what she does. But hey, don't take my word for it. Please. Check it out for yourself. Try to get the name of the therapist, a number. They'll suddenly go out of business or move out of the country or *die*. You won't get it out of her, I guarantee it. Katherine would never go to therapy with me; it'd be like an embezzler volunteering for an IRS audit."

It's all more than I can sort through; I don't know what to believe.

"She says you're cheating," I say softly, though even I'm not sure how that matters anymore.

He gives an ambivalent shrug.

"Yeah, fair enough," he says. "*I* would call it escaping, but sure. I've found a great, non-insane woman and I'm getting the hell out of this wreck while I still can. Before I'm put behind bars for supposedly pushing my wife and her kid down the stairs—or *fucking suffocating her*! So yeah, my cheating, I guess there's one true thing she's said. Even a broken clock tells time twice a day, as they say."

"*Her* kid? You're not Leo's father?"

"*No.*" Dave seems surprised by my ignorance. "Katherine and I got together when Leo was, I don't know, *three*, or just about."

I gaze off into space, troubled and trying to put everything together as quickly as it's coming. I realize suddenly that I *believe* Dave. He doesn't seem to be thinking up answers the way Katherine sometimes does; somehow Katherine's stories had never felt entirely right. It had been a subtle thing, and one I'd suppressed or explained away, but now it's plain to me. I'd always wondered just a little, deep down, if she was telling me the truth.

A question occurs to me suddenly.

"Do you know who Max is? I mean, I know Leo has a stuffed giraffe he calls Max, but—"

"Leo calls his giraffe Max?" Dave asks with a keen look of curiosity.

"Well . . . yes . . . you know the stuffed animal I'm talking about?"

"Oh yeah, I know Leo's giraffe. We're well acquainted, but around us, he's Mr. Longneck."

Dave ponders the discrepancy with interest, though I can't see that it matters much. I press on.

"Is there someone else named Max? Did—did Leo have a brother named Max? He seems at times to be talking about someone, besides his giraffe, named Max, but then he says he's not allowed to talk about it."

Despite my previous harsh accusations, interrogations, and candid talk of his affair, it is only now that Dave begins to look uncomfortable. Hand on the raised trunk lid, he deliberates for a moment with a grimace on his face. Finally, he cranes his neck at the house as though checking for someone at the window before speaking in a lowered voice.

"Yes. Max was Leo's older brother. He died, two years ago, August. He drowned in the pool of a house we'd just moved into. Leo was the one who found him."

"Oh God," I whisper, putting a hand to my mouth. "Oh no. Oh, poor Leo."

"They were apparently playing hide-and-seek, and on Max's turn to hide, he went in the pool. He was obsessed with that pool, always begging to go in, but he didn't know how to swim. He could only go in if one of us took him in. I was busy with work, and pools aren't really my thing. Katherine, she maybe took them in a couple of times, but she's not the most *energetic* mother, as we both know.

"Anyway, one afternoon, I come home from golfing and Leo's in the garage, crying and trying to get a pool floatie down from a shelf. I ask what's the matter, and he says Max is in the pool and he won't come out. I knew right then."

I feel dizzy, nauseous. I put a hand over my eyes, trying not to visualize the scene in my mind, but it intrudes. There is Leo standing at the edge of a pool, small and distraught, peering down at the shape of another child, dark and motionless, at the bottom.

"I just thank God Leo didn't go in after him," Dave continues almost at the same time that I have the thought myself. "I have dreams all the time about finding them both in there."

"Where was Katherine when this happened?"

Dave gives the house another glance, this one baleful, then he shrugs as if the answer were obvious.

"Sleeping. Knocked out on pills and sleeping so hard that Leo couldn't wake her up. He tried. *I* had a tough time waking her up before the paramedics came, had to throw her in the shower. Then that became the story, that she'd been in the shower when he drowned. *That's* why Leo's not allowed to talk about it."

He gives me a meaningful look.

"He was coached. We told him, if anyone asked, to say she was in the shower. It seemed like the right thing to do at the time. Probably it was, but it's also probably the ten minutes of my life I'm most ashamed of."

I give him a questioning look. Telling a child to lie is, of course, nothing to be proud of, but with so much on the line, it seems at least understandable.

"Katherine told Leo that it was their fault, both of them, Leo's and hers, that Max drowned, and that if he didn't say what we told him to say, they would both go to jail. The kid's three years old, for fuck's sake, his brother's lying there dead, and then his mother tells him it's his fault and that he might go to jail for it, scares the absolute shit out of him. And I didn't stop her. I went along with it because the cops were on the way, and we really needed him to stick to the story, and if fear was what it was going to take, so be it."

I'm appalled and sad, so sad for Leo. It comes back to me, the way he'd acted when Audrey's aunt, the police officer, had shown up to the open house, how strangely he had behaved, how he'd refused to go in a room if she was there. It had seemed so out of character and irrational, but what if it was because he was afraid she might know about his supposed crime and take him away to jail?

"Did Katherine ever tell him the truth? Or you?" I ask. "Later? That it wasn't his fault and he wouldn't go to jail?"

Dave tips his head from side to side uncertainly. "I told her she should. Told her she was going to fuck him up for life if she didn't. I kind of rode her about it for a while. Then she told me that she did it, but did she really? Who knows? My guess is she didn't. She still needs him to keep her secret. It's still unmentionable. And . . ." He gives me a thoughtful look. "He doesn't call his giraffe Max around us."

I take a deep breath, troubled and overwhelmed.

"*Why are you telling me all this?*" I ask. I'm not sure whether I mean, why me? Or, why tell *anyone*? Or maybe I mean, why are you doing this to me? Burdening me with this horrible knowledge? Maybe I mean them all.

"Probably guilt," he says, shutting the trunk of the car. He turns around and leans against it, folding his thick arms across his chest and looking thoughtful. "You know, I never wanted kids. I'm a fairly selfish person. I just want things pleasant and easy: work, golf, a nice bourbon in the clubhouse after, a beautiful woman on my arm, nice and simple. I was stupid and I thought that I could have Katherine, and *she* would have her kids, and it'd kind of stay separate, and I'd be the good guy 'cause I'd provide for them, but she'd be *responsible* for them. Then one kid *dies*, and the other . . . *fuck!*"

He puts his hands out before him as though holding the damage between them, surveying it with horror. "I just never signed up for this. I never wanted this much power—for good *or* for bad. I mean, I'm just a fucking *guy*."

He rubs his chin for a moment, combing fingers through the bristles of his beard.

"Now I'm leaving to go get that good, simple life, but Leo, he's gotta stay. And selfish as I am, I still understand that when I'm gone, that leaves one less person who knows what really happened, one less person who can set him straight. I sure as hell don't trust Katherine to do it."

His gaze jerks over to me. "And I'm not asking *you* to do it. I'm not putting that on you. I just . . . want someone else to *know*. It would just feel like another betrayal to take the information I have and leave with it."

"Do you know who Leo's real father is? Or where he is? Would *he* maybe want to know this?"

"Name's Hest—Jim, if I recall correctly. Lives in the city somewhere, big Wall Street guy, tons of money, but no, he doesn't want anything to do with them. He's got another family, did the whole time. Katherine thought she could get him to leave and marry her, but it sounds like she got too pushy—perhaps *crazy* too, would be my guess, maybe tried to accuse him of, oh, I don't know, suffocating her, pushing her down stairs—whatever the case, he shut her out hard. Sent his lawyers after her with a choice between a lawsuit and a buyout."

He pulls his car keys from his pocket.

"Anyway, I should get going. After what *you* told me, I think I need to make a call to my lawyer."

He jingles his keys in his cupped palm. "Sorry you had to hear all this. It's more than *I* care to know. I just wanted to say, be careful. You like Leo, you want to look after him, fine, great. He deserves to have *someone* around who gives a shit about him, but lie low, play dumb. She can be real charming, until she's not."

He starts to walk around to the driver's-side door. "And you should probably make an angry gesture at me, kick my car if you like, before you head up to the house," he says, opening the driver's-side door. "She's probably watching and she'll be suspicious. Tell her you told me to go to hell."

He gets in the car and after a moment backs it down the driveway.

When I arrived, I wanted only to get past him without interaction. How can it be that now I almost wish he weren't leaving? I turn and face the house and, suddenly, everything looks different.

· XXXI ·

FOR a while, I went on leaving the fallen soldiers right where they fell, but this, I quickly realized, was foolish. The bodies were being found and arousing the suspicion and ire of the German companies. What's more, it was a terrible waste. The village was running out of everything. Shoes were wearing thin, larders were running empty, pocket money was a memory. The soldiers were heavily armed and outfitted. They had leather boots in good condition, warm socks, and wool coats; they had cigarettes and chocolate and money, often a variety of currencies depending on where they'd been and where they were going. And, of course, they had blood. Great flowing quantities of it. I'd never done anything but subsist, and it occurred to me that, for the first time, I might store up so that I did not have to hunt every time my belly hungered.

I began hauling bodies home to the woodshed behind the house to drain and store the blood and to sort and salvage every item of value. It was a bitterly cold winter, and the deep pack of snow kept the shed icy cold, no concern about the stench of decay wafting. I drained the blood into tin milk pails and let the bodies stack up in a corner to dispose of later. I cut the identifiable German coats into swatches of nondescript fabric, and in greatest stealth left a rucksack stuffed with the cloth outside the door of the couturier and another full of boots outside the *cordonnier's* shop. Soon men could be seen going about town in the boots of German soldiers, and the footwear became a sort of symbol of the French Resistance. Because that's what people believed, that French assassins were hunting and killing Germans and, if not significantly impacting their numbers, hurting at least their morale and giving the French in the region a sense of hope and pride.

To my students, I brought the chocolate and candies and any other food items I found, but the frenzy of strenuous nocturnal activity took its toll on me during the day. I struggled to the school each morning, yawned all throughout my instruction, and then dragged myself home afterward to sleep away the hours before nightfall.

"Madame!" the children began to tease me. "Why are you so tired? Do you have a secret beau?"

Jean-Luc Fevrier and Alain Seydoux made a game of guessing the identity of my mysterious amour. This game was made all the more entertaining for the fact that most of the young, marriageable men were gone soldiering. Is it Monsieur Auber, the stooped old librarian? they guessed. Monsieur Durand, the baker's one-eyed assistant?

"C'est Monsieur Leroy!" they exclaimed, dissolving into giggles—the fat and bald *poissonier*, who smelled perpetually of fish guts. Even the orphans, who had begun, bit by bit, to feel more at home here in the village, laughed at this, their legs kicking merrily beneath their chairs.

Anais also began to wonder about me. I sat at the bar one evening, just up from my afternoon nap, yawning as I talked with her. She tilted her head at me.

"You're tired, Anna. From the sound of it, you hardly ever sleep. Why don't you go home and get a really good night of the stuff?"

"No, I'm not," I protested with a yawn. "I just got up from a nap. I need to wake up is all. Give me another espresso, if you want to help."

"You know, Anna," she went on, "you're a bit like a thousand-ton train. It can take quite a bit of force to get you going, but then it takes just as much to get you to stop."

She leaned forward in front of me, elbows on the bar top, chin on one fist. "You're doing so much for us. The children, the teaching, the hunting. You're not even from here, yet you're practically carrying us all. When's the last time you painted?"

I laughed aloud at this. "Who knows? There's no time for that, Anais. Don't be ridiculous."

"It's not ridiculous, Anna. It's who you are. Coincidentally, it's who we are too, the French. The Germans do not win only by taking down our flag, but by getting us to cease being who and what we are."

I contemplated this for a moment, and contemplated too how much I liked my friend, how clever and kind she was.

"I can't do what you say," I answered finally, smiling at her. "But I do appreciate you saying it."

"Well, then at least go home and get some sleep."

"Do you need an escort?"

It was Monsieur Seydoux who said this. He'd stepped up to the bar with his empty wineglass for a refill, his third or fourth of the night, despite his family certainly having better uses for his francs.

"Not a good time for young ladies to be walking about alone at night."

Anais and I exchanged looks of loathing.

"No, thank you," I said with icy politeness. "I'm not going home just now."

"Well, where are you going, then? At this time of night?"

"I'm thinking that's her business primarily," Anais shot back. "Besides, there are things beside Nazis that a woman must guard herself against."

For an instant, Monsieur Seydoux gave Anais a subtle, vile grin, as though savoring some pleasant memory, and I feared for an instant that Anais's fist might come across the bar top at him, but then the man put his hands up in a gesture of disarmament.

"Just trying to make sure that my children's teacher does not come to any harm. They're very fond of you, you know."

"I'm glad to hear it," I said flatly and without turning toward him. "I'm fond of them too. Thank you for your concern, but I assure you, I'll be fine."

Monsieur Seydoux nudged his glass forward on the counter for his refill, but Anais, hand on the neck of a half-full wine bottle, gazed at him coolly and said, "We're out."

LATER THAT NIGHT, I STRUGGLED home an hour or so before dawn with two soldiers in two sacks slung heavily over my shoulders.

I'd encountered a pair of them, spying at the windows of a farm-house, preparing to break in most likely. Neither of them was especially large, so I'd decided to take them both, but I was regretting the decision now, as I stumbled along in exhaustion toward my home.

The moon hung like a shard of glass, thin and sharp, in the clear sky, and the snow was dark and blue around me. A flickering smell of smoke had been nagging at me for days, and it stopped me several times in my tracks, seeming to come suddenly from right under my nose. At other times, I would think I caught a glimpse of movement just there, behind a tree, a shadow slipping into another shadow, Czernobog, per-haps, come at last to say hello, to poke his smoking dragon's snout in my coffers and tell me it was time to pay. I would pause for a full minute or more, gazing about in tense silence, sniffing the air, but the shadows never stirred when I was watching them and the smell would vanish, and eventually I'd move on.

When I finally reached my property, I pushed open the door to the shed and hefted, first one, then the other sack over the threshold and into the dark, before lighting an oil lamp on one of the counters. The shed was a sight. It had been a few weeks since I had last disposed of any bodies, and a pile of them, clad only in underwear, formed an odd tri-angle in one corner. Buckets of Lugers, ammunition clips, knives, boots, and frozen blood rested on the floor beside them, and a deer and a fox were on the floor waiting to be dressed and butchered. I opened the first sack and was just hefting the body, boots first, out of the opening, when the door to the shed, which I had left open, creaked suddenly closed.

My heart leaped into my throat, and I stumbled backward onto my skirts.

Out of the shadow behind the door, Monsieur Seydoux's face, pale and black-eyed in the flickering lamplight, appeared. Despite the cold, a sheen of sweat could be seen on his forehead, and he was weaving slightly. A small smile would come onto his lips and then fall away. He had clearly gotten more to drink somewhere after Anais had cut him off.

"What are you doing here?" I asked, trying to conceal my fear and draw the burlap of the sack pointlessly back over the boots of the soldier.

Monsieur Seydoux opened the shed door and peeked outside, looking for anyone else who might be about. Seeing no one, he closed the door again, and the odd smile came back to his lips. "What are *you* doing here? What is this?"

He gestured around at the scattered details of my slaughterhouse: the bodies, the weapons, the blood. I surely did not look innocent either. The front of my dress must have looked like a butcher's apron. My hands were stained crimson. I prayed that there was no blood on my mouth.

"I'm doing my part for the Resistance," I whispered, trying desperately to keep my voice calm. "Helping to protect the village."

My mind was working quickly at the situation and trying to imagine possible outcomes; they were few and none were good. I had a guess as to why drunk, lusty Seydoux was here. Looking for me, he had found both less and more than what he'd been seeking. Now that he'd found everything, I'd have to either trust him somehow with my secret or kill him. Both options seemed impossible. Monsieur Seydoux was anything but trustworthy, but he was also the father of four of my students, with a wife and baby at home. Could I really kill him?

Seydoux took a step forward into the room and then another. There was the familiar, sensual look in his eyes that I recognized from many late nights in the café.

"There's more to you than meets the eye, isn't there?" he said, still moving forward. "And there's plenty for the eyes to begin with."

I imagined that his questions might have been very different had he been sober, but as usual, drunk, he had only one thing on his mind.

I rose from where I sat sprawled on the floor.

"You must not tell anyone," I said. "If anyone found out it would ruin everything, put people—*put the children*—in danger."

"Of course," he said, now stepping close to me, reaching over the body bag that lay between us on the floor, and taking my hand. "I won't tell anyone. You and I, we are both good at keeping secrets. You have nothing to worry about."

His fingers entwined with mine, and I felt as though I would be sick. I pulled my hand back.

"Thank you," I said, looking away.

He reached out and stroked the side of my chin, and I recoiled at his touch.

"There's blood on your face," he said, and reached for my face again. "Let's go back to the house and get you cleaned up."

I did not like the sound of that. I didn't want Monsieur Seydoux in my house, but I did want us both out of the shed and away from all the damning evidence, as soon as possible, so I led the way to the door.

We crossed the snowy yard and I paused outside the door of my house before opening it.

"I'm very tired, as you can imagine," I said. "If you don't mind, I'd like to go in and go to bed. I'm very grateful to you that you are going to keep my secret. The consequences, if anyone found out, would be very bad."

"Yes, yes, of course," he said, nodding expectantly at the door. "We will go in and go right to bed. And yes, the consequences would be very bad. For you. If anyone found out."

He reached forward and turned the knob, and the door to my home opened before us, the inside dark with shadow. I stood there, still, on the threshold. Then felt Monsieur Seydoux's hand come up and rest against the small of my back.

"If say, the Germans, right down there, found what I found. In your shed. The consequences would be terrible."

I turned a troubled gaze toward him, and he looked blankly back.

"Neither of us wish for this to happen," he said in a soft, insidious tone of friendly reassurance. "I promise, I will do everything in my power for you. Surely you will not refuse to do what is in your power for me?"

He pressed the one hand more firmly against my back and extended his other palm forward as though inviting me into my own home. I stepped forward into the house, and he followed, shutting the door behind him.

"I *will* do what I can for you, Monsieur Seydoux," I said, turning to him. With a smile, he stepped closer and pushed a lock of hair back from one side of my face.

"I will keep *your* secret, so long as you keep mine."

He put a hand on my waist and leaned forward to kiss me.

"I won't tell anyone that you got Anais pregnant, or that you came here to my house tonight looking to do the same to me."

His shoulders slumped, and a look of pained disappointment came over him.

"*Anna*, there is no need for things to become unpleasant. Love is an enjoyable thing. I promise I can make it enjoyable for you. Why not? Why not simply enjoy it?"

He put his other hand to my waist and stooped down so that he could peer up coaxingly into my face. "Then we will carry our secret like friends, mine safe with you, yours safe with me. That also can be enjoyable. Just ask Anais."

I took a step back and pulled his hands from my waist. When I spoke, I worked with great effort to keep my voice measured and not unfriendly because I wanted, more than ever, to murder him, but still I knew that I must not. Everything was held in the most precarious of balances, and if anything tipped just a little, if things escalated, I felt sure I would kill him.

"I have made you the best offer you are going to get from me, Monsieur Seydoux. Consider what you discovered in the shed and be reasonable. You are the father of several of my students; I do not wish for anything to happen to you, nor do I wish for your reputation to be damaged before them."

Monsieur Seydoux took a soft step back and studied me for a moment, gauging my resolve. His eyelids lifted and fell almost as though he were fighting off sleep. Then suddenly, he lunged at me, one arm going around my waist, the hand of the other taking firm hold of the back of my head, trying to pull me forcefully to him. I caught him a blow across the face with the heel of my hand, and he staggered back, doubled over, with a hand to his now bleeding nose. I felt the wolf in me crouching down to spring again, to take his throat in my teeth and release the life out of him, let it spill across the floor. But I held. I thought of the children, his children, my children, and I held.

"*Ohhh*, foolish woman!" Seydoux snarled, face still to the floor. "I've been so nice. I offer you friendship, but you prefer to make an enemy."

"I prefer no such thing. You've had too much to drink tonight, Monsieur Seydoux. You're not yourself. Let's count it all to that. In the morning, you will forget everything you know about me, and I, likewise, will forget everything I know about you. Anais will forget too. I can promise you."

He turned finally and started toward the door. On the way, he kicked a small table that held a vase of flowers, breaking the leg and sending the vase tumbling to shatter on the floor.

"*Idiote*," he spat at me as he opened the door. "A couple of bar whores, who would believe you? And who would care?"

My answer—"We will find out if we must"—he didn't hear, so loud was the slam of the door behind him.

IF I HAD BEEN ANY less tired, I might have sat up the night worrying over my encounter with Monsieur Seydoux, replaying it and wondering what to do next, but almost the instant he had gone, all the adrenaline flooded out of me and a powerful fatigue took its place, and I collapsed into bed, knocked down into an oblivion of sleep.

The sleep was a brief one, though. In it, Czernobog waited for me, billowing like a massive pyre and pulling my children, the students and orphans, one by one into his hungry depths. The shrill screams of the children echoed off mine with strange, unearthly dissonances, and I woke up to find Czernobog still there, outside my bedroom window, leering at me as his white flaming wings beat the air around him.

Shocked suddenly awake, I leaped from my bed to the window. The figure was no longer there; instead, I saw that the shed was on fire. Flames were roaring up into the glittering winter dawn, and bright sparks were flicking out, threatening to catch the roof of the house on fire as well. Throwing on coat and boots, I ran outside, but there was little I could do except pitch small, ineffective buckets filled with water from the pump into the furnace and watch as, first, one side of the small building crumpled and fell inward, and then, like a house of cards, all the rest slid and fell and was consumed.

When the fire had finished with the small structure, I picked through the blackened timbers and ash, searching for whatever remained and wondering how the fire had started. Had that bastard Seydoux done it? Or had I left the oil lamp burning? Distracted as I was, it was certainly possible that I'd forgotten to put it out.

I worried that the fire might attract help from my neighbors. Much of what had been in the shed had been burned away to nothing—the German uniforms were nowhere to be seen, and the deer and fox had been reduced to a scattering of bones mixed with small scraps of shriveled and burnt hide—but a good deal remained. The other bodies, the soldiers, had been blackened and charred, but not so thoroughly destroyed. The buckets of blood had boiled and bubbled out in the fire, spilling what looked like dark cherry juice and tar, and the clips of ammunition were melted and sooty, but they too could still be recognized for what they were.

I was just throwing aside a fire-gnawed beam, and discovering beneath it a tipped-over bucket of guns—stubby Lugers and Mausers and a few long rifles as well—when I heard the chug of a motor on the road. In alarm, I dropped the gun I had just picked up and ran toward the road, hoping to head off anyone who might be coming to help.

I could see from a distance that the driver was a man I recognized from town, a skier and mountain guide who had organized some other guides to begin patrolling the region, watching out for German troops. Another man in the seat behind him might have been one of those guides, I wasn't sure, but beside the driver, in the passenger seat, was Seydoux.

While they were still a short way off, I saw Monsieur Seydoux pointing past me to where the smoke was still rising thinly behind my house, and though I called out and waved, the car drove past me, the men inside barely dignifying me with a glance. I turned to follow it. The vehicle bumped and jostled over the snowy knolls in the field and pulled up right alongside the smoldering ruins, and the men got out.

Running back toward the fire again, I could see Monsieur Seydoux doing a great deal of pointing and talking, and the other men walking around and around the rubble, studying it.

When I drew up close to them, one of them, the driver, squinted up at me from where he was crouched, poking with the barrel of a gun at a charred hand. The third man had also pulled a gun from the rubble and was turned toward the forest. He tested the gun with a shot aimed at a squirrel and missed, but looked pleased that the gun had fired.

"Who should we send your body to?" the man squatting in the rubble asked me. "Who are you working for? I want the highest rank. Who would really get the message?"

The jarring question stopped me mid-step.

"I don't know what you're talking about. What has he told you?" I asked, tossing my head at Seydoux. "He's a liar. Whatever he's said, it's a lie. He came to my home to try to . . . to try—and when I refused, he did this."

"This?" the man said, gesturing again to the human remains before him. "He murdered French soldiers and put their bodies in your shed. He gave you German weapons and German money and then burned the building down around them?"

The man laughed. "I've known Seydoux since we were boys. A lazier fellow I never knew. You will not convince me that he is so industrious as all that, even in the service of his bitte."

"They're not French, those bodies. They're German. I'm working with the Resistance. Seydoux knows this perfectly well."

"When did you come to Chamonix?" the driver of the car said, rising to his full height and coming toward me.

"The spring before last."

"Hmm, right before the war began. Interesting timing." The man looked off for a moment as though considering it. "Your French is sloppy. What language did you speak when you arrived here?"

"She spoke German," Seydoux chimed in. "Everybody knows it. The

Chambruns' little German pet. I was always suspicious. It's why I came here."

I glared at him. "We both know why you came here."

The driver seemed uninterested in this line of conversation.

"Why do you live all the way out here? So far away, so private?" This was a rhetorical question, and the driver did not give me a chance to answer before he went on. "So, you're trying to tell me that a woman who has been here for less than two years and arrived speaking German has become a trusted member of the French Resistance? Who do you work for? What are their names? Who can vouch for you?"

I must have looked guilty then because, for a moment, my mouth could only open and close, searching for an answer that would not make me sound guilty too, but there wasn't one.

"Where did you come from?"

Another question for which I did not have a satisfactory answer.

"I—I was in the woods . . . for a very long time."

"In the woods," the man echoed, and then looked to the other two men. "And before that?"

I didn't answer. I couldn't.

"My guess, despite your reluctance to say it, is that you came from *Germany*, where they speak *German*."

"No!" I said, shaking my head furiously. "I did not come from Germany."

"You're lying!" the man barked. He turned to Seydoux. "Do you have any of those cigarettes you found?"

Seydoux began to dig in the pocket of his jacket.

"There were so many!" the driver marveled, glancing back at me.

Seydoux pulled out a pack and held it out for the man to take one, then he held it out to the other man, who took one as well. He produced a lighter toward which both men leaned to light their cigarettes. The lighter bore the red swastika on its side and had come from the stash I'd had in the shed. I had Nazi lighters, cigarettes, money, and no good answers for any of this man's questions. My alibi about the French Resistance had fallen immediately apart. He clearly did not believe me. There was no reason he should.

The man took a puff from his cigarette, then turned back to me.

"I suppose you know, better than anyone, what the Germans do to female spies and saboteurs."

"I don't know anything about Germans except what it's like to kill them."

The man smiled. "Good answer. It's a lie, like everything else you've said, but it's your first good one."

The man tilted up his cigarette and studied it, then he grabbed suddenly for my neck, got hold of me, and plunged the glowing tip of the cigarette into my cheek. I screamed so loudly that a flock of dark birds lifted out of the trees, cawing, and took off through the air. The pain went on and on, and I heard the sizzling of my skin. Then the cigarette pulled away, and I fell to the ground, pressing my face against the snow and moaning in agony.

"They burn them," the man said. "With cigarettes. They burn them over and over again. And then they kill them."

I looked up, nearly delirious with pain, but prepared to fight. French or German, reasonable in his suspicions or not, I would kill him if he came near me again. Seydoux, where he stood, had gone white, and seemed to hover on the brink of protest. I wondered if he had begun to believe the story he'd made up, or if he knew that I was innocent and was growing uncomfortable with the lengths his revenge had brought us all to.

"But *we* are not Germans," the man said. "We have not their barbarism. Thanks to God."

I saw Seydoux let out a breath. He looked back and forth between me, where I lay still groaning in the snow, and the man who spoke.

"Get out of here," the man said. "Get out of Chamonix, now, and do not come back. If you do, even the smallest child will know how to recognize you. By end of day, I promise every French man and woman in this town and in the valley below will know what to look for to spot the traitor."

For a moment, I squeezed my fists against the snow and writhed with rage, willing myself to spring up and tear the man to pieces, tear all of them. Damn the costs. They could not take from me my home, my village, the children. I would kill them. But the man shouted, "*Go!*" and I knew that I would not kill them as I wanted to. I had not yet become so savage, and so I clambered up out of the snow and started off through the trees.

I was no more than a hundred yards away into the trees when the flames started. I turned back and sank to my knees in devastation and wept as I watched my beautiful little house burn. Inside the house, I knew, Paul's paintings that I'd hung on the walls were igniting, the pigments of trees and peaks and rivers spitting and spattering like hot grease in a pan. A window frame fell, and the glass shattered. Fire licked at the flowered curtains in the kitchen window, and I wept and wept as the flames flapped and darted, a frenzy of orange-tipped vultures dancing over the collapsed frame of my house, feasting on my every possession and the last of my foolish hopes of ever making a home among people.

· XXXII ·

AT the door, I ring the bell and wait at least a full minute outside. I feel a strong impulse to turn around, get in my car, and leave before Katherine opens the door—are they even having a meeting with their lawyers? Is that really why I'm here?—but I know I can't just leave. Besides, Leo is in there. As much as I'd like to drive away and never look back at the Hardmans' house, I can't do that to Leo.

The door finally opens, and Katherine is there. Her eyes are heavy with makeup, but I can tell that they are swollen and bloodshot beneath. She's been crying.

"Hello," she says in a falsely cheery voice.

The lighting in the front entryway is dim, and in it, her pupils are shifting subtly, swelling and shrinking. Dave's story is confirmed at least in that detail. I wonder what she has taken, and how much.

"I'm so glad you're here," she says. "Dave just left and, of course, it was awful, so I'm still a bit worked up."

She is moving nervously and excessively, hopping as she adjusts a shoe, opening the closet door, avoiding my eyes as much as possible.

"What happened?" I say, but it's a perfunctory response. I don't particularly want to hear the answer.

"Oh, he's trying to deny the affair, asking me to reconsider. Try a separation instead of divorce."

Her words come out in a sloppy tumble. She stumbles forward, putting on her other shoe, and braces against the wall.

"He even offered to start going to therapy again."

It's embarrassing, this situation, listening to lies and knowing they're lies but having to pretend that I don't.

"Oh, I meant to ask you, Katherine, do you have the number for your therapist?" I'm trying to make the question sound as innocent as possible, but it comes out haltingly. "You've gotten me thinking that it . . . might be helpful to have someone—*a professional* to talk to about some things in my own life."

Katherine stares blankly at me for a moment, still hunched over and with her hand on the heel of the shoe she is trying to get on.

"Oh . . . well . . . it's only for couples, this therapist," she says. "But maybe I could get a referral from her. If I ever see her again, that is."

"Oh, right," I say. "That makes sense, of course."

"Anyway, it's all just an act." She lets out a sudden laugh of derision.

I'm confused. What's all just an act?

She goes on. "Dave wanting to go back to therapy. It's all just an act, that's what it is. Right before we meet with lawyers, right before he has to pay up, he suddenly cares about our marriage again? I'm not stupid. I'm not falling for it. This is the right choice. You were right."

She suddenly takes my hand and squeezes it thankfully. It's a shock of physical intimacy I've not had in years and am not prepared for, especially not now. Tears continue to seep from the corners of her eyes.

"I don't know how I can ever thank you enough."

"Please, Katherine. It was your decision. You're doing the hard work, not me."

For a moment, I can't do anything but stand there uncomfortably, waiting for her to release my hand.

"I'm sorry, I'm such a mess."

"Anyone would be emotional right now," I say, taking the opportunity to break from her grasp and get her a tissue from a box on an entryway table. I hand it to her, and she presses it to her eyes.

"Now my life can finally be okay," she murmurs into the tissue. "Things can finally"—she puts her hands out in the air, presses them down slowly—"be calm. I just can't handle things being so crazy all the time. I'm glad he's gone. I just need a minute to pull myself together."

"Take your time."

I put my coat on a hanger in the closet, and Katherine pulls a coat out. She fumbles with it for a moment, trying with what appears to be great difficulty to find the correct armhole.

"Where's Leo?"

"He's in the bath upstairs. I had him take a bath because I didn't want him around with Dave here and being crazy."

"I see. That's smart."

She takes her purse from the closet and struggles to get the strap onto her arm. Purse on at last, she grabs for her keys and glasses where they lie on the shelf above the coats. The keys clatter to the floor. I bend down and pick them up, but I don't give them to her. She should not be driving in this condition.

"Actually, Katherine, do you have just a minute? There is something I wanted to talk to you about. Won't take long."

I can tell she wants to leave—where is she going? I wonder. Where has she *been* going all these evenings that I've been here with Leo?—but I move toward the kitchen and I'm holding the keys, so she follows.

"Do you mind if I make a pot of tea?" I ask, setting the keys on the counter and turning the burner beneath the kettle on low to give us more time. I've grown comfortable in the Hardmans' kitchen over the last few weeks. Katherine gives a vague nod and shoulder motion that could be yes or no or neither, but I pull two mugs from the cupboard and two tea bags from a glass canister anyway.

Katherine sits at the table with her arms laid out in front of her. Her eyes are glazed, and her head nods slightly.

"Have you given thought to what you'll do next?" I ask, hoping this conversation starter will take. "Now that you and Dave are splitting up, will you and Leo stay here in Millstream Hollow?"

"No, no. We'll sell this house and go back to the city. It was a mistake to come here at all. We thought the quiet would help, but it makes everything worse. Nowhere to go, nothing to do but sit around and stare at the trees. Think awful thoughts."

With that, at least, I can sympathize.

"That's a shame," I say, and it hits me that all of this will mean Leo leaving the school. In all likelihood, after this year, I'll never see him again. I'm surprised by how deeply this upsets me.

"We'll miss Leo at school. I'll miss him. He was doing so well there."

"I had everything: a great career, connections. I never should have left."

I turn toward her. She's staring into space, her arms splayed out on the table, one hand cradling the other.

"I can have it again," she continues. "I don't need Dave. That sad sack. That fool."

She turns her palms up where they rest on the table and then lays her head in her palms.

"*Ms. Collette!*"

Leo is standing in the entryway to the kitchen. He's wrapped in a bath towel, shivering, water dripping onto the tile beneath his pruney, blue-mottled feet. I glance at Katherine—still lying with her head on the table—and then go to him and scoop him up into my arms.

"Mon petit, look at you. You're so cold, your little lips are turning blue. Let's get you dressed."

I hurry him from the room before he can notice his mother. He is curled into himself and shivering inside his towel as I carry him up the stairs.

"Tu deviens une *prune ridée!*" I say, holding up one of his wrinkled, translucent fingers.

In his room, I help Leo get his clothes on. He pulls sweatpants up over his alarmingly thin legs. He shivers and his teeth chatter. He is just poking his head, messy with matted, wet hair, through the neck of his pajama shirt when we hear the front door close. I remember the car keys that I left on the kitchen counter and run out to the landing, where a window looks out over the driveway. Katherine's car backs down the drive and into the street.

From the kitchen, a soft whine from the kettle rises into a shrill, steady whistle, almost a scream. Vlad the Impaler is barking next door.

I SPEND THE EVENING WATCHING Leo thoughtfully. I can't get it out of my head, what Dave has told me, and I vacillate between feeling certain it's all true and wondering whether I'm being made a fool of, playing somehow right into Dave's hands. As Leo eats his dinner of microwavable chicken nuggets, fries, and broccoli, and then later, when we sit at his little art table in his room and draw, I find myself studying him, searching his face or his expressions for clues as to what's true. His face is too evocative, though, anything could be imagined in its paleness, the thin little point of his chin, the dark rings around his eyes like cup stains on a table, the large, dark solemnness of his eyes.

He finishes a drawing, and I look over to find that it's a cat, and a vaguely familiar one at that, with patches and blotches all over its flank.

"Leo," I say, stirred from my brooding and recalling another drawing I once saw of this animal. "Is that your cat? The one that ran away? What did you say his name was?"

"Puzzle," Leo says, and begins writing the name, minus a *z* and an *e*, in large, wavering letters at the top of the page.

"Do you remember the picture you drew for me the very first time we met? At the school? It had Puzzle in it. Do you remember that?"

Leo nods.

"I remember you kept it, rolled it up into a little scroll, and tucked it away in your pocket. Do you still have that picture? I'd really like to see it again."

I expect the answer to be no, but to my surprise Leo nods and runs over to his bed. Max the giraffe is lying against the pillow. Leo takes him up in his hands and returns to the table with him. My brows are knit in confusion, but Leo gives me a *be patient* look and sets to working one of the sleeves of Max's tiny brown T-shirt up off one of the animal's arms. I tilt my head, trying to get a look at what he's doing, and see a rip in the fabric under the arm of the stuffed animal. Leo puts his finger inside the rip, digging around in the stuffing, and after a second he begins to inch out a small scroll of tightly rolled paper.

"*Ahhh*, I see," I murmur. "*Clever.*"

When he's worked the scroll all the way out of the stuffed animal, he grins at me with self-satisfaction and then unrolls the scroll, smoothing it against the table with his palm. It is indeed the drawing he made for me on that first day that we met, but I understand it now as I had not then. A woman, a cat, and two small boys.

"That's the drawing!" I exclaim with a smile. "The very one. That's how I first knew you were such an *artiste*. And you've gotten even better since then."

Leo just smiles, his arms folded on the table before him. I hesitate for a moment and then take a chance.

"Is that Max, then? Your brother?"

Leo's eyes shoot up to my face, but he's calm. He nods.

"You know . . ." I continue, speaking slowly and carefully, "Dave told me all about Max."

Leo is watching me intently, his eyebrows heavy over his eyes with caution. I go on.

"And he said it was okay for you and me to talk about Max, that you didn't have to worry about getting in trouble."

Leo contemplates this, looking down at the table and the picture on it. Then he looks up at me.

"Do you want to see another picture of my brother?" he asks with quiet eagerness.

"*Yes*," I say, the tears almost starting in my eyes. "I would *love* to."

Leo takes up his giraffe again and sets once more about digging around in the rip. How much, I wonder, does he have hidden in there? He catches hold of and then works out a small folded square of thicker paper. It's a photograph, folded twice in half, and I feel a terrible anticipation as he begins unfolding it on the table.

It won't flatten completely, and so Leo pushes it over toward me and holds the edges so I can see it. It's a picture of two children, one around the age Leo is now, the other a toddler, two or maybe three years old.

Both are dressed in sweaters and coats and hats with fleecy earflaps down. The big kid, who looks very much like Leo—same large eyes and unruly hair, but sturdier and fuller-faced—is sitting on a park bench with the other child, who must *be* Leo, sparsely toothed and grinning, perched on the older child's lap, though apparently slipping. The older boy is squeezing his brother about the middle, in part to keep the child from falling, but also out of sheer obvious affection. He nestles his face close and lovingly against that of the toddler. Behind and around them, a tree spreads limbs loaded with white and pink blossoms.

It's a beautiful photograph, and it shows quite plainly that Max loved his little brother, Leo, very much, perhaps to a degree that few older brothers do. I'm getting emotional just looking at the picture, but I need to stay cool in order to talk to Leo. I turn my face to the side, blink heavily, and take a few steadying breaths.

"It's an *amazing* picture, Leo," I say when I've collected myself. "Look at the two of you! You look so much alike. Both so handsome. What else do you have hidden away in that giraffe?"

"Nothing in there," Leo says, "but there's more pictures in the desk downstairs. That's where I found this one. Mom—I mean, Katherine—doesn't know I took it." He scrunches his face guiltily at this.

"I'm sure it's okay," I say. "You *should* have a picture of you and your brother."

"But you won't tell her, will you?" he asks, looking suddenly very anxious.

I quickly shake my head. "No. No, I won't tell her."

He relaxes, looks again at the photograph.

"It looks like you were really good brothers," I say. "You can see it in the picture that you really loved each other a lot."

The gentle smile that was on Leo's face fades.

"I wasn't a really good brother," he says softly.

"Why would you say that?" I ask.

He gives a small shrug but doesn't answer. I study him for a moment, trying to figure out how to proceed. I want to know what he believes about Max and his part in what happened—I *need* to know, but the confidences of children are hard won. It's so easy to make a wrong move and lose their trust forever.

"You know," I go on carefully, "Dave told me what happened to Max. It's so very, very sad. I'm so terribly sorry. You don't . . . Leo, you don't think that any of it was your fault, do you?"

Leo picks the photograph up from the table and begins folding it up again as it was.

"Leo?" I say, but he doesn't look at me. "You *don't* think that what happened to Max was your fault, do you? Because you shouldn't. It was not in any way your fault. Dave knows that too. He said he was very worried that you might think it was your fault."

With the photograph folded, Leo begins pushing it back into the rip in his stuffed animal.

"*Leo?* Leo, sweetie, do you hear me?"

"It *was* my fault," he says so softly I can barely hear him.

"Oh no, Leo," I say, the tears rushing again at my eyes. "No, no, no, Leo. It was not your fault. You must not think that it was your fault."

I reach for his small hand hanging limp at his side.

"But *it was!*" he shouts with sudden fury. "*It was my fault!*"

I'm astonished. I've never seen Leo angry like this before. He snatches the drawing off the table, crumpling it in his fist, and then runs to his bed and scrambles up to curl on his side, clutching Max the giraffe tightly against himself.

Heartbroken and at a loss, I get up and go to the bed, taking a seat on the edge. Leo seems to curl more tightly into himself, steeled against anything I might say.

"Leo, I don't know what you've been told—"

Leo's hands go up to his ears, blocking out my words, but I just talk louder. Now I'm the one almost shouting.

"—but what happened to Max was *not your fault*. You were three years old. *Nothing* is a three-year-old's fault, Leo. *Nothing!*"

"It was my fault!" Leo says, turning his head over his shoulder and shouting at me. His face is red, and his eyes are wet and running with tears. "My mom told me so, and I might even go *to jail!*"

"It isn't true, Leo! *It isn't true!*"

The louder and more insistently I say the words, the more tightly he curls into himself and presses his hands to his ears, and his hands do not fall away until about thirty minutes later, when he has fallen asleep. I'm there beside him on the bed through all that time, unsure whether to give him space or comfort him. I end up just sitting right up against him, my hip against his back, and after he falls asleep, I reach over and carefully adjust Max's small T-shirt, putting his arm back in the sleeve so that the rip in the fabric is again concealed. Then I get up, feeling weary and bereft, and go downstairs in search of a desk.

After opening a few doors downstairs that I had never had reason to open before, I find a room with the beginnings of a home office: an expensive-looking desk and chair, a green table lamp like the kind they have in libraries. This *must* be the desk where Leo said he found the pictures of his brother. There's a sliding glass door beside the desk, and when I sit down heavily in the chair, I can see outside to the backyard, where a light snow is beginning to fall in the darkness. The neighbor's yard is visible as well, where that utterly inexhaustible dog, still aware of my presence and still agitated by it, is running back and forth, *still* barking.

I begin opening drawers. The center drawer is empty. Top right drawer, empty. Bottom right, empty. Is everything in this house empty? Everything in this family? Does everything appear to be something but actually contain nothing?

I pull the drawers on the left side open one at a time, top to bottom, expecting emptiness, but the bottom drawer has a different heft to it. Inside the drawer I find a shoebox and behind it a large blue-and-white-striped cosmetics bag. I pause for an instant and listen, afraid that Katherine has somehow returned without my noticing and is about to walk into this room to find me snooping about in her things. The only sound, though, is the tireless, agitated barking from the yard next door.

I pull the box out of the drawer, set it on the desk in front of me, and take the lid off to find birthday cards. "Hope your day is *super!*" shouts a masked and caped superhero on the front of the card. Beneath that one, a T. rex takes a bite out of a giant number 4. Two of the cards are addressed to Max from "Mom, Dave, and Leo." An older one, for a third birthday, is addressed curiously from "Mom and Dad." Below these, I find a birth certificate for a Maxim Steven Mizrahi from Mount Sinai Hospital in Manhattan with only Katherine Rebecca Mizrahi listed as parent. *Leo Mizrahi*, I think to myself. That must be Leo's real name. Leonardo Mizrahi. I find the name lovely and somehow more fitting. Much better than Hardman.

Beneath the social security card, there is a large kindergarten class picture with two dozen grinning children. It takes me a minute, but I finally spot Max. His hair, usually wild like Leo's, is neatly combed and slicked down. Below the class picture there is a newspaper clipping, just a small, thin rectangle with two columns of fine type. It's the newspaper report about Max's death. *Child, 5, Drowns in Family Pool.*

I read the article, and it tells me the same story that I've already heard from Dave. The mother of the unnamed child, the article reports, was showering when the child went into the pool. Whether the child fell or went in intentionally is stated as being unclear. There are a few details I had not known. The home, I learn, was in Old Westbury. The child was just two days away from his sixth birthday. The article seems to make a special point of describing how the drowned child was discovered by his younger brother, that the younger boy tried to reach the drowned child with a pool net before alerting the mother. I find myself enraged at the journalist. Surely, I've read dozens of articles just like this one before without reacting in anger, but this time, knowing the child concerned as I do, those horrific details about "the younger brother" making the discovery seem like perverse excess on the writer's part, inserted to add pathos and intrigue to a back-page article, to tug at the reader's heartstrings but to no real purpose. There's no delicacy, no care for the child who was *Leo*, not just some nameless "younger brother," some especially tragic *element* to the story.

In anger and sadness, I set the article aside and flip through the other assortment of papers in the box, looking for the other pictures Leo said he'd found, but aside from the class picture, I don't find any. This must be the desk drawer Leo was talking about. What are the odds of there being another? I pull out the striped cosmetics case from the back of the drawer, wondering if the photographs might be in there. When I unzip the bag, though, I find it full of white-capped prescription medicine bottles, nearly a dozen of them. My eyes instinctively flit to the door again, but no one is there. I'm alone with this.

Gingerly, I turn the labels up to read them. Diazepam, oxycodone, Demerol. No antibiotics here, no diabetes or heart medications. These are all pain meds. Strong ones. The labels feature a handful of different doctors' names and varied diagnoses: Dr. Jonas, Dr. Schietzmann, Dr. Laghari, Dr. Reddy, neck trauma, migraine, back pain, sciatica. Some of the bottles are empty, some full, most are somewhere in between. I knew that Katherine took pills occasionally for a bad back, but this is something else. No one could possibly need this much pain medication. All the doctors, all the different causes—and the *dates*. There must be hundreds of pills here, and there isn't one prescription that is more than a few months old. "Do not operate machinery," the labels warn; "Risk of profound sedation, respiratory depression, coma, death"; and, of course, "Keep out of reach of children."

Did Leo find this bag? I wonder. Surely, he must have. If he was snooping around in drawers, it's unlikely that he opened a box and then disregarded the bag next to it. The thought—a young, curious child stumbling upon a bag stuffed full of opioids and barbiturates—fills me with terror. Against my will, I picture Leo unconscious and blue, foaming at the mouth from overdose, having popped some candy-like pill in his mouth. And I now have to put the bag right back where it was, right within Leo's reach, unless I want Katherine to know that it's been found, and suspect that I was the one who found it. What would she do? If ever there was an occasion to turn on someone, "get rid of them," as Dave said, this would be it. And then Leo would be gone. I would have no way of reaching him, being there for him.

Everything Dave has told me seems to be true. Leo believes he is to blame for his brother's death. He has been told this. Katherine is a liar and a manipulator and a danger to her child. I get up and stand at the sliding glass door, looking out, trembly with adrenaline and anger. I look out at the yard where light from the neighbor's porch cuts their yard in two sections, one light, one dark. Extraordinary how close they can be to each other, light and dark. Extraordinary how you could stand in that light, everything visible, plain as day, and then take one step to the left and suddenly its darkness, blindness. Light and dark, truth and lies, love and hate, all just jammed up right next to each other. The choice between the two a matter of only millimeters.

I think of Leo standing beside that pool two years ago, looking down at his brother, who won't come out; Leo facing his mother, wide-eyed and scared, as she tells him that what's happened is his fault, their fault together, that they'll go to jail if anyone learns about what they've done; Leo hiding in the cloakroom from a police officer he thinks has come to take him away; Leo alone in this house with Katherine, or in an apartment in the city, after Dave leaves and takes with him everything he knows.

In the yard next door, the German shepherd has spotted me in the window and ceased his frantic laps. He stands now with claws hanging over the fence, looking me dead in the eyes and barking. His black gums gleam with saliva, and his sharp teeth snap the air. I think of Leo scared to play in his own backyard because of this dog. This *snarling, barking, vicious, lunatic dog*. Everything around Leo vicious. Everything barking and snarling, cold, and lying, and betraying. Not a shred of mercy anywhere, not a shred of care or compassion. I feel the warmth in my stomach, the yawning of hunger paired with a boiling *rage*, and I look at the dog, and I think, Well, okay, Vlad? You want to work something out between us? Why not? One less vicious, snarling thing for Leo to be afraid of.

I reach for the handle of the sliding glass door, my chest beginning to heave with fury and anticipation, and I think, Really, why not?

· XXXIII ·

THE men burned my home to the ground in the sparkling first light of a January morning. But they did not drive me from the village. I watched from the trees as the black smoke rose into the crystalline blue sky. Then I began climbing up Mont Blanc.

I knew of an abandoned ski chalet a mile or so above the village and I made my way there. It was stone with a wide, vaulted log roof that slanted right down against the mountain slope. Inside, I found a wide, bright dormitory, full of dusty, rotted mattresses, and I threw myself down on one and lay there for days, moaning from the pain of the burn on my face. The windows of the chalet were grimy, steps were missing from the stairs, and patches of vibrant mold crept across the wallpa-pered rooms. Rodents scrabbled about at night until I started catching and killing them. It was perfect; a place just like myself: empty, aban-doned, dark. It held no pretense of hominess or civility, no cupboards to hide the absence of food. It was a dank, barren cave for a monstrous creature. I wasn't a person; I was the Nacht Bestie. I didn't need a home, only a den from which to set out on my prowling and to which I could return when done. Whatever they believed about me, I would go on guarding Chamonix, Anais, and the children.

At night, I descended from the chalet. Slipping among the trees, I checked on the orphanage. It pained me horribly to think of what the children might have been told about me. After all their teacher had taught them about courage and resistance and hope, to then be told that she was a spy. The sense of betrayal was too terrible to imagine. And Anais too, she had certainly been told the same story. I felt sure she would never believe it. She would see right through Seydoux, but what kind of position would that put her in? What would it mean for her if everyone believed that her closest friend had been a German spy?

Sometimes I wished that I had killed Seydoux and the other men, but again and again, I came back to the fact that they were Frenchmen in a town and country that needed all the Frenchmen they could get, and also to the lonely, sad knowledge that Chamonix belonged to them as it never had and never would to me. Anais would grow old and die there. My students would grow old and die there, and what would I do? Eventually, I would have to move on. It was my fate to lose everything, to watch everything eventually go up in flames. Czernobog, the god of endings, would be my only lifelong companion.

I went on hunting, both animals and soldiers. The animals I left at the doorstep of the orphanage or the café. The soldiers I threw dead in the snow behind the chalet. I didn't bother to conceal them. Wolves fought over the carcasses at night, and a pretty spotted lynx pawed delicately among the icy remains during the day. If somehow the Germans ever reached my new dwelling place, they would easily find the picked-over bones of their fellow soldiers. Let them. I didn't care. Up on the high slopes, I had only myself to worry about and I could take care of myself.

It went on like this for weeks. Then one day, I woke around noon to see a spindle of smoke curling blackly up into the air from somewhere below. I moved down the mountain cautiously. I hadn't been near the village in daylight since the morning I'd been driven out. I no longer had the telltale burn mark on my cheek, but plenty of people would recognize me nonetheless.

A dim wailing could be heard from a long way off. The column of smoke widened and blackened the closer it came to the earth, and white specks of eerie ash drifted down from the sky. The outer fringe of the town was quiet and still, but I could hear a commotion coming from the square at the center of town. I took a narrow, cobbled side street and held back in the shadows of doorways and narrow alleys when I was close enough to observe.

The townspeople were gathered in an agitated congregation in the square. Men and women wandered and turned aimlessly, bleating and wailing like sheep in a pen harassed by wolves. The women were crying, and several men had lurid injuries that were dripping blood down into their eyes or onto their shirtfronts and coat lapels. Among them I saw Jean-Luc Fevrier, just twelve years old, holding a rag up to his bloody forehead.

At the edge of the square, what had been the tavern was now a gaping black mouth, craggy and soot-blackened and billowing smoke. Some men, Seydoux among them, were taking buckets of snow and throwing them into the smoldering heart of the fire. Monsieur Bonard, the tavern keeper, was laid out beside the fountain. His wife was washing the red pulp at the center of his face, and his children were huddled about them, holding one another.

I leaned against a wall, trying to make sense of what I was seeing, and my finger felt a smooth, still warm hole. It was a bullet hole. Now that I was looking for them, I could see, all around the square, the buildings and houses speckled intermittently with bullet holes.

There came a low, aching wail of anguish and everyone in the square turned in its direction. At the last house on the far opposite side of the square, a man had just discovered the body of his wife. She'd been hiding—from the Germans, it now seemed evident to me—on the side of their house, holding their baby daughter in her arms. A stray bullet had hit her in the head, and she'd collapsed with her child in the snow.

I drifted with the others, who in their grief paid no attention to me, toward the wailing man, but when I saw the body—his wife laid out, legs bent strangely, eyes upturned to the sky, and the baby squirming and crying against her chest—I thought of the orphanage and turned in its direction.

"*No!*" a man's voice rang out.

It was the man. The driver of the car, the alpinist who had burned my face. He'd seen me and broken away from the group tending the fire.

"*Spy!*" he shouted, his face contorting with rage. "She works for the Germans!"

Seydoux turned from where he was tending the fire. When he saw me and realized what was happening, a look of dismal weariness came to his face, as though he were being drafted into some game he'd grown tired of playing. His gaze went with dread from me to the other man.

People turned frightened gazes toward me, and I looked back at them with equal fright. Then I started to run. From the corner of my eye, I saw the man begin to run also. I had to get to the orphanage. I had to know if the Germans had gone there too or if the children were still safe. I pounded down side streets, dodged around corners, my feet slipping on the slick cobblestones. All the time, I could hear the steps of the man following behind, and his voice crying out loud and furious, "*Traitor! Spy! Stop her!*"

The houses beyond the square seemed to be unblemished by bullets, and as I drew closer, I dared to hope that the orphanage had been left alone entirely, but then the building came into sight. I could see the front door of the orphanage open, darkness beyond. Why was the door just hanging open like that? It didn't look right, and the flowers at the corner of the flower bed right next to the front walk were upturned and smashed as though stepped on.

I was almost there—thirty yards more—when I heard the hammer click of a gun, and then my arm exploded. The whole world burst upward in white, like a blown dandelion, and a rain of burning stars showered down around me. I was thrown forward against the side of a statue of St. Joan, the dirty snow on the rim of the base scalding my forehead with its cold. I looked down at my arm: a bouquet of torn flesh and blood, bone and tendon, a beautiful mess of gore. Blood—*my* blood—poured lavishly down the side of my dress.

I could hear the man's steps approaching again, and I turned from where I'd fallen to face him. He was cocking his gun again, lifting it to his eye. The pain in my arm was so intense I could barely see straight, but through the swirling vertigo of pain, I set my hand down on a paving stone and felt it jiggle loose under my hand. A second shot cracked out, and another bullet ripped through the lower left side of my chest. I felt something inside of me burst, a taut, stretched drum torn and falling slack, and suddenly, as if I were underwater, there was no air.

"*Stop!*" a woman's scream rang out high and agonized.

The clap of the gunshot had brought Anais out from the orphanage to its doorway, and she stood there bent forward with the force of her scream.

"*Do not shoot her!*"

At the end of the black tunnel of my vision I saw the man with the gun look toward Anais. I wrapped my fingers around the paving stone, pulled my arm back, and threw it straight at his head. It caught him at the hairline, and he threw a hand up to his head and tumbled backward.

I cradled my chest in my good arm and pulled myself to standing. My eyes felt heavy. I dragged them up to a sky that was emptying of blue, draining of color and meaning. The birds flew upside down, and the clouds were ash falling softly like dirty snow over everything. There was a shuffling of feet on the snow, Anais had come running, but Monsieur Seydoux was holding her back.

"Get your hands off me!" Anais shouted and fought like a badger to escape the grip of his arms.

The man on the ground was stirring, lifting his head off the street and feeling around for his gun, which had fallen from his hands and bounced a few feet away. I took my last look at Chamonix, the cobblestone streets, café awnings, and fountains, the white mountain slopes rising up beyond the rooftops, Anais struggling and fighting and cursing on my behalf.

"I have to go, Anais," I tried to call out, but my voice made almost no sound. "Please, tell the children."

I turned from the man splayed out on the ground and bleeding, the townspeople huddled in the alleys, whispering. I turned and began, as best I could, to run again.

"*Anna, no! Don't go! Please!*" I heard my friend cry out. "There's been a *mistake!*"

She was right. There had been a mistake, but I was the one who had made it and it couldn't be undone. Half running, half dragging myself, suffocating and dripping blood like a bread-crumb trail, I ran away. I ran and ran and ran.

I never learned what happened to the Jewish children—Jacov and Hadassa and Michiline and Mendel—whether they lived, or they died.

· XXXIV ·

HOURS later, I'm on the couch in the Hardmans' living room. I'm flipping through television channels, trying to avoid thought. During my stays at the Hardmans', I confess, I have been seduced by the appliance's cheerful, if artificial, company. It has a sort of sedative power, and at times I find myself watching it with a kind of fascinated horror. It is especially helpful for calming oneself, should one find oneself in an agitated state, after, for instance, dispatching a neighborhood bully.

I flip the channel and land on a sitcom: calculatedly ordinary people in a calculatedly ordinary middle-class setting, rolling eyes at one another and slapping things out of each other's hands to the delight of a crowd that seems to have been prepped with laughing gas. I flip again. Music videos: young people skulking and jumping, hair whipping the air, smooth bellies punctuated by the dark commas of belly buttons. Another flip, and it's the news. The New York Stock Exchange has seen a record-high trading day, a politician speaks sternly about cities crippled by crime, the Bills are soon to play the Jets. Then, an international segment: an unfolding coup attempt in an Eastern European country has sent the communist secretary-general into hiding. I'm about to change the channel again, my finger hovering over the button, when I hear a strangely familiar voice from the television. It's a strong voice, loud and confident, shouting in a language close enough to Russian that I can make out the gist: "*We want our money for our labor! We want food for our children!*"

The screen shows the back of a tall, solid man in a dark wool winter coat. He's shouting to a crowd, and whatever he shouts, the crowd shouts back. "*We want light and heat!*" the man sings out to the crowd. "*Bread without cards!*"

The camera moves, the man's face comes into view, tawny-skinned and with thick black brows and beard. I cannot believe it. It's Ehru. It's my brother, my adopted brother, from forever ago. My brother, whom I'd always imagined as living ever on in the dark heart of the Carpathian forests, splitting wood and defending with relish his wife and child from bears and wolves. It would seem he has left the woods. There he is, organizing an uprising, rallying a civilian army against some tyranny.

I want to know so much more. *Where is he?* What cause is he fighting for and why? But I wasn't paying attention at the beginning of the segment when the details were given and it's over now, unlikely to be repeated. Who in America cares about food shortages and regime changes in Eastern Europe when the Bills are playing the Jets? All I can do is sit there stunned, asking myself a thousand questions I can never have answers to. Eventually one question, not a logistical one but a sort of philosophical one, sticks and will not let me be. Ehru was on television. Ehru was known by that crowd. He had their trust. He was their leader. How did he dare to become so enmeshed in the lives of others and the events around him? How did he dare to be so visible? And why? What could be worth the risk of marrying himself to this struggle? One struggle among the thousands of constant ugly, hopeless struggles taking place all the time and all over the world? I had done it once, become involved, and I had learned my lesson. How had Ehru not learned the same? Against the time line of forever and with stakes as high and lasting as his, why not lie low? Why not move on, find a quiet, peaceful place, and let the vremenic fight their own hopeless battles? At the same time, I know the answer. Ehru was always reckless. For a long time, it had seemed like madness. Maybe it had been, but on that last night that I'd spent with him, when we'd built a coffin for his child soon to be born, and he'd spoken with such calm, clear joy of the family and the future to come, full no doubt of both fortune and misfortune, his recklessness had no longer been mistakable for madness; it had been courage. I'd watched him carry his love off into darkness so full of reckless courage, and it had pleased me sometimes afterward to think of it. I'd liked to imagine Ehru at peace with his wife and child, and whenever I did, the same words always came to my mind as the ones his brother had said on the night he gave his life for Ehru's joy: "*Go! Live!*"

EVENTUALLY I FALL ASLEEP, AND the fireworks of light leaping from the screen work their way strangely into my dreams. I'm standing at the window of Piroska's hut with someone. It's Vano, but then at odd moments it's Ehru, then it's both, as if they were images seen through binoculars, sometimes in focus and one, sometimes splitting apart into two. Bright bursts of light outside dissolve against the dark trunks of the trees. The hut now seems to be partially underground, and dirt slips through the cracks in the chinking.

"Your time is almost come," Ehru says, in his voice that always did sound like the voice of a commander in some army. "Are you ready?"

"Time for what?"

It's Vano who answers me in his low, gentle voice.

"For emptying, for the death of all you know. Naked we come into this world, it is said, and naked we leave—the time is coming when you'll be stripped of everything and walk empty-handed into the new. Are you ready?"

"How can I possibly know?"

Vano, then Ehru, then Vano again smiles at me, a tiny rivulet of sweat slipping down into his eyes. "Are you tired of what is? Are you so tired of it that you would be ready to hand it over, if asked, for something—*anything* else?"

Missiles are raining down overhead, showering us in a hail of fizzling blue or red or white embers, and the dirt goes on whispering as it slips through the cracks.

"I *am* tired," I murmur, and I feel it, the fatigue of nearly two centuries, the countless heartaches and bitternesses that have filled that time. "Everything is falling apart. I'm tired of trying to hold it all together when everything seems only to want to fall apart."

"Then you are ready," Ehru says with firmness, and I feel a terror at his words, as though I have just been called up to some front line.

A large, weasely missile explodes in the sky and its embers work to burrow through the thatch roof, and I wake to the sound of keys turning in the front door lock.

I sit up and rub my eyes, disoriented. It's dark but for the erratic, shifting light of the television doubled in the glass of the sliding door. The light hits the trees outside, and they look for an instant like pale figures standing silently just beyond the glass. I look at my watch and see that it's just past eleven. I struggle up from the couch, wanting only to leave. I don't want to give Katherine a chance to lie to me. I'm afraid that I might just call her a liar to her face and ruin everything, and I'm equally afraid that I won't, that I'll nod and smile and go along with it, as strategically I should, and then feel disgusted with myself for it. I just want out.

Katherine comes in with her coat still on and walks from the door to the living room slowly, like a tightrope walker. She sits down at last in an armchair beside the couch and gazes at the TV.

"I'm very sorry that I'm so late," she says. Her voice is effortfully even, like the stillness of her posture in the chair and the fixedness of her gaze on the TV. I wonder what this act is about, what her strategy is now.

"It's fine," I say, stepping carefully around the glass coffee table. "You have a comfortable couch."

I make my way across the room toward the entryway, where my coat hangs in the closet.

"You know about Max," Katherine says.

I stop at the threshold of the entryway and turn around.

"Dave told me that the two of you spoke."

I blink, afraid to say anything. She's still looking straight ahead at the TV, where a woman mops up a spill with an unbelievably strong paper towel, and I'm glad her gaze is directed there and not at me. Surely my consternation would show on my face. I'm wondering how much of what Dave and I discussed he's told her about, and *why*. Why would he do that when he, himself, advised me to "lie low, play dumb"? I'm thinking also that I should have known never to step between warring spouses. How foolish could I be?

"I do," I say finally, "know about Max. Just a little. Just that he was Leo's brother and that he died. Dave confirmed what I had guessed from a few little things that Leo said—*accidentally*. I'm terribly, terribly sorry for your loss, Katherine. I can't imagine how painful it must have been—and continues, surely, to be."

"I prefer for Leo not to talk about it. You disagree with this."

Is this a question or a statement? I can't tell, but I am distinctly uneasy with the way this conversation is going. Katherine, knowing more than I do, has the clear upper hand, and I'm feeling very much on my heels.

"Where would you get an idea like that?"

"That's not really important. I want to know. You're a teacher, you work with children. What's your opinion?"

It feels like a trap. Somehow, I must avoid walking into it. But then there is Leo. I have an opportunity, likely the only one I or anyone will ever get, to tell Katherine what would truly be best for him, to plead with her to do what Leo needs. Trap or no trap, I have to say it.

"Well . . . if you insist . . . I suppose I think that Leo probably should have at least *someone* with whom he can talk about it."

"Should that someone *be you*?"

"*What? No.*" I feel heat rush into my cheeks. I'm not sure what she's insinuating, but it isn't good. "I would think that person might be *you*. But I could understand if you felt that it was still too painful for you. Then maybe it would be best for it to be someone else, someone who understands the situation and cares for Leo."

"Someone like you?"

"Katherine, I'm not sure what you're trying to suggest. I never asked for this or wanted to be . . . *involved* in any of this."

"Then it probably would have been best if you had not had a conversation with my soon-to-be ex-husband and shared your opinions of my parenting choices with him. He seems to think he has you on his side in this matter."

"*What?* Oh, no, no. Absolutely not. I did not offer Dave my opinion, one way or another, and I have *no* interest in taking sides of any kind. *You* asked for my opinion, and so, with misgivings, I gave it, but this is your home and your family. You do whatever *you* want. From here on, I'm staying out of it."

"*Deal*," she says tartly. "Now, should we talk about the worst thing that's ever happened to you and discuss how well you handled it?"

For a moment I just gape at her, then I turn and get my coat out of the closet.

"I have no idea what I would do in your position, Katherine," I say, as I work my arms into the sleeves. "I only want to help, if help is needed. I'm not judging you or taking sides."

She says nothing, and when I let myself out the front door, she doesn't look up, just goes on sitting perfectly still, staring at the television.

I'M FUMING AS I STEER my car down the dark country road home from the Hardmans'. I'm angry and disgusted with Katherine; I'm angry and distrustful of Dave. I want nothing to do with either of them. I've *never* wanted anything to do with them, but as always, when I toss them mentally into the garbage heap, vowing to be done with them once and for all, Leo steps forward in my mind. I think of him as I left him tonight: curled on his side, clutching Max and crying, with his hands balled into fists against his ears, shouting with such vehemence that his brother's death was his fault, his mom told him so, and he might even go to jail for it. I can't toss Leo aside, but how can I keep one without having to deal with the other?

Up ahead, in the glow of my headlights, I see the Emersons' mailbox, a green and brown fish with a mouth that opens to receive the daily letters and print ads. The long gravel driveway that winds back to the Emersons' farm is there just beside it. I need to be up early in the morning for school; still, without really deciding to, I find myself pulling over.

More than anything, *absurdly*, I want to lie in that toasty barn against the soft, warm flank of one of those cows and drink. I maneuver the car as far off the road, amid the concealing brush, as possible. I don't want it seen and I don't want it hit. I take the small canister of WD-40 from the glove box, then I get out and start walking.

The moon over the trees is a waning crescent, a Cheshire cat's smile. My breath ascends in thick plumes of the same color, a pale, mineral vapor rising up to the stars. The back side of the barn looms ahead of me. I've come up to it and the Emersons' modest brown-shingled house from the rear this time. Through the glass slats of the louver windows, I see a light on in a wood-paneled hall. I stop and watch from the shadowy arch between two trees. A door opens. An elderly white-haired woman in a flowered nightgown, May Emerson, comes out of a bathroom. The light behind her flicks off, then the hall light. The house is dark again. I don't move for a moment. It's not a good situation. May might have gone to bed, or she could have gone to the kitchen for a glass of water in the dark. She could be standing at the sink just behind one of these dark windows, at this very moment, looking out at the night as she takes slow sips.

I wait until it seems that the choice is to go now or just turn around and go home. I move along the edge of the trees, then break away from them and head for the barn. In the shadow of the barn, I know I won't be seen, and I go around the side to the barn door. The doors slide smoothly. No need for the WD-40 after all. I guess they've been lubed up more of late than they have in the whole of their history.

The sweet smell of hay and the warmth hits me, and the response is Pavlovian. My mouth is suddenly flush with saliva. I go into the last stall on the left—I have given all the cows -ora names: Cora, Lora, Mora, and so forth. This particular cow I have taken to calling Dora. I slump into the bristly hay beside Dora. One of her ears flicks, batting away a dream fly. Bone-tired in body, mind, and soul, I sink against her velvet hide and drink.

• • •

I HEAR SOMEWHERE, FOGGILY, A voice.

A bird warbling. A birdlike voice, clucking.

"*Ladies!*"—chattering in a cheerful, singsong voice—"*Chickies!*"

Another warble. Words.

"Give 'em up now, ladies. You know the drill."

My eyelids peel away from each other painfully, and I see a sliver of indigo-blue sky through a crack in two distant wood slats. My eyes are coated in sandpaper. Something sharp is poking uncomfortably into me somewhere.

"Now, ladies, I know you're hidin' more somewhere in here. If I step on an egg 'cause you've gone and hidden 'em in the straw, well, that won't do either of us any good, now, will it?"

A bird sings its morning song nearby, and I jerk upright, panic jolting through my body.

I fell asleep.

I slept all night in the barn.

The Emersons are awake. One of them could be on their way to the barn for milking right now. If I'd slept for much longer, I might have woken by one of them poking me in the shoulder. Fresh waves of panic break over me one after another after another.

I look down. Dora is still lying with her head on her forearms.

Across the barn, the cow in the opposite stall is standing, gazing at me as her mouth methodically works a clump of hay.

My limbs are stiff. In my panic to escape, I push against Dora's broad back to stand. It doesn't matter if she wakes now, all the cows are awake. But she doesn't wake. She doesn't move at all. I push against her again, and everything inside, each cell of my body tingles with despair.

"*No, no, no, no, no,*" I whisper, running my hands over her hide. Her body is stiff. The vital warmth I've enjoyed all these nights is dulled and fading. I cover my mouth with my hand before I even look. Then I step over her, look down, and look away. Her eyes are glassy, brown marbles, seeing nothing. I fell asleep drinking from her, and like a tick or a leech, I just went on drinking all through the night.

"*Aha! So that's your new spot, is it, Beatrice?*"

May. Dear God, she's just outside.

Well, ma'am, I guess the jig is up.

I can't go through the barn door. She's in the chicken coop. Maybe she wouldn't come out, but if she did, we'd run right into each other.

I look up in the direction of the loft doors, the source of the light that first pained my eyes upon opening them. I climb out of the stall as silently as I can and then climb up the ladder to the loft. From up on the ladder, I can see Dora's full shape curled into itself on the floor of her stall. Asleep forever because of me.

I crawl through the hay in the loft to the doors, then I crouch behind them and squint through the crack. Thick white flower petals are drifting down slowly from the sky. At least, that's what the absurdly oversized snowflakes look like at first. Everything is white. The trees, spindly the day before, are engorged—obese with snow. A quilt of unblemished snow covers everything—the ground, a good twelve-foot drop from the loft doors, and my path past the Emersons' house and into the trees. I have white-painted myself into a corner and now I'm going to leap down onto the paint and walk across it, leaving outlandish footprints behind me. I won't be able to close the loft doors behind me after I jump either. They will be blowing in the wind like two big hands waving goodbye.

I hear a metallic clink that could well be milk pails—a second voice, deeper than the first, but indistinct. I open the doors slightly. There's nothing else I can do. It's leap or climb down and wish the Emersons a good morning. When I hear the noisy rattle of the barn door being thrown back along its metal track on the opposite side of the barn, I leap.

I land on all fours up to my shins and elbows in snow, but at least the snow is useful in making my landing soft and silent. Then I am running lightly and furiously like a fox for its hole. I don't slow down or look back until I have run through the woods and emerged on the other side. The road has been erased beneath the snow. What's left is a broad sleigh path through the woods.

I have no idea what time it is. The sky is the dark, bruised blue of predawn. Thomas and Ramona will be at my house at seven thirty. Is that an hour from now or twenty minutes ago?

I push forward to where I think my car should be with an awkward hopping gait, pulling my legs out of the wells that form around them with each step. Up ahead is a white hillock that I recognize as my car mostly by the earlike protrusions of the side-view mirrors. I run to it, pulling my mittens from my pocket so I can begin scooping the snow away from the passenger-side door with my hands. As I do, I remember the can of WD-40 that was also in my pocket and is no longer. I scoop, straining my ears the whole time for the sound of a car or truck rumbling down the road. The Emersons out to catch a thief. Have they discovered Dora's body yet? Almost certainly they have. The loft door, then? The tracks? Are they following them now? Calling the police? Do police get involved with dead cows? They probably do. Cows are money.

At last, I get the passenger-side door open, crawl across the seat, put the key in the ignition, and turn. It cranks and cranks but doesn't catch.

"Oh please, ma vilaine fille. Pretty, pretty, pretty please."

The engine roars. The dash lights flicker as the engine wavers, almost dies but doesn't, then they come on and stay on.

"*Oh merci,*" I whisper, my breath fogging the air before me. "Merci, merci."

The radio clock says 7:12. *Dear God,* eighteen minutes until Thomas and Ramona arrive with their father. The car chugs, low and puttering, but it continues. I grab the scraper from the floor of the passenger seat, crawl back out the passenger door again, and get back to work clearing the snow from the car. It's much more efficient with the scraper, and I'm almost done, just pushing the last deep, blocky drifts off the trunk, when I hear a distant scraping sound coming from the road behind me and growing louder each second. A truck is coming, moving slowly through the snow. *The Emersons.* They are about to drive up and find me here where I have no business being, helplessly digging my car out of the snow, where *it* has no business being, with a trail of footprints leading directly from it to their barn.

I pry open the frozen driver's-side door of my car, get in, and sit there trying to come up with an even remotely plausible story. The sound of the scraping grows. It is thunderous. I can hear each rock caught beneath the steel plow blade and scraping the earth, dragging furrows into the ground.

I watch in the rearview mirror, waiting to see the Emersons' beige Chevy pickup come into view. Their faces—that will be the worst part, the part I must prepare myself for. They will be confused, shocked, and dismayed that someone could do such a thing. They've always been so trusting, always treated their neighbors with trust and respect and took it for granted that their neighbors would do the same. I close my eyes and brace myself.

The scraping is a roar. It's right upon me. It roars and scrapes past and then comes to a stop. I open my eyes. A man in a flannel jacket, orange nylon vest, and hunting cap is climbing down from his snowplow, looking back in my direction. This man is not Henry Emerson. I don't know this man. He's a snowplow driver, a completely unfamiliar snowplow driver. He jogs back toward my car, a concerned expression on his face. I roll down my window.

"Y'okay, ma'am?" he shouts over the steady rumble of his idling vehicle.

"I'm fine," I call, then I wave reassuringly to him. Still, he comes all the way to my car. "I'm fine. Thank you!" I say again through the window I've lowered just a crack. "My drive will be much easier now that I can follow you."

"You sure you can get movin' in this?" He glances down at my tires in their deep beds of snow. The green digits of the radio clock read 7:26.

"Well, now that you mention it . . ."

"I'll just go back and rock you a bit while you give it gas to make sure we can get you out of here."

"I would appreciate that."

"Just do me a favor and make sure you're in drive so you don't back over me."

"Ah, yes. That'd be no way to repay you for your help."

He disappears to the rear of my car, then I feel the car bobbing and I press the gas. The car is in fact stuck. The man comes up to the window again.

"Now let's put it in reverse, and I'll rock the front."

We do this, and the car comes free.

"Thank you!" I call from the window.

He gives me a thick-gloved thumbs-up and then turns and jogs back to his plow. I follow him for three-quarters of a mile, watching the clock obsessively—7:29, 7:30, 7:31—and sweating. My tire tracks blend invisibly with those of the plow. That at least is a relief. The Emersons won't be able to follow a trail directly to my door.

As soon as I turn into my own drive, I see that another vehicle has already made its way through this snow. I reach the roundabout and see the Snyders' green Jaguar idling, with its dome light on and thick plumes of smoke ascending from the exhaust in the frigid air. I am, by now, five minutes late.

I glance in the rearview mirror at my face, and find pretty much what one would expect of a woman who has just passed the night in a barn. My hair is matted, glistening with melted snowflakes and specked with stray pieces of hay that I work quickly to pick out. I look down, not even sure what clothes I'm wearing. The light gray slacks that I put on yesterday to watch Leo are dark to the knee, sopping wet from trudging through the snow. I'm a mess.

I take a deep breath and step out of the car.

"Bonjour, mes chèrs!"

Dr. Snyder, getting out of the car, does not hide his concern.

"Everything all right?" he asks, wide-eyed, and places the straps of Ramona's backpack on her shoulders.

"Everything is fine here," I say, picking a piece of straw from my coat and trying ineffectually to smooth my hair. "I must look a sight! A neighbor, an elderly couple down the road, needed help this morning, digging themselves out of the snow, for a—a doctor's appointment. It ended up being quite the project. So sorry to keep you waiting."

"Oh goodness. Are they all right now? I could drive over if you think they could use more help."

"That's so kind of you, but they're all set now and on their way."

"Your pants are wet," Ramona says, peering up at me.

"I know," I say, "and cold too. Let's hurry inside where it's warm."

I gather the siblings and make for the door before Dr. Snyder can ask any more questions.

"Goodbye!" I call back over my shoulder. "Drive carefully, the roads are atrocious!"

· XXXV ·

I ran for miles like a bleeding, hunted animal before collapsing in the snow. The exit wound of the gunshot in my chest—a ragged hole through which you could have passed a line of thick rope—was just above my bottom rib, and one of my lungs had most certainly been punctured. Each hard-won breath was a new stab wound.

My left arm hung uselessly at my side. The flinty shards of mangled bone still protruded from the flesh. The bleeding from both injuries had stopped, though, and when I finally lay down, the snow kissed my injuries painfully.

I lay there so long that I should have frozen to death. My skin grew stiff and blue, and I wondered as I looked up at the darkening sky beyond the tops of the trees, the stars just beginning to grow bright, what would happen if I just lay there—if I never got up. Would I freeze like an ice cube? Would the wolves come gnaw my flesh as they had gnawed the bodies of the soldiers, but with me fully conscious, feeling each tear of teeth? Would that pretty lynx come stepping among the trees to perch on my chest and nibble with her small, sharp teeth at the tip of my nose? My stiffly parted blue lips? Would I thaw and carry on in the spring? If I could have just lain there and died, I would have done it, but the knowledge that I would not pushed me to my feet, and I went on.

I moved south, avoiding French and Germans alike. I snuck into barns, and after subduing the suspicious lowing of the cows, I fed from them and slept among them for warmth. My wounds healed painfully, my flesh itching and burning as it regenerated. In two weeks, a dry cough was all the evidence left of my chest wound. The innards of my arm had already folded themselves inside again, tucked themselves neatly beneath new, perfect skin. All I did was survive. I did not think. I did not feel. I did not know where I was going, only away.

I arrived eventually in Marseille, a southern port town. In Chamonix I had grown accustomed, even in wartime, to the pervasive and pristine stillness and beauty of life in the mountains. No matter what strife transpired in the valleys, the austere peaks were unmoved and lovely. In Marseille, one of the few unoccupied ports in Europe, all was dust and movement and confusion. Ship masts bristled in the bay, lobsters clicked their claws against the sides of metal tubs, the sunlight shifted and glimmered restlessly on the water, and in the streets crowds of people from all over Europe bustled day and night, making frantic arrangements to try to flee the war.

I looked the part of a war refugee; I was filthy, still wearing the torn and bloody clothes I'd been shot in. Not knowing where else to go, I sat along the edge of the street, as so many others were doing, and people put coins in my hands. Eventually, I had enough money to get a room in a hotel, but the hotels were so crowded that people had to share beds with strangers and even the bathtubs were rented out for people to sleep in. I spent one night in a room full of women, with a large, restless bedmate who snored to wake the dogs. The next night I returned to the streets, which were hardly less restful than the hotel rooms but cost nothing.

It made my skin crawl—the crowds and the filth and the misery. Everywhere I turned, I saw burned villages, men with slashed faces, dead mothers in the snow, my Jewish children lined up by soldiers in front of the orphanage and shot, or guns discharged at the floorboards, a hail of bullets and the small bodies jerking and bouncing where they'd hidden underneath.

Slowly but steadily, day after day, the money in my palm accumulated, and just to get away from Marseille and the teeming, miserable squalor and chaos, I bought a ticket and boarded a steamship. I didn't know where it was bound, nor did I care. It was a bad choice, though. A ship moves, but on it, you are so still. You're trapped with your losses, your burned villages and dead children, and your guilt.

Conditions on this ship were nothing like the ship I'd been on when I was a girl. The vessel was so massive that it felt as though you stood on solid ground, and it moved quickly with no concern for the winds, but it was just as crowded and miserable as Marseille had been. People from dozens of countries and speaking as many languages were fleeing the war, and the cabins for the poor, though far cleaner and more sanitary than the ship of my childhood, were packed like hog pens, and the people in them were dirty and ragged and terrified.

The sea was full of unseen enemies: Italian manned torpedoes that could sneak up silently on a ship and plant bombs on its very hull without ever being detected, and sophisticated German U-boats, the locations of which were betrayed only by a slender periscope sticking up above the water. The soft sputter of warplanes came and went overhead, and there was the intermittent and not-too-distant sound of the bombs raining down on Malta. People spoke with terror of a ship called the *Athenia*, a passenger steamer like our own bearing hundreds of civilians, which had been sunk off the coast of Ireland. The Germans never admitted to having sunk it, but everyone knew it was them, and what was to keep this ship from the same fate?

I didn't care about any of it. Let a torpedo rip through our hull. Let the water rise and splash around our throats. What did any of it matter? The whole world was just a sad theater of horror and pain, and within it, death was a mercy. Why did all these people wish so earnestly to live? If they had any sense, they'd stop running; they'd turn and face death and be done with it.

I didn't eat, didn't drink. I didn't want to. I wasn't trying to starve myself, though I would have been glad if it had been possible, I simply couldn't put effort into my own continuation. I refused.

The days passed, and I lay in my berth, doubled over in an agony of hunger and despair, cramps gnawing at my ribs, the small, invisible heralds of insanity gnawing at my brain. The seven passengers who shared the tiny cabin eyed me and, fearing disease, pushed off into the other corners as far from me as they could as I moaned and tossed and babbled. My fingers and lips cracked and bled. Eventually, my cabin emptied, the other passengers managing to squeeze in elsewhere rather than remain in close quarters with a diseased madwoman.

I woke one night from cloying dreams overflowing in blood, panting the dry, sour breaths of a mummy. I fell out of my bunk to the floor in the pitch black. I lay there for some moments, scratching my nails against the floor planks, feeling the moisture hidden deep inside the wood. I couldn't even salivate anymore.

Half sleepwalking, half hallucinating, I stumbled out to the lower deck. It was cold. The sea sprayed an icy, needling veil of water against my skin and a faint drizzle of rain fell from above. The moon was obliterated behind a thick, rolling fog. Now and then, a star would glimmer through the haze for an instant before being snuffed out again.

I dragged myself along the railing. The ship pitched softly in the waves like a dancer. The sea sang strange music, calling me to dance to it, to climb over the railing and dance out into the air, to swim in it. The stars played peekaboo, like children they called me to catch them, to run out into the dark and catch them. *I'm going to catch you*, I sighed.

Up ahead a soft sound stirred. A star hiding. I listened without knowing I listened. I pulled my body through the shadows toward the sound without knowing I moved. When the sound was right in my ear, I stopped. It was coming from the dark enclave where the lifeboats were stored. I slumped down to the floor just around the corner from the sound and listened thoughtlessly.

There was a *whisk, whisk* sound, the soft, rhythmic motion of fabrics rubbing against each other. I dreamed of linen sails billowing in the wind. There were hushed, ecstatic gasps of stifled breath. I felt a dog panting at my feet. I reached out to pet it. It licked my hand with a warm, velvet tongue. The panting crescendoed, with a final rising coo, a swallow warbling in the eaves. I shielded my face from its beating wings as it took flight.

A man's shape rose from the darkness. There was the metal clink of a belt buckle being fastened hastily, then the shape departed, slipping away quickly into the darkness of the ship deck. The soft, trembling breath of something living continued in the shadows, a rustle of clothing being adjusted. I crawled around the corner, hands groping the blackness for the dog or the swallow, finding instead the soft cotton of a skirt. *I'm going to catch you*, I sighed.

The warm living thing started in fright, gasped not as a dog or a swallow would gasp, and I clawed my hands up to something long and slender, warm and tender as a roasted gooseneck. I sank my teeth into it.

Something clawed at me, wrenched furiously at my hands. The salty, warm broth poured forth. I drank and drank and drank. The swallow flapped and flapped, trying to fly away. It dug its talons into my skin. It gargled and sobbed and gasped out strangled cries, flailing and flopping beneath me. The warm wet ran down my chin, down my neck. I drank. I drank so deeply I forgot to breathe. The flapping of the swallow's wings died down to a weak shudder. The claws loosened at my wrists. The body lay limp and pliant in my arms. The rushing river of blood slowed to a trickle. I sucked greedily, but the blood was all but gone. I sucked and sucked, trying to draw the marrow from the bones.

My mind became aware, slowly, dimly, of the hard little shape of buttons under my fingers, a seam running along beneath my palm. The swallow was clothed. The swallow was much too large to be a swallow, too small to be a star. It had damp skin and long, soft, loose hair. I pulled a fold of cloth up before my eyes, then a mass of tangled curls. I looked down in a panic and saw a smooth cheek turned down and away on my lap. I turned it toward me and saw eyes, nose, a mouth, a young girl's face, a beautiful young girl, sixteen, seventeen at the most. Her face was framed in blood, as though she'd nearly been submerged. Her hair was slicked in it, glued in dark red coils against her cheeks and neck.

My mind reeled. Where was the swallow? Where was the dog? The star? Where was I? How had I gotten here? How had this happened? The blood was everywhere. It was pooled on the deck floor. It was spattered against the side of the lifeboat. I looked like I'd bathed in it. I put my hands to the girl's face, wrapped them around her throat, feeling for any soft drumbeat of life. Cold. Still. I'd sucked her dry, so dry she was already blue. I pulled her up into my arms and clutched her tight, as tightly as I could, as though I could squeeze the life back into her limp body. She felt like Anais in my arms. I wept into her dark, wet hair. I told her I was sorry. I whispered it into her deaf ear over and over and over again.

I threw her over the side, the words of the woman on that other ship so long ago coming back to me. "There's no rest to be had in the sea." But what else could I do? The sea would be gentler to her than I had been. I found a mop hanging on a wall and, in the soft rain, did what I could to mop the blood up, then I threw the mop over as well. My bloody shirt I took off and hand-washed in the dirty rainwater that had accumulated in one of the lifeboats. It had been bloody to begin with, and many passengers on the ship wore similar souvenirs of the violences they had escaped.

At last, I ran shivering and clutching my wet clothes, through the darkness, back to my cabin. The worst part, the truly despicable part, was that I threw up. I'd gorged myself. I'd eaten too much too fast, so much it had killed her, and then I threw up half of it. I threw up enough blood for her to live on right back into the sea.

I spent the next few days huddled in my cabin waiting for a knock at the door; when none came, I finally ventured out of my cabin for a few minutes in the sun. I stood at the railing, staring at the white-capped sea and gauging the distance from where we'd left her. The ship moved so fast. She was hundreds of miles away by now. I felt her loneliness out there. I looked down at the water and the waves slipping past and imagined what it would feel like to fall as she had, to look up and see the stars bright around the dark silhouette of the ship's funnel, to see the murderer's face—*my face*—pale and wild over the ship's railing, then to fall. To fall and fall and fall.

When a voice close beside me said "Miss," I jumped with surprise.

I turned and found an elderly woman, her hair gray beneath a tied handkerchief and her wrinkled cheeks tear-stained. Beside her was a deck officer. It was he who had just spoken to me.

"I'm sorry to disturb you, miss, but it seems this woman has become

separated from her granddaughter. I'm taking her around to ask if anyone has seen the young lady."

He turned to the old woman and held his hand out to her. Muttering in an unfamiliar dialect, and wiping the tears from her cheeks, she
placed a small black-and-white photograph in the man's hand, and he
gave it to me to examine. It took everything in me not to shake or begin
to cry, to instead feign calm and direct my eyes steadily to the face in the
picture. The photograph reminded me of what I already knew: the girl
was beautiful and she was young.

"Have you, by any chance, seen the young lady?" the officer asked.

I shook my head. "I'm sorry, no. I haven't."

I held the photograph out for him to take again, but before he could,
the old woman, who could not understand any of what we had said,
suddenly took my hand.

She pointed a bent arthritic finger at the picture, tears flowing down
her cheeks. "Irka, Irka," she said, stabbing the picture with her finger
and crying and still clinging to my hand. "Kde je moje Irka?"

My eyes filled with tears, and I closed them, certain that, by my body
language alone, I was all but confessing, but instead of arresting me, the
officer took gentle hold of the woman and softly transferred the photograph and the woman's grip back to his own hand.

"Thank you for your help, ma'am," he said to me apologetically and
then coaxed the woman on to the next huddle of passengers.

I stumbled back to my cabin, and when the ship reached its next
port, the port of Alexandria, I got off.

· XXXVI ·

THE morning is an inelegant scramble. There is no time for baking, so the morning snack is whatever I can scrounge from the cupboards, which turns out to be bowls of Marnie's weight loss cereal, topped with sliced bananas.

I bring all this to the classroom and get the children set up with their breakfast. Leo's seat is empty. There's nothing new about that, but today everything connected to that empty seat seems entirely new. For the first time this morning, the events of the previous evening return to me. The cosmetics bag filled with prescription bottles; the picture folded and stuffed inside Leo's giraffe; my conversation with Dave in the driveway, when he seemed to so effortlessly unzip, as if with a single motion top to bottom, everything I thought I knew about Katherine and their family. Max and the pool and the lies and the guilt. Then Katherine so icily censuring me for talking to Dave and judging her parenting.

All those other times when Leo was late, I'd been imagining Katherine tired, puffy-eyed, and upset from Dave's latest abuse, struggling through the morning, struggling to get everyone dressed and in the car, all with an aching back. Does she even have a bad back? And migraines too? A neck injury? Sciatica? As all the diagnoses on all those pill bottles claimed. Now I look at Leo's seat and think of Katherine swimming slowly up through those sleep-inducing substances toward conscious-ness; I think of the fragile chemistry equation coursing through her veins, determining whether she wakes up at all. Whereas I once hated the thought of Dave there in the home with Leo and Katherine, now I hate the thought of Leo and Katherine there alone. What if one morn-ing she doesn't wake up?

From the phone in the hall, I call Leo's house. I don't know what I will say. As the phone rings without answer, I'm pacing, the phone cord looping around me as I turn back and forth. Down the hall the front door opens. Rina steps inside, dusts the snowflakes from the shoulders of her coat, and takes it off. There is no answer. I hang up.

"Everything okay?" Rina asks, seeing my worried expression. With one hand, she balances her coffee mug and tucks her keys into her purse.

"Yes," I say, still pacing with the phone in my hand. "No. I'm not to-tally sure. Rina, if I needed to run out and check on a situation, would you be able to watch the children just for a little while, perhaps a half hour?"

Her eyes go wide with girlish alarm. "Um, okay. Just one thing, there is a couple coming by for a tour this morning. Their appointment is at nine thirty. That's why I'm here early."

I glance down at my watch. It's a few minutes past nine now.

"Could we call them perhaps and push the appointment back?"

"Well, they're coming all the way from New Rochelle, so my guess is that they've probably already left."

I let out a frustrated breath.

"What's the situation?" Rina asks.

What *is* the situation? I don't exactly know. Leo isn't here, but he's often not here. His mother isn't who I thought she was; she isn't a good mother. And I'm going to run out in the snow and do what about that?

"It's nothing," I say finally. "I'm sure everything is fine. I'm just being ridiculous."

THE SNOW FALLS FAST AND heavy. The light at midday is dim, and the world outside becomes like a photo negative: ghostly grays, blacks, and whites blurring softly into one another. We build a fire in the library hearth. The logs pop and snap, sending their warmth out into the room, and the children watch from the windows as the snow piles in the bare branches of the trees. Birds—large black crows—land on the tips of the pines, rocking them, and cascades of snow slide down, like miniature avalanches, to the ground. The birds, alarmed, take flight.

The couple who was to come for a tour got halfway from New Rochelle and then pulled over at a gas station to call and reschedule. Leo also never shows. Rina watches the snow pile up nervously. She asks if we should consider calling the parents to pick up the children early, in case the roads become impassable later.

I'm not concerned about the snow, though, at least not in regard to the children. I am quite concerned about the snow in regard to *me*. What am I going to do now that I have, by my own stupidity, eliminated the Emersons' barn as a feeding option? And even if I hadn't committed the colossal blunder of killing one of their cows, the snow that is spread across everything like an incriminating layer of fresh paint makes it impossible for me to access the barn without leaving a trail.

While the children are eating their lunches, I call Leo's house again, hoping to eliminate at least one anxiety from my mind.

"Hello?"

I'm surprised to hear an answer.

"Katherine, it's Collette. I was just calling to check on Leo since he wasn't at school today. Is he not feeling well?"

"No. He's feeling fine."

There is a long pause that feels rather insolent and it seems like she might simply leave the matter at that, but at last she goes on.

"It was so snowy today, and the morning news said the roads were pretty bad, so I just decided to call it a snow day and stay put."

She clears her throat and continues. "Is it a policy that we should be in communication if Leo's going to be absent?"

A *policy*? As if she were dealing with HR or some federal bureau?

"No, not anything as formal as a policy. It was just a—a friendly check-in. I—well, I know you've been going through a lot lately, and with

Valeria gone, I just wanted to see if—I don't know, if you needed any help."

"That's kind of you." From her voice, though, it doesn't seem as if she finds it kind. "You know," she says, and hesitates. "I could be mistaken, but it almost feels as though you've gotten the impression that I'm not capable of taking care of my own child."

"Katherine," I say, flustered. "No. Not at—"

"I want to be very clear in my gratitude for the help you've provided with childcare." She is speaking slowly and very clearly, as though performing an elocution exercise. "But I also want to be clear about the fact that *I* am Leo's mother. *I* am capable of making decisions regarding him, and I'm generally not going to appreciate having those decisions questioned or contradicted."

"Katherine . . ."

I take a moment, thinking carefully about what to say. I don't know what any of this is. Does she mean the things she has said? Have I actually offended her? Or is this a move of some sort, a strategy to provoke conflict for some endgame I don't understand? Is she simply "done with me," as Dave described, and now wants me minding my own business? I realize that it doesn't matter either way.

"I'm very sorry if you feel that I've overstepped my bounds in any way. I didn't mean to imply anything about your parenting. I . . . I meant only to be helpful."

"Great," she says, as though I'm a receptionist confirming a hair appointment.

There is a pause and then she says, "Have a nice day," and the line goes dead.

THE REST OF THE DAY I feel dazed, gnawed on. It's hard to focus on anything, but after naps, I manage to get the children bundled up in their snow bibs and boots, their sweaters, hats, and mittens, and we go out into the snow to play. We build two snowwomen. Marnie sets a platter of fruit and vegetable facial features out on the back steps for us: carrot noses, strawberry mouths, black olive eyes, various tubers for ears.

The children work with diligent intensity, their cheeks as red as the strawberries, their cheeks as red as blood. They climb on me and pull at me, and I try all the while to forget that they are little sacks of blood running around on short legs. Their pulses animate their skips and laughter and give off a strong bloody scent; without thinking, I find my toe tapping to the beat of the nearest pulse—a song I'd like to get out of my head but cannot. I think of the Greek figure Tantalus—from whom we get the word *tantalizing*—that poor sot whom the gods condemned to an eternity of hunger with food ever just out of reach. How many times must he have studied that branch, heavy with ripe, gleaming fruit? Licked his lips? Reached? And how many times did the branch bend away? And *ha, ha, ha, ha*, what an amusing diversion it must have been for the gods! How they must have laughed.

When we finish the snowwomen, we begin work on an elaborate city of snow forts. A few of the parents do come early for their children. Audrey's mother arrives at two, and Audrey drags her to the back windows to see the rudimentary white architecture sprawled across the back lawn. She and Thomas had become especially absorbed in the project, and when it was time to come inside, they made me swear that they could continue working on it the next day if it was still snowy. Audrey's mother flicks her eyes at the window, coos disingenuously, and then urges Audrey to hurry up before the roads get any worse.

By three thirty the last of the children have departed. Only a minute or two after they've gone, the doorbell rings again and I answer it, expecting that someone has forgotten a lunch bag or scarf, but instead Henry Emerson is standing on the doorstep.

"*Henry!*" My voice is overloud. I've nearly shouted in the poor man's face.

Henry Emerson is a long-faced man with age-spotted cheeks that flap loosely when he speaks and lift up like curtains being pulled back when he smiles, which he does often. His face looks especially long in the blue plaid hunter's cap he's wearing now with the earflaps turned down. His Chevy is idling in the drive behind him, a snowplow rigged up to the front.

"Henry," I say again in the calmest voice I can muster, "nice to see you. What can I do for you?"

"Good afternoon, ma'am."

Henry has known me for five years and has never called me anything but ma'am.

"We have had a bit of a situation this morning."

His voice is hesitant and stern. He is reluctant to get to the heart of the matter, but determined. They've found me out. How, I wonder, will a man as mannerly and kind as Henry Emerson articulate the accusation he has come to deliver? I brace for it.

"Oh, really? I hope everything is all right. It's not May, is it?"

"Oh, no. May is just fine."

He kicks the toe of his boot, getting the snow off.

"Well now, I don't want to alarm you, and to tell the truth, I don't have the whole thing figured out entirely in my own mind, but it seems that there may have been an intruder on our farm last night or early morning, maybe."

"Oh no," I say. "How frightening. The house? Was it the house? Was anything stolen?"

"No. No. It looks like he just got into the barn, and well, like I said, I don't have it all pieced together myself, but, well, one of our cows is dead."

My eyes go wide with what I hope is a convincing show of horrified disbelief.

"Now, I only come over to tell you because I know you're over here all alone and you got the little ones here during the day, and I don't wish to alarm you, but I just wanted to alert you."

"I appreciate it."

"And, I'm sure you won't, but if you *do* happen to see anything, or hear anything out of the usual, or even if you just get nervous, May and I want you to give us a ring. Do not hesitate. I am more than happy to come over with my shotgun and take a look around. Doesn't matter what time, day or night."

"Thank you, Henry. That is kind of you."

The old man gives me a stern nod. "Well, we're neighbors and neighbors look out for one another. Will you promise me that you'll call if you have any concerns? May and I would just rest easier."

"I promise. Thank you, Henry, and I'm so sorry about what happened. That's just so bizarre and horrible. What are you going to do about it?"

"Oh, just lock her up tighter at night, I guess, and keep the shotgun by the bed."

Through all of this, I am nodding like a bobblehead doll. My head is close to falling off from sympathy.

"Had the police out this morning . . ."

I can feel the heat run up into my face; I only hope he doesn't notice.

"But my goodness, if it idn't the strangest thing they ever seen. Millstream Hollow's finest can't seem to make heads or tails of it any more than I can."

He has been looking down this whole time, working absently at the snow caked onto his shoe, but he suddenly looks up and his tone turns direct.

"Now, one more question," he says, and holds up a gloved thumb at shoulder level, "and maybe you can guess what it is . . ."

There is a pause then that feels infinite and unbearable, until I finally say, "Where was I this morning?"

Henry's face cracks into a sudden smile, and he lets out a guffaw of deep, earnest laughter.

"That's rich," he says when he has gotten his laughter under control. "'Where were you this morning?' Oh, my word, that's funny. Can I plow *the drive* for you, ma'am?"

"Ah, yes. That would be very helpful, Henry."

"'Where were you this morning?'" he repeats mirthfully. "You teachers, so quick on your feet. My word. All right, then," he says, starting toward his truck, "and don't forget—anything amiss, you call us!"

"I will call you if anything is amiss."

"You have an excellent day, ma'am. And bring those kids by sometime! It's been too long."

"I will do that. You have a good day too, Henry. Give my regards, and my condolences, to May."

The truck scrapes its way noisily around the circular drive, with Henry inside waving as he drives past, and I close the door and lean heavily against it. "*Where was I this morning?*" How could I say something so idiotic? Why not just say, *Henry, have you ever considered that I might have killed your cow?* I close my eyes in disgust and let out a breath, then, because the children are gone, I crumple to the floor like a demolished building. There were police at the Emersons' barn this morning. *Investigating me!* I think of all my nights spent in the barn. My concern was only to conceal my presence from a kind and unsuspecting elderly couple, not a forensics team. Who knows what kind of evidence of my presence I left behind without realizing it? I still don't know what it is I'm doing every night, where I'm going. What if the police discover the answer before I do? But could Henry and May Emerson ever possibly consider me as a suspect for even one moment if it were suggested to them? If the police came to them and said, we caught your cow-killer, here she is, your neighbor, the preschool teacher, would they even entertain the idea? Certainly not, I tell myself, though certain is not how I feel. The more pressing concern for me, however, is figuring out how I'm going to avoid starvation or bloody rampage without the Emersons' cows.

It's been a ragged day. I don't know how I made it through and I can't imagine how I will make it through the next one. Everything inside of me and everything outside too feels like a hopelessly tangled knot, like when a child goes to sleep with gum in her mouth and wakes up with it in her hair and there is nothing to be done with the gnarled rat's nest but to cut it out. I don't know why this hunger keeps growing, why it must be so unreasonable. I look down at the dark green knit of sweater that covers my stomach—*treacherous organ*. Before I can hold them back, tears of exhausted frustration begin coursing down my face. I dig my fingers angrily into the flesh of my belly, which even now is conveying its incessant hunger.

"What do you *want*?" I moan in anguish, digging harder and harder into the skin. I would rip my guts out of my body if I could, be bloody and done with the entire apparatus. "*What* do you *want*?!"

When the pain of my clawing fingers reaches a satisfying intensity, when I have punished the insurgent member to my satisfaction, I release. I lift the bottom of my sweater and look at what I have done. The pale skin is splotched with large red fingerprints. In certain spots purple bruises and the deep red half-moons of fingernails are visible. I feel a strange mix of anger and sadness. This rebellious, unruly body, and this violent, despotic will to subdue it. How is it that one person can be, at once, within the same body, both incorrigible prisoner and sadistic prison warden? I'm so tired of this endless battle. I'm so tired.

What do you want? I ask of my groaning stomach. It occurs to me that I have never really asked this question, or perhaps I have just never actually listened for an answer. I've been so busy fighting my hunger and barricading myself from my nighttime impulses that I've never permitted myself to engage with them, follow where they lead, learn. I remember something Ehru said to me that last evening in Piroska's hut before everything ended in fire and devastation. "Your body always knows what to do," he'd said, "if you can only move your mind out of the way."

All right, then, I say to that bound and gagged part of myself that I've been so forcefully beating back to no avail. I stand up, put on my winter coat, my gloves, a hat. Where do you go each night? Why? What do you want? I'm listening. Show me.

THE WHITE IS THICK OVER the ground and the pines are shaggy with it. Between them, the deciduous trees hold empty arms up to the sky as if in their frailty they can do nothing but beg for mercy. I feel the same. Together we are starving in the darkness, sinking, brittling, growing gaunt, our only hope some mysterious clemency that may never come.

I step out of the kitchen door, the one that is always open in the mornings, armed with only a flashlight and my intuition. My body is getting up out of my bed so many nights, making its way down the stairs and out of the house and then on to wherever. My body *must* know the way. My body must tell me.

I head in the direction of the Emersons', where I found the glove along the way, the only clue I have. The shadows amid the trees are lengthening, and the snow is blue inside them. Sounds are muffled and the woods are perfectly still. I try to do what Ehru told me. I try to put off my mind. It's difficult. My thoughts chatter and clamor in protest, not wanting to be cast aside, but I just keep asking my body quietly, gently, where are you going every night? What do you want?

I hold the flashlight out in front of me like a divining rod. It might be foolish, but I try closing my eyes and just following wherever my legs take me. It's difficult in these conditions, but when I open my eyes again, the trees are familiar: the jack pine bent beneath the weight of snow, the finely spoked knot in the trunk of an ash that looks like a sea anemone. This is where I found the glove.

I'm tempted here to shove my intuition aside, look around, investigate, but instead I close my eyes again, move slowly in a direction that feels right, or that I am perhaps convincing myself feels right. I shuffle forward slowly and carefully until, quite suddenly, I have an almost electric sensation that I'm about to fall, as though I've just missed a step on a staircase. I jerk back and open my eyes. I see a wine-colored glove crusted with snow and resting in the crook of a low branch. On the ground before me is a strange, out-of-place-looking mound: needled pine branches heaped up and topped with snow. I take up one of the pine branches and toss it aside. Then another. Then another.

When, with a final motion, I have cleared away the last of the pine boughs, I draw in my breath sharply and step back, chilled. Here it is, at last. I've found it: the place my body has been taking me. Part of me would cover it up again, walk away, pretend never to have seen it at all.

It's a hole. Not round, though, as one might naturally expect a hole to be; rather it is a sort of boxy haphazard pit, quite deep, with loose dirt carelessly strewn in piles on every side. It is *my* hole. I have dug this hole. There can be no doubt about it. Just the sight of it fills me with the strangely mixed horror of both the inconceivably alien and the dreadfully familiar. So, this is why my hands, on those mornings, have looked like garden spades of human flesh. The pain, the dirt, the torn nails.

I stare at the hole, crawl around it, feel the dark turned earth inside for ten minutes at least, trying to comprehend it. Why have I done this?

My dreams of Vano return to mind.

"Are you ready, Anya?" he asked me. "Are you ready for the new thing that the world waits to give you?"

I asked him in my dream, "Is it death?"

I wonder it again now. An ending, an emptying, a cup poured out. Could this grave—for what else can it possibly be but a grave?—be some instinctual preparation my body has been working feverishly at for what it knows is to come? Could the god of endings, for once, use his destructive powers for my benefit? Have I managed, at last, to outwit Czernobog by desiring the end he brings? Take it all, and good riddance. Burn me up to ash. It *was* a miscalculation—what my grandfather chose for me all those years ago. This world and all its darkness and pain without end. I never wanted so much. Never had any use for it or it for me. I only ever needed a little.

I sit down in the snow and look down into the rich, black, loamy depths, with bewilderment and tenderness, at this thing—my door, my season, my gift coming soon.

Then, from nowhere, and for no articulable reason, I'm overwhelmed by the desire to dig.

· XXXVII ·

It's a strange thing to suffer in a beautiful city; the beauty of the place is made dark in the mirror of your pain, and your pain is made beautiful in the mirror of the city. Afterward, the memory becomes dreamlike, as full of turbulent passion as a doomed love affair, which in hindsight becomes lovely, though you know that at the time it was hideous and horrible. Alexandria—*Al-Iskandariyyah*, as she called herself—was that place for me.

It was called the pearl of the Mediterranean, and like a pearl, the city seemed not constructed but naturally occurring: a white and shimmering wonder conjured from the slow mingling of sand and water and time. In Alexandria, the unceasing wind was crusted with salt, and the light poured down hot and blinding from the sun to reflect off the sand and the white stone buildings and the white drapery of the peasants' kaftans in the markets, so that it hit your eyes from a thousand angles and pervaded everything with a sun bleached drowsiness. Somewhere beyond all that light, the endless blue of the sky became eventually the endless blue of the sea, and from those distant vertices sudden storms rushed in to throw the city briefly into darkness, tamp down the dust with rain, and then rush off again.

Living there at the fulcrum of so much vastness made one feel small and unimportant in a way that was a great relief. Somewhere, in tight, dark cities far away, a great many people were arguing and fighting, dying and suffering, but in Alexandria the war seemed like a disturbing dream faintly recalled after a sweat-damp midday nap. The nearest front was hundreds of miles away at the border with Libya, where the Italians and British scuffled in the sand to claim the empty desert. In our own Port of Alexandria, two British battleships had been blasted, but even this act of war was unspectacular, done at night by manned torpedoes beneath the silencing waterline—out of sight and out of mind and then quickly forgotten.

In Alexandria, there were no huddled and desperate war refugees, no lost-looking orphans, only the ever-present poor who stood in the streets and sold handkerchiefs to women so that they could wipe away the thick dust that accumulated on their faces and in their nostrils with every breath. In the cafés, Egyptian men played backgammon with water pipes in their mouths, uniformed officers smoked cigarettes and drank champagne, and foreigners in swimsuits lay on Stanley Beach like dead fish, letting the sun turn their pale limbs brown, while the voice of Umm Kulthum swam out of radios and thrown-open windows.

I walked the corniche, a busy strip of promenade that hugged the waterfront, limping through the bright days like a kind of inverted ghost. Instead of a soul with no body, I was a body with no soul, a walking monument—a gravestone—for those I'd harmed or failed to help: my children, Anais, the village, the girl on the ship, her weeping grandmother. I'd once been consumed and sickened by my hatred for the world and the evil of the people in it, the monks in the monastery who had beaten Vano and Ehru, the men from the village who had come for Ehru and taken Vano's and Piroska's lives, the men who'd exiled Paul for his fits and visions and later for being a Jew, then it was the fascists, the Germans, and the Italians whom I despised. But now I was sickened and consumed by hatred for myself. I was one with the world. Cut from the same ugly cloth. Dangerous and destructive and not to be trusted with anything good or innocent. In the mornings, I woke to the same feeling of disgust that had tucked me into bed the night before. I despised myself and I despised the world, and I could escape neither.

I took a room in a boardinghouse on the Boulevard Saad Zagh-
loul, where the honking of motorcar horns mixed with the braying of
donkeys, and the streetcars chugged and clanged their bells day and
night going to and from Ramleh Station. Rent was due at the end of the
month and I told myself I would find a way to make money by then, but
all I did was walk out to the citadel in the evenings, stand on the battle-
ments of the bleached stone fortress with the wind whipping the loose
strands of my hair, and look out across the darkening Mediterranean. I
studied the choppy black water and thought about the girl on the ship
whom I'd killed.

When I threw her over the side, she had plummeted down to the water like an anvil. The sound of the wind rustling my dress was the exact
sound I had heard as she fell. Again and again I imagined it, her sinking
down through the blackened blue, skirts pluming around her like the
sails of a capsized ship, the curls wreathing her head like a wet crown of
seaweed, sharks gliding darkly in the middle distance.

During those days, I thought seriously about attaching some kind
of anchor to myself and dropping, just like the girl, off the side of the
citadel into the sea. The anchor would sink to the bottom and I would
sink with it, and there I would remain, out of the way, harmless, watching the days—only a dim light filtering down through the murk—come
and go above me. Would my flesh eventually dissolve in that salt bath,
I wondered, and if it did, would I die then, or would my consciousness
be parceled out equally into each tiny part? Would a million pieces of
me circulate, distributing my mind with the ocean currents? Would I,
in essence, become the ocean? Or would I remain in one piece, floating
at the end of my leash, growing ever hungrier, ever more ravenous, until
I became some red-eyed, mindless, gnashing Charybdis, catching and
devouring hapless swimmers who made the mistake of diving too deep?
No, I decided, the bay wasn't a deep enough grave for me. A monster
such as myself belonged somewhere less accessible, somewhere deeper,
farther, lonelier.

Back in my rented room, new nightmares moved into the already
crowded space of my dreaming head. I dreamed about the girl. I killed
her over and over again, never realizing what I was doing until it was

done. Sometimes, when I turned the face toward me, it was one of my students dead in my lap, sometimes it was Paul, sometimes Vano, or my father. I'd wake myself with my own screams.

On one of these nights, I was startled awake by insistent rapping on my door. Disoriented and with my damp dressing gown clinging to me, I opened it to find the Egyptian proprietress of the boardinghouse, a stout woman with deep-set eyes and protuberant cheeks, standing there, looking resolute. Beside her and clearly embarrassed was a lanky young expat, a man with dirty-blond hair, a rugged bone structure, and soft brown eyes, who had been recruited to translate from Arabic to French the proprietress's request that I stop disturbing her guests at night.

"My sincerest apologies for this intrusion, miss," he continued in German-accented French after his official message had been communicated. "I was made an unwilling accomplice in this errand. If you hadn't noticed, the lady can be *quite* forceful."

He nodded pleasantly to the woman, who was looking sternly back and forth between us, to convey that her message had been delivered.

"I'm sorry," I said, dragging a blanket from the bed and wrapping it around myself. "It's nightmares. I'd like them to stop as much as she, I'm sure. Tell her, please, that I'm sorry. I'll do my best to be quiet."

He spoke again to the woman, who took my hand and patted it, looking now both stern and begrudgingly tender. The woman spoke again to the man, going on this time for quite a while and gesturing repeatedly to me with one hand, while still holding my hand fast with the other.

"She says that, for nightmares, you should take bread and herbs, soak them in beer and kapet—"

"Kapet," the woman said, nodding, emphasizing the single word that had been understandable to her.

"Which is a kind of incense, it seems, in common use here."

The woman continued speaking, making at one point a circular motion over her face, which caused the man some confusion and he clarified the point before turning to me.

"And then, you should," the man went on uncertainly, "rub that . . . on your face . . . before going to sleep."

"Rub that on my face?"

Doing his best to keep a straight face, the young man turned to the woman and confirmed this last detail again. She nodded and spoke again in Arabic.

"That's what she says. Time-tested remedy. Alternatively, she has a crucifix that she says you are welcome to borrow. Either should . . . keep the demons . . . away from your body while you are sleeping. She says."

From the man's gentle smiles and the way he stole soft glances at me from beneath the fringe of hair that fell forward into his eyes, I could tell immediately that he was drawn to me. There was a shy hungriness in his eyes, and like a coin tossed into a wishing well, it fell echoing down into my emptiness.

His name was Josef Hirzel, and he was the son of a well-to-do family in Berlin. He'd fled Germany to avoid military service and had been disowned as a result. Josef was a poet and artist, who had chosen Alexandria for his exile because of the city's famed beauty and because he loved the Alexandrian poet Cavafy.

Josef made great and gentle efforts at courting me. He would coax me down to the cafés that lined the corniche, where we spent afternoons beneath the shade of the umbrellas. For a while he would try to make conversation, and then, finding me uncooperative, he would move on to reading a book or writing in his journals while bringing a cigarette from his mouth to an ashtray and back with long, strong fingers like those of a pianist.

I lacked the energy or care to refuse these efforts, despite the fact that Josef, by his nationality and even more by his gentleness, caused me great discomfort. Somehow, in France, on those dark, snowy nights in the forest, it had never occurred to me that there might be Germans like Josef: men who would rather flee and write poems in poverty than march in the rigid lines of the occupying forces, singing hymns to the fatherland. How many Josefs had I killed—*and with pleasure?* How many artists or poets scratching in their journals by candlelight and hoping only to survive until the war was over? I could never know. And even if they had all been such, would it have made a difference? Both eager and reluctant soldiers alike follow orders. Would I spare the men and give up instead Jacov, Hadassa, Mendel, Michiline?

I had come to Alexandria exhausted from moral calculations, but here they were, dredged up again. Some days I sought to flee the past. I wanted to think of nothing. Like a jungle beast I wanted my violences to have no meaning and no consequences. On those days, the scratch of Josef's pen, the intermittent clearing of his throat was an irritant that chafed abrasively at the conscience I wished to deny I had, and complicated my numb embrace of beastliness. On other days, I condemned myself savagely—judge, jury, and hangman—and sank without defense or justification into the damnation of the past. At those times, Josef's presence was a torment. He became host to a legion of ghosts haunting me sweetly.

He never knew all the conflict he stirred in me. The better and kinder he was, the more stubbornly I barred him entry to my inner world. I would not begin anything ever again. To begin was to set forth the spark that would grow and leap into the blazing bonfire of the end. He was patient, though, seemingly content to read or write while I sat in silence, feeling the wind move against my skin and watching the hypnotic motion of the waves sweeping in and out along the beach on the far side of the corniche.

One day I caught a glimpse of a painting in the book he was reading.

"May I see that?" I asked, initiating conversation for perhaps the first time.

Josef handed me the book and in it I saw a print reproduction of an unimaginable painting: a forest from a dream or a fairy tale. A bright blue tree bent and hanging like a willow with a sunflower-yellow sky thick around it and peeking here and there through the arms of the tree. Foregrounded in the air, butterflies and other colorful winged insects teemed twinkling like stars. The painting was silly and reckless and dreamy and extraordinary, as it had no right to be. What right had art to be so joyful, when everything real was trash?

"What is this?" I asked in a voice almost of disgust.

"Redon," Josef said, missing my tone and pleased by my interest. "That's a painting by Odilon Redon, a French symbolist painter. It's magnificent, isn't it?"

"People paint like this?" I asked, grudgingly transfixed by the photograph.

"No," Josef said with a laugh. "He does. Not many like him. How could there be? He has the skill of an old master and the vision of a child."

"What is the medium? It's too bright to just be oils or tempera."

"You're right. He *mixes* oils and pastels, sometimes with charcoal or pen and ink also. He's a madman, a mad genius." Josef studied me for a moment curiously. "How do you know so much about art?"

I hesitated, reluctant to share any part of my history with him.

"My husband was a painter. And so was I."

Josef tapped his cigarette against his ashtray and kept his eyes on it as he asked, "What is he now, your husband?"

I gazed ahead hard at the sea, the waves doing their tireless pacing, back and forth along the shore.

"He's dead."

I could feel the invisible force of the dance taking place between us, the hidden gravity of each word, but I did not want to dance.

"I'm very sorry," Josef said, though most certainly he was not. "It must have been very recent."

"Why do you say that?"

"You hardly look old enough to be a widow."

"It was decades ago. I'm actually a very old woman."

He laughed. "You're marvelously preserved then." He crushed the spent end of his cigarette in the ashtray. "And why do you say that you *were* a painter?"

"Because I used to paint, and now I don't."

"Would you like to?" he asked, and then looked up from the ashtray, that innocent desire plain in his soft, brown eyes. "Would you like to paint, old woman?"

· XXXVIII ·

I return to the woods the next afternoon, this time with a shovel. The evening before, I had felt self-conscious, silly even, as I pulled up the first scoop of dirt and tossed it aside. But then I scooped another, and a great burning purposefulness came over me. I felt like a child working urgently at some imaginary endeavor, scooping and mixing and baking mud pies without a hint of irony. I'd not experienced anything so mesmerizing in ages—while I dug, the hunger fell away, and the fear, the anxiety, every care—and I would have tunneled my way to the center of the earth just to go on feeling the peace, even joy of it.

Awake, I was more careful of my hands and my nails, and I added several inches of depth to the hole without doing anything like the physical damage I had done in my sleep. Best of all, afterward I did not dream or wander. I went home and slept a sound, blank sleep in my bed for the first time in a long time.

The shovel makes a lovely, cold shearing sound now as I dig. The sweat bristles on my scalp. My neck becomes slick with it. I throw my hat down in the snow beside the hole and keep digging. I have the nagging thought as I dig that I am perhaps, here right now, slipping—that I'm standing at the edge of some psychological whirlpool that descends to who knows where, and the edge where I stand is very, very slippery;

it would take almost nothing to lose my footing. Would I even know it if I had slipped? And what if I have to slip? What if part of letting go of the old, as Vano described it, includes the old logic, the old sanity even? For how can you cling to proper reason and also go down into a door in the earth where you've been told a gift, new and unforeseen, waits for you?

I throw my gloves down beside my hat, for probably the same reason that I did in my sleep. They're distancing me from the digging, from the hole. The frigid air numbs my fingers quickly, and the shovel handle is rough in my palms, but I want to feel it like an extension of my hands.

The hole descends in cubic feet—a rectangle three feet deep, then four. I stop somewhere after that because I know that I can't dig forever. At some point it must be complete, but I'm not ready. I sense too that there was perhaps a reason why I never brought a shovel. I wanted to feel the dirt in my hands, the soft, cool soil, the small stones, the tiny threads and filaments of roots. The shovel is faster, yet I feel like I've missed out on something. I wanted the sweat, the grueling labor—the cracked nails? The pain? The hands unusable with muscle fatigue the next day? Maybe. I don't know. It seems that maybe I did. It seems that maybe some part of me wanted or needed my blood to mingle with this soil, to make it mine, to make it mo.

A sound. The sudden crunch of footsteps on snow some hundred feet to my right snaps me awake from what might have been almost a trance. I freeze, but inside me my heart has taken off running like a frightened rabbit. My shovel is poised before me in my palms, which have begun to blister and bleed against the wood grain. Moving only my eyes, I look to the right and see in my peripheral vision a dark figure moving toward me in the darkening shadow of the trees.

"Afternoon!"

It's a woman's voice that calls out to me, a large, formal voice, with a hard edge beneath the pleasantry.

"Good afternoon," I call, stabbing the shovel down so that it sticks upright in the snow. I wipe the sweat from my brow and stoop to retrieve my gloves before the person draws near and sees my bleeding hands. I take deep breaths, trying to slow my heart.

Once my gloves are on, I exhale, collecting myself, then turn toward the voice, but when I see the woman, dressed all in navy, gold badge on her chest, walkie-talkie on her shoulder, pushing thin branches aside as she makes her way toward me through the trees, I break out in fresh sweat.

There's a crackle of static from the walkie-talkie, a man's voice robotic-sounding over the radio waves, as Audrey's aunt—Officer what's-her-name—approaches. It seems she's not recognized me yet. She's tilting her head toward the voice on the walkie-talkie and pulling out her badge.

"Officer McCormick, Millstream Hollow PD."

"Ah yes, Officer McCormick. Samantha, was it? Audrey's aunt? I'm Collette LeSange. Audrey's teacher. I met you at Audrey's open house."

"That's right," she says, and I realize from her absence of surprise that she had, in fact, known who I was as she approached. The hard formality had not been from lack of recognition.

Her nose is red from the cold, and jet-black hair spills out from the bottom of her navy police-issue winter hat. She wears little makeup, but her green eyes are bright and pretty despite their stony expression.

"How are you doing today?" she asks without a hint of interest in the quality of my most recent twenty-four hours. She is too busy studying the fruits of my labor, which are splayed out uncomfortably in front of us.

"I'm well. Thank you. And you?"

"Hell of a day. Hell of a day."

She looks up at me. "Where you from?" she asks, and for a second, I'm confused. "The accent."

"*Ah, yes.* Pardon. France. I'm originally from France."

"Oh yeah? Which part? Paris?"

"Um, no. I lived in Chamonix, and then later, in Lozère."

Her face is blank, so I clarify. "They're mountain regions, one in the Alps and the other in the Massif Central. Have you been to France?"

"No. Always wanted to. I studied French in high school, but you know how that goes. I've pretty much got bonjour to show for it. I love that Audrey's learning French. Maybe someday she and I can go to France, and she can order for me in all the restaurants."

"That sounds lovely," I say, encouraged by the turn of the conversation and the routes it might open to more genial topics. Through all of it, though, Audrey's aunt has stood beside me with her hands on her hips. She has not taken her eyes from the hole.

"Someday, perhaps," I murmur, searching for a way to keep the conversation going.

"Cold day to be out in the woods if you don't have to be," she says at last.

"It is. What brings you out in the cold? Is it part of your usual patrol? These woods?" My private property, I think but don't say aloud.

"No. No, it isn't, but the Emersons—you may have heard—had a bit of a disturbance at their place yesterday, so I'm just taking a little hike"—she scans the darkening tree line—"looking around for anything unusual."

She looks down at the hole again, and I think that *unusual* is a very good word for the thing, or the non-thing—the vacancy stretched out darkly in front of us.

"*Did you?*" she says, turning to me.

"I beg your pardon?"

"Did you hear about what happened? At the Emersons?"

"Oh, yes. Yes, I did. Just a bit. Henry—Mr. Emerson stopped by yesterday afternoon. He didn't go into great detail, but he did say there had been an intruder, and something about a cow? A cow was injured, or something like that?"

"*Killed.*"

I shake my head in bafflement. "*Killed?* But then just left there?"

The officer nods vaguely. Her hands are still at her hips, and her eyes are still on the hole, her head moving slightly to take the measure of its depth, its width, in a way that is making me tremendously uncomfortable. Then suddenly she looks away, off to the side at the branches blackening in the falling light.

"That's just . . . that's just so strange," I murmur. "Has anything come to light?"

"Eh, well, some tracks that came out on County D, a few other minor details, but yeah, it's weird. It definitely is . . . *weird.*"

There is something about the way she hits the last word that makes me think she is applying it to more than just the incident on the Emersons' farm.

I'm finding it suddenly difficult to swallow. I've had enough of the chitchat. I want out of this interaction as soon as possible.

"I'm starting to get the sense," she continues, "that this is kind of a weird town. There was that break-in at the cemetery. You may have heard."

My expression, at this, is noncommittal.

"*The cemetery* of all places," she goes on. "I mean, the money's all sitting in the vault right where it should be at the Millstream Hollow Savings and Loan, the guns are all accounted for at the pawnshop. Instead, it's the barns and cemeteries we gotta keep an eye on."

"I suppose wealth and boredom make for more interesting crimes," I offer with a laugh that I hope sounds natural.

She gives me an appreciative lift of the eyebrows.

"It would seem so, wouldn't it? You know, I just transferred to Millstream Hollow from the Jersey City PD. Helping with my mom—Audrey's grandma—she's getting up there. I was afraid that I was going to be bored out of my mind out here. Just enforcing hunting licenses every day. I'm like a dog, you know, can't be cooped up in a boring little apartment all day. I gotta get out and run. You know what I mean? So, truth be told, I'm kind of enjoying all this."

She pulls a flashlight from a holster at her hip, flicks it on, and shines it into the dark recesses of the hole.

"So, what is this?" she finally asks in a cut-the-crap tone. "What are you doing out here?"

"Uh, well. It's a bit hard to explain."

Her flashlight beam remains fixed on the hole, but her eyes, green and catlike, flick to me—no trace of warmth.

"You see, the children and I"—I gesture back in the direction of the house—"we're going to be doing a—well, a science experiment of sorts. We're going to bury some—some trash, and, you know, leave it there. Then a few months later, we'll dig it up again. To—to see what—uh, what's the word? *Biodegrades* and what doesn't. Sort of an environmental science thing."

She nods her head slowly. "Huh. Guess you got a lot of trash. That's quite a hole."

"Yes, well. We'll have a section for plastics and another for paper and kitchen scraps, metal, then we'll compare them and draw conclusions— and, you know, small sample sizes are problematic in scientific experiments. Trying to get them started on the proper methods for scientific inquiry early."

"Jeez, I guess so. We never did anything that scientific when I was in preschool. Think we just watered some plants or something. A bit of a hike for preschoolers, isn't it?"

"A bit, yes. Science and exercise all in one lesson—the proverbial two birds with one stone. They're used to it. We often go for long walks."

This woman, with her endless questions and penetrating, stony gaze, would have made an excellent Vichy guard at one of the checkpoints into the zone libre.

"All right," she says, her tone finally returning to some approximation of courtesy, "well, it's getting dark. Would you like me to accompany you back?"

I try not to laugh at the thought of this little woman escorting me safely home. "Oh no. That's very kind of you to offer, but I'm sure I'll be fine."

"Okay, well, I don't like to tell people how to live their lives," she says, turning back to me, "but you might think twice about coming all the way out here by yourself for a little while, you know? Both of these incidents occurred within a couple miles of your property. We can't rule out the possibility that it's the same person and that they live or are hanging around this area for some reason. We want to keep those little ones safe."

"Goodness, do you really think so? The idea that they might be connected never occurred to me."

"Just a possibility, but all possibilities have to be considered."

She pulls a card from a coat pocket and hands it to me.

"That's my card just in case there are any disturbances, or you think of any helpful information. You be safe and have a pleasant rest of the evening."

"Thank you."

Officer McCormick of the Millstream Hollow PD heads off in the direction of the Emersons' farm, the light from her flashlight skipping off the dark snow. I wait until she's out of sight and then I move from tree to tree, snapping off branches to lay over the hole to keep it from filling again with snow. As I do this, I replay our conversation. She knew about both the Emersons' and the cemetery. Could she possibly have suspected me of anything? She is a hard person to read: flinty and unsmiling when you expect warmth, jokey and familiar when you're feeling on guard. I was nervous enough when I believed that I was only dealing with the Millstream Hollow PD, a five-man outfit of diligent doughnut eaters at best, but Samantha McCormick, energetic police dog from Jersey City, who has been in my house, who has now discovered me working at my most private and bizarre obsession, she fills me with dread.

I lay the branches across the hole until it's completely obscured beneath evergreen boughs, looking something like a funeral pyre, then I start to leave. I walk some fifteen paces back in the direction of the house before I stop. I turn back around, look and listen as far as I can in each direction to be sure that the police officer is nowhere nearby, then I walk back to the hole. I stand above it for a moment, looking cautiously left and right again, then I stoop down beside it. I push the branches back at one corner. I remove my glove. I reach down and scoop up a handful of soil. It's cold and firm, clumped and damp against my palm, and between my fingers.

I'll dig just a little bit more. Just until nightfall.

IT'S LATE INTO THE NIGHT, the moon high and full overhead, when I finally tear myself away from the digging and the hole. When I stop, I do so only because I realize I must. I could go on and on, but I need sleep. I need to wake up rested and refreshed. I haven't exactly been putting my best foot forward lately, and I sense, or perhaps imagine I sense, a subtle watchfulness about the parents, a conversation broken off midsentence when I come near, a quick exchange of glances not intended for me. Maybe word's gotten around about the morning I was late to school and showed up with pants soaked to the thigh and bits of hay stuck in my hair, or maybe it was enough that I broke down in tears at the open house and wept on an infant's face. Either way, I don't want to give anyone further cause for gossip or speculation, and so, full of a peculiarly strong reluctance to do it, I leave the hole.

I'm striding over the lawn, my boots crunching the crisp remnant of snow, when I look up at the house, come finally into view, and notice something odd. It was still daylight when I set out, and a few lights had been left on: the entryway light, which is glowing faintly from deep within the first floor, and the light over the kitchen island, which Marnie must have left on. But for some reason, the dormer windows of the basement, just above ground level, are lit softly from behind their curtains.

I last went into the basement a few weeks ago to bring up the Christmas decorations. It would be unlike me to have left the lights on, and if I had, I would have certainly noticed before now. They would have been plainly visible on all the nights that I returned home late from Leo's.

Could it have been a child? I'm wondering as I draw closer to the house. Could a child have gotten it into their head to sneak down into the basement? It would be quite the terrifying adventure, full as it is of extremely old curios: antique furniture, tools, farm and carriage equipment, much of it quite dangerous and not anything a child should be poking around in. Could one of them—for some reason, Octavio comes first to mind—have managed it without my noticing?

Then, in the frame of the yellow window, the shadowed shape of a man rises suddenly to standing. It moves quickly across the length of the basement and disappears into shadow again. For a moment, I struggle to believe my senses. Did I really just see that? My heart rate doesn't question it, though; it's begun hammering in my ears. There is someone in my house. I didn't leave the lights on in the basement; no child has stolen down there. Someone is *in* my house. I don't know what to do. For an instant, I recall the warnings of both Henry Emerson and Officer McCormick, advising me to keep an eye out for an unsavory character who may be hanging about the area, but then I remember, with a flush of embarrassment, that *I am* that unsavory character.

I continue toward the house, more careful now to step quietly. I approach one of the basement windows and lean forward, putting my eye to a thin crack between the window frame and the edge of the curtain beyond. I can see the naked basement light bulb and the gray-blue slats of the stairs, and on the floor beneath the bottom step, a black duffel bag lying open. Am I being *robbed*? The idea fills me with curiosity. Could some fool of a common crook have found his way into my basement? At the very thought of a petty thief in my home and the gallon and a half of blood chugging through his impudent trespassing body, my stomach warms and churns. I'm very hungry, and well, don't trespass against others if you don't wish others to trespass against you. How to proceed, though?

I creep around to the kitchen door, open it as softly as I'm able, and then move without a sound across the kitchen. If the presence of the intruder needed to be confirmed, it is now by the rustling and rummaging sounds that are coming up through the floor from below. The person seems very confident that he is alone in the house, the better for me to take him by surprise. I don't want to kill this person, just feed from him and ideally scare him into a more respectable line of work. But I also don't want to get caught. He must not see my face, and I'll have to make sure that the experience is so horrifying and bizarre that he would never dare tell the story to a soul. We're off to a good start already considering that the man's story would have to begin with, "So there I was, burglarizing a house one night."

The basement door, when I have crept quietly up to it, is ajar, and soft light reaches dimly up the stairs from the bottom. The noises are louder. There's the scrape of a heavy carboard box sliding across the concrete floor. Softly, gently, I glide the door farther open.

So there I was, burglarizing a house one night, the story will go, *and I was down in the basement, when suddenly . . .*

I reach my hand along the wall, feeling for the light switch, flip it.

. . . when suddenly the lights went out, and I was in total darkness.

As I step through the blackened doorway, I notice that the noises from below have stopped abruptly. There are a few slight creaks on the stair as I make my way quickly and lightly down, but I don't mind. They serve to build anticipation. The intruder has been momentarily blinded by the darkness. I haven't. He's gone still or perhaps ducked behind something, but I'll find him. Already my hidden teeth are pushing forward, reaching out for their next meal, and I don't bother to restrain them. It would be nice, really, if the man had a flashlight; if in a small sudden circle of light, he got a good glimpse of the teeth before he felt them.

From the bottom of the stairs I see him, a tall black figure, a large man, standing perfectly still off to the left. I'm channeling all that I once learned about hunting from Ehru, all that I once used in the snowy woods of Chamonix, but for an instant, something draws me up short in hesitation. For just an instant, the darkness and unshrinking stance of the figure sends a stab of uncertainty, of *fear*, running through me. What if I'm mistaken? What if this isn't just a man? *What if it's* . . .

"*Anya?*" a distinctly Slavic voice whispers in the darkness. "Anya, ty okhotish'sya na menya?"—Are you *hunting* me?

Laughter floods the space, deep and warm and dimly familiar.

I fumble for the light switch at the bottom of the stair, and the lights come up bright and blinding.

"You're louder than a rooting pig," the large man says, switching from Russian to French and still laughing. He's squinting and holding a beefy hand up to shield his eyes against the light, but I can see a thick, dark beard, and in the beard, a patch of chalk-white hair.

"*Agoston?*"

"A little girl no longer, but still fond of a good tussle in the dark. I must always be on my guard with you, eh?"

I'm aghast. It's been ages since I thought of Agoston as anything but a memory. In my mind he's forever perched atop a carriage, *clop-clopping* away from me, into the woods.

"Agoston, what are you doing here?" I ask, gaping at the man. "Why are you . . . in my basement?"

"It is *Philippe* now," he says, putting his hands to his hips and turning this way and that, surveying the open boxes he has gathered around himself. "Though, now that you mention it, I do prefer Agoston. The French have such ridiculous names."

He strokes his beard thoughtfully, seeming somewhat at a loss amid all the mess.

"And," he goes on, "it is, technically, not *your* basement, but your grandfather's basement, and he has sent me in search of a teeny, tiny needle in a quite large haystack. Have you, by any chance, noticed any boxes around here that hold documents predominantly?"

A SHORT TIME LATER, AGOSTON and I are sitting in the dining room. Beside him on the table is a small shirt box that we had finally located high on a shelf.

We'd opened it to find a stack of miscellaneous and all very old deeds and documents. Agoston had carefully rummaged through the fray-edged, crumbling pages, and then had given a small crow and pulled one from the stack. It was yellowed, folded, and wrapped in a loop of thin red cord. Across the top, the word DEED was printed in ornate letters. Agoston unfolded it and read, and I read over his shoulder. It was a bill of sale from 1909 for a property in Tropico, California. A Mr. George Benton was signed as the landholder.

"California?" I said, looking to Agoston. "What's this about? Who's George Benton?"

"He is your grandfather," he answered, folding the paper again and replacing the cord around it. "And he's going to be glad to see this."

"Grandfather owns land in California?"

"Your grandfather owns many properties in many places, but he is not much of a bookkeeper. As a result, it is my lot to spend a good deal of my time scurrying hither and thither over the face of the earth, hunting down scraps of paper. Fortunately, I'm not much for sitting still."

He put the deed back in the box and replaced the lid.

"I'm going to take the whole box and save myself future trips."

We'd gone upstairs then, and Agoston had retrieved from the entryway a wine bottle set next to the keys for a rental car parked in the drive, all of which I would have seen if I had come in through the front door instead of the back.

In the dining room, he opened the wine bottle labeled "Margaux 1931" and poured the deep currant–colored liquid into two glasses that he pulled from the china cabinet. A smile came to my face as he poured. There was no aroma of currant or dark fruit or raisin. The smell of this was more metallic, more savory, more *bloody*.

"Fine stuff," he said, lifting one of the glasses and setting it before me on the table.

I put the glass to my lips and drank gratefully.

"I thought you were a common thief," I said. "I was looking forward to drinking *you*."

"Well, then, I'm glad I could offer you a substitute."

We'd lapsed then into amiable silence, taking sips from our glasses, but looking across the table, seeing a man I last saw wearing a waistcoat and trousers now wearing a knit sweater with patched elbows and blue jeans, I want to talk. I have a million things to ask him, but whether I have the courage to ask them, I'm not sure. Agoston beats me to it, though.

"How are you, Anya?" he says, leaning back in his chair contentedly. "Your grandfather has told me a little. What little he knows. You're not much of a letter writer, it seems. He says most of his go unanswered."

I sit back in my chair, turn my wineglass, eyeing the inky liquid inside. The light from the chandelier overhead does not penetrate it, only gleams along its surface.

"He feels ignored, does he?" I say with a tart suck of my cheeks. "*Abandoned?* Perhaps in another hundred years, we'll be even on that score, and I'll begin a faithful correspondence."

I'm surprised by the bitterness that rises in me suddenly.

Agoston smiles, seeming mildly entertained by my sharp tone.

"I don't know what he feels, but I would be surprised if it was any of that. He's an old leather-hided bastard. He pays no attention to scores, and he's not one to dwell on injury, whether sustained by others or inflicted on others. Maybe he owes you an apology, maybe he doesn't, maybe I do. I'm happy to give it if it helps you, but you won't get one from him. He is never sorry for anything, whether it is something he has done or something that has been done to him."

"How nice that must be, to never feel you've done anything wrong."

"It isn't that, Anya. Wrong, right, you've done them all. All the things you've done are a little of both. Wrong things come out right, right things come out wrong, then with enough time, they switch. Over hundreds of years, you see this. What are you to apologize for? In the confusion and profusion of it all, it is impossible to sort. The line cannot be traced. Your grandfather can't keep track of his property deeds; he's certainly not going to keep track of the good and ill he's done over many hundreds of years, worry over the balance of his little checkbook, and he's right. It's impossible."

"What about motives?" I insist. "You can't know how things will come out in the end, sure, but you can know why, in the moment, you're doing a thing and whether, by doing it, you're seeking a person's benefit or profiting from their harm."

Agoston gives another small laugh.

"*Civilian* concerns."

My eyes go wide in indignation, but before I can speak, he holds up a hand. "I'm *not* saying you're wrong. Please, hear me. The world needs civilians and their concerns, their moral calculations, but your grandfather and I, we were warriors for hundreds of years in a world that was nothing but war. We are warriors still, at heart—"

"Where were you and Grandfather warriors?" I interrupt. "When?"

Agoston laughs lightly and leans forward in his chair.

"Ah, stories and stories and stories we could tell you. When were we not and *where* were we not?" He brandishes an invisible weapon, something like a spear, I'd guess from the grip of his hands, over the table in front of us.

"I can still feel the weight of the bodies of the Saxons at Moravia, weighed down beneath eighty pounds of mail, hanging from the end of my rogatina. You had to shove them off quickly, to avoid being likewise skewered. But what was the point I was making?"

He sits back again in his chair, a faint, joyful gleam still in his eye.

"Ah yes, motives. Your grandfather and I are warriors, and warriors have a different calculus. Motive is too fine an idea, too delicate for our rough blades and blundering hands. We cannot work with it, and we cannot change no matter how the world does. Eh, maybe *I* can. I've always had something of a soft side, but your grandfather, no. He was designed perfectly for war. If there is no war—no winners and losers—he will make one. You speak of motives; his motive is always the same: victory, checkmate, protecting his army, defeating his opponents.

"For my part, I do not say that you are wrong to consider motives, but the remedy for both the civilian and the warrior is, as far as I can tell, the same: do your best in the moment, and then let it go."

Agoston takes a drink of blood, then looks to me again kindly.

"Despite what you might call his callousness, your grandfather cares for you, Anya, in his way. I am sure he believes he has done you naught but good. Children, to him, are only small, weak soldiers: they need hardship, injury, deprivation to become strong because *strength* he prizes above all. Now that you are grown and strong—hunting *me* in your basement, for instance—he would like to know more of you, *see* more of you. He sent me with an invitation. He wishes you to come to Bordeaux. *If you like.* Of course, it is up to you. To visit or stay, the choice is yours, but he thinks it might . . . *benefit* you. To be among your own kind. Doesn't it ever get lonely, surrounding yourself only with vremenie?"

"I've never even wanted to *be* my kind, why should I want to be among my kind?"

This answer comes quickly because it's long been true, but it suddenly also feels glib. Agoston's question, such a simple one, has actually cut through me like sharp shears through fabric, though I don't want to let on. This brief conversation with Agoston, I realize suddenly, *has* felt like air to one suffocating, like food after years of starvation. To think that he and Grandfather can speak to each other candidly like this anytime. To imagine, for a moment, that I could.

"It is nice to be able to talk to someone without having to keep all the lies straight," I add after a pause. "When did you become such a conversationalist anyway, Agoston? In my memory, you were this huge, silent figure who loved to terrify me and then laugh about it."

"Terrify you? *No*, surely not. I practically *doted* on you. But if I was silent, it was because we did not share the same tongue. English is an awful language, all knees and elbows. I can still barely get directions in it."

"Then you're living in Bordeaux with Grandfather?"

"For the most part."

"Tell my grandfather that I thank him for the invitation."

"You won't come?"

"No. I'm not ready. I'm still too mad. Whether I should be or not."

"You are still young, Anya, but you look ahead to a long life. A tougher hide might be of value to you too."

I'm silent for a moment, trying to decide whether I'm offended by this or not, but Agoston sits there serenely. His gentle expression tells me that he does not mean to offend but to help me, help me hurt less, have more happiness. I'm not offended, still I feel the urge to test his hide, see whether it's really so easy to let go as he makes it out to be.

"You know about Piroska, I suppose? That she was killed."

He does indeed look suddenly pained. He blinks heavily.

"I know what was done to her, yes."

"Not everything," I say. "I didn't even tell Grandfather everything. It happened before my eyes. It was slow and ghastly."

One of Agoston's eyes gives a slight twitch, and he blinks again. He knows that I am baiting him, horribly, but he does not resist, just listens.

"One of the boys too. There were two boys who lived with her in addition to myself, you may recall. He wasn't a boy when it happened, but it was . . ."

I look away for a moment. Somehow the thought of Vano's death is still painful and horrific.

". . . it was awful."

"I am sorry, Anya," Agoston says gently. "Piroska was like a mother to me also. I would have spared her all suffering if I could. This is a hard, cruel world, and transformations in it are always violent and painful."

"Transformations?"

"Yes, like your own. And mine. It was not easy or painless for you or I to become what we are. It was not easy for Piroska to become what she is."

"What she is? She's *dead*."

"Eh, maybe. Maybe not. Conservation of mass. Nothing disappears. Piroska least of all. I don't know what Czernobog did with her, but her goodness cannot be unmade. That is my sense anyway."

"*Czernobog?*" Just saying the name makes my stomach twist. "You know Czernobog? The god of endings?"

"Of course. The god of ashes, destruction, woe. And Belobog, the god of light, life, good fortune. I grew up in the same place you did, only many hundreds of years earlier. I know them."

I sit up, suddenly urgent.

"May I ask you a strange question?"

"I would take pleasure in it," Agoston says, lifting his glass toward his mouth. "Make it very strange, the stranger the better."

I pause for a moment, not knowing which question to ask, where to begin.

"Have you ever seen them? I—I believe I've seen Czernobog. In fact, I have felt, ever since I learned of him, that he has pursued me, even here. He's taken things from me, so many things from me. I hear him when he's close, like a roaring fire. Sometimes I see ashes in the air and smell smoke. The smoke alarm, even, *in this house* has been going off at strange times. It isn't fire, and it isn't the batteries. It makes me feel, at times, like I'm crazy. I don't want to believe it, but just when I stop, it comes again. I've wondered so many times if it's all in my head. I don't know what to think, but I live in almost constant fear. Do you— What do you think? Do you think it's all in my head, or do you think I'm experiencing something real?"

Agoston looks thoughtful for a moment.

"It is impossible to know, with precision or certainty, what is in your head and what is outside of it when you are speaking of gods. The supernatural cannot be known as other things are. It does not behave consistently like molecules or light, which can be measured and studied, but creatively and unpredictably, as a person behaves. By its consistent behavior, we can come to many conclusions about light, but about people, our conclusions are always at least partially wrong, and more often very wrong. Unless you have cause to doubt your sanity across more areas of life than this one, I think it is fair to trust what your senses tell you about Czernobog, but I would advise you to be slow in your conclusions.

"Many people in many places have come to conclusions about Czernobog—certainly, they call him by other names. They have experienced this force or this person, just as you have and I have, and at first, they only described him as they experienced him, but with time and many conclusions, some true, more false, they began to *create* him. Where you and I grew up, they called him Czernobog, they painted him black, and to him they attributed all their strife, misfortune, loss. *Is that his name, though? Is that who he is?*"

He gives a shrug and an ambivalent purse of the lips before going on.

"For my part, I am not convinced that he and Belobog are even two, but like joined twins, my people cut him apart. Like a child calling the giving, hugging, generous aspects of his parent by one name and the disciplining, punishing, medicine-dispensing aspects of the same parent by another. Perhaps this is right and true; I have doubts.

"Like you, I have sensed the pursuit of both Czernobog *and* Belobog for most of my life—not singly, but as one; I have heard and seen strange and terrifying and wondrous things, just as it seems you have, but I have noticed a pattern—and this is a conclusion, mind you, so place no blind trust in it—but the pattern I have seen is that the Emptier must empty before the Filler can fill, a space must be cleared for a gift."

"*A gift*," I murmur, and Agoston looks at me curiously. "Oh, it's just something Vano said too. A friend. I'm sorry to interrupt. Go on."

Agoston takes the last drink from his glass and holds it up for us to see, empty and stained in the chandelier light.

"Well, we children do not like emptying, clearing. We do not want Czernobog's darkness, only Belobog's light. Even us very old children.

We forget that light, without shadow or variation, is blinding. We malign and fear and slander the Emptier, Czernobog, the Dark One, the god of endings. Perhaps we would do well to wait, like children learning patience, learning trust, and see what fills the space he clears, what light breaks into his darkness."

· XXXIX ·

THE picture Josef had showed me by Odilon Redon stirred up thoughts of painting. In my mind, I resented art and no longer felt entitled to the pleasure of it. Who could make art when civilization was on the brink of collapse? Who could make art when they'd just committed murder? But my hands had no such compunctions; they hungered greedily for brushes and palette knives, wood frames and canvas, and so we began. Josef and I would sit on the boardwalk and paint the white froth of surf where it crawled up onto the sand, or the Egyptian women wading into the water, the thin, bright cloth of their gallabiyas spreading around them like water lilies.

Josef managed to obtain some pastels and a Redon print—this one a vivid and delicate bouquet of red poppies in a sea-green vase—which he gave to me, and with the pastels, I drew the fruit vendors beside their crates of burnt-orange persimmons and pink prickly pears. I drew a pretty little Egyptian girl who wore a scarlet hijab as she sold combs to passing gentlemen outside the shops on the rue Fouad. I offered the drawing to the girl, and the expression on her face was of such deep astonishment that it could have been mistaken for fright until she hugged the picture to herself seriously and fled on legs that seemed too thin to be capable of such speed.

For my room and board, I persuaded the boardinghouse proprietress to accept a portrait of her building, one of the many lovely multi-
storied neoclassical structures characteristic of the British Quarter,
which would have looked at home in London but for the Islamic arches
and tiled muqarnas that ornamented the facade.

When we worked, Josef would lean close to praise some detail of my
painting, or to get my opinion of his perspective or value, and I would feel
his eyes lingering on my face, but I never acknowledged his gaze or returned it. He was so innocent and kind, his love so plain and unguarded.
There was a small part of me, etiolated and barely conscious, that desired
him, but there was another part, strong and vicious, that forbade it.

Now and then, Josef called me "old woman"—a joke, but the joke
was on him. Everything he thought could not possibly be true about me
was, and everything he imagined was true about me was just that, imagined. He had fashioned me in his mind like one of his beautiful poems,
but he had no idea who I really was. He believed that I still grieved my
dead husband and that with love and patience he might bring me out of
mourning, but the sweeter Josef's care, the more sadistically the beast
inside of me fought.

I decided to stop seeing him and told him so with the listlessness
that had become my manner. He seemed, at first, confused and disbelieving.

"Why are you saying this?" he asked as we sat at a table of a café on
the quay of Port Neuf. He'd brought a new book of prints to show me,
and it sat untouched beside his ashtray, the wind of a building storm
whipping the cover back and forth. He reached across the table for my
hand, something he'd never done before, but I pulled it away.

"You must know that I care for you very deeply," he said. "If I haven't
made that clear, it was only because I didn't want to be pushy. I thought
it best to give you time. Perhaps I've been too subtle as a result. But I
want to make plain now that my intentions are honorable and earnest.
You are more than anything I've ever dreamed of."

"No, Josef," I said, without looking at him. "You are mistaken."

"About what?" he asked with a pleading smile. "About what am I
mistaken?"

"About everything," I said. "About all of it. There can be nothing between us."

He wrote letters after that and slipped them under my door, letters full of questions and promises to remedy whatever it was I found lacking in him.

"I am too tall, perhaps," he wrote. "Easy enough. I hear there is a doctor in Abu Qir, entirely without scruples, whom I believe I could enlist to take two inches off at the knee."

"I am poor," he wrote in another letter. "Perhaps that's it. And if so, you're right! You do not deserve poverty. You deserve a life of palatial luxury. I will get a job as a banker, a shopkeeper, a very useful spy for the Allies. I'll infiltrate Hitler's inner circle, anything to give you the life you want, anything to have your love, which I value more than poetry, more than art."

I did not answer his letters. I avoided him completely until a day when, leaving the boardinghouse, I opened the door and found myself face-to-face with him as he was returning.

"*Please*," he said in a stricken whisper. "Please. One word, something, anything. Tell me what's wrong, what you find so unendurable about me, just please not this silence, this wondering. I beg of you. It's too much."

I stepped outside. With shaking hands, Josef lit a cigarette and waited for me to speak as I stood watching a streetcar pass.

"There is nothing wrong with you, Josef," I said finally.

When he put his hands to his head in anguish, I went on. "There's nothing wrong with you. You are *perfect*. You are a perfect, good man."

He looked up hopefully and took a step toward me, but I looked away.

"If I were someone else—a different woman—I would . . ."

He squinted at me, disbelieving, despairing, wanting me to finish the sentence, but I didn't.

"That *can't* be *true*," he cried. "If it were true, you wouldn't be doing this."

"It is true, Josef. It *is* true. I see you, standing here before me, a perfect man. But I don't want *anything*. I *want* nothing. You have not understood this about me. I have no love to give you."

He closed his eyes.

"It's your husband? Are you still grieving? There's no hurry. I can wait. I can wait *years*! And with no expectation, only hope that eventually you might . . ."

"It isn't my husband. It's me. I have no love to give to you or to anyone. It's as simple as that, and it cannot be changed or waited out."

"Then don't love me," he said stubbornly. "Only let me love you. I don't need anything in return."

"It's not possible. I would not simply not love you, Josef; I would destroy you. I would kill you."

"What *is it*?" he asked me, looking intently into my eyes as if some answer lay there, some clue hidden in the pattern of the iris that he could find if he looked hard enough.

"There is something. Something that you're not telling me, something that would make this make sense, but I don't know what it is and so it doesn't. It doesn't make sense, and *that* is what is killing me. If it only made sense, I could accept it."

"You want to know the something? The something is this: I am not a good woman. I'm a bad woman. I'm a cursed woman, and if you understood that, you would not be asking me to begin something with you."

He laughed with exhausted sadness. "You're not a bad woman. You're not a bad woman." He reached up tenderly to touch my hair, but I turned my head away.

"You don't know anything about me," I hissed wrathfully. "You like the way I look. You gaze into my blankness and imagine all sorts of wonders. They aren't there. It's your imagination, your poetry. It's garbage. Let me save you the trouble of finding out the hard way."

He looked startled, shaken.

"I've given you what you asked for," I went on. "Now we'll see if you keep your promise and accept it."

I didn't wait to see whether he would accept it. I left Josef and the British Quarter and a bill with the landlady that I didn't have the money to pay, and moved to a dilapidated boardinghouse deep in the Arab Quarter, where the streets ran like thin ribbons through the stacked labyrinthine buildings that stood shoulder to shoulder and never permitted sunlight to lift the gloom between them.

In this building, the dust accumulated in corners like miniature sand dunes, there was a hole in the second-story floor that I had to jump across to reach my room, and a mother cat and her tiny kittens lived on the stairs and left their dark, dry droppings on the steps. Somehow, I found it soothing. I liked the cool shadow of the sharply winding streets choked with market stalls and the damp clothes hung on lines like draped banners, the thickets of colorful fanous lamps that the lantern vendors lit each evening. I liked most of all that I didn't have to worry about meeting Josef in the hall, at the washroom, or outside in the streets.

The habit of painting rushed back hard like an addiction, regardless of my deserving it or not deserving it. I went out painting every day. At the El Qaed Ibrahim Mosque, I covered my head and wrapped my feet in burlap bags, as required of infidels, to climb the tightly spiraled stairs of a tower that let out onto a veranda from which I could paint, to the north, the crescent of the beach and the traversing Stanley Bridge, and to the south the ruins of the ancient Roman amphitheater. I took my finished paintings down to where the tourists walked by the seashore and laid them out on the walk beside me to sell while I sketched in my sketchbook. The cost of living in the Arab Quarter was extremely low, and the European tourists spent as they were used to spending in Europe, and I easily made more than enough to get by on.

I began to see, here and there, the little girl with the bright red hijab whom I had drawn on the rue Fouad. If she saw me, she would run up to me shouting, *Fannan! Artist!* And then paw at my easel, eager to see and appraise my work. If she happened to find me out while I was still painting, she would stand quiet but steadfast at my elbow, close enough that I could feel her breath on my sleeve, and stirring only to run forward and offer her combs to some passerby, then run back to my side.

This should have been very irritating, but the girl—Halla was her name—was so calm and genuinely fascinated by the work; and she had beautiful, intelligent eyes like golden-brown agates and a bright, sweeping smile that reminded me of the white sheet sails of the fishing boats and that seemed to be her natural resting expression. I could not have begrudged her anything if I had tried.

When she followed me one day out to my dusty view of the Sera-peum and began, with a stick, to draw our shared subject—Pompey's Pillar, tall and lonely and unmistakable, in her sketch—in the dirt beside me, I tried my very best to ignore it. No more students; no more children—but of course, I couldn't.

In irritation, without smiling or giving her the slightest glance of encouragement, I handed her a small canvas panel and my tin of pastels. I could feel the intensity of her overjoyed smile burning through my cheek, though I refused to look at it. I just pointed at the scene before us, and we both got to work.

I don't know how she found me, but the next morning when I left the boardinghouse, the girl was waiting for me. She leaped down from her perch atop a stack of rice bags on the other side of the road and fell in step with me as I made my way to St. Mark's Coptic Orthodox Cathedral. When I had settled on a spot, I held out a panel and the pastels to her, but she just stood beside me, smiling amiably and eyeing the brushes and oil paints I'd set up in front of me. She said something that I did not understand and pointed at my setup, then smiled again. Her smile was soft, not manipulative; she was not accustomed to getting her way by it, she just wanted to paint.

So, we switched places that day and because oil painting is less intuitive than drawing with pastels, her picture, several hours later, was a mess. She peered over my shoulder at the drawing on my panel and clapped her approval, then she looked to her composition, laughed, and hung her head, unpleased with her results.

I struggled to pull together a few terse reassuring words in Arabic. "Good" and "It's difficult."

She smiled broadly, a little artist utterly without ego. I felt the smile that had formed sympathetically and involuntarily on my face and dropped it. I would not teach her. I would not *know* her. Perhaps tomorrow, I reasoned, after experiencing for herself the difficulty of painting, she will give up, run off and play with her friends, go back to selling combs, and I could work in peace again.

On our way back to the Arab Quarter, Halla spoke to a vendor who gave her two dates without payment, and it occurred to me that the child had not eaten since we had set out five, maybe six hours before. I bought her a bowl of *kushari*, an odd aromatic street food of rice, lentils, macaroni pasta, and fried onions all drowned in a tomato broth. The girl ate the large bowl down to the bottom, smiling and savoring it as though it were an outlandishly sumptuous feast, and for the first time, I began to wonder about her, where she lived and how.

· XL ·

THE last day of school before the winter break arrives, and with it our holiday party and recital. From the minute the children arrive, they are delirious with excitement. Annabelle has some sort of glitter gel smeared across her cheeks and more glitter dusted in her intricately braided hair. Audrey has brought a tube of red lipstick from home and informs me with elation that she has permission from her mother to wear it during the performance.

None of the children can move without hopping, running, skipping. They can't speak without gasping. They bounce and twirl and sing all around the classroom. Even Leo, usually my most subdued little one, is downright silly. His laughter, a gravelly but infectious burble of un-controllable joy, spills out over the din regularly, followed more often than not by a small conniption of coughing. One of his customary chest ailments seems to be gathering force, though it's not affecting his mood any. If only my own spirits were so high.

Agoston departed the same night that he came. Off on Grandfather's business to a bit of land in Tropico, California. I was surprised by how sad I was to see him go, and surprised further when that sadness did not dissipate the next day or the next. "Did it get lonely living among vremenie?" he had asked me. If it wasn't before he asked, it certainly became so afterward. And the truth was that it had been before.

The snow has fallen only lightly since that first heavy dump, but it has stuck. The cold has kept the thick garnish of white perfectly intact for days. I'm not sure whether this is more fortunate or unfortunate. The Emersons' barn has of course been out of the question, but I suspect that if it weren't for the snow, I would likely have been tempted to try it again and equally likely to have been shot by Henry Emerson for my foolishness.

I'm not doing well. My head pounds, the lights are all too bright, my hands are constantly shaking. Sometimes it is all so much that I feel the need to scream. I can feel the accumulating deficit building up in my brain. At odd moments when I am drifting off vaguely into abstract thought, I see a flash of movement, catch a whiff of child, and some part of me starts, the way it did when poor Mona fluttered her wings in my peripheral vision. I'm like a lion in a zoo: a thickly muscled, sharply fanged, ravenous hunter forced to lie lazy and depressed behind a pane of glass, while on the other side fat, fleshy babies and toddlers writhe and swarm, smear greasy fingerprints, and make faces. The glass between myself and my children is a brittle pane of self-control, which I have erected myself, but it's splintering. For that reason—for *them*—I'm glad that two weeks of vacation are upon us. For myself, I feel nothing but despair. I wish I would have thought to ask Agoston about this strange, insatiable hunger. He seemed to have answers for everything. I consider, a few times, sitting down to write a letter to Grandfather—he might know something about it as well as Agoston would—but each time something keeps me from doing it.

Marnie comes in early on the day of the recital to make orange cranberry cinnamon rolls for the morning snack and to painstakingly ice three Yule log cakes that the parents and children will enjoy after the Christmas performance. She also bakes some things for me to eat over the break, which I, of course, will not eat over the break.

Sweet and motherly to the bones, Marnie is perpetually concerned by my lack of husband and my weight, and she expresses the latter concern, the only one she feels she can remedy, by baking rich pies and casseroles and leaving them about. Rina is not here today. She has left early for Boston, in the hopes of making it in time for the birth of a niece.

The children and I spend the morning rehearsing. They practice lining up at the sides of the stage in the correct order, filing onto the stage, taking up the correct formation, bowing at the end, and filing offstage again. We run through the group dances and songs. The girls are desperate to wear their costumes, and I have to keep moving the sequined tutus to more and more unreachable locations to foil them.

"Ma petite," I chide Annabelle at one point. She is incurably fixated on the snowflake costume and blue sparkly tap shoes for her solo. "How will you feel when you drop a cinnamon roll in the lap of your white costume and then cannot wear it for the performance?"

"I'll be careful," she whines.

"Indeed, you will, careful enough not to put it on until it's time."

She relinquishes the costume ruefully, two fingers clinging to the fabric for as long as possible. I take it to my room and hide it in my own closet.

After rehearsals, there are cinnamon rolls, and after cinnamon rolls there is E. T. A. Hoffmann's "The Nutcracker and the Mouse King" read aloud on the rug before a fire, and after the book there is a nap.

Last week I promised Annabelle that on the day of the performance we would practice her solo during nap time. When nap time comes, she pleads with me, and though I hate to go back on my word, I must. I'm simply too dangerous. Her pulse, as she hops up and down and whines, rumbles in my ears like close thunder, and my blood teeth shift softly, mistaking the child for my next meal. I tell her that, unfortunately, I have too many other things that I have to attend to and she can choose to practice alone or nap with the other children. She heads off alone to practice.

I leave Annabelle and make for the dance studio where the recital will be, but on my way, the phone rings.

To my surprise, it's Katherine. At drop-off and pickup, she and I have exchanged nothing beyond the most basic pleasantries since our last conversation, when she basically accused me of undermining her parenting.

For a moment, I'm afraid she's calling to say she won't be at the recital, but when I ask whether she'll be there, she says, "Oh yes. I'm looking forward to it. Leo's been talking nonstop about his dance of the candy canes."

"Yes, he's been working very hard on it. You may want to arrive early to save your seat. These parents can be rather cutthroat."

"I will. Thanks for the warning."

There is a pause. Then we both rush to fill it and neither of us can be heard.

"You go ahead," I say uncomfortably.

"Well . . . I just called because . . . I owe you an apology."

"Not at all, Katherine," I hurry to say, my stomach lurching with discomfort.

"No, I do. After all that you've done for us—for *me*, I—well, I didn't treat you the way you deserve. Dave told me that he basically forced you to talk to him. Even when I got angry, I knew you hadn't done anything wrong, but I let myself get all worked up anyway. It really wasn't fair to you."

"It's all right, Katherine, really. You've been under a lot of stress. I couldn't even imagine—"

"It's more than that, though," she insists. "It's a thing I *do*. I feel so ashamed all the time of all the things that I'm messing up, *especially* as a mother. You know, I could be a bad woman and not feel half the shame that you're expected to feel for being a bad mother. No one has any compassion at all for a bad mother, least of all the woman herself."

For a moment, I'm at a loss. Katherine *is* a bad mother, a horrible, neglectful, maybe even abusive mother. I'm certain of it. But what if she's certain of it too? What if she despises herself for the things she's done to Leo as much as I've come to despise her for them? Where *does* "compassion" fit in all this? These are all thoughts for another time, though. Right now, I'm happy to patch things up to the extent they can be patched and get off the phone. I have things to do besides weigh Katherine's guilt or innocence.

"You're right," I say. "It isn't very fair. Perfection just seems to be expected of mothers and not a lot of grace is given to them." Then, because

I feel I have to say it, though the words feel wrong coming out of my mouth, I add, "You're not a bad mother, Katherine. No one's perfect."

"But then," Katherine continues, "if I open up to someone kind or allow them to help me, I find myself becoming horribly self-conscious. I start to feel like all my failures and inadequacies are on display, and then I start to imagine that I'm being judged for them and I get defensive, even angry at imagined wrongs. But they *are* imagined, and they're imagined just so that I can have an excuse to shut that person out and run off to hide again.

"That's what I did to you. Usually, I would just hide and feel more ashamed, but this time I wanted to apologize and let you know that you didn't do anything wrong. It was all me and my crap. You've been nothing but kind and helpful, and I repaid that by attacking you. It was totally wrong of me, and I'm sorry. I guess I've never been very good at relationships."

"Well," I say, "while I don't believe this needs to be said, if you need to hear it, I forgive you. I know what difficult circumstances you're dealing with and it's not my intention to judge you. I'm certainly in no position to judge. We're all miserable failures, I guess. In our own ways. I've never had any illusions on that point."

"Thank you," Katherine says. "The truth is, I can't afford to push you out. You're the only thing like a friend I've had in a long time, and you're a good one. I told you that I'm a good judge of character, and I know that you're a very good person—Leo loves you so much. With Dave gone now, I realize I can't do it all on my own. I'm going to need all the good people I can get."

Something about the turn this conversation has taken makes me uneasy. I'm willing enough to receive Katherine's apology and happy to hear her speak with some self awareness about her own unhealthy behaviors, but I'm reluctant to be reestablished as someone on whom she can rely. Part of me does want to help Leo in any way I can, but part of me also wants nothing whatsoever to do with his mother.

"It seems smart to confront this reluctance you say you have to letting people in. It's a trait I share with you, if I'm honest. But I'm also confident that you can handle what's ahead."

"Thank you," she says quietly. The line is silent for a moment, and I'm wondering if we're done and I can get back to the numerous tasks still before me, but then Katherine speaks again.

"There is something else I wanted to talk to you about, though it's kind of scary for me to do so."

I'm silent. The things I should say—*Of course! Go on! Do tell!*—I simply cannot muster. I feel only dread at being taken deeper into Katherine's confidence.

"You may know or you may not," she goes on, "that I've been struggling for a while with a dependency issue. Pain pills. It started with a prescription for my back, but since then, it's gotten out of hand."

"I see," I murmur, following Dave's advice to play dumb.

"The reason I'm telling you is that with all the changes in my life, I feel like I want—I *need* that to change too. For the first time in a long time, I don't want to take those pills anymore. I don't want to be foggy and forgetful and out of it, and I can't afford to sleep half the day away. I don't think I can make it through everything ahead like that. I need to be clear. I need to be me. The real me. Leo needs that from me. I'm all we have now."

"That's really good, Katherine. I agree with you that that problem would make everything you're trying to do much harder. I'm glad you told me. Please let me know what I can do to support you in that."

"Dave found a place, a program, I guess you would call it—he's willing to pay for it all too. He's actually being very generous about the whole thing. Anyway, he put my name on the wait list a while back, against my will at the time, but now it seems like the right thing."

"That sounds great. I really think you should do it, and if you need someone to care for Leo while you're there, please, just let me know."

"I'm so grateful for your offer because that's just what I wanted to ask you. As I said, my name was on the wait list and it usually takes a really long time to get in, but they just called today and said that a spot had opened unexpectedly and if I can make it, it's mine."

"Oh."

"It's so horribly last-minute. You were the only person I could possibly imagine asking or even telling about this whole situation."

"When would you go?"

She hesitates. "Almost immediately. Tonight."

"*Tonight.*"

"I know. It's so last-minute, and it's absolutely fine if you can't do it. I shouldn't even be asking; it's such a terrible imposition, but I just had to try because if I could somehow swing it, it could be such a good thing . . . for all of us. I would pay you, of course."

"Don't be silly," I mutter, then pause, thinking. Katherine doesn't know that I know about all her lies. All those therapy and doctor's appointments that never were. Is this a lie too? The apology, the confession? Where would she want to go for days on end, *at Christmas*? Of course, it must be a lie. But how could it be? The guilt, the self-reckoning, and what if it's not? What if Katherine could get clean and actually wants to?

"Katherine," I say after a moment, "I agree that this sounds like an opportunity to be seized, but I wonder whether I'm the best person to watch Leo. After all, Christmas is in three days. Shouldn't he be with family?"

"There is no family for him to be with except me."

"What about Dave?"

"Dave is in Tokyo. On business. Family man no longer; he can work right through every holiday just like he always wanted to. I just really feel like if I don't do this now, I might not do it at all. If it's not a good time for you, or if having Leo would be inconvenient, please, let me know. I'll look in the phone book for a sitter. I'd prefer he be with someone I know and trust, but I'll do whatever it takes. It's worth it."

I'm silent for a moment, fretting, weighing. The idea of some stranger out of the phone book spending a week with Leo is horrifying, but the idea of him staying with me is full of complications, not to mention *dangers*—I am *so hungry*. But if I could manage to white-knuckle my way through, and if Katherine is telling the truth and could actually get well, what might that mean for Leo? I must admit too that the thought of spending a Christmas not alone as I was dreading but with Leo is painfully lovely. There could be sledding and hot chocolate, somehow I'd find presents for him, and on Christmas morning, in pajamas and with hair awry, he would open them.

"Well . . . are you sure you wouldn't prefer that I come stay with Leo at your house? He would be more comfortable—"

"I absolutely would ordinarily, but there's a bit of bad timing there too. We're in the process of selling the house, and the real estate agent has scheduled an open house here tomorrow. Flyers have already gone out. God willing, there will be lots of people passing through, and the house needs to look just so. After the open house you could definitely bring him back here if you wanted to. I know it's so much to ask . . ."

I'm silent, faltering on the cusp of what I know will be acquiescence. "You'll bring his things today, then?"

"I will, yes," she says. "Thank you. Thank you. I don't know how to thank you enough. My hope is that, one day, Leo will thank you too."

WHEN THE CHILDREN WAKE FROM their naps, the commotion in the house rises to a frenzy. Mr. Castro, who has offered to help with sound and lighting, arrives early, and Tchaikovsky's suite becomes a racket drifting down the staircase as the man acquaints himself with the cues and transitions. Sophie's mother and sister have volunteered to help with costumes, and soon they're in the bathroom with a queue of little girls lined up to have Audrey's garish red lipstick applied to their small pixie mouths.

Katherine, as promised, is early as well. She has a neat navy pantsuit on over a white blouse. Her clavicles stand out starkly above the neckline. For a while, she stands in the hall looking sober but more lost than ever. I suggest that she help Sophie's mother with hair, and she seems grateful for the direction as she takes the package of bobby pins that I hand her and heads off to the bathroom.

The rest of the parents arrive and settle in their folding chairs on one side of the studio, and Mr. Castro lowers the house lights. The blue stage lights come up and twinkle against the huge glitter-encrusted snowflakes of the stage backdrop. I'm in the hallway with the children, who stand in a hushed but giddy line. The first song comes on over the speakers.

I'm holding a finger up to my mouth and whispering, "Mes enfants!

C'est la musique," when Audrey's aunt, Officer Samantha McCormick but in street clothes, comes walking down the hall. Officer McCormick gives me a polite but not overly polite nod—caught off guard, I have no idea what expression I give her and only hope it's not one of abject horror—waves to her niece, who waves back, and then slides past us and into the recital room to join the audience.

"Chut! Chut! Suivez-moi!" I say, remembering myself, and the children and I file into the darkened studio.

There's a frenzy of loud clicks and flashbulb flares from the parents' cameras as we enter. The children crane their necks, flash gap-toothed smiles at their parents, and wave. Katherine, in a front-row seat, waves to Leo, who begins to wave back but is arrested by coughs and instead covers his mouth. Audrey's aunt stands in the back of the room, where she is chatting with Audrey's mom. Her legs are planted strongly, and her arms are crossed at her chest. Even at a child's recital and in street clothes, she looks the part of a police officer. Everything about her declares it. I take my spot sitting on folded knees just in front of the stage area, where I can direct the children.

First is the dance of the flowers: Sophie, Audrey, and Ramona, dressed in tulle and sparkling with sequins, take the stage, where they leap and spin and prance as the audience oohs, and the camera flashes hop like lightning across the room. After the flowers, Annabelle takes the stage for her tap solo. Throughout the dances, the parents laugh and snap their pictures. They wave and blow kisses. Bouquets wrapped in crinkly cellophane lie on the empty seats beside them or on the floor at their feet.

The boys perform the dance of the candy canes to wild applause, then all the children go up for the tea dance, and then I'm holding the mic up for Octavio as he thanks the parents for coming and informs them that tea and cake are waiting downstairs.

There's the scraping of folding chairs against the floor, then the children are running, proud and excited, to their parents. The room is full of the shouts and exclamations of praise given and received. Mothers and fathers hug their little ones and kiss their glitter-strewn cheeks as the children clutch their flowers.

Everyone is happy and exhausted as they file out of the room. Katherine and some other parents are getting a picture of the candy cane boys all lined up in a row. I hang back, helping Mr. Castro get the lights and sound equipment turned off and packed up. I'm not sure how Leo will react to the news that he's staying here for the holidays, and I prefer not to be there when he and Katherine discuss it.

Later, I find them in the dining room. Leo is sitting at the table, eating his slice of Yule log. Katherine is standing behind him eating nothing and wearing a wan smile as she listens in on a conversation between Sophie's mother and Annabelle's. Audrey's aunt is nowhere to be seen. I come up behind Leo's chair and smooth his wild hair. He looks up, mouth stuffed with cake, grins, and goes back to it.

After a moment, Katherine leans toward me and whispers, "I'll be leaving soon. It's over in Dobbs Ferry, about an hour's drive, and I'd like to get there by six. I've got Leo's bag and some Christmas presents in the car. Where would you like me to put them?"

I don't really want anyone else to see Leo's luggage being brought into the house. This isn't a boarding school, and I'm not keen to start putting ideas into the other parents' heads.

"You stay with Leo, and I'll bring in the bags and take them upstairs to his room."

"Oh no, please," Katherine says. "You've got guests. I can do it."

I imagine it's a toss-up as to which of us is more desperate for an excuse to leave this room.

"I know where they go," I say. "It'll just be easier that way."

She fishes her keys out of her purse.

"His overnight bag is in the trunk, and the presents are in the back seat. You're sure you'll be able to get them all? It's really no trouble."

"I'm sure. I'll be right back."

I go outside, relieved by the cold after the crowded warmth of the dining room, and for the briefest moment, with the snow falling against my hot skin, I feel the impulse to run. How I wish to run and run, through the woods, away from all of this. The world has grown smaller, though. There aren't nearly as many places to which a person can run for peace and solitude. I think of the hole. I'd like to run to it, to throw myself in, tuck myself snugly beneath a blanket of grass. Peace and quiet forever. If it is a grave, a place for a new transformation, how will I know when the time comes for me to climb in? I wonder.

I pull my sweater more tightly around me and pop the trunk. There is a large duffel bag inside. To make sure I'm grabbing Leo's luggage and not Katherine's, I unzip it at one end and glimpse a familiar pair of blue-and-yellow-striped pajamas.

Behind me I hear the front door open. I glance over and see, with a sinking of the stomach, Audrey's aunt coming down the front porch steps. I set the duffel down in the trunk and feign searching for something. I have no wish to share with her that one of my students is staying with me. I have no wish to share anything with her. I only hope she's leaving.

She pulls a pack of cigarettes and a lighter from the inner pocket of her coat and lights a cigarette.

"I know, I know," she says to me, though I've barely even looked at her. "But I'm down to a pack a week, so, you know, could be worse."

"Life today involves far too little risk," I say with a smile, trying to be amiable. "We should all smoke and forgo seat belts at a minimum."

She smiles and picks at some bit of tobacco on her tongue.

"I'll never give it up completely," she goes on. "It's too valuable. Keeps me in tune with the addict mind. We've all got a bit of addict in us, don't you think?"

"That's probably true," I say, then rummage, rummage.

"Most crime, in my opinion," Samantha McCormick continues without encouragement, "comes from that same kind of addict mentality. Some want or appetite that feels so urgent that it just drives every other thing—consequences, the feelings of others—out of consideration. Criminals want what they want really bad and right now. Just like me." She takes a drag from her cigarette and then exhales a long cloud of smoke. "I totally get it."

"That's a very interesting . . . perspective," I offer politely. "You seem to think very deeply about your work."

She shrugs and sends another plume of smoke up into the darkening sky, and I go on half-heartedly pretending to find something in the trunk and hoping that the conversation has come to its close. After a moment, though, she goes on.

"Probably not necessary anymore, though. Here in lovely, quiet Millstream Hollow. Not too many criminal minds to stay in tune with, at least not this kind," she says, holding up her cigarette and gazing at it. "Here, people rob cemeteries and cow stalls, and I've yet to form any theory as to why—"

My breath catches in my throat at this, and warmth runs up into my face, but I just swallow slowly.

"So, I guess now it's just plain old smoking."

She glances over and from amid all the parents' expensive SUVs and even the Snyders' green Jaguar, she picks out my car, the old Datsun.

"Oh, baby!" she breathes. "That *car*! It's so great. Do you know who it belongs to?"

"The Datsun? It's mine."

She walks over to the car, takes another drag of her cigarette, and begins walking around the car, examining it.

"I'm sorry, I just love these weird old vintage cars. So much personality. Reminds me of the cars you see in those old British spy movies."

She squats jauntily beside the bumper, rubs a thumb along the dent.

"That's a bummer," she says, looking up at me. "If it weren't for that, I'd say it was mint."

How does this woman manage it? I'm wondering. Manage always to hone in on precisely whatever it is I'd prefer she not see.

"I'm not too concerned about resale value," I say.

"What happened?" she asks.

"Just a little fender bender. A while back. I haven't gotten around to having it fixed."

"Huh. That's funny. I noticed this car back at the open house—it's definitely got a distinct look—but I didn't notice the damage."

To offer a response—a *defense*—is what one would do if they were lying. So, I just say "hmm" and go back to rummaging through the trunk.

"I know a guy who runs a shop in town. He could fix it up for you. If you like I can give him a call. And anyway, you don't want to be driving around with a busted headlight." She raises her eyebrows at me. "Get a ticket."

I don't want her or any guy of hers anywhere near my car.

"Oh, the headlight works. The damage is purely cosmetic, but thanks for the recommendation. I'll let you know. It's not at the top of my list of to-dos at the moment, but if I do decide to fix it, I might ask you for that phone number."

"Yeah, I guess not everyone is as detail-obsessed as I am. Just kills me to see a fantastic car like this with a nasty ding in it."

Officer McCormick drops her cigarette butt on the ground in front of where she still squats by the dented bumper.

"All right, well, I'm taking off," she says, standing and then smashing the cigarette butt with the toe of her shoe. "Thank you again for your hospitality. That was really cute."

She winks up at the second floor of the house where the recital took place.

"Thank you for coming."

She gives the car one last look and then walks off to her own car. I take a few deep breaths and pull the duffel bag from the trunk. Does Officer McCormick share her philosophies of the criminal mind with anyone who happens to be standing by while she has a smoke? I wonder as I open the rear door and pull the gift-wrapped packages from where they are stacked on the seat. Or are her words really as freighted with insinuation as they seem to me? It's so hard to tell. For a moment I was near panicked, imagining that Henry Emerson was hot on my trail, though such an idea seems laughable now. But Samantha McCormick is no kindly neighbor; it's her job to be suspicious, and from where I stand, she seems to do her job well.

Juggling the presents and overnight bag, I nudge the door closed with my hip, then struggle momentarily at the front door before getting it open.

Inside, I hurry up the staircase and to the bedroom—third one on the left, at the far end of the hall from my own. It's the room that I stayed in as a child. The past hangs thick like a residue and I hope that Leo doesn't feel it when he enters. I drop the duffel on the bed and stuff the presents in the closet.

When I come back downstairs, Katherine is standing with Leo in the entryway. Her back is to me. I pause on the bottom step, stuck in an awkward compromise between joining them in their conversation and respecting their privacy. Katherine is kneeling before Leo, speaking to him quietly. I can't hear what she says, but I can see the expression on his face. It's oddly calm, his eyes distant and unfocused as though he has climbed deep down into himself and is listening to her from some-where at the bottom of a ravine. He's thinking intently. It's visible on his face. What is he thinking? What does he make of all this?

He asks a question—"why" or "when," I can't tell for sure—his eyes still unfocused. Hesitantly, she puts her hands on his arms, a strange, robotic gesture of affection, but his body remains stiff. It comes to me clearly that this is an important moment in Leo's life. The time his mom left him with a babysitter for Christmas, but also, maybe, the Christmas his mom went to rehab and everything began to get better. I wonder which way he will remember it in the long run.

Katherine stands, turns around, and sees me hesitating on the bot-tom step. I come over and stand beside Leo, put a hand on his shoulder.

"Be good for Ms. Collette," Katherine says. There is a sheen in her eyes, a slight sparkle of tears. She's avoiding my seeing them by speak-ing to Leo and then checking her purse for her keys, which, of course, I have. I hold them out to her, and she takes them from my hand.

"I put a bottle of cough syrup in Leo's bag," Katherine says, blinking and finally looking at me. "I noticed his cough was sounding bad today."

"Oh, good. Yes, I had noticed that too. Oh! And also—can you give me the number for the . . . well, where I can reach you? Just in case."

Katherine puts a hand to her forehead, aghast.

"That would certainly be helpful, wouldn't it? My goodness, could I possibly be any more scattered?"

I'm holding my breath as she looks down, mentally searching her person—pants pocket, jacket pocket, handbag—for the number. Will she produce it? Does it exist?

At last, she digs a day planner out of her purse.

"If I can just find where I wrote it . . ." she murmurs, flipping pages. "Aha!"

She finds a pen and copies the number onto a blank page, rips it from the planner.

"Thank you again," she says, handing it to me. "Really, I can't thank you enough."

"I have confidence in you, Katherine," I say, hoping that all this is real, and that if words have any power, like magic spells, to conjure a desired reality, these ones may do so. "This feels like a—a real turning point . . . toward a better life. I think you'll discover how strong you really are as you struggle to do . . . what's best."

She looks down at her hands and smiles, neither of us sure what to do with such bumbling and ungainly effusiveness.

"Thank you," she says. "I'd better be on my way."

I nod.

"Be good," she says to Leo again, squeezing his shoulder. "I'll see you soon."

Then she turns and walks out the door.

· XLI ·

MY hopes that Halla would abandon painting were not fulfilled. The next morning, she was there sitting on the same stack of rice bags, wearing the same dingy dress, the same red hijab, and the same wide, sweet smile. This time I bought a bag of dates on our way, and this time she was not content merely to help herself to my paints and brushes: she sat before the canvas and held the brush out to me, pointing at a feature of the vista before us with that open, expectant smile on her face, plainly requesting instruction.

I huffed, and then I instructed her—only what she specifically asked and with no special warmth. She would nod seriously and then do her best to imitate what I had shown her. At the end of the day, she gazed at her painting, tilting her head to the side appraisingly. It wasn't good, but it was better, and she knew it.

I should have been glad when, the next day, my student was not waiting for me in the morning, and I was thus able to paint in silence and solitude, but instead I felt unsettled and vaguely distracted all day. I found myself at various times thinking I'd spotted her in a crowd or coming around a corner, and then, when I was sure it wasn't her, my thoughts would wander to surmises of where she might be and what could have caused her not to show. I felt a nagging schoolmasterly disappointment at the thought that she might, in fact, have simply lost interest in painting, and throughout the afternoon I caught myself muttering, "Just as well," and "Why should she?"

By evening, however, I was searching the faces in each huddle of children in earnest for Halla, having over the course of the day imagined a number of calamitous possible explanations for her absence. I did not see her. Just as well, I said again to myself as I entered the dusky vestibule of the boardinghouse.

The relief I felt the next morning when I walked out into the street and saw my small pupil sitting on her stack, waiting for me, was undeniable—though I surely would have denied it—but it quickly gave way to alarm when I saw that one of her eyes was blacked and the hem of her dress was rusty with spattered bloodstains.

"You're hurt," I said, owning up finally to the advances I'd made in Arabic.

Her answer was more than I could understand, but it had included the verb "to sell," and she held up her box of combs, and I understood. In spending all her time painting, she had neglected to sell her combs. She was no self-employed entrepreneur, of course, I thought, angry at myself for my own stupidity; the person who expected to receive the money at the end of her day of work had received nothing, and Halla had been beaten for it. I lifted the hem of her dress where the bloodstains were concentrated; her feet and ankles were covered in red lash wounds as from some kind of whip. It took me a moment to collect myself. I felt sick with fury at whoever had done this to her and at myself for causing it through my carelessness and naivete.

Halla seemed far less affected than I. She hopped down from the rice bags, took my hand, and pulled, that bright smile on her face as always. She waved for me to come. I did not yield, though.

"I want," I said to her in Arabic, pointing to her combs. "How much do they cost?"

"Two cents," she said, looking hopeful.

"Give me twelve," I said. It was something like three or four fewer than she had with her in the box.

She gave me the combs with a laugh, and I tucked them away in a compartment of my easel, then we headed off together to find some worthy subject, Halla humming and skipping much of the way.

AFTER THAT, WE FELL INTO a routine for a little while. In the mornings I bought some sizable number of her combs, a different number each day so no one would get wise but enough to count as a full day's work, and then we set out. I let her have the easel and I rested my canvases against a wooden board on my knees. We split the brushes and shared the paints. At the end of each day Halla sent her paintings with me, despite my suggestions that she take them home and show her family. When the canvases began to pile up, we laid them out to sell to passersby. Halla's first painting that showed some degree of growing skill sold to a European couple outside King Farouk Palace for five dollars—more money than she had ever had at one time.

I had brokered the sale, and when I gave the money to her, Halla reacted as if I had placed a live toad in her palm instead of bills. Her eyes went wide and an astonished laugh burst from her mouth.

"This is mine?" she asked, disbelieving. "*This* is mine?"

"That's yours," I said each time she repeated the question, which was many.

"They gave *this* money for my painting?"

"They did, indeed. You're a professional artist now."

For a moment she just gazed at it in wonder, but then she became sober.

"Will you please keep it for me?" she asked, holding it out to me. "Keep it safe?"

I was surprised, but then I thought of the bruised eye and the marks on her feet.

"Of course," I said, taking the money back from her. "Just let me know when you would like it."

THE FOLLOWING WEEK, SHE SHOWED up with another black eye, but when I asked what had happened, she only shrugged and changed the subject. She sold another painting the following week for three dollars, and I added the new profits to the old.

"With the money I am getting," she said one day when we were sitting on the Stanley Bridge, painting the sea, "I am going to go to the place you come from."

"Where is the place I come from?"

"Over the sea," she said, pointing ahead. "Where everyone is rich. I don't know what it is called, but I'm going to go there. Are you going to go back there someday? If you go, maybe you can take me with you."

"I came from a country called France. You're right, it is over the sea, but not everyone is rich. There are plenty of poor people there too, but they can't afford to leave so you don't see them."

"I don't care. I will go there anyway. I would rather be there than here."

"Why is that?" I asked her.

"Many reasons. They paint. I only ever see your kind paint."

"Well, you paint already. Why do you have to go over the sea to do what you're already doing? Why can't you be a painter here?"

She shook her head. "Here, people like me don't paint. People like me only sell combs or work in shops or beg or do worse things. I want to leave here. It's not good here for me."

I knew that there were certainly Egyptian painters and artists of all kinds, writers and poets, but I knew nothing about the class rules she seemed to be speaking of. Could she become a painter here in Alexandria? I didn't know.

"How much money must I have to go there?" she asked, interrupting my thoughts.

"I don't know. It's complicated."

"Why?"

"Well, for one, you're very young."

"No," she said, turning to me and wagging her head with conviction. "I'm not young. I'm thirteen."

I laughed. "Well, in Europe that's considered very young."

"I won't go to Europe; I'll go to France, where you are from."

"I'm sorry, I didn't explain. France is in Europe. It's a part of it, and in

Europe there are perhaps more rules than here, at least when it comes to children. For instance, you aren't supposed to work until you're sixteen years old. You're too young to go alone or to live alone. You would have to be adopted."

"What does that mean? Adopted?"

"A family would have to let you live with them, like a daughter."

"What about you? Could you adopt me?"

I nearly choked.

"What about your family?" I asked, dodging the question. "Wouldn't your family miss you? Wouldn't you miss them?"

"I don't have a family. Senet, my friend, would miss me, and I would miss her, but that is all."

I realized by my own lack of surprise when she said this that some part of me had suspected this was the case all along. I was silent, feeling sorry for Halla and guilty for my unwillingness to help her in the ways that she wanted. I couldn't possibly adopt her. I couldn't possibly take care of a child. There were a thousand reasons why it was completely, disastrously implausible. I was dangerous, not to be trusted or relied on. And I didn't want to besides. I didn't want anyone depending on me or even knowing me in any substantial way. This thing with Halla, which I refused to call a friendship, was already more than I wanted.

"It could be just like this, couldn't it?" Halla said simply, squinting ahead into the sunset with her brush poised before her canvas, calculating her next stroke.

I felt breathless and agitated, looking dismally into that same brightly dying light. All thought of my own painting vanished from my head.

"I could go with you and live with you and we could sell paintings?" she continued. "I am good. I would not be trouble for you."

She was right. With incredible ease and with no understanding of European culture or law, she had found a reasonable solution to every complication except the most important one: that I could not possibly say yes.

"I suppose in theory that could be possible," I said hesitantly, then added, "but who knows if I'll ever leave? I'm quite happy here."

It was an excuse, a way to put her off. I knew I would eventually leave, and I certainly wasn't happy in Alexandria. Happiness was not something I was capable of. If I had been willing to take her, to adopt her as she suggested, she wouldn't need money either. My paintings sold well and living in Egypt cost almost nothing. We could leave the next day, but the plain truth of it was that I wasn't willing. It felt ugly to frame the situation in such callous, self-centered terms, to just say I was happy and that was that. Halla's reasons for what she wanted seemed far more legitimate than mine, but I couldn't tell her the truth, that the care of her was far more than I could psychologically handle, that I was entirely unfit for such responsibility, that she shouldn't depend on me.

She seemed not the least bit disturbed.

"That's okay," she said with her large, sweeping smile pointed at the sea before her and her canvas. "I would like best to go with you, but if I can't go with you, I will find another way to go."

· XLII ·

THE other parents and children linger a while more. Feeling indulgent, I give Leo another slice of cake. Soon he and the other children are running through the rooms and halls, chasing each other, wild with sugar and excitement. When Sophie corners Leo in the hall to tag him, Leo holds his arms up in front of himself and giggles helplessly with his head tipped back.

He is so different now from the silent, sedate little boy I met on the day of our first interview. He's still pale and unwell-looking, with those dark wells beneath his eyes, but he's happy, animated, and he's an artist. It's true what they say about kids, they are resilient, and yet, they are also terribly fragile—not breakable but impressionable. Like soapstone, nearly impossible to shatter but *so* easily carved.

I sit at the table with the remaining parents and mutilate a slice of cake with my fork as they talk of their upcoming flights or car trips to Philadelphia, Buffalo, Binghamton. They ask me what my plans are for the holidays, and when I say that I will just be here enjoying peace and quiet, they pretend to envy me. How nice that sounds, they say. Why do the holidays have to be so hectic? But there's concern in their eyes. It's just like Thanksgiving: the same questions, the same answers, the same sympathetic eyes, but this time I'm not pitying myself. For better or worse, I won't be alone, and though this frightens me, it fills me also with an anticipation that almost feels silly.

Eventually the parents stand, the children are called from their game. Marnie comes into the dining room to fetch the Yule log remains. I hug each of the children and wish them a happy holiday, and then the clattering and laughing and clomping of the children putting on boots, coats, and mittens in the mudroom dies down. The parents call farewells across the drive to one another. Car doors slam with snow-muted thuds, and the children wave from the windows of SUVs and sedans as they drive away.

It's suddenly quiet, just Leo and myself.

I look down at Leo, who's waving happily out the window. There's a rivulet of snot running down from his nose. At the same moment, my stomach turns noisily, my mouth flushes with saliva, and, as if a fog suddenly lifts from my brain, I realize with dismay what I should have known all along—this was a *terrible* idea.

Now that the choice is made, now that he's here in my home and will be for the next several days, maybe more, it's clear. I'm *hungry* with a terrible, frightening, uncontrollable hunger; even now, strong hands are kneading my inner organs painfully. I *never* should have agreed to Leo staying with me. It was a mistake, a terrible, terrible mistake.

I look at Leo and feel a surge of panic to get away from him, to get him away from me. I take him to the art room and set him up with his pencils, then I run down the hall to the kitchen. Marnie is still there, bending down in front of the oven, pulling steaming pies out to set on the wire racks at the island in the center of the kitchen. When she turns and finds me standing there, she's startled and nearly dumps the pies on the floor.

"Good Lord, you gave me a fright!" she breathes, setting the pies down on the island. She puts her now free hands to her heart, trying to regain her composure.

"I'm sorry, Marnie. I didn't mean to scare you."

"My lands, you dancers sure do move quietly. We bakers aren't nearly as good at sneaking up on people," she says, giving her hips a pat.

She runs me through the provisions she's leaving, for which I'm suddenly grateful as I would otherwise have nothing to feed Leo: a roast turkey, sectioned in the fridge, but she'll leave "a nice plate out" before she leaves, biscuits, glazed yams, and here on the island an apple pie and a cottage pie with beef and potatoes.

I listen and nod appropriately, all the while trying to summon the courage to ask her to stay, trying to piece together a compelling reason why she should forsake her own family and remain in this dreary house for Christmas. *To protect Leo from me, to guard his room at night, to keep me out! But you'll need something to protect yourself with too. Surely there's something around here we can fashion into a stake.*

A tempting proposal, no doubt. Aside from the unspeakable truth, there is nothing.

"You all right?"

I look up from my thoughts to find her gazing at me, her head cocked in concern. I'm not all right. I'm the furthest thing from all right. I'm lonely and exhausted and horribly afraid. I want to collapse sobbing in her warm, floury arms. I've fended for myself, strong and alone, for so long. I'm tired of it. And one thing I know is that the only thing against which I cannot defend myself is myself. I need someone stronger than myself to protect me from myself, to listen as I spill out everything, to fix it all, to rescue the little boy quietly drawing upstairs.

"I'm fine," I manage to whisper. "Thank you, for everything. It all looks delicious."

"Is there anything else you'll need before I go?" She's still looking at me strangely.

"No. No, thank you, Marnie. You've done so much. I hope—I hope you have a wonderful holiday with your family."

I turn away quickly, afraid of what would happen if I looked her in the face. I walk out of the kitchen and slowly down the hall, trying to think of someone I might turn to or call. Agoston, whom I would desperately like to talk to, is somewhere in California. Grandfather, thousands of miles away in Bordeaux, also comes to mind, though with less eagerness on my part, but, as Agoston said himself, he thinks of children only as little soldiers in need of hardship and suffering in order to grow strong. Besides, I've heard the general theme of my grandfather's advice plenty of times before in his letters. "Why you choose to live hidden among vremenie, instead of boldly among your own kind, why you lock yourself in a cage of vremenie morality and weakness, and then chafe at the tight quarters, is beyond me."

His remedy to all ailments is the same: throw off the shackles of compunction, live boldly and fearlessly, take what you desire. That others—innocents—sometimes pay the price for one's ill-considered boldness, one's desires, seems, still, to be largely lost on him. No, there's no one.

I hear Leo coughing again from all the way down the hall. It sounds deep and croupy and convulsive, worse than before, worse than it's been in a long time. I reach the doorway of the classroom and stand there for a moment. Leo is hunched at his desk, humming contentedly. I watch him and try to calm the rising panic in me. This is Leo, I think. I could never harm him. But a vision of the attic flashes in my mind, the blood smears on the floor, the torn limbs and heads. Then there's Dora's stiff, motionless bulk in the barn in the morning. I don't always have to mean to do harm to do it.

Another coughing fit seizes Leo, and his shoulders hunch with the force. It passes; he goes on with his drawing and his humming as a stream of snot creeps perilously close to the edge of his upper lip. He wipes it with the back of his hand.

"Oh no, mon chou, don't use your hand!" I grab a tissue from a box nearby. "Here's a tissue."

Keeping Leo at arm's length isn't an option. I'll just have to be vigilant, self-controlled, strong. I can do this. I'm not an animal, not just a walking appetite; I'm a moral being, capable of reason and restraint.

"Leo," I say, dropping to one knee beside his chair.

He has arranged the small wooden figure on the desk in a position—leaned forward, arms extended out to the sides—that reminds me of one of the steps in Annabelle's tap-dance performance. He looks up from his drawing.

"Katherine told you that you are going to stay with me, yes?"

When did I start calling her Katherine? I wonder.

"Your mom," I amend, rolling my eyes at my own misstep.

Leo nods.

"How do you feel about that? Is it okay with you? I would understand if you were disappointed. You could tell me."

"Well," he says, his eyes lowered and despondent, "I am a little sad."

"You miss your mom?"

"Yeah. But there's another problem."

"What is it?"

"*Santa.*"

I'm caught off guard, but immediately relieved. "*Ah?* What is the problem with Santa?"

"Santa will take all the presents to *my* house, but I won't *be* there."

"That's no problem at all!" I say, waving a dismissive hand at him. "I can go call Santa on the phone right now."

"You can? At the North Pole?"

"Of course! I'll just tell him that you're here and that your presents should be delivered to this address. Would that put your mind at ease?"

He nods and wipes with the back of his hands at the tears that had begun sparkling in his eyes. I get up and walk out of the room. I hear him scamper from his seat and then he stands at the doorway, as I walk to the phone and make a show of picking it up and dialing.

"Yes, hello . . . *Gumdrop*. Merry Christmas!" I silently mouth the word *elf* to Leo. "Gumdrop, I know this is not the most opportune time, but is Santa available for just a moment? I have something very urgent to discuss with him."

Leo's mouth is wide with amazement.

"Thank you. I do appreciate it." I drum my fingers against my arm as I wait for Santa to come on the line, check my fingernails.

"Ah, yes, Santa! Oui, bon soir! Joyeux Noel! Oui, merci. Well, Santa, I just wanted to let you know that I have Monsieur Leo Hardman—ah, yes, certainly." I put a hand over the phone and whisper to Leo, "He's checking the book."

Leo puts his fingers to his mouth and bites his nails in anxious anticipation. The ascending tones of the dead phone are ringing in my ear and the recorded operator is telling me again and again that she is sorry, but my call cannot be completed as dialed.

"Yes, of course he's on the nice list!" I say when Santa at last comes back on the line. "I could have told you that. Anyway, Santa, I just wanted to let you know that he will be staying with me this Christmas Eve, so if you would be so kind as to deliver his— Yes, yes, precisely. *Exactly*."

As I talk, Leo is creeping slowly down the hall, his eyes wide and impressed.

"Same address, yes, County Road M, Millstream Hollow, New York, yes, you've got it! Thank you *so much* for your time, Santa. I realize how busy you are. Yes, he is such a sweet little boy. I agree."

Leo is dancing and spinning with joy in the hall.

"Okay, thank you. Au revoir!"

I hang up the phone.

"Satisfied?"

"*Yay! Yay! Yay!*" Leo cries, pumping his arms in the air.

I take Leo upstairs to show him his room. He takes my hand as we climb the staircase, and then he wants to open every door along the hallway and poke his head in to investigate. He has a watchful air. His movements are slow and careful, and he asks me questions about each room.

"Who sleeps in here?"

"No one."

"How come it has a bed? Did someone used to sleep in here?"

"Yes, someone used to sleep in here, but not for a long, long time."

He gazes around the room silently then, as though doing calculations in his mind, evaluating the energy of the room, deciding whether it is a good, innocent room or a malevolent one. He looks up at me, the childish wariness still on his face.

"Was it a nice person that slept in here?"

"Oh yes, it was. It was a sweet, adventurous, good little boy just like you. The two of you would have had so much fun playing together."

Not true. This was Agoston's room, but how could I possibly explain Agoston to a child?

Leo and I reach his room. It's one of the house's several turret rooms, large and octagonal, with five shuttered windows on one side. Opposite the windows, two twin beds dressed with ancient ivory linens and hand-sewn quilts stand beside each other on one side. A large round rag rug covers the middle of the floor and there is a wooden rocking chair on it. Some unfathomably old toys are arrayed on the shelves of a bookcase.

Leo runs to the rocking chair and climbs on. I take a wooden yo-yo from a shelf and demonstrate for Leo, who grabs it and promptly has it in knots. Abandoning the yo-yo, Leo takes up a wooden case bound with leather straps and two buckles. He undoes the buckles and blocks tumble out, each one with a portion of a larger scene intricately painted on it.

"What is it?" Leo asks.

"It's a puzzle. Actually, it's six different puzzles, one for each side of the blocks."

"I never saw a puzzle like this before."

"This is how they were before the machinery was invented to cut cardboard into all those teeny, tiny pieces."

I put a couple of the blocks together to show Leo.

We work silently, fitting the picture together. In it, a pretty blond girl sits before a gleaming banquet table in a golden palace hall.

"What's that picture of?" Leo asks, tilting his head.

"It looks to me like the story of Marienka. She was a very spoiled girl who wanted only one thing, to live in a golden palace. Eventually she got her wish, when the dark king of the mines married her and took her to his palace, but in the palace, everything was made of gold—even the food, and poor Marienka had to live in a palace full of food that she could not eat and splendor she could not enjoy. She got her wish and quickly realized that it was a foolish wish."

"Wow. That's a sad story."

Leo begins turning the blocks over to make a different picture.

"You know, I stayed in this room when I was a little girl," I tell him.

He gives me a look of surprise.

"Will it be all right for you?"

"Sure," he says, and goes on flipping and rearranging the blocks. As he crouches on all fours over the puzzle, he begins to cough. He sits back on his haunches for a moment. His mouth forms an O, and his tongue sticks out through it as the sharp barks erupt from him. His eyes bulge and water.

"You all right? Should I get your inhaler?"

He lifts one hand to wipe spit from the side of his mouth. He shakes his head, too focused on the puzzle to think about anything else.

I, on the other hand, feel sick with anxiety. The house is so silent, the hours ahead so dangerously vacant. I think with sudden longing of the Hardmans' jumping frantic television, the commercials full of white smiles, the inane sitcoms with their hysterical laugh tracks, and music videos full of cars driving into the sunset. What I wouldn't give for a television, an idiot noisemaker to do battle with the silence and the heavy downward pull of reality, the black hole that is hidden somewhere in this house and drawing everything inexorably into itself.

Suddenly, *I* feel scared of the house with its insinuating silence, its rows of rooms like watchful eyes. I have to get out. I have to get Leo out. I have to clear my head. I have to *eat*. Something occurs to me, an idea both crazy and brilliant. There is absolutely no way I could risk sneaking into the Emersons' barn again to feed. It would be suicidal. But it has just struck me that walking right into the barn with their permission is perfectly feasible, especially with Leo accompanying me.

"Leo, what do you say we go visit the Emersons' farm and sketch the cows in the barn?"

"Yeah!"

I jump up, relieved by Leo's enthusiasm. Mr. Emerson himself invited me to stop by just the other day. He said it had been too long, and I couldn't agree more.

WHEN WE ARRIVE, MR. EMERSON is splitting wood in front of the house, and making an impressive show of it for a man in his late seventies. The can of WD-40 that I may have left behind comes suddenly to mind, and I have an instant of panic thinking about the possibility that the can was tested for prints: the Emersons know that it was mine and that, somehow, utterly illogical as it seems, I am connected with the death of their cow. But then Henry turns his broad, full-cheeked smile toward our car, and all my fears are gone. He deftly lodges his axe in the stump and walks toward us, pulling his gloves from his hands as he does.

"Evening!" he calls.

"Good evening, Henry," I answer, stepping out of the car.

"What a nice surprise," he says, taking my hand in both of his and shaking it. "What can I do for you, ma'am?"

His brown eyes are watery in the cold wind.

"Well, Henry, we"—I gesture to Leo, who is still sitting in the passenger seat of the car—"we were wondering if we might do some drawing in the barn."

Henry leans forward to look through the driver's-side window of the car. He smiles at Leo and waves, and then crosses his eyes and sticks out his tongue. Leo's giggle, inside the vehicle, is muted by the glass.

"Well, nothing in the whole world would please me more!"

"Speaking of which, has anything new come to light regarding your . . . your recent incident?"

"Nope. Nope," he says, putting his hands on his hips and gazing out over the snowy hills that recede into the west, belted sporadically with fences. "It is just the darndest thing. But we haven't had any trouble since then, so we're just figuring it was . . . I don't know, just some freak incident, I guess."

"Well, I'm glad to hear you haven't had any more problems," I say. The irony of my words is not lost on me. I am almost literally champing at the bit to get into that barn. I feel faint from hunger, weak and frail, like a thin, leafless branch trembling in a cold wind. My teeth are chattering faintly.

Leo cracks the driver's-side door. He has gotten out of his seat and crawled across mine and now is climbing down out of the car.

"Well, hello there, young sir. Good day to you." Henry extends a large, liver-spotted hand out to Leo, and they shake. Leo looks to me and smiles bashfully.

"And what might your name be?" Henry asks him. "Or should I just call you young sir?"

"Leo."

"Leo*nardo* da *Vinci*! Well, I'll be! I guess I shouldn't be surprised that Mr. Leonardo da Vinci wishes to engage in some artistic ventures in our barn."

Leo looks to me again, his tongue crawling out at the side of his mouth in awkwardness.

"*What?*" he says to Henry, who chuckles.

"You'd like to draw in the barn, is that correct?"

"Yeah! Are there cows here?"

"There most certainly are, and if you will follow me right this way, I will introduce you to them."

Henry winks at me, and then he and Leo start toward the barn while I fetch our supplies from the trunk. It's a bit warmer today. The snow has melted down to patches here and there.

"I hope you brought your *colored* pencils," I hear Henry say, "because these cows have been known on occasion to spontaneously change colors. Have you ever seen the movie *The Wizard of Oz*?"

When I reach the barn, Henry is standing in front of the first stall with Leo, holding the standing cow at the neck and letting Leo run his hand over her hide. The other cows poke their heads out curiously from their stalls on each side of the center aisle. There is one face fewer on the left side than on the right.

"Now, you *never* want to go behind a cow," Henry explains to Leo, "and a horse is even worse because take a look at these beauties." The old man leans down and lifts the cow's front leg, showing Leo the hoof. "This sweet little lady—Mabel is her name—now she's a sweet ole gal, but she'll knock your block right into the next county if you get within kicking range. I got another sweet ole gal just like her in the house," Henry says, referring to Mrs. Emerson and winking at me. Then to Leo, he goes on. "So you have to be really careful. Can you do that for me, young sir?"

Leo nods, and Henry pats him on the shoulder before heading for the barn door.

"And can you do one more thing for me, please?" he asks, turning back to us. "When you finish here, can you come up to the house for some hot chocolate? I know May would be delighted to make this gentleman's acquaintance."

At the mention of hot chocolate, Leo's eyes light up. He grins and nods vigorously.

"Thank you, Henry," I say. "That would be lovely."

"Enjoy yourselves!" he calls, sliding the door closed as he leaves.

I push a couple of hay bales over in front of the first stall for Leo and myself to sit on, and we set up our easels before them.

"Okay, Leo," I explain before we begin, "this will be an exercise in speed. We must try to catch the general form and motion of the cow. She isn't going to hold still for us. She'll be constantly shifting and moving. The shadows and light will change as she moves too. The more you try to control the image and get each part perfect, the more imperfect the whole will become. So instead, we will make as many brief sketches as we can."

Leo goes to work, his little brow tensed in concentration. I sit next to him for a couple of minutes and watch. Many of my students are self-conscious about being observed while they paint, but Leo seems not to even notice my presence beside him. The world beyond the page or canvas falls away for him just as it does for me.

He's not heeding my advice. He's working and reworking the muzzle of the cow even as the cow's muzzle is working and reworking a mouthful of straw. The cow's jaws move in a lazy circle, and its lips grope, fingerlike, at the bits of escaping straw. Leo sets down lines and then scrubs at them with the gum eraser. I can measure his growing frustration by the increasing force he applies to the eraser.

There is a subtle, stubborn streak in Leo that I have only ever detected in his art. I take it for a good sign. There is so little in Leo's life that is within his control, and that stubbornness, I suspect, means that in his art, if in nothing else, he feels powerful.

Leo turns to me, his eyes doleful.

"Mon chou," I urge gently, "remember, quick, loose lines. Don't overthink it. Feel it. Trust your body, your hands and arms and eyes. And here, use this."

I take a slightly dull 4B pencil—a softer, darker graphite—from the pencil case and hold it out to him. You cannot avoid bold, dark lines with a 4B. Hesitantly, he hands me his beloved HB, which he has sharpened as usual to a fine, delicate point.

"Fast and loose," I say again. I lift my own pencil to my paper and draw the lead across it in loops and quick curves. My hands are so jittery that I doubt I could manage much beyond a loose sketch. Leo watches intently, his mouth ajar due to his congestion. I can hear the phlegm rattling in his chest with each breath.

In thirty seconds, a cow emerges from the sparse, sweeping lines on my page. Leo looks up at me, a small smile lifting the side of his mouth.

"A cow," I say. "You see?"

Leo doesn't answer, but turns purposefully to his own paper.

"One minute," I say. "It's a race against time. Give me the barest suggestion of a cow in *one* minute. *Vite! Vite!*"

He draws and his motions are delightfully quick and loose. He laughs as he swirls his pencil recklessly across the page, and it occurs to me how very strange Leo is. The things that delight other children, trucks and dolls and TV shows, Leo has little interest in. He takes pleasure in art, almost as I do. He loves it and is frustrated by it, doggedly pursues the beckoning nymph of it *already*. If he continued like this, he could be making indistinguishable copies of Velázquez at eight, just as Picasso did. At twenty, he could *be* the next Picasso. What might he be at *my age*—at two hundred? Three hundred? There is likely no adequate comparison to draw upon.

"Très bien! Ten seconds!" I say, playfully counting the ticks on my wristwatch.

"Five, four, three . . ."

Leo races to scribble dark splotches on the side of the cow where the spots are.

"Two, one! Time!"

Leo holds up his drawing triumphantly, and I applaud. He turns his head and coughs over his shoulder as I study the picture.

"This is exactly what I am talking about. So wonderful and loose. I adore it."

He turns back to me and smiles, his eyes dewy from his coughing.

"It's kind of fun, isn't it?"

"Yeah," he says, his voice froggy.

"Want to do another one?"

"Yeah."

"Okay. I'll give you three minutes this time, so you can work with value—the light and dark—as well, but keep it just as fast and loose."

Leo sets the drawing pad on his lap again, his pencil poised above it, waiting for the signal.

"Go!"

As he draws, I wander down the center aisle, peering into each pen, trying to decide how best to feed without Leo observing. The hunger is so acute, it feels like it will split me in two. My brain feels like a brick inside my head, heavy and with sharp, grainy corners scraping against the bone of my skull.

"Two minutes," I call back to Leo. He is so fixated on his drawing and the cow in front of him that I think I could feed right next to him without his noticing. I duck swiftly under the wood slat and into the last stall, where the smallest of all the cows, the one I have called Cora, is standing.

Unlike on the nights when I visited the barn to slip among the drowsy or sleeping cows, the cows today are alert, standing and nosing at the scrubby hay in their troughs. I lead the cow gently by her collar back into the farthest corner, cooing softly and trying not to look past her at the empty stall across the aisle where another cow used to be. I position her between myself and the entrance to the stall, so that if Leo should happen this way, her body will be between us. She lows softly. Her broad pink tongue flicks out against my wrist. I stand up and look over the tops of the stalls at Leo. He is hunched over his drawing pad, lost in concentration.

I kneel beside the cow, put one arm over the bony ridge of her back like a friendly embrace, and then run the tips of my fingers quickly over her neck, looking for the pulse point. I find the spot, set my mouth against it, and the instant before I puncture the skin, I use the hand that is draped over the animal's back to pinch her hide, drawing her attention away from the sensation of breaking skin. The hide is thick and insensitive, though, and my hand is at an awkward angle that makes it hard to pinch with much strength. It doesn't work. The cow feels the puncture and jerks forward, mooing loudly in alarm. I have to scramble along in my awkward squat to stay with her and avoid her heavy hooves coming down on me.

I drink frantically, trying to get as much as I can as quickly as I can. She tosses her head and swings her neck, trying to shake me off, lowing in protest all the while. As though sensing her agitation, the cow in the next stall begins to low too, then a third and a fourth. The cows go back and forth, a murmuring call-and-response of alarm.

"I'm done!" Leo's voice comes to me from closer than it should. I fall away from Cora, wiping my sleeve quickly across my mouth.

"I'm done," he calls again, even closer this time.

When I stand, Leo is there in front of the stall, holding up his sketch-pad. The cows are still lowing back and forth. They pace their stalls in agitation.

"What are you doing?" he asks.

"I dropped something," I say, wiping my mouth with my sleeve again. "Something fell. I was afraid she might get it—eat it."

I climb out of the stall and brush the dirt and hay from my knees. "Cows will eat anything. They're—they're like goats. Did you finish? Let me see."

"Mr. Henry said we're not supposed to go in there."

"Sound advice that you would do well to heed. Show me your picture! I can't stand the suspense!"

"Why are they mooing like that?"

"I don't know. They must be gossiping, or . . . discussing the quality of the hay perhaps."

There is a sudden loud shearing sound. The barn door slides open, and wan, snowy light cascades in. Henry is standing in the doorway, looking quizzically at his complaining cows.

"What's all the fuss?" he chides Mabel, then strides down the aisle toward us, shushing and checking over and under each cow as he does, running his palm across the wet leather of their muzzles.

"They giving you lip?" he asks when he reaches us.

"Honestly, I'm not sure what happened. It was very strange. One of the cows here"—I have discreetly inched us a stall down from Cora's—"I'm not sure which one, began mooing, and then the others joined in. Could we be bothering them by being here?"

"Well, that doesn't seem likely . . . One of these ones, you say?"

"Yes."

Henry ducks into the stall next to Cora's and examines the cow inside, running his hand along her spine, tossing her ears back and peering inside them.

"Or maybe this one, did ya say?" he asks, pointing to another cow that is not Cora.

"Could be. I really can't say for sure."

Then he climbs into that stall and gives the cow the same examination. Finally, he steps out again and shrugs.

"Could have been a bug bite maybe, though I don't know what would be out and biting in the dead of winter. Could be they're just a bit jumpy these days." He stands beside us pensively for a moment with his hands on his hips, looking at his cows, who have finally quieted down, then he turns to Leo.

"So how's the drawing coming along, Da Vinci?"

Leo smiles sheepishly and holds his sketchpad up in front of his face so that he can simultaneously display it and hide behind it.

"Sakes alive! That cow looks like it's about to walk off the page!" Henry turns to me with a look of genuine amazement and says under his breath, "My word, I was expecting stick figures."

The drawing is a far cry from stick figures. I can't help but be proud.

Leo is now peeking out over the top of the sketchpad, watching Henry's reaction with pleasure.

"You are quite the talented fellow. Do you give lessons? I can only draw Pac-Man."

Leo begins to speak, but his voice comes out a croak and then becomes coughing. The sketchpad trembles in his hand and then presses against his knees as he is doubled over by the fit.

"Goodness," Henry says, "that doesn't sound good."

I realize that he's right. I was appalled early on by the Hardmans' seeming indifference to Leo's health, but I realize that I have also grown used to his constant sickness, his coughing, and my own position of helplessness beside it.

I kneel beside Leo and take his small, heaving frame in my arms.

"Are you okay?" I ask. "Do you need your inhaler?"

He shakes his head between coughs. His face is flushed red from the strain, and when he stops coughing at last, snot is again creeping down from his nose.

"Well, I'm going to give you some cough medicine at least," I say, pulling a tissue from my pocket and handing it to him. He blows his nose and sinks down on a bale of hay. His eyes are droopy, the bags beneath them deep and sallow. From my bag, I dig out the bottle of cough syrup, pour the bright purple liquid into the tiny plastic cup, and bring it back to Leo. He makes a face and puts up a hand to resist the medicine.

"I don't like that stuff," he says. "It's yucky."

"No, it isn't, it's . . ." I search the label for a flavor and find a cartoony cluster of grapes. "Yes, you're probably right. It probably is yucky, but it will help your cough and make you feel better, and you simply must take it."

He grimaces, covers his mouth with both hands, and shakes his head.

"Leo," Henry speaks up from beside me, "I'm right there with you. I hate taking my medicine. You know what helps me get that awful, nasty stuff down?"

Leo's hands are still covering his mouth and he doesn't answer, but his eyebrows lift in curiosity.

"Hot chocolate. What say you drink that little cup of yucky stuff, and then we dash into the house and get you a big mug of hot chocolate—with marshmallows and whipped cream? You think that would clear the yuck out of your mouth?"

Leo looks glumly at the cup, but then he takes it from me and, with one final grimace of despair, drinks the syrup down.

· · ·

THE EMERSONS' HOUSE IS WARM and full of a subdued golden light from the many small Tiffany-style lamps that are tucked here and there around the kitchen and adjoining dining room. May Emerson is a vigorous older woman who refinishes old furniture and sells it at roadside antique shops. As a result, she's always busy sanding or painting something and is often to be found wearing a tool belt.

When we enter, she's standing at the kitchen table, an upholstered footstool in front of her and a staple gun in her hand. Straight pins are clenched in her teeth. She smiles and greets us, the words garbled incomprehensibly behind the pins. She squeezes the trigger of the staple gun, and there's a quick clap of sound not unlike an actual gunshot. Leo jumps slightly beside me. May moves the staple gun, presses it again, and another clap resounds through the room. Then she lays the gun down, takes the pins from her mouth and sticks them in a pincushion, and comes around the table to us, smiling broadly.

"Would you look at this little gentleman!" she exclaims. "And what might your name be?"

"May, you won't believe it, but this here is Leonardo *dee* Vinci, and I got the drawings to prove it. Now, I promised this little Renaissance man some hot chocolate," Henry says, clapping Leo firmly on the shoulders, "with *all* the fixings."

"Then I guess you better deliver, hadn't ya?" May says, giving us a wink.

The two of them exchange something like a two-second staring contest, and then Henry chuckles and says, "I guess I better," and makes his way to the small alcove of the kitchen. When he's past May, he winks back at us. "She doesn't let me get away with a thing."

"Doesn't stop you from trying," May sings back sweetly without breaking the smile she is directing at us.

The old pair are like gleeful performers in a well-rehearsed vaudeville show. I've never seen two people take more pleasure in teasing each other.

"Let me get all this junk off the table, so the two of you can have a seat," May says as she ushers us over to the table. She scoops up a varied armful and dumps most of it on a shelf of a large buffet set up against the wall. Sitting on top of the buffet is a small can of WD-40, which momentarily stops my heart until I force my gaze away from it.

Henry, in the kitchen, is fumbling in the cupboards, opening and closing cabinet doors.

"May," he calls, "where might the marshmallows be located?" He lifts the lid and peeks inside of each of a half dozen ceramic canisters on the counter. "And also those little Swiss Miss packets?"

"*My goodness!*" May exclaims, turning and hustling into the kitchen. "It's remarkable how such a big, strong, capable man can be rendered so utterly helpless by a little old kitchen. Scat!"

She waves her hands, shooing Henry away, and he joins us at the table, where he gives Leo a mischievous look.

"Works every time," he whispers.

"I heard that," May calls.

THE EMERSONS INSIST THAT WE stay for dinner. I demur briefly and perfunctorily before accepting the invitation. Really, I'm unspeakably glad to stay. Surely, I was hoping for this all along. I don't even want to think about returning to my own house, pulling up the dark gravel drive, the many windows of the house staring down at us like the glittering eyes of a spider, still and fat and waiting in its web to scuttle forward at the subtlest twitch of a strand. I don't ever want to go home.

Dinner is a pepperoni pizza taken from the freezer, mixed vegetables strained from a can, and three black olives apiece. Leo is alarmed at the dark olive juice that threatens to soggy the crust of his pizza, until Henry distracts him by waving an olive-crowned pinkie finger his way.

"You're a bad influence, Henry," May chides her husband playfully. "One evening with you and this very well-behaved boy will be an out and-out hellion."

Henry only wags his olive pinkie in her direction.

After dinner, there is a homemade apple cake with streusel topping, and then Mr. Emerson brings out an old wooden marble run he built for his own children years ago. He shows Leo how to race the marbles down the tracks. Both he and May seem delighted to have us, and so we linger longer than we should.

The cozy wood paneling of the house, the carved and painted ducks and needlepoint decorating the walls, the living room in which a small television set with rabbit ears is playing *Wheel of Fortune* to an audience of two old armchairs, all of it combines to make the safest and most peaceful atmosphere I've been in in ages. In this warm old farmhouse, things like me are nonsense. Anything frightening or destructive exists only in the innocuous form of a ten-minute spot on the evening news, captured and caged in the small, staticky screen of that beat-up TV.

I look over at Leo. He's clapping and laughing excitedly as the marbles take their furious turns down the track. When they fly out the chute at the bottom, he snatches them up and puts them back up at the top, hopping up and down and crying, "Faster! Faster! Faster!!" Mr. Emerson, who's managed to get his big farmer frame down on the floor beside him, helps him catch the renegade marbles and chuckles at Leo's elation. Mrs. Emerson sips from the decaf she has made us and smiles over at the two of them. She sighs contentedly now and then.

I don't mean to, but I find myself for that hour or so adrift in a haze of longing, so thick I can't find my way out of it. I am longing for a child, yes, a child just like Leo. When he turns to me and laughs, when he stands next to me, drinking water from a glass and dripping on my pants, when he hops and turns an anxious look my way and we rush off to the bathroom, it is so close. I could almost imagine that I had one, that Leo was my son.

Katherine, Leo's actual mother, flits through my mind. She has surely reached the rehab center by now. I imagine her sitting quietly on a strange bed in a strange room. Strangers mill the halls and sit to her right and left at breakfast. I wonder if she is experiencing discomfort yet? It's probably too soon. When the pain does begin, will she think of Leo—*her* son? Will she use the thought of him to steady her? I hope so. I hope, whatever her character flaws or failings, that nevertheless she loves him and wants to care for him well. More than anything, I want Leo well cared for.

"He's such a sweet, happy boy," Mrs. Emerson sighs.

"Yes. He is."

"Looks just like you. Somehow, I never realized one of them was yours."

I glance at her and then quickly back at Leo and Mr. Emerson.

"Those blue eyes and dark hair. Spitting image."

A moment passes in silence and I'm trying to get myself to speak. It's the first time I have had it brought to my attention how alike Leo and I look. I'm surprised I never noticed before. I should set May straight. No, no, he's not mine, I should say, but somehow, I just can't get the words out of my mouth. Then the moment is too far past and it would be stranger still to correct her so late.

May asks, in the guileless way that only the elderly can, "Where's his daddy?"

I swallow uncomfortably and look down at my hands, which are cupped around my coffee mug.

"I—I don't know."

True. Not untrue.

"I don't mean to pry, honey. I have such sympathy for all those single mothers out there. It's a hard life. Well, he's a fine boy."

It's much too late to correct her. I'll just pretend I misheard her, clarify if it comes up again. I smile uncomfortably and look down into my lap.

We go on watching them, and sipping from our mugs in silence, until finally, Mrs. Emerson yawns discreetly, and I come to my senses.

All but jumping to my feet, I apologize for lingering so late. They insist that they were happy for our company and to please come by anytime. I thank them again and we leave, and that warm, simple feeling, the safe, wholesome patina of the house extends outward from it, across the yard and the Emersons' orchards and fields upon which a light snow is beginning to fall. I climb in behind the wheel of the car and navigate it over the cumbersome snowdrifts, Leo belted in the seat beside me, and the feeling of warmth and safety lingers until we reach the end of the drive and the dark road unfurls before us into the night, and then that feeling is gone as though it had never been.

· XLIII ·

THE next day, feeling anxious and surly, I suggested that it might be time for Halla to take her money.

"You have quite a bit of it now," I said. "Nearly fifteen dollars. You could do a great deal with fifteen dollars."

"Is it enough to go to France?"

"Not quite."

"How much do I need for that?"

"Well, you would need probably twenty just for the boat, but then you would need more money for afterward. You wouldn't want to arrive with empty pockets. You'll need to eat."

"So how much then?"

"The more the better. I wouldn't attempt it with less than eighty dollars. But isn't there something you could use the money for now? Isn't there anything you need more urgently?"

"There's nothing I need more than to leave. If I make my paintings better, do you think I would get more money?"

"Well, that is, theoretically, how it is supposed to work, but more often a thing is only worth what a buyer is willing to pay or a seller is willing to take, and that seems to be especially true with art."

"Then I will just have to be patient. I am very patient. Like I think, maybe, you will decide you don't like it here anymore and you are ready to go back where you came from and take me with you, but this might take a very long time, so I am patient."

Her words, which truly did sound patient and sweetly innocent, rubbed me, and for the rest of the afternoon I was quiet and irritable, trying to focus on painting and block the girl beside me from my mind.

She sold another painting that day, and this time I did my best to haggle for the highest price I could get. I pointed to Halla where she sat before the easel that I had bought her, as much for her benefit as to be able to use my own again, and explained to the interested gentleman that she had aspirations of going abroad to art school someday, the Académie des Beaux-Arts, perhaps. He handed over ten dollars for a genuinely lovely portrait of the Roman amphitheater.

"Now how much do I have?" Halla asked when I reported it to her.

"You've made nearly forty dollars."

"How much more do I need for eighty? For getting to France and for food and things when I get there?"

"You need another forty, but you also need a plan. Like I told you, they might not even let you go alone."

"Are you still happy here?" she asked.

"Yes, I'm still happy here," I snapped more shortly than I meant to.

For a moment she was silent, thinking hard. "Is it a long trip? The boat ride to France? Maybe I could save up even more money and you could go with me *just* on the ship and then leave me there and come back."

"Halla, I couldn't possibly just leave you there. It's dangerous. Who knows what might happen to you? Children can't just be left alone to run wild."

For a moment she just looked at me and neither of us spoke, but it seemed that we both understood the unspoken. I remembered Halla's feet hatched with bloody abrasions and the black eyes she'd had on more than one occasion. She was already left to run wild here, and worse. If someone attacked her here, there was no one apart from me to protect her. She could fail to show up tomorrow, never be seen again, and I would never know what had become of her. I didn't even know where she lived or what she did during the hours we were apart. Of course, she had no fear of danger; it was dangerous for her here. Young as she was, she seemed, again and again, to be the more reasonable of the two of us, the one more acquainted with stark reality and more guided by pragmatism rather than inscrutable emotion. But even if she was right, reasonable and right about everything, and even if she deserved every bit of what she wanted, I simply couldn't give it to her. I just couldn't. I *just* couldn't.

THAT EVENING, WHEN WE RETURNED to the Arab Quarter, Halla ran off as usual down an alley that teed off the larger street where my boardinghouse stood, but instead of turning into my building, as I usually did, I let her get some distance ahead and then I followed her. Halla was determined; she would reach her goal of eighty dollars, and likely soon. I needed to know, finally, all the things I'd been avoiding learning about her: where she went when she left me, how she lived, and with whom. I wanted to know how bad it was, or perhaps that it was, in fact, not bad at all. She was a child; maybe she'd been lying all this time. Maybe she wasn't really an orphan. Maybe she lived with her own loving family but wanted to run away for some small, silly reason, the way children often do.

She took a left, running with her box of combs clasped in her arms, past colorful stalls of spices and vegetables. She bounced up short flights of stairs that passed beneath elegant archways. At one such stair, she opened her box and took a coin from inside to give to a beggar sitting at the side of the stair, and then continued on. She turned again, down a narrower alley, dirtier and more crowded with people milling about and squatting around cooking fires or seated along the sides of the path, begging. Plumes of smoke and tiny bits of ash from the cooking fires made everything hazy in the wan light.

Another left, and she vanished briefly from my sight. I came around a corner and glimpsed her hijab among the milling peasants and stalls of the vendors, but then lost her behind a pushcart overloaded with heaped bags of *aish baladi*. The cart stopped and she reappeared, making her way down the narrow lane to where it ended at an intersection with a larger, more heavily trafficked road.

On the far side of that upcoming road was a squalid, decomposing sandstone dwelling in front of which dozens of children, skinny little girls all of them and none wearing the hijab, loitered—begging or playing in the dirt or just sitting vacant-eyed, watching the bikes and mule carts rumble past them.

With a sinking sense of dread, I felt it confirmed that Halla did indeed live in an orphanage with these malnourished and dirty little girls.

A girl about Halla's age with a large and very dark floral-shaped birthmark across her face leaned against the wall of the dwelling. When she saw Halla coming, her face lit up and she waved. Halla waved back, and the girl beckoned her to come. This, I thought, must be the friend Halla had mentioned. The only person who would miss her or who would be missed by her. I felt a small surge of bittersweet happiness at seeing someone smile brightly at Halla, so plainly pleased to see her.

Halla started to run to her friend. Still some distance behind, I followed and watched, expecting her to slow, any second, as she approached the busy road. At any moment, she would slow and then stop, look before crossing the steady traffic—I kept expecting it, right until the moment when I knew with a sudden sick lurch of panic that she would not. For some reason, like an illogical nightmare, she kept running, her eyes on the friend ahead. She kept running straight out into the road.

I saw the girl on the other side turn her head. I saw her mouth open, her eyes widen, and at the same moment that I knew with absolute certainty what the alarmed expression on her face meant, I felt a scream rip from my own throat, loud and long, as though trying to fill all the air in all the world with her name.

"*Hallaaaaaaaaaaaaaaaaa!!!!!!!!!!!*"

A hideous beast on wheels flashed across the road—a bike, bulging and heavy, laden with goods for delivery—and then was gone, and Halla vanished with it. I ran forward screaming, sick in every part of myself, desperate to discover some optical illusion, some magic trick that had caused her to vanish, or to wake up from the nightmare I was in. But when I got there, she was lying in the road. She had not vanished; she had fallen, been hurled by force. I was not the first to reach her. The children from the orphanage as well as several men who had been nearby had formed a tight, fretting huddle around her.

"*Halla! Halla!*" I cried in delirium, pawing at the men's shoulders, trying to see past them—*get* past them—to Halla, who lay crumpled and bloody in the road. With incredible speed, the huddle of men lifted Halla's small frame and began carrying her gingerly into the dwelling on the other side of the road, which they all seemed to know was where she belonged.

I followed them—a strange, foreign woman, weeping uncontrollably and being paid no attention—as they carried her through the open door and into a parlor lit softly by beaded boudoir lamps that cast flickering light from the corners. The men set Halla down on a fraying green velvet couch, and one of them tilted her head gently to one side, to examine the wide, bloody crack in her skull that poured blood like a faucet onto the upholstery and floor. The other girls were gathered, wide-eyed, around her, and her friend, the one who had called to her, sat beside her on the floor, clutching her hand and wailing.

I stood frozen by the door, crying into my clenched fists, wanting to run forward, but paralyzed in despair and confusion, hoping that any moment a doctor would appear and make her well, though I knew by looking at her, by the profusion of blood, the sag of her eyes, the stillness of her chest, which was taking its last, limp breaths, that no doctor would save her even if one were to come.

Some of the men looked Halla over, lifting her eyelids to study her pupils or the crack in her skull, but there was a strange remoteness to their care. They seemed uncomfortable, all of them, in this space. A large, veiled woman appeared from some dark, rear part of the building, and at her appearance all the men left but one. The man who remained spoke to her in a way that suggested she was Halla's caregiver, but when a moment later a blond soldier came stumbling out of the darkness, peering about with perplexity and working to get an arm into his jacket, this last remaining man turned and, with a look of disgust, left as well.

The large woman went to where Halla lay and looked down at her, but it was with as much sympathy as one might show for a broken umbrella. She seemed equally distressed by the blood on her couch.

The soldier was joined by another, who was, with effort, struggling in the dim light to buckle the clasp of his belt. I stared at the men in dumb, blank incomprehension, as though two zoo animals had just appeared in the room, and seeing me and my stare of disbelief, they looked abashed; one pulled money from a pocket and set it on a side table, and then they both slipped out the door past me.

I looked around the room but could not comprehend it; the horror of it was too great, the deranged despair I would feel upon comprehending it too wide and deep to fit in my psyche. The young girls who stood in frightened clusters around the room and gathered around the couch, none of them wearing the hijab, some only in short tunics with their skinny bare legs exposed: they were not orphans, or they were not only orphans. This was not an orphanage. I could not speak the word for what this place was or what it had made of them. What it had made Halla.

Some women from the street pushed past me as they entered the room, more willing than their husbands, it would seem, to enter a house of ill repute in order to tend to an injured child. If I had been in a functioning state, I would have run to Halla, knelt beside her, and begged her to live, but I could do nothing. My body was shaking so hard that a step forward would mean collapse. All I could do was stand there sickly, deaf, blind, splintering beneath the truths that were forcing themselves into me. She didn't have to be on that road. We could have left long ago. I could have taken her away at any time. Day after day, I had listened to her talk about her desperation to leave. Day after day, I told her no. Day after day, I had left her to this life and consigned her to this death.

A thought occurred to me briefly: What if I walked across that room and picked her up? What if I carried her away and out to the lonely desert where I could bury her and wait for her? I could adopt her still, the way I should have in the first place. We could still go to France. She could live, but only forever. All or nothing. Too much or not enough, those were our only choices.

"Forgive me," I heard myself moaning. "Forgive me, Halla. Forgive me. Oh, dear God, forgive me."

The misery and shame of that room unhinged me. I felt myself tee-tering on the brink of implosion, a wild, raving lunacy. I did not say goodbye. I did not give her even a last look. With what small trembling strength I could muster, I turned and stumbled out the door. I fell in the street and vomited there. Somehow, stumblingly, I made it back to my room.

As soon as I could, I left Alexandria.

I carried Halla's memory, like ashes, in the ossuary of my own shame. I sought silence and stillness in their purest, most punishing distillations—a place where I might bury us both—and when I found that place in the empty expanses of Lozère, I remained there, in a netherworld of my own making, for a very long time.

· XLIV ·

I'M driving through snow, or is it ash?

Soft, gray flakes fall against the windshield of the car as Leo and I make our way back to my house. The wipers stir them back and forth across the glass, and they dance, but they don't melt.

As soon as we turn down the long, dark drive toward the house, the hole in the woods announces itself. I could point to it, I'm sure, with logic-defying accuracy. It's an absence, an emptiness, a lack, and yet its presence is almost more powerful than my own. It calls to me. It weeps. Is it time, Vano? I ask silently. Time for courage, as you said? Time to face the god of endings, *the Emptier*, as Agoston called him, with courage?

Of course it would be now. Of course, when I have Leo here with me, that would be the moment that the turning teeth of the lock align, the door opens, and freedom finally invites me. But a season must be more than a day, mustn't it? My season, my destiny, my ending will have to wait until Leo is back with his mother. *Please*, I beg my hole in the woods, my door, wait for me. *Please*, I dare even to ask the god of endings. I'm not resisting anymore; I'm not running, only wait for me.

The house is everything I had feared, shadowed and cold, treacherously silent. As we pull up to it, my busted headlight flickers and goes out, and the darkness encroaches that much farther.

Leo is curled up in the passenger seat, sleeping uncomfortably with his head against the door. I would prefer that he stay awake until he's safe in his bed with the bedroom door locked and me far away in my own room. I am dangerous. My feed in the barn was hurried but adequate. I do not feel hungry now, and yet I'm not sure how much it matters anymore. This hunger is not reasonable. Some meter, gauge, or gasket within me is surely broken. Fill the tank with gas, but still the signal light blinks empty.

There are few things harder to impede than a child determined to sleep, though. Leo does not wake when I try to rouse him, so I carry him from the car, into the house, and up the stairs to his room. His coughs echo intermittently through the silence. I lay him on the bed and pull pajamas over his heavy, pliant limbs. His whole body is warm, and his forehead simmers with a low but distinct fever. I try to rouse him enough to give him another dose of medicine, but he will not wake enough to take it. Sleep, I've always believed, is the best medicine anyway, so I tuck the covers up around him and then flee to my room down the hall.

My hands rattle the glass shade of a hurricane lamp as I fumble with the knob in my bedroom. I don't know what to do. I'm afraid to go to sleep. I'm afraid of what could happen. I could *kill* him. Like Dora, I might drain him to the dregs and then lie down and go right on sleeping, not realizing what I had done until morning. But a week without sleep isn't possible.

What if I were to dig? Every night that I've gone out and worked at the hole, I've slept afterward without disruption. If I were to go out and spend just a little time digging, as my body so desperately wants to, could I trust that the result would be the same? That I would not get up and wander in the night? It's the only thing I can think of that might help.

I get up and dress hastily. Outside Leo's door, I pause to listen and make sure he's snug and asleep and will not need me while I'm gone. Poor boy, mother in rehab, brother dead, father who knows where, and caretaker absconding quietly to go dig her own grave in the moonlight. Poor boy, what is this world you've been set down into? Why is it we never get a choice about how, where, when, or with whom we enter the world?

I grab the flashlight from the counter in the kitchen and then the shovel from just outside the door where it leans against the wall. Above me, as I cross the grass and move into the thickness of the trees, that moon, that downturned face with its softly pitying expression, as if it were a spectator, a theatergoer watching the small comedies and trage-dies unfold again and again on the tiny world below. Do you know the ending, Moon? Have you seen this one before? Is that why you watch with that look of resignation, your face white as if from the light of a cinema screen?

I can feel the pull so clearly now. There's nothing subtle in the way my hole draws me. I find myself skipping along, running like a leaf blown in the wind, and I tell myself it's because I must be quick—can't leave Leo alone for too long—but it isn't that. I can't wait is all. I urgently need to see it, be reunited with it, climb down and press my fingers deep into the soft, cold parting grains, feel it against my cheek. What is happening to me? I wonder, and not for the first time, but my misgivings can only be brief because my body has taken over and is moving fast and with certainty, my mind only clinging like a helpless passenger.

Exhaling billows of white drift up into the cold, I come running up to the edge of my hole. I throw the shovel aside to begin pulling up the branches that cover the hole, and then my eye is caught by something I hadn't noticed before. Just outside the hole, at the top of it and where I could not have seen it so long as the snow lay thick on the ground, a small, squared-off slab of gray is reflecting ghostly moonlight.

My heart rises to my throat; it's my father's gravestone. It was here all the time. It was here even as Officer McCormick and I stood five feet from it, talking about the cemetery break-in. Did she know what had been stolen? Did she know about the stone? I fall to the ground beside it, take it up in my hands, and cradle it, laughing and crying like a mad-woman.

The *feel* of it, after all these years—soapstone has such an unusual texture to it, smooth and waxy like no other stone. I run my fingers over the letters my father carved with his expert but dying hand, then the ragged letters I carved with mine, and I can do nothing but weep, like that little girl alone in the woods again.

Eventually, I place the stone back where it was, at the top of the grave, and get to work digging, peering up at it every now and again, fearing that a gift so unexpectedly given might be just as quickly and inexplicably withdrawn. After who knows how long, after a couple of feet, when I have dug my hole so deep that it's taller than I am and will take some work to climb out of, I lift a shovelful of soil, toss it up over my shoulder, and know suddenly that it's finished. I could not thrust a single additional stroke of the shovel if I wanted to.

I pitch the shovel out onto the ground beside the hole and stand there for a moment inside it, letting my body feel it, awaiting my body's instruction. I cannot die tonight—Leo still sleeps back at the house— but I'm feeling for a clue of what will come next, what I will do when the time comes. My body is strangely silent, though. I sit down in the hole, feeling the cold of the ground through the fabric of my pants. Then I lie down, stretching my body to its full length, trying to coax a reaction from myself.

I lie in the hole, looking up at the moon, breathing the cold air into my lungs, and imagining the weight of dirt pressing down on me, my flesh dissolving. I listen again for any intuition, but there is only silence. The instinct is gone. I realize it suddenly. I feel nothing. Like a child trying to suck her thumb years after she's been threatened and bribed into giving up the ecstatic drug: the magic, the feeling is gone.

I stand up. With effort I climb out of my hole. I suppose it's good that my body didn't direct me after all. This is not the time to die, and if the impulse had beckoned, would I have been able to resist as I should, as I *must*? The time will come. Patience now. As Agoston said when we sat together in my dining room, what's needed is to wait, like a child learning patience.

I pick up the shovel and make my way back to the house. As an extra precaution, I go into the entryway, where the Christmas tree stands in the crook of the staircase. By the glow of the lights twining the boughs of the tree, I pull a handful of bells from where they are hung on the branches in decoration. I'll hang them around my bedroom doorknob just in case. If I do happen to get up in my sleep, maybe their jingle will wake me.

Passing Leo's door upstairs, I hear him cough, a sharp, grating sound, as if his lungs were rusty metal. I pause in the hall and listen, but everything returns to silence, and I finally continue on to my room. There I loop the bells around the doorknob, then open and shut the door to try them out. They jingle festively, despite their morbid purpose.

I climb into bed and lie there for some minutes, staring at the door, at the little bells, wondering whether now I dare go to sleep. The knob and the bells expand until they take up my entire field of vision. The silence is so silent it begins to have a sound, a pulsing, like the steady hiss of a candle flame. I feel my head fall forward and jerk back.

Once.

Twice.

Then there is a gentle knock at the door. The bells shiver. The doorknob turns back and forth inexpertly until the latch pops and the door floats open. The hall yawns darkly behind it. A small, dark-haired head finally peeks around the corner, almond eyes squinting and bleary in the light. The emaciated frame of a young girl steps forward into the room.

"*Halla?*" I whisper in disbelief.

My eyes blur with tears, and a growing ache fills me until it feels uncontainable, as if it might tear me open.

The girl closes the door behind her and then runs lightly across the room and climbs up onto the bed, and I take her joyfully into my arms. There's a crack on the side of her skull where her hairline meets her temple. The hair around it is matted and wet with blood. I hold her close, weeping without restraint.

"Why did you leave me there?" she asks in that guileless voice of hers, not accusing or demanding, only asking.

"I'm sorry," I say when I've stopped weeping enough to speak. "I left because . . ." I search my memory and the deepest parts of myself for what I have always known is true. "Because I was a coward and because I was ashamed. I was too selfish and scared to care for you, and because of that . . ." Weeping overtakes me again, and I struggle to speak. "You . . ."

Halla's warm hand comes to rest on mine.

"But why did you leave me *after*? Why did you leave me dead?"

I study her for a moment, confused. "What do you mean, *after*?"

"I wanted to go. I wanted to live. You knew that. Even after what happened, you could have taken me with you. Why didn't you do it?"

"You mean . . ." I struggle to speak the words. "You mean . . . *change* you? Make you . . . *like me*?"

"Yes," she says, her face as certain and stern as when she would speak of going to France.

"No. I couldn't possibly. How could I do that to you?"

"Easily. So easily. You would have only had to choose it. No one cared about me. No one would have stopped you. I wanted to go with you, across the sea. I wanted *more* life—to see and experience all of it, every bit, but instead I got so little. You could have given me life forever with you, but instead, you left me there, left me, dead forever. *Why?*"

"To—to *trap* you in this life forever with no hope of escape? Halla, you can't understand what such a choice would have meant? How frightening forever is."

"Perhaps it's *you* who doesn't understand the choice; it's very simple really. Nothing forever, or *everything* forever. You left me there to die. You chose, for me, nothing forever, but *I* would have chosen *everything*, all the good and the bad, all of it. Everything, however difficult or complicated or painful, is better than nothing. Though you're right, it is more frightening."

For a moment I just look at her, baffled and somehow bested, once more, by this girl and her uncanny certainty.

"I don't know, Halla. I don't know what to say. I hear you, and I'm sorry. Can you forgive me?"

Halla's stern face shifts, like a flower opening, into her beautiful smile. She embraces me, and the relief of holding her is like ice on a burn. I put a hand to her coffee-colored forehead, and when I take it away, it's red and wet with blood.

"You're here now anyway," I whisper softly to her. "I'll make it up to you. We can paint every day the way we used to."

"No," Halla says, drawing away. "Take me to your door."

"What?"

"It's time. The door is open. Take me."

"I don't understand."

"Yes, you do. Your season has come, the gift you were promised. It's time for you to go, but this time you won't go alone. You'll take me with you. You won't make the same mistake again."

"But, Halla, my door is a grave—my grave. Perhaps I'll see you on the other side."

"You can't know where your door leads. All you can do is keep your promise and take me with you."

I don't know what to say. I don't understand anything except that I've missed her. I didn't let myself feel it. Even as I punished myself ruthlessly for her death, I somehow never grieved her; I tried to forget her instead. Now it overwhelms me, the pain of her death, the pain of the briefness of her beautiful life.

"Promise. You won't leave me behind again," she whispers, looking up into my downturned face.

"I promise," I whisper, though I have no idea what this promise means.

She climbs up to her feet.

"Come on, then!" she says, beckoning me toward the door. "Hurry."

With a flail of spindly limbs, Halla jumps down from the bed and runs to the door, takes hold of the knob, and starts turning. The bells *jingle, jingle* with her efforts to turn the handle.

"I can't get it," she says, grimacing. "Help me, please."

Jingle, jingle, go the bells as she goes on struggling.

Jingle, jingle, jingle.

"I'm not sure," I say. "There's something . . . I don't think I'm supposed to . . ."

"*Please*," she insists, "I can't open it."

"All right," I say, still hesitant, though I can't say why "Hold on. I'm coming."

I get up from the bed and walk across the room, take the doorknob in my hand.

Jingle, jingle, jingle, jingle.

It's the feel of the cold metal of the doorknob in my hand, and then the bolt of dread it sends through me, which throws my eyes open wide. I'm up out of my bed. I'm standing before the bedroom door, which, in my sleep, I've opened. The hall before me recedes into blackness. My hand is still on the knob, and the bells are still tinkling lightly, but there's another sound also that's coming from the hall: coughing.

For a moment, I'm too at a loss to make sense of it, still trying to sort dream and reality. I'm searching for Halla, who was here a moment ago but is suddenly gone. I lean forward to peer out into the hall and find, instead, Leo, in pajamas and bare feet, standing in the dark, eyes closed and coughing.

Me here, him there—how close have we just come to disaster? The thought makes me feel sick.

"Leo." My voice is groggy, confused. "What is it? What are you doing out of bed? Are you feeling worse?"

"Max. I can't find Max."

Tears are glistening on his cheeks, and from the sound of his voice and his tightly clenched eyes, I think he is also not entirely awake.

I finally come to my senses enough to go to him and put my hand to his forehead: it burns like a live coal. I drop onto one knee before him, gently pulling him into my arms and checking and rechecking the frightening heat of his forehead.

"Max must be in your bag. Don't cry, we'll find him."

"No!" he wails, eyes still closed. "I can't find him!"

I pick Leo up and carry him back to his room. It's not easy, though. He's sick and delirious with fever also, it seems. He squirms in my arms, kicking his legs restlessly and calling out for Max the whole way down the hall.

When we get to his room, I try to lay him down on the bed, but he won't lie down. He sits on the bed disconsolately, mouth open, hands limp in his lap.

"Where's Max?"

His eyes are closed, and his voice is strangely even, as if he has not asked me this half a dozen times already. I'm in the closet on hands and knees, groping along the dark floor for his overnight bag.

"Mom?" Leo turns his blank, sleeping face in my direction. "Mom?" he says again.

For a moment, I don't know how to respond.

"Leo, it's me, Ms. Collette. Your teacher. You're staying with me, remember?"

"Mom?" he calls again. "*Mom?*"

I finally relent. "What is it, Leo?"

"Where's Max?"

"I'm looking for him, my sweet. I'm looking."

I find the bag, unzip it, and begin rummaging furiously through the contents.

"But I can't find him, Mom. Can you help me find him?"

There is something suddenly chilling in the phrase. I pause and think about the story Dave told me. Leo and Max playing hide-and-seek on a summer day. How long must he have searched before he looked in the pool? Did he stand beside the bed where his mother slept, calling to her, asking her for help? I push the thought from my mind and go on searching.

My fingers run over coarse jeans, the soft fabric of a flannel shirt, little bundled pairs of socks. I reach the bottom of the bag, but I go on searching, begging any animating spirit that might exist in the cosmos to let me suddenly feel beneath my fingers the nubby fur of a giraffe, because it's a *giraffe* we're searching for. It is Max, Leo's stuffed giraffe, not Max, Leo's dead brother. It can't be possible that a little boy's dreams could torture him as mercilessly as that, that they might force him to relive something so ugly as an old game of hide-and-seek.

"Mom?"

I can't find Max. He's not here. I dump the whole bag on the floor and start going through the items again, one by one. Leo's voice behind me is hollow and flat.

"Where's Max, Mom? Can you help me find him?"

"I'm trying, Leo. *I'm trying.*"

"I *can't find* him," he says, his voice sliding down finally into tearful despair.

I grab a handful of clothing and throw it in frustration. A shoe hits the wood paneling at the back of the closet with a dull thud.

Max isn't here. Brother or giraffe, he's not here. There's nothing I can do to make this better. There's nothing I've ever been able to do to make anything better. With the sudden, breathtaking force of an avalanche, my disgust overwhelms me: the countless small accumulated angers and griefs at the brutality of the world, and my impotence before it, are shaken suddenly free, gather in one massive drift, and sweep down over me, swift and crushing. I despise it all. Every rock, every tree, every rising and setting of the sun, I would tear it all down if I could. Better nothing at all than all this pain and helplessness.

I press my face into the heaps of clothing, tears of rage dampening the cloth. Then, out of the silence, there's a sound as high and sudden and frightening as a smoke alarm, but it isn't that, it's Leo. He's scream-ing and sobbing between screams.

"I—CAN'T—FIND—MAAAAX!! I—CAN'T—FIND—MAAAAA AAX!!"

The screams crumble into coughs, deep and racking and painful-sounding, and all at once it occurs to me how like all the other adults in Leo's life I'm being: crying in the closet, consumed with my own selfish cares, while Leo deals with his pain and his sickness alone.

I pull myself up off the floor and go to him. He's wriggled off the bed and sits slumped beside it, eyes still closed, alternately coughing and crying now into the side of the mattress. I sit down beside him, pull him into my lap and arms. He struggles, but I hold him anyway. I can't stop my tears and I don't bother trying anymore.

Leo coughs again so hard that he gags. His eyes roll up in his head, and his body curls forward, rigid around his straining lungs.

"Leo, breathe! *Breathe, Leo!*"

Strands of saliva run down from his mouth and into his hands, which are cupped at his mouth and wringing with panic.

"*Breathe, Leo!*"

I grope along the surface of the dresser for his inhaler, find it, press it to his mouth, and pump twice slowly. I can see his chest fill visibly with air like a balloon being inflated. For a moment, his arms and legs sag against me in exhaustion, but then he begins crying again softly.

"Leo," I say, "do you want to go to your house and get your giraffe? Get Max?"

I don't know if he can hear me. I don't know if it will help, but I'm desperate. I can't give him his brother, but if a fifteen-minute drive to his house to find a stuffed animal will calm him, I'll gladly do it. His eyelashes flicker, and then he nods.

"Yes? You want to go get your giraffe from your house?"

He nods, eyes still closed.

"Yes," he says in a soft whisper.

THE CAR FOLLOWS THE WHITE path of its single headlight through the blackness of the back roads. The gold disks of animal eyes shine between the trees. Leo's breathing, from beside me where he is wrapped in a quilt, is so wet and rattling that I can hear each exhalation. Sometimes he coughs and those coughs go on alarmingly until his little body can't handle them anymore and he somehow stops from sheer exhaustion. I reach over to feel his forehead again, even though I know that it is blisteringly hot despite the medicine I managed to get into him.

Vlad is not there to greet us with his barked threats when we reach Leo's neighborhood. Instead, he watches us silently from a lost-dog flyer that's taped to a streetlamp and flapping in the breeze as we drive past.

When we pull up to the house, Katherine's car is in the driveway. The sight of it—a beige Saab with seams gleaming like running water in the moonlight—hits me like a punch in the gut. Why is Katherine's car in the driveway? Why is it not an hour's-drive away at rehab in Dobbs Ferry? She's here, and my astonishment at the fact is an indication only of how great a fool I am. I've been lied to again.

Someone got as far as the Hardmans' front stoop with a snow shovel but did not manage to actually shovel the snow. It's thick and dirty across the drive, pocked with footprints going up the front walk. There's no open house sign, no for sale sign. Of course there isn't.

Leo lies in the passenger seat, unmoving. His breath is wheezing but regular. I think he's asleep, but just in case, I whisper, "I'll be right back with Max."

I leave him in the warm, running car, in the driveway beside Katherine's, and approach the house warily. I take my copy of the Hardmans' key from my pocket but find that I don't need it. The front door is unlocked. When I slip inside, the interior is as disheveled as the exterior. Cast-off shoes form a hapless pyramid in the corner of the entryway. There's a heap of clothing on the bottom step of the stairway, a book on the second. A throw pillow lies on the living room floor beside the couch, and curled rose petals litter a tabletop where drooping flowers stand in a vase, stems swimming in murky water. The supposed real estate agent will have some cleaning up to do before the supposed open house tomorrow.

My eye is drawn to a small folded square of white paper that lies on the slender table just inside the door. There's a mirror hanging on the wall above the table, and the white square is doubled in its reflection as if for emphasis. Somehow, I have a sense of what it is even before I pick it up.

On the outside of the paper, in a faint, delicate pencil script, is a name. I fear that it's Leo's name—what poisonous words would she print indelibly in his mind?—but it isn't. It says *Dave*. I glance at the words inside, but a fragment of a sentence is all I can stomach—*When you find this, you'll be rid of me, at last*.

It's a suicide note. Katherine's final words to the living are addressed not to her son but to her husband of only a couple of years.

Katherine has done it again. Lies and lies and lies. There was no program, no wait list, no plan to get clean, nowhere to be by six. Likely there was no remorse for attacking me. No real desire for my friendship. The apology was a magnificent calculation as well. She needed a babysitter to keep Leo away from this, her grandest feat of theatrics. She needed to flip a person she had alienated as quickly as possible back to her side so she could get from them—from *me*—what she needed, and she used compassion and care for her son, a thing she seems totally devoid of herself, to get it.

I set the paper back where it was and move toward the stairs. I catch the scent of smoke; it seems to hang thickly, like a fog, along the ceiling. Czernobog has beaten me here. Naturally, he would. The moon shines down through the skylight, through the smoke. It washes the room with pale light and makes the carpeted white steps of the floating stair look like snow-covered stones ascending in a dark stream. I feel alert, almost jittery—pupils dilated, ears pricked up for the slightest sound—and at the same time unbearably tired. This thing that I have somehow become a part of, and that Leo has always been a part of, it's sick. It's noxious. I'm fed up. I'm enraged. Damn you, Katherine, I think as I climb the moonlit stairs. Damn you.

I move down the dark hall, a shade among shadows. I search the air for the stench of death—it's remarkable how quickly decay begins its greedy work—but it isn't there; instead, the strong smoke smell mingles with the burn of alcohol and the sour foulness of vomit.

I reach Katherine's bedroom door, which opens to silver-lit darkness. The white popcorn ceiling with its odd geometric angles and steep slant bright with moonlight gives the room a tomb-like feel; it's the inner depth of a pyramid, a mausoleum, some performative death theater. The bed is empty, covers rumpled. A liquor bottle with a blooming rose on the label stands on a low bedside table, tall and kingly amid short pill bottles and a phone off its cradle, the dial tone stuttering softly.

The faint light that I saw from the street is coming from around the corner to the left. Cautiously, I peer around the corner. There's a built-in vanity with a round, spidery web of cracks in one corner. Then, farther to the left, there is a bathroom with the door open. A light in the shower shines hazily behind the dimpled glass of the door, and there is Katherine, sprawled out on the thick shag of a bathroom rug in front of the toilet.

She lies on her side in a silvery nightgown that's fallen down so that one small, shapeless breast is exposed. Her arm is thrown out long on the rug, and her head rests in the crook of the elbow. The tendons along her bicep stand out, ropey and thin and blue-veined. There's an orange prescription bottle and a small dribble of vomit like a chain of islands clumped on the rug beside her. I don't know where she is in the process.

She isn't dead, but she's close. Far out past the point of no return. I can smell her foul blood, thick with bourbon and a strange bouquet of unnatural chemicals, crawling through her slowly.

I stand just outside the bathroom, outside the dim ring of light, and study her. This scene that she has created right here is, like everything else, a manipulation, designed, it would appear, for Dave. Leo and I are only bit players in this production.

"I feel so ashamed of all my failures as a mother," Katherine had said to me, and I felt sympathy. I understood the feeling of carrying the crushing and constant weight of all my failures. But she was lying about that too. It was just the most convincing thing to say, for who could possibly say such a thing and have it be a lie? *What kind of monster?*

My eyes drift to the vanity, and my face is caught in the broken glass, refracted to me in skewed thousandths, many-eyed, terrible. What kind of monster? I think as I look at myself. Katherine, me, we're both monsters, truth be told. There's a difference, though. What is it? I look back at Katherine, study her.

"You don't even care," I hear myself whisper aloud. "You don't care about the harm you do, to Leo, to anyone. You don't care at all. That's the difference."

A small gurgle from deep inside Katherine's throat makes me catch my breath and study her watchfully for a moment, but she's still motionless and silent.

"Don't worry about Leo," I say softly to Katherine, heedless of whether she can hear me or not. "He's going to be okay. I'm going to make sure of it."

I look down at Katherine for the last time—that body fragile as matchsticks, the mind inside a match head already burnt, blackening, about to go out—then I turn and leave.

In Leo's room, I find the small stuffed giraffe, Max, on the floor beside the bed. I carry him down the hall, feeling the soft synthetic fur, the thick plush: all the pain and grief and tragedy accreted on this thing of string and cloth and stuffing, but how much Leo loves it, needs it, is soothed by it. That, I suppose, is how the brave do it, they just put it all together, the good and the bad, and they hold it tight to themselves, and walk on with it. It seems that I have been an extraordinary coward after all. All this time, I thought I was so wise, cursed with clarity about the true nature of things, while others walked around foolishly happy and half-sighted. But it was me. I was the fool. The scared, stubborn fool, who preferred nothing forever to everything. It's a terrifying choice, but the Halla from my dreams was right when she called it a simple one. Nothing or everything? Well, which is it, Anna, Anya, Collette? What's your choice?

It's a hard choice still. I'm still so afraid.

I go down the stairs and out the door to drive Leo away from this place forever, to usher in something new and terrifying.

Czernobog, the god of endings, the Emptier, is coming. I can hear the billowing of his flames, and the sweat from his heat drips down the end of my nose. He's coming just as he always has, earnest-faced, arrayed in cinders and smoke and finality, yet this time I won't run or resist. Perhaps with him, as Agoston believed, the god of beginnings comes also, joined twins unsplit. For once, I'll wait for them like a child learning patience, like a child learning trust. I'll apologize for my foolishness in misunderstanding and dreading the Dark One for so long. It turns out that I *did* make a deal with him: the taking of anything sets into motion its eventual loss; nothing that *is* can resist becoming what *was*; to begin presumes the acceptance of an end. The god of beginnings-as-much-as-endings keeps those contracts without malice. He lends out generously and collects exactingly, and I've finally agreed to his terms: all that I had—the school, this house, this life—and all that I was—clenched and frightened, distrustful and ungrateful—will end tonight, and in the space that's cleared, I'll take hold of something new, though its eventual and likely painful end is assured. Something, even if it must eventually end, is better than nothing. This time, I'll hold what I'm given tenderly but loosely; I'll accept that it's mine only for a season.

But first I need to prepare. There are rituals to endings. I need the stone. It wouldn't do to have it there perched beside the hole, indisputably declaring the thing's purpose. I'll have to hide it, but first, I want it close, like Leo wants Max close. I want to trace the inscription, the lovely and then less lovely chiseled words, carved out with the last of a father's and a child's earthly strength and love. Such a lucky stone. How many gravestones find fitting use twice? Did my father know somehow? Was he an unwitting prophet? Or was Vano's gentle spirit somehow present, guiding invisibly our hands and our chisels to carve the premonition? It was just my father's favorite poem, that's all.

"One short sleep past," reads the line in the stone, "we wake eternally. And Death shall be no more. Death, thou shalt die."

We wake eternally.

Vano was right, as always. A new way, a gift I could never foresee. And his beloved spirit—I can feel it near me now like a hand in mine, a gentle midwife, speaking reassurances and coaxing the trembling laborer through the loss of all that was and the birth of the unimaginable.

LEO IS VERY SICK. BURNING fever, lethargy, horrible cough.

It could be pneumonia, for all I know. The wet rattle deep in his chest certainly seems to suggest the presence of fluid in his lungs. Wouldn't that be convenient? But if not, no matter; he is still a weak and sick asthmatic child. He could go in the night and nothing would seem implausible, only sad.

I stand in the doorway watching him sleep. It's dark in my old room but for the soft glow of the night-light I lit for him. He lies there so small in the bed, curled around Max, quilts pulled up to his chin. His mouth is open, and he's snoring, his head thick with mucus. I'm anxious. I'm frightened. I need to think it all through now because there will be no time later, and I have to get it right, everything down to the smallest detail. All my hope depends on it.

I wonder if Katherine is gone yet. What a terrible bit of dark luck, they'll say, that mother, miles away, dies of self-inflicted overdose on the very same night that son dies in bed of respiratory failure. But coincidences are far more common than we tend to believe. As one who's had time to view longer stretches of the pattern of phenomena than most, I've observed that randomness rarely looks random; chaos is often bafflingly ordered. The EMTs who will come here, who'll rush up the stairs with their stretchers and defibrillators, who've seen every kind of horrible and bizarre, they'll surely know this better than any. And besides, who will be left to ask questions? No one.

But through all that's to come, I'll know the truth. I'll be holding my breath in the rush of ambulance, the frenzied noise of emergency room, in the soft silence of funeral parlor, and then standing in the cold beside Leo's tiny, open grave (the grave I've dug for him, if I can manage to pull it off right). I'll be treasuring a secret, hoping, waiting for the coming moment that will change everything.

Leo's breathing catches on mucus, and he nuzzles his head against the pillow, sniffing and snorting, struggling to breathe. He coughs once, twice, finds some sliver of passage for air and rolls over.

I'll perform the exchange from the back of the knee, where it will be less noticeable. Someone *will* notice. I expect it, but that someone will supply his or her own more rational explanation, because what cannot be cannot be. My body, Ehru had assured me, will know what to do. I'll be gentler than I have ever been in all my life. Unlike me, Leo will not remember a thing. My little artist, my son.

When I step into the room, when I lift the bottom of the quilt and turn it aside, exposing his thin, pale leg, I'm crying. All the fear and hope and fear. All of my long, sad life, everything I am, everyone I've loved, all the death I've seen or caused, whatever good, whatever beauty, it all converges. I drink from him, and I give to him, and it is all transmitted.

* * *

AT FIVE FIFTY-THREE IN THE morning, I call the police.

"Nine-one-one, what's your emergency?"

"I need an ambulance. *Please*, send an ambulance. A little boy. He's staying with me, but he's not breathing. *He's not breathing!* I came in this morning, and he's not breathing."

"We'll send an ambulance right away, ma'am. Where are you located?"

"Twenty-One Hundred County Road M."

"Is that a house?"

"Yes. Yes, it's a house. *Oh, God, please, get here.* I think he might—I think he might be . . . *Oh, God, please, please get here, please!*"

"Ambulance is on its way. Just hang on, ma'am."

It's quiet and horrible in the house until the ambulance pulls wailing into the drive, then everything is a blur. The police arrive shortly after the paramedics. I look down from my bedroom window and see what I should have anticipated I would see but did not, Officer McCormick in the driveway. She's talking with another officer. They're poking around my car. The doors are open. They're wearing gloves.

They cut Leo's shirt down the middle with scissors and a large man with meaty fists pumps Leo's naked ribs. A woman prepares the paddles that will attempt to shock his heart into beating again, but of course, it's futile. His heart stopped beating hours ago.

I'm sent out of the room, and I stand and then slump down in the hallway, sobbing. It's no act. I'm sick with fear and uncertainty. I have never done this before and never seen the end result of it done. When we buried Ehru's baby, she looked dead. Did she in fact live? I realize that I don't know. What if I got it wrong? What if my body is broken and does not know? What if, instead of giving him life, I've simply taken his? We grow from seed just like every other thing. Some bit of flesh, some magically endowed kernel is planted deep within some fertile bed, where it lies dead, decomposing, shying, and nestling into its skin, curling around some invisible ember, and then, from somewhere, a soft breath blows, and in the dark, the ember begins to glow. Or that at least is the hope, but how do I know it will take? How can I be sure? Some seeds never bloom. *What if? What if? What if?* I feel close to collapsing, disintegrating under the unbearable weight of what-ifs.

A medic comes down the hall carrying a body bag, and looking at it, I feel as though I were the one about to be zipped up inside. I would *prefer* that it was me. I think of Leo sealed up in that plastic cocoon, and I can't catch my breath.

An officer—*not* McCormick—comes to take my statement. He

introduces himself as Lieutenant Hendrickson. He is stoic but not unkind as I explain how this boy, who is not mine, came to be staying with me.

"His parents are divorcing," I explain. "His stepfather recently left, and so I've been helping his mother with childcare."

"Where is his mother?"

"She's been having some . . . trouble—painkillers, sedatives. I agreed to watch Leo so that she could go to a treatment center. She's there now."

"Do you have the name of the treatment center? A number?"

As soon as he asks me this, I realize I've made a misstep. I do have the number, tucked, if I recall, in the pocket of the pants that I wore yesterday. If I had it, why wouldn't I call? The answer is that I knew she wasn't there, but I can't give that answer to this man.

"I don't," I say. "I asked her for the phone number, but then she forgot to give it to me, and I forgot to remind her. You see, I've been watching Leo somewhat regularly, and she never needed to give me a phone number before, so I think it just slipped both our minds."

"Okay, no number, no name—*anything* you can tell me about this treatment center? She say anything *at all*?"

"Uh, Dobbs Ferry. She said it was in Dobbs Ferry. I'm sorry, that's all I know. I wish I could be more helpful."

"You have the Hardmans' home phone and address?"

"I do, yes."

"Can you jot that down for me?"

I nod and hurry over to the bedside table to write the information down on a pad of paper that I keep in the drawer beneath the phone.

Lieutenant Hendrickson strides over to the door and calls a deputy in from the hall.

"Get a phone book," he says to the man who enters the room, "then I want you to call whatever drug treatment centers you can find in Dobbs Ferry to locate the deceased's mother, Katherine Hardman."

I hand the slip of paper with the Hardmans' phone number and address to the lieutenant, who takes it without a glance.

"This is the home phone and address," he continues to the officer. "We might as well check there while we're at it."

I listen to their conversation and take deep, steadying breaths; the revelation of the second half of this twin tragedy has now been set in motion. Things are only going to get more complicated.

"Phone book, ma'am?" Lieutenant Hendrickson asks me.

I've already pulled one from the same bedside table drawer and placed it beside the phone.

The deputy nods and heads over toward the table.

"What about the boy's real father? Do you know anything about him? His name, where he lives?"

"I heard it once, but I can't remember. From what I've been told, it seems like he's no longer involved in their lives."

With the deputy set at his task, Lieutenant Hendrickson steps back over to me and resumes his questioning, asking about Leo's health and how he had seemed when I put him to bed the night before. As I'm answering, Audrey's aunt comes into the room, holding in her gloved hand a sheet of watercolor paper, which I had completely forgotten existed until this moment.

"What is this?" she says, turning the paper my way so that the portrait is visible to all. No greeting, no condolences, no glint of friendly recognition in her eyes.

I summon everything in me to remain calm.

"It's a portrait. A painting."

"Is this painted in blood?" she asks.

The lieutenant to whom I had been speaking raises his eyebrows.

"It is," I say. "Strange, I know, but I have a friend in the city, an artist. He paints using blood, all voluntarily collected, of course."

"Whose blood?"

"It's my blood. He drew it from me. Bizarre, I know, but he's actually quite talented. As you can see."

Officer McCormick gives me a skeptical look, then turns it over to the lieutenant.

"Who's this friend of yours?" she asks. "What's his name?"

"Sergio."

"Sergio what?"

"I'm sorry, but I don't know. I only know his first name."

"Where is just Sergio?"

"He's located in the Bronx."

"Where in the Bronx? Do you have an address or phone number?"

"I'm sorry, but I don't. He's a friend of a friend, really. Maybe if I looked at a map, I could find the general area where his studio is, but I was brought there and I'm not sure I would know how to find my way back again."

"Who's the friend of a friend?"

"Her name is Dream."

"*Dream?*" she snorts with disgust. "For fuck's sake."

"I'm sorry, I realize this all might sound strange, but I'm an artist myself and I have many artist friends, and well, they can be an eccentric lot. I'm not sure what Sergio or that painting could possibly have to do with anything anyway."

"That's what police are for, ma'am, to decide what anything has to do with anything, so you don't have to."

She cups the Christmas bells hanging from the doorknob in her palm. "What are these?"

"Bells," I say. "I'm a deep sleeper. I wanted to be sure that I'd wake up if Leo came to the door in the night."

"Bells. 'Cause you're a deep sleeper." She gives a small, irritable laugh.

"I'm sorry," I say. "I'm not sure exactly what's going on here. I've just been through the worst experience of my life and now I feel almost as if . . . as if I'm being interrogated or harassed. I'm a little at a loss."

"No one is trying to interrogate you, ma'am," Lieutenant Hendrickson says reassuringly. "We do have to be thorough in investigating the scene, just to make sure we understand what's taken place, but *some of us* sometimes forget that we're in Millstream Hollow"—he turns a stern eye toward Officer McCormick as he says it—"and *not* the Bronx."

Officer McCormick's face is expressionless for a moment, as if she has fallen asleep with her eyes open.

The phone lets out half a ring and we all look to it, but the deputy has already answered it.

"I'll be walking the perimeter," Officer McCormick says to the lieutenant. "Ma'am," she offers with overdone courtesy to me, and then turns and walks out of the room.

I have a feeling I know where she's going; when she gets there, she won't find a grave, but a very deep hole neatly divided into several sections labeled "plastic," "metal," "glass," "organic." A preschool science experiment, and nothing more.

Hendrickson, at least, seems mollified. He resumes asking polite questions, "mmm"ing and nodding at my answers and scribbling them down on his pad. We're coming to the end of things when the deputy hangs up the phone, crosses the room, and pulls Lieutenant Hendrickson aside.

"Found Katherine. That was Saint Joseph's on the phone." The deputy glances my way, then speaks to Hendrickson in a low voice.

"Oh, you've got to be kidding me," Hendrickson says.

The lieutenant turns back to me. His face is morose.

"This thing just keeps getting worse," he says.

"What do you mean?" I ask.

"Katherine Hardman's beaten us to Saint Joseph's Hospital. She wasn't at any treatment center. Apparently, she was taken from her home by ambulance some hours ago. Her ex-husband found her at home, mid-overdose. They're calling it an attempted suicide. The hospital was trying to locate the boy, husband gave them your number."

"*What?* But she was—but she." I'm confused, but not for the reasons he thinks I am.

"I don't understand," I whisper. "I don't understand."

He watches me sympathetically as I try to make sense of what he's told me.

"Her *ex-husband* found her? She said he was in—in Tokyo on business." I realize as I say it how little it ever matters what Katherine says.

"*Attempt?*" I ask. "Does that mean she survived? She's *alive*?"

"Yeah. She's alive. Sounds like he found her just in time."

I'M AT HOME. THE POLICE and paramedics have finally left. The tears have dried to tight bands across my cheeks, and I'm sitting in my bedroom, listening to the silence and staring stupidly out the window at the crows that fly heavily among the trees. I'm not hungry. I feel terrible in a whole host of other ways both emotional and physical, but the howling, pleading desperation of an insatiable appetite is not among them. I hadn't noticed it until now. Has my body, finally, gotten what it was after? Could it have been Leo—that small, lifeless body wrapped in plastic and wheeled out on a stretcher—toward whom my hunger was driving me all along?

Katherine is at the hospital. I wonder if she's been told about Leo. What's the protocol for informing family members, who are themselves in delicate medical condition, of tragedy? I should go to see her tomorrow or the next day—how would it look if I didn't?—but I can think of nothing I'd rather avoid more. What if she knows that I was there that night with her? What if she hears my voice and remembers? I could deny it, of course, play dumb. In all likelihood, she *was* hallucinating at the time. But that's the least of my concerns. How could I even look her in the face after everything? After all the lies and betrayal, but, more important, after what I've done? What words could we possibly pass between us?

I let the day go by and then another. The next morning, though, I finally force myself to call the hospital—perhaps her condition has changed, perhaps visitors are not allowed yet, perhaps the whole building has burned to the ground in the night.

Visiting hours are ten to noon, I'm told.

I get dressed. I wash my face. I consider putting it off for another day, but instead I get in the car. For once, I need something from Katherine; for once, I'm on my way to try to discreetly extract what *I* want from *her*.

At the hospital, I sit behind the steering wheel for a while. Finally, I get out of the car and go into the lobby. In the gift shop, I buy a potted begonia and clutch it tightly against my chest as the elevator climbs up to the fourth floor and my stomach moves in the opposite direction.

When I stop at the desk to ask if someone can point me in the direction of room 427, a late-middle-aged nurse gets up and offers to walk me there. The woman is very tall and she's chewing gum casually, but I can see by her expression that she knows the situation.

"Poor woman," she says, cracking her gum loudly as she leads me down the hall. "Poor, poor woman."

"How is she?" My voice is a low, cracked whisper.

"She's stable—*physically*, at least."

"So, she knows, then?"

The nurse looks me in the eye and nods with her lips pursed.

"Is she awake, do you know? I don't wish to disturb her if . . ."

"Not sure. She's been sedated off and on. Her husband is here with her, so if she's asleep, he can tell her you came by."

Before I can react to this, we're there. The nurse raps lightly on the door with a knuckle, then opens it.

Katherine lies in the bed, her hair dark against the homogenous sickly pallor of the bedding and her skin, which nearly matches the pale mint of her hospital gown. Her face is turned, eyes closed.

Dave sits beside her bed, looking very large for the hospital chair, long legs forward and bridged one over the other at the knee. He has a Styrofoam coffee cup in one hand, a business magazine in the other, and reading glasses on his nose, which make him look like a different and more studious person, an even stranger match for Katherine and her dramatic games. I wonder if this—this pitiful scene right here with her husband—*ex*-husband—was exactly what Katherine was after the night she did it. She left him a note with who knows what recriminations in it. She must have called him too, and he came. And now here he is, back at her side.

Dave looks up at me and the nurse. He gives me a brief knowing frown, and a nod and hello to the nurse. The shades are drawn and the room is dim. The quiet is stippled by the beeps and blips of monitors. Katherine is strung up like a marionette to a half dozen machines.

I stand there hugging my potted plant, hoping that the nurse will take a very long time at what she's doing, straightening the sheet, tucking a loose edge of it up under the mattress, but she's efficient, and in less than a minute, she's tidied the bed and jotted something on a clipboard hanging beside it.

"I'm going to bring a tray in," she says to Dave. "Doughnuts, fruit, omelet. We're going to try to get some food in her today. Would you like me to bring you one too?"

"Thank you, no. I'm fine," Dave says.

The nurse leaves, and I set the plant on the bedside table and then for a moment Dave and I just gaze at Katherine, the unspoken star of the show, the one of the three of us who I now realize was always doing the talking, the scheming, the breaking things, the making things happen, while Dave and I watched stoically and braced ourselves. Even now it seems she could suddenly spring up in bed, like a Hollywood starlet bursting out of a cake, arms high over her head, a wink and a *ta-da!* But she's motionless except for the faint rise and fall of her chest with each breath.

Dave removes his glasses and, getting up from his chair, tucks them wearily in his shirt pocket.

"I'm going to go get some more of whatever this is," he says, lifting the Styrofoam cup in his hand. "I don't imagine you want to stay in here. She's out of it anyway. Join me? I'll buy you a cup, though you probably won't thank me."

He's right, the thought of being left alone with her, though it's what I came here for, is horrifying. I glance at Katherine once more and then follow him out the door.

"You know," he says as we make our way down the linoleum hall to a hot-drink vending machine, "you might be the one I feel most sorry for in all this. And Leo, of course."

I shake my head no. I don't deserve anyone's pity.

"What happened is . . ." he continues, "well . . . personally, I'm all out of feelings. I'm completely empty, nothing left—but *you*. I can't imagine what this has been like for you. Leo never deserved any of this. And you didn't either."

For a moment, the tears bite at my eyes and my throat tightens, but then I blink it all back.

"Deserved," I say slowly, turning the word and the idea over. "I'm not sure what the word means anymore. I'm not sure I even understand the concept. What do I deserve? What does anyone deserve? How can you ever know?" I look to him in confusion. "Where's the ledger? To get what you deserve: it's a concept that only exists in the mind."

"I guess," Dave says, laughing gently at my sophistry as he feeds quarters into the machine, "what I was trying to say is that you were only trying to do a good thing, and you got a lot more than you bargained for from it."

"Oh, I understand, and I'm not trying to be difficult. I guess I've just realized recently that *I've* been obsessed with this idea that you speak of—getting what one deserves, or not—it had made me bitter. But that's because it just doesn't make any sense to begin with. What you deserve and what you get: there's no way to measure them. You get the world and the world gets you, who's swindling whom?"

"I don't know," Dave says, putting a warm cup into my hand and then placing his own beneath the dispenser, "somehow it still feels like, if nothing else, a kid deserves to be safe and loved."

Hot brown liquid pours noisily from a white tube, slapping against the insides of his cup.

"Yes," I say, gazing down into my own. "You're right. Children do deserve *perfect* love, but it isn't because they're perfect, which means it has to be some other word besides *deserve*; but I don't know what the word is. But then it's true for adults too; after all, we're just the warped remains of imperfectly loved children. None of us gets the perfect love we ought, but maybe that's what life is for, to give us time to collect it in bits and pieces, a little here, a little there. Maybe we're supposed to put it together ourselves slowly."

Dave laughs at me again, but it's a kind laugh.

"I'm sorry," I say, and put a hand to my forehead, the tears welling up again. "I sound like a crazy person. I've got a lot I'm trying to make sense of right now."

"Well, your theory sounds plausible, and if you're right and that's what life is for, I'd say that Leo was able to get some of those bits and pieces from you. I know you meant a lot to him. I'm not sure anyone's thanked you for that. I'm not sure anyone's going to."

He looks dolefully down the hall toward Katherine's hospital room.

"I want to ask you something," I say, summoning the courage to do what I have really come here to do. I thought it would be Katherine whom I would ask, but now it feels right—infinitely preferable, in fact—to ask Dave.

"I want to offer something, actually. You know how much I care about Leo."

Tears begin to fall down my face at this, and I feel horror at the thought that Dave might be manipulated by tears yet again by another woman, but they are also completely genuine. I couldn't hold them back if I tried.

"My property is very large and quiet. I wanted to offer you and Katherine a resting place for Leo there."

The tears fall in earnest now, nearly uncontrollable and making it hard for me to speak. Dave grabs a handful of tissues from a box that rests on a nearby counter and hands them to me. I press them to my eyes.

"I really loved him very much," I whisper. "It would cost you nothing and you would always have complete access. Please, just talk it over with Katherine."

Dave puts a large hand on my shoulder and squeezes gently, then takes it away.

"I'll talk to her about it. Thank you."

We turn and start back toward the room. At the door, we look in. Katherine still lies motionless in the bed, eyelids lowered.

Dave says, "I'll make sure she knows you came by and offered your condolences."

He's letting me off the hook, and I'm grateful.

"Wish me luck," he says darkly, and then edges past me through the door and into the room, where he resumes his station in the chair beside her and reopens his magazine.

I CLOSE THE SCHOOL. THE police investigation, despite Officer McCormick's subtle antagonisms, amounts to nothing. The deceased is an asthmatic child with the beginnings of pneumonia. The blood of the portrait is not his, nor does it connect to any trail of unsolved murders, only a bunch of strung-out artists in the Bronx. The "grave" is clearly not a grave but an ambitious preschool science experiment at an ambitious elite preschool. Open and shut.

The parents offer condolences and half-hearted protests, but I know that they're spooked and glad for the excuse to enroll their children elsewhere. Rich people are easily frightened by things money can't fix.

I see many of them at the viewing. They weep, press tissues to the corners of their eyes, and walk up to the casket out of obligation, glancing in long enough to appear respectful and then moving on. None of them want to see a body so nearly the size of their own children, a small, smooth-cheeked face, lost deep in a dreamless sleep.

I too move past the casket quickly, pausing only long enough to tuck Max under Leo's heavy arm. I want it there for him when (*if?*) he wakes. I don't look at his face. I can't. I'm too afraid that I'll see the death, fixed and immutable there.

I feel all eyes on me, or perhaps I only imagine them. Neither the police nor Katherine have faulted me. There was no evidence of foul play, and Katherine has scarcely been soberly conscious for any period of time long enough to form an accusation even in her own mind. Besides, Dave wouldn't tolerate it, and my guess is that Katherine would do nothing to risk losing his support right now.

The two of them sit at the front of the room. Katherine leans heavily against Dave, gripping his hand in her own bony fingers and staring at the floor. I glance toward them as I walk away from the casket. Dave gives me a soft nod as I pass by, but Katherine's eyes remain fixed on the carpet at her feet.

It will only be Katherine and Dave, a minister, and some hired pallbearers at the grave site, which is on my property near a bent-over jack pine and a strangely spoked ash. The gravestone they chose for Leo was delivered the day before. The gravestone I have chosen for him is still hidden away. None of them will know who it was who dug the grave, and none of them will wonder—some gravedigger, done with his work and gone. Who cares? I won't be there. It only feels right to give Katherine privacy for her last moments with her son.

I leave the wake before anyone else. Chitchat and hors d'oeuvres afterward would be unendurable. As I walk out, I pass a collage of pictures of Leo and his family on an easel propped up in the entryway. There are no pictures of Leo's father. There are no pictures of Max. I wonder at that. Even now, at this raw moment, when both sons are gone and surely both are being grieved, Max can't be shown or spoken of. Likely Katherine doesn't want to deal with the questions his picture would provoke, or perhaps with the emotions. It strikes me as terribly sad, though, almost as sad as the deaths themselves, that Max must stay a secret even now at his little brother's funeral.

There are professional black-and-whites of Leo as an infant, Leo chubby-cheeked with a party hat and a fistful of cake at his first birthday, petting a dolphin at SeaWorld. Then I notice one photo in the bottom corner. Leo nestled under his mother's arm. They're both dressed nicely for some special occasion. Katherine is healthier, fuller-cheeked, her eyes sparkle. The picture is folded oddly at the bottom right corner, Katherine's arm cut off by the fold.

I take it from the collage and unfold the corner, then take in my breath. There is Max, probably close to his last birthday. He is *so beautiful*. Dark, wild hair like Leo's, but he looks above all like Katherine, the bones in his face narrow and delicate like hers and with large, olive-green eyes. There's a gap between his front teeth, advertised loudly by the great, wide grin on his face.

It hurts to look at him, and it suddenly makes some sense to me why his pictures have been hidden away. The life is too strong in them. It's blinding. I want this picture. If Leo makes it through, I want him to have this picture to go with the creased and worn one that hopefully is hidden still inside Max the giraffe.

I look around. No one is near. I take the photo and tuck it into my purse, then I leave.

I DON'T REMEMBER BEING BORN, of course, but I do have some recollection of being reborn.

He wasn't there when I woke up, Grandfather. He said I came early. It's not an exact science. As with babies and seedlings, a due date is really just an educated guess. They come when they're ready.

I was underground, in the pitch-dead dark for a day and a half. I didn't know if I was alive or dead or in a nightmare or in hell. I tried to claw my way out. When he found me, my nails were nearly torn off, my fingers were fat with splinters and blood, and I'd come close to drowning in dirt. He said I whispered to myself for weeks.

I can't let that happen to Leo, so I'm waiting. From dusk till dawn, in nights black as tar, in the freezing early-spring rain, I'm sitting out here, shovel and crowbar by my side, hope—frightening, terrible, reckless hope—in my battered, frightened heart, waiting for a faint sound, a soft vibration coming from deep beneath me. The cracking of a chrysalis, black butterfly wings straining against their brittle shell to unfurl in dark velvet.

My new thing coming to me. My way that I have never gone nor ever thought I would.

He'll be frightened. I'll have to work fast.

He'll be hungry. I won't give him possum.

The arrangements are made, the documents forged, the tickets paid for. We'll go to France, to Bordeaux. It's time I see my grandfather; it's time to try life among my own kind. I'd like my grandfather to be there when I explain things to Leo, just as he once explained things to me. I saw an incredible strength in you, I'll say. I thought that if any might have some use for eternity and all that this blistering world, brimming with light and shadow, holds, it might be you.

How presumptuous is the gift of life? What arrogance is implicit in the act of love that calls another into existence? This world, my love, I give it to you. All of it. You're welcome, and I'm sorry.

A sound: a stifled scream, like the roots of trees on fire.

My child stirs in the earth.

ACKNOWLEDGMENTS

It's a commonly shared understanding among writers that most books begin as crap. Some remain forever as crap in drawers or boxes under beds, but some undergo a series of transformations that ideally result in something better. Those transformations are a collaborative effort: a blind and disoriented writer, who has lost all ability to see their work accurately, listens to the advisements of her sighted readers and then, still blind, returns to the book to gropingly address what her dear readers have described.

As a result, I've come to believe that the quality of a book is directly correlated to the quality of its author's most trusted readers. It can certainly come out worse than those readers merit—the author is still at liberty to muck it up—but it's unlikely to be better. By this calculus, the potential for this book was truly limitless. No astigmatic writer has ever had more tireless or trustworthy readers and friends to guide her.

The prize for most drafts read, most detailed notes given, and best attitude in spite of it all must go to Garrett Fiddler. If you'd been paid for your editorial work, you would be a rich man now. Runners-up include the other members of the Tuesday Night Casbah Chicken Club: Cam Lay, Adam Miller, and regular TNCCC guest Kij Johnson, whose mastery is still a very high bar to strive for. To Tom Lorenz for genuine enthusiasm and encouragement from the very beginning (when I most needed it), for very good editorial advice, and for saying you could see it, sitting there on a shelf someday. To Laura Moriarty for being an ever-available and ever-encouraging champion and guide to the novelist just setting out; I promise to pay it forward. To my wise, caring, thoughtful, elegant, and ever-available agent, Jennifer Gates, who liked the things I liked and put so much work into this book's success. To my incredible and passionate editor at Flatiron Books, Megan Lynch. How did I get so lucky? I ask myself this all the time.

To all my compatriots at KU for all your insights: Divya Balla, Jason Balthazar, Jason Goodvin, Jennifer Pacioianu, and many others. To Erin Harris for so much smart editorial feedback that made it better. To Cassandra Minnehan, Johnnie Decker Miller, and Laura Dickerman—eager, smart, and gracious readers; Alyosha Bolocan for all things Slavic, Russian, and eight; and officer Noelle Burns of the Kansas City Police Department. To the Rouleaus for some incredible quiet writing days in a beautiful cabin in the woods.

More crucial even than readers are cheerleaders (though many of you were both!). Thank you to the crew who kept singing those fight songs and never once let the pom-poms droop—despite it being a very long game. The aunties Patti, Peggy, and Theresa, and the top-of-the-human-pyramid, captain of the squad herself, whose opinion was worth nothing, biased as it always was, but whose faith and encouragement were and always will be everything, Rita Thomas, aka Mom.

Thanks to dear friends, patient listeners, and ceaseless encouragers: Emily Garcia, Tori Morgan, Kate Penkethman, Kara Shim, and Crystal Kelly. And to my junior cheer squad, who celebrated and suffered all the ups and downs right alongside me and also gave me something to write about in the first place, my sons, Henry and Luca, whom I love so intensely it's scary: I promise the next one won't be so bad. And to Peter, my fellow artist, who sacrificed even more than I did, while only being able to enjoy the writing highs vicariously. Perhaps you should have married a doctor, but I'm sure glad you didn't.

There have been so many friends and helps along the way that I'm absolutely sure I'm failing to name many. Chalk it up to paucity of memory, not gratitude. Thank you, thank you.

ABOUT THE AUTHOR

JACQUELINE HOLLAND holds an MFA from the University of Kansas. Her work has appeared in *Hotel Amerika* and *Big Fiction* magazine, among others. She lives in the Twin Cities with her husband and two sons.